PARTY PLANNING CAN BE MURDER

PARTY PLANNING CAN BE MURDER

ADDY WINTERS
BOOK ONE

KERRY SCHAFER

KERRY ANNE KING

WRITE AT THE EDGE

Copyright © 2025 by Kerry Schafer

Published by Write at the Edge publishing, Colville, Washington

Book cover design by Steven Novak

Paperback ISBN 979-8-9922807-0-8

To the Dream Team - you know who you are

Fox Valley, Washington
Thursday
June 13, 2024

CHAPTER 1

GRANDMA GENEVA IS UNDENIABLY DEAD. If this were not the case, she would not be in a coffin and the rest of us would not be here to mourn her passing.

But the idea of her death and the yawning chasm her permanent absence will leave in my life still feels theoretical and unreal, thanks to the analgesic effects of denial. It's not so much her death that's bothering me at the moment; it's her funeral, planned and executed—and I mean the word executed with all of its murderous connotations—by my mother and my aunt.

"Jesus took her too soon," Jeannie Goertzen wails when we first walk into the church. She flings her arms around my mother and bursts into loud sobs. "Such a tragic loss."

I open my mouth to ask if you can really call it tragic and too soon when your number comes up at ninety-five and change, but before I can get the words out, Vic jabs me in the ribs with his elbow. Breath whooshes out of my lungs with a

1

loud whooping sound that carries, especially through the foyer of a church where people in various shades of black clothing are murmuring in subdued voices and dabbing at decorous tears.

The whoop gives everybody a reason to stare—and glare—at me openly instead of darting surreptitious, vaguely disapproving glances in my direction. It also serves the purpose of diverting some of their grief into gossip. Two of my mother's friends, making it clear that you can be a mean girl at any age, don't even bother to try to keep their voices discreet.

"Can you believe what she's wearing?"

"Addy you mean? I'd believe anything."

"As if Bethany doesn't have enough of a cross to bear without her daughter trying to attract all the attention today, of all days."

"Even if this wasn't a funeral, she's not exactly built for a dress like that. Am I right?"

My face flushes hot with shame as my childhood wish for the power to magically *poof* myself into invisibility resurfaces. To be clear, I'm not ashamed at all of my bright yellow, polka-dotted sundress or the implication that it's inappropriate, not just for the occasion but also for my not-so-skinny body. Geneva asked me to wear this dress, and I'm happy to honor her request. Also, let's face it. I was born chubby, and I've stayed chubby. I've had thirty-one years to get used to not being slender and graceful.

What shames me is knowing that I've once again embarrassed my mother in front of her friends. I've never managed to live up to her—or their—standards of...well...anything. My twin brother Vic, on the other hand, can do no wrong.

Unfortunately, shame is a terrible motivator and has never, ever kept me in line. In fact, it tends to have the opposite effect.

I sashay over to the gossip session, exaggerating the sway of my hips in my admittedly skimpy little dress, and pitch my voice to carry.

"Stephanie! How absolutely divine to see you. How is Rose? I haven't heard anything about her in ages!"

This is, I know, because there's not much to write home about from the women's prison in Purdy. As long as the trial was ongoing, we heard plenty about Rose's innocence and Stephanie's suffering, but now that Rose has been found guilty by a jury of her peers on several counts stemming from real estate shenanigans, it's as though she never existed.

Stephanie Markle gasps and clutches her pearls—not metaphorically, but literally. She's wearing a double strand that hangs down over cushiony bosoms onto a belly that you'd think might make her think twice about making digs at my comparatively svelte self. She gasps, covers her mouth with her free hand, and stares at me as if I'm a monster, even though it's her daughter who defrauded a bunch of seniors of their life savings, certainly not me.

"Addy. Must you, really?" Aunt Rachel reprimands, ostensibly into my ear in a whisper, but she's hard of hearing and always misjudges her own volume. "You've drawn enough attention to yourself with that ...get up...you're wearing. You don't also have to cause a scene."

Her mild-mannered, nearly silent mouse of a husband, Uncle Newsom, looks at me in alarm, silently pleading that I stop this somehow.

It's too late, of course. The scene has already been caused, and Aunt Rachel is about to add a keg of gunpowder to the blaze. It occurs to me to turn around and walk away—not just from this scene I've created but the funeral itself. I'd much rather be curled up on the couch at home, watching one of Geneva's favorite movies, or writing down my memories so they don't slip away from me. But I loved her, and she gave me one last mission to complete for her, and I'll be damned if I let her down now.

As for the scene in progress, Stephanie Markle has a good eighty pounds on me and I figure she has a lot of nerve commenting on my weight. This is not something I'm inclined to let pass, but I notice Vic's elbow armed and ready and decide to keep my mouth shut, settling for glaring at them all defiantly.

"How can you?" Annie Galbraith demands, trying to put an arm around Stephanie's waist and then opting for shoulders instead. It's a long way around that circumference and her arm is too short. She dabs at her eyes with her free hand. "With your poor, dear grandmother's dead body still warm in her coffin. Such a tragedy."

Vic's elbow notwithstanding, my mouth opens. "Geneva was ninety-five and lived a good, long life. She wanted to die. So *tragedy* is maybe not the right word. And if she's still warm in there, we've got a bigger problem than what I've worn to the funeral."

Stephanie and Annie both gasp in sheer horror, as if I've summoned the antichrist rather than just stating what we all know to be the truth.

I look at Aunt Rachel and say, "Don't even start with me."

Of course, Aunt Rachel will be perfectly justified in calling out my inappropriate behavior, and Mom will join in, and for years everybody in Fox Valley will rehash the scandal of the time Addison created a scene at Geneva's funeral. And all of that before I even do the truly scandalous thing Geneva has tasked me with.

Why, oh why, can't I learn to just keep my mouth shut?

Just before everything blows up, Ricky Hayes glides over in his self-effacing black suit and slicked-back hair, a soothing smile on his face. Not too much of a smile because Rick, born and raised in a family undertaker business, is ever conscious of the proprieties of grief and has years of practice placating fractious relatives.

"It's time for the family to be seated," he says, laying a proprietary but very respectful hand on Aunt Rachel's arm. "If you would allow me the honor?"

With one final glare at me, she allows herself to be escorted to the front of the church, Uncle Newsom trailing behind her. When Rick comes back for Mom, I fully expect Vic to go with her, but he opts to stay with me.

"Nice work, Addle Brain," he says, the use of my childhood nickname a reassurance that our twin bond still holds firm. He takes my arm, and the two of us walk to the front of the church.

I'm aware of the eyes following us and of the comparisons that go with them.

Could twins be more different than those two?

Vic certainly did get all the attractive genes, didn't he?

And the intelligence, too, from what I hear...

It was Geneva who hugged and consoled me when I overheard these things as a child or read me the riot act when I was old enough to adjust my own attitude.

"Don't let them make you less than you are, Addison Winters," she would tell me. "You're every bit as smart as Victor and just attractive enough to be comfortable without your looks getting in your way. You'll grow into yourself, and you'll outgrow this town."

Most of the advice Geneva gave me over the years turned out to be true, but this bit, not so much. Here I am, still in Fox Valley. And if I'm as smart as Victor, those brain cells are hiding somewhere and haven't shown themselves yet.

Geneva usually got her way, but Mom and Rachel and Fox Valley, together, were sometimes too much, even for her. Take this funeral, for example. She made it crystal clear what kind of event she wanted to honor her passing, and it wasn't this.

"I want a party," she'd said. "Music. Food. Dancing. An open bar for guests. You can make a toast to the memory of my life, and you can tell funny stories if you wish. But make it a celebration to mark the fact that I won at life and have returned to the energy beyond."

My mother and my aunt absolutely refused to honor any part of this. "Funerals are for the grieving who are left behind. Geneva, for once in her life, is no longer the center of attention," Mom said.

Aunt Rachel agreed. And then they proceeded to consult with the staff of *Ever After*, the local funeral parlor, with the result that today is the antithesis of everything Geneva said she wanted.

First thing, she's in a coffin. She wanted to be cremated and her ashes scattered in the ocean. This she also wrote into her will. But Mom and Aunt Rachel both take the Bible very literally and get all kinds of cringey about the idea of cremation and ash scattering.

"What happens at the resurrection if she's all burned to bits and then the bits are washed around in the ocean?" Mom asked when I protested.

"You do know that people don't stay...intact...in their coffins," I'd countered. "Cremation ashes or dust and bones, what's the difference?"

"At least there won't be bits of other people and...fish and algae and whatever mixed in," Mom said. She's never been one for logic.

"Imagine," Aunt Rachel agreed. "You get bits of Geneva and bits of other dead things, and they all come together and then she spends all of eternity as some sort of awful fish person."

"Pretty sure if the powers of the universe can resurrect somebody at all, they can be trusted to put them all back together properly," I said.

"*God*, honey," Mom protested. "Say *God*. Don't say powers of the universe. You sound like you're from California or something."

Vic just shrugged and said, "There's no point fighting about it. We all know they're not going to change their minds." And so, here we are at this misguided funeral.

Another thing Geneva always hated was open caskets, one more request that her daughters have ignored. At least her body is screened from me by our family seated in the first row, so I can avoid staring at her directly. We're supposed to be up there, too, but Vic very wisely steered me into the pew behind Mom and Aunt Rachel so we wouldn't be tempted to continue what we'd started.

"Worse than staring at a naked person through a peephole," Geneva's voice says now, so loud and clear that I startle and look to my left, half expecting to see her ghostly form in the pew beside me, but Vic is sitting there, unbothered, apparently, by a voice from beyond the grave. He glances at me, frowning slightly, an admonition to stop squirming and behave.

I do my best, staring determinedly at the mole on the back of Uncle Newsom's head, wondering if I should tell him to go see a doctor. Is it cancerous? Pre-cancerous? Or just one of those old-person protrusions, unsightly but nothing to worry about?

As if he feels my eyes on him, Uncle Newsom shifts position just enough that I can see the casket right between his shoulder and Mom's. People are walking by it to pay their respects before they are seated. Or, alternately, gawk, which would have been Geneva's word for it. I myself can't help gawking a little, trying and failing to make the wax doll in the casket look like its real counterpart.

At the time of her death, Geneva's hair was a vibrant pink, gelled to stand up straight on top of her head, but it's either been dyed post-mortem or maybe covered with a wig because now it is gray and tamed, lying thin and meek across her scalp. As for makeup, whoever did hers for the funeral has been reading those "makeup for mature women" articles. Mom kept emailing them to Geneva, whose response was, "Over my dead body," and now here we are.

I know for sure Mom purchased the skirt and sweater set Geneva's corpse is clothed in because she tried to make me go shopping with her and got outright huffy when I suggested jeans and one of Geneva's more obnoxious T-shirts. I was a fan of the one with a picture of the devil on it and the slogan OH SHIT, SHE'S UP. I went looking for that shirt so I could have it, and it was nowhere to be seen. Pretty sure it wasn't sent to Goodwill, either, but I stopped short of combing through the trash.

Other things that are wrong with this funeral:

The ceremony is in a church instead of at the community park. The music consists of slow, mournful hymns accompanied by an organ. People are somber and tearful and dressed in dark colors. The preacher, well...preaches. All a far cry from Geneva's big party. She'd wanted a live band playing rock and roll. Open bar. Good food, laughter, and positive energy.

"Maybe you can put my ashes in a cannon with a bunch of confetti and blast it out into a park," she'd said. "Would fireworks be too much, do you think?"

But now, here we are with the full-on traditional church funeral, and it's time for me to do the last thing she asked of me. The minister sits down, and I stand up. Knees quaking, I get to my feet. Vic, probably thinking I'm headed for the restroom, stands up to let me out. I make my way up onto the platform, followed by whispers and rustling as everybody sits up straighter to see what Addy is going to do next.

Pastor Holliwell pops back out of his chair and touches my arm. "I think," he whispers, "that it's really time for the eulogy. Your Aunt Rachel is doing that."

Aunt Rachel is, in fact, out of her seat and halfway to the pulpit, staring daggers at me. I smile at her and then at the minister, pat his arm gently, and begin to unfold the handwritten letter I've been clutching since I took my seat. It's soggy from nervous sweat, and I have a moment of panic that it will tear, that the ink will have run, that it will be unreadable. But I get it open and set it down in front of me so people won't see how badly my hands are shaking.

I take a deep breath, look out at the church full of people, and dive in.

"I have a letter here from Geneva. She gave it to me before

she died and made me promise to read it to all of you. I suspect I'm not the only one she extracted promises from, but it's pretty easy to break faith with the dead." I let my gaze rest on my mother, who shifts in her pew uncomfortably and looks away, and my brother, who glares back like he wants to strangle me, and Aunt Rachel, who has retreated to her seat rather than make a scene. But I know she is running emergency responses in her head, one of which is likely "tackle Addy and beat her into submission with a shoe." Surprisingly, Uncle Newsom smiles at me and nods.

Bolstered by that unexpected sign of encouragement, I clear my throat and begin to read.

"Friends—and enemies—because, let's face it, some of you aren't overly sad to see me go. You know who you are, and you might as well stop pretending to be mournful right now. I'm watching you.

"If you are sad at my passing, let it only be because you'll miss me. Have a drink, shed a few tears, and then go find some other people who light up your life. No more of this nonsense about me being taken too early, either. First, I wasn't taken; I went of my own free will. Volunteered, you might say. Second, I died at precisely the right moment in time. What does that mean? Maybe that all time and space would have come to a screeching, jarring halt if I'd continued on. Who knows? Well, at least when I wrote this, I didn't know, but I bet I do now. How cool is that? Are you jealous? You should be. I now have all the answers.

"I'd like to believe that Addy is reading this at the party I asked for, but I'm going to guess that my beloved daughters objected and my send-off is some stuffy thing in a church. That's okay, girls. I know. Death is hard for you, and you do take things seriously. No hard feelings. I won't haunt you, my loves, but I do wish you could learn to lighten up. Speaking of which, don't you just love Addy's dress? She wore it to please me. The rest of you could benefit from some brighter colors. Just saying.

"Anyway. While I would love to think you're all having a good time right now, I guess it doesn't matter. I'm at the best party ever, a party of one, just for me. Think about it. I'm discovering eternity and the answers to all the questions while you all are crammed into those uncomfortable pews.

"Well, that's really it. I didn't have much to say; I just wanted to get in the last word from beyond the grave. I suggest you skip the graveyard event and go do something fun."

As I've been reading, murmurs and mutters have run through the congregation. The sobbing has largely stopped. Some people are staring at me in outrage, as if I've written this missive myself—and in their defense, they probably think I have. Mom's face is scarlet. Aunt Rachel has hidden hers in a handkerchief. Uncle Newsom is still smiling.

"Goodbye, everybody. Look me up when you get here," I read.

And that's it.

Geneva's gone. I've read her letter and I wore the yellow dress, but I was too much of a coward to fight my family to give her the party she really wanted. It's too late now. I've failed. And her absence, her complete and utter goneness from the fabric of my life, is suddenly a huge, gaping black hole that makes me feel utterly alone and bereft.

I do not want to be close to my mom and Aunt Rachel right now or look at the judging eyes of the other mourners. Besides, my knees have gone too wobbly to take me down the stairs, so

I escape out the side door and into a back hallway instead. I'll make my way around to the back and stand there instead of returning to my pew. Or maybe just make a run for my car and get out of here.

Aunt Rachel has just started the eulogy, after which there will be a final hymn. Then, the decorous pew-by-pew exodus, like airline passengers deplaning only more slowly and with emotional baggage. They'll linger in the foyer to console my mother and Aunt Rachel about both Geneva and me. I don't need to be here for that.

Caught up in my thoughts, my eyes blinded by tears, I very nearly trip over an old man in a wheelchair parked right in the middle of the dark hallway. Barely have I righted myself, rubbed my bruised thigh, and caught my breath when he says, in what is definitely not an old-man voice, "I want a proper send-off party, and I need you to help me."

CHAPTER 2

THERE'S no mistaking that voice, only I can't reconcile it with the emaciated figure in the wheelchair.

"Leno?"

"In the very feeble flesh."

He's bald, his once gloriously wavy red-gold locks not just shorn but vanished. His skin is stretched tight over his bones; his eyes are sunken. The rest of his body matches. His arms are skeletal, the hands resting on the arms of the wheelchair are claw-like.

"I didn't know you were in town," I say, trying not to stare at the wreckage of the most beautiful boy I've ever known.

Normally, when Leno visits Fox Valley—which isn't often—social media is abuzz before he ever boards his flight, fans are waiting for him when he gets off in Spokane, and by the time he hits Fox Valley the gossip mill is busily reporting Leno Sightings in real-time.

He was already legendary at Fox Valley High. That face!

That hair! *That voice.* Whether he was crooning out ballads in the hottest rock band in high school history, reading out loud in English class, or just being stupid with a bunch of kids in the hallway between classes, almost any girl—and some of the guys—would have knelt and kissed his feet if he'd asked. And that was *before* Leno and the Lonely hit it big and his fan club expanded into the stratosphere.

"Been keeping a low profile," Leno says, in that voice that still curls my toes no matter what he looks like. "Trying to avoid the media. It's been alarmingly easy. If *you* didn't recognize me, nobody else is likely to."

I have too many questions and not enough oxygen. *What happened to you?* That's a big one that I obviously can't ask. Or shouldn't, anyway. Drugs, eating disorder, mental illness—any of the reasons my imagination conjures are things you don't ask about.

Why are you at Geneva's funeral? That one is better. Maybe followed by, *can I call 9-1-1 for you? Give you a ride to the ER?*

But there's also history between us. A betrayal as deep as the Mariana Trench. If he needs a ride somewhere, then one of his acolytes can help him. There are a bunch of otherwise normal women in the world, even in Fox Valley, who call him Lord and Master, which is, I guess, what happens when you're a big-deal rockstar with a last name like Masterson.

I slap a Band-Aid on my suddenly bleeding heart, summon my coolest, most business-like voice, and say, "Given that you have a million groupies out there who would be delighted to do anything for you, I'm not at all sure what you want from me."

"I deserve that, I suppose," he says. "Please, Addy. Could we talk somewhere, do you think? Other than this creepy back hallway? Pastor Holliwell tried to cast a demon out of me here. The most terrifying experience of my lifetime."

Laughter catches me unaware, and I press both hands over my mouth to silence it. The last thing I need is for some funeral goer wandering the hallway to hear me. "He honestly thought you were possessed?"

"Possessed and leading all Leno and the Lonely listeners into the thralldom of the devil. Yes. Last time I set foot in this place. Until now."

"Well, technically, you've not set foot now, either."

"Oh, my wheels, you mean? You noticed. How perceptive of you."

"I still don't understand why you're here."

Anybody who didn't know our history might think I've asked a question. Leno doesn't make that mistake.

"Practicing for death," he says, leveling an intense gaze at me. "A funeral rehearsal, if you will. But I need to talk to you, Addy. Could we please go somewhere else?"

"Like one of the classrooms, you mean?"

"I was thinking more like *Grounded*, if you don't mind being seen with me."

I stare at him, wordless for possibly the first time in my life.

"I get it," he says. "I don't blame you. I'm not exactly photo-op material these days, not the guy you want to be out in public with."

That shakes my brain loose from the shock and disbelief problem it's having, and I exclaim, "Oh my God. You think it's *that?*"

"The wheels and impending death are sort of a buzz kill. Plus, sooner or later, the media is going to figure out that I'm me, even with this excellent disguise. Paparazzi, reporters. And they will put a repulsive spin on the pretty woman and the dying man. So, yes. Maybe I think you don't want to be seen with me."

Pretty. He called me pretty. He also said the big D word again.

My heart is bewildered and confused, sending me urgent queries: *Are we hurt and resentful? Flattered by the attention? Excited to see him again? He did say pretty...*

But I recognize manipulation when I see it, and I tell my heart to stand down and back off. I am not going anywhere with Leno, dying or not. I'm not falling for his charm. I'm not going to be manipulated into anything. I'm going with my family to the graveyard to watch Geneva's body get put into the ground when what she really wanted was for her ashes to be shot out of a cannon. I don't owe Leno an explanation, certainly not tea and sympathy. I won't say another word. I'll turn around and walk away.

Right. Like my big mouth will ever let me get away with that.

"If I remember correctly, *you* were the one who didn't want to be seen with *me.*"

"Addy," Leno pleads. "We were in what, junior high? What do you want from me?"

"You could start with an apology."

"All right," he says. "I'm sorry."

I'm not letting him off that easily. "You're sorry for what, exactly?"

"Please, can we not do this here? Yes, I was a dick. And now I'm a dying dick and I don't have a bunch of time to make it up to you."

Again, I think about the cemetery. Watching Geneva be put

into the ground. Covered up with dirt. Leno's request gives me an out.

"Oh, fine. *Grounded* it is. But if the paparazzi catch me playing hooky from Geneva's funeral, there's going to be hell to pay."

"God," he says. "You're right. I really am still—what did you call me back then? 'The most insufferable, stuck up, insensitive, manipulative bastard ever to draw breath?' Of course you need to go to the graveyard. I just...I was afraid if I didn't talk to you now, I'd lose my chance. You'll walk off and I'll never see you again."

Which, to be fair, is exactly what would have happened.

I gesture to his wheelchair, which is an electric version, not one of those low-profile, lightweight affairs. "Will that contraption fit in my trunk?"

"It folds up pretty compact," he says. "But I have my own car. If you'd be so kind as to help me stow the wheels, I can drive. My legs work fine for driving; I'm just too weak to wander around."

"We'll have to sneak out the back," I say. "If I'm seen, I'll be captured, hog-tied, and dragged to the cemetery behind the funeral procession."

Leno laughs at the image and motors down the hallway. When we reach the door, I hold it open for him to roll through, blinking in a flood of glorious daylight.

"This way," he says, and I follow him to what may be the shiniest set of wheels ever.

The car is low and sleek and dangerous looking, yellow and black like a hornet. I don't know cars, but I know this one is expensive and the only one of its kind ever seen in the town of Fox Valley.

"Just a tip from a middle-class plebe. This is sort of an attention-getting rig. Maybe not quite the thing for a guy flying under the radar."

His pale lips quirk into a half smile. "I couldn't bring myself to part with it. Few pleasures remain to me, and this is one."

"You drove here? From New York?"

He laughs bitterly. "No. I came by private jet. I paid a guy to drive it up for me and flew him back. Money can buy you anything. Except, you know, happiness—or health. I'd take you for a ride, but you may need your own wheels for a getaway."

"If the press finds us, you mean?"

"That. Or if I drop suddenly dead."

I clear my throat. "Right. Or that. Fine. I will meet you there."

I leave him to his smoothly purring, sexy ride and traipse out of the parking lot and into the street, where I parked my own set of wheels. Her name is Jezebel, and she's a gas-guzzling, rusted, dented old harridan of a Crown Vic. I've thought about buying a new car, new*er* anyway, but I'm not in the habit of casting off a loved one just because they've become erratic and unsightly.

Jezebel was my first car love, the vehicle I purchased with my first post-high school job, and I'm still fond of her. She doesn't return the sentiment, however, always acting up at the worst possible time. Now, for example, she refuses to start, not even making a groan of pretense when I turn the key.

To be fair, I might have left the lights on. So I have to get out in my high heels and my teeny-weeny yellow dress and flag down a jumpstart. And the first available person I see is Deacon Smythe, whose first name is, improbably, Smith, and I can assure you, this is not because his parents had a sense of humor.

When I wave my arms and trot over to him shouting, "Jezebel needs a jump start," I'm pretty sure that the way his eyes widen in shock and horror and his face gets all red has nothing to do with my car. Anyway, I gesture at the Crown Vic and he gets up to speed and brings his Subaru over. He is very careful to keep at least two feet of distance between my sinful flesh and his dried-up, leathery self, but he does his charitable Christian duty and Jezebel rumbles to life.

I take a second to send a quick text before I shift into gear.

> Addy: Guess what I'm doing?

> Britt: Texting during your grandma's funeral? Behave. 😞

> Addy: Relax. Texting from my car. Read Geneva's letter to the masses and had to escape the lynch mob.

> Britt: Really sorry I missed that. 😞 Seriously— sorry not to be there for you.

> Addy: How's your dad? How did the appointment go?

> Britt: Won't have the scan results until later, but the doc is optimistic about the chemo.

> Addy: 🙏 🙏

> Addy: Guess what I'm doing next?

> Britt: Going to the cemetery?

> Addy: Meeting Leno Masterson at Grounded.

> Britt: ...

> Addy: Anyway, need to go. He's waiting.

> Britt: Don't. Go to the cemetery.

> Addy: I'm not—I'm going to Grounded.

> Britt: Punctuation, dumbass. DO NOT GO WITH LENO.

> Addy: Sorry. Driving. Laters!

Britt is my best friend, and I love her. She's not perfect like Vic, and she has no problem with breaking a few rules or flouting societal conventions, as long as nobody notices. She missed the funeral because her dad has cancer and she drove him to an appointment in Spokane today. Which is all horrible and awful but a small, good thing at this moment because she's not here to stop me from doing what I've decided to do.

CHAPTER 3

LENO IS ALMOST DONE with his coffee and has crumbled a pastry to pieces without, as far as I can tell, eating any of it by the time I walk into *Grounded*.

"Thought you stood me up," he says when I slide into the chair across from him.

"That's your job," I say.

He grimaces. "I did say I was sorry."

"Why don't you work on a real apology while I grab a coffee? Unless you're in a hurry to get out of here, in which case, spit it out and I'll sit down and listen."

"I've got nowhere to be except the beyond," he says. "Plenty of time to get there."

"Would you stop that?"

"What?" he asks. "Dying?"

"No, the freaking death jokes. They're not funny, and you're starting to sound self-pitying."

"I am?"

"You have a right to it, I guess, but you don't have to rub my nose in it if you don't mind. It's not helping your cause."

He bursts into an open-mouthed, belly-laugh guffaw. A lot of eyes turn in our direction. Two middle-aged ladies next to us put their heads together and start whispering. One of them pulls out a phone, and they both get intently absorbed in watching something, with frequent glances up at Leno and me.

Apparently oblivious to the fact that he's no longer under the radar, he wipes his eyes and smiles at me. "This is a thing I always loved about you," he says.

"My rudeness? Also, since I ceased to exist in your world in junior high, I don't think there's anything about me that you've always loved."

Geez, Addy. Can you knock it off with the self-pitying comments? You're worse than he is, with less cause, I tell the part of myself responsible for running my mouth. I'm pretty sure it still isn't listening.

"You've always been the person to blurt out the truth," Leno says. "Do you know you're the only one who ever had the nerve to tell me what an asshat I'd turned into? Well, you and my brother. Credit where credit is due and all that."

"I didn't think you were listening," I say. "It would have been difficult to hear me over the clamor of your groupies."

"Oh, I heard you. I was just too stupid to let on. Go get your coffee. I'll try not to expire in your absence." He grins, and I feel myself grinning back, the bitterness of years falling cleanly away.

Too fast, damn it. I know when I'm being manipulated. But in this case, maybe I don't mind so much. It feels good to let this shit go.

Kathy, everybody's favorite barista, has my drink ready for

me by the time I've paid the kid at the till. "Who's the dude?" she asks, her fingers grazing mine as she puts the cup directly into my hand. "Little old for you, but hey. JoJo was out having a smoke and said this guy drove up in a Maserati. For real? Did you go and find yourself a sugar daddy?"

"God, no. Old friend. Just catching up."

"You okay?" she asks, her deep-brown eyes searching mine. "Funeral over already?"

"I sorta skipped the burial part."

"Nice," she says. "I know that wasn't what Geneva wanted. Good for you, staging your own private protest."

"Thanks, Kath. You're the best." I return to the table, clutching my frosty, custom-designed caramel macchiato.

There's a big red heart on the cup that matches Kathy's lipstick perfectly. Which is a thing I probably ought to do something about one of these days—not the lipstick, but the possible misconception. Sit her down and explain that the one time last year when she kissed me and I kissed her back, it was an alcohol-induced experiment and while I like her very much, she's definitely in the friend zone and I'm still firmly in the land of dating men, just as soon as I can find a man I actually want to date.

But this is my favorite coffee shop—actually, it's the *only* coffee shop in Fox Valley—and I do appreciate my custom drinks and expedited service. So, maybe it doesn't hurt anything to keep on letting Kathy believe whatever makes her happy. I take a big slurp of my beyond-perfect drink before turning my attention back to Leno.

"Okay. You've got some explaining to do."

"It went to my head. The sudden fame thing. I mean— going from the nerdy, gawky new kid to rockstar dreamboat pretty much overnight? I betrayed my only real friend, and I really am sorry."

"Thank you. Now that we've got that out of the way, what's all of this shit about needing me? If I remember correctly, you also said something about a send-off party."

"Right, that." He blinks and clears his throat. "You've likely deduced that I might not have much time left on the planet."

"It's possible that you've mentioned that."

"A year ago, I felt perfectly fine. Chemo, radiation, a ton of toxic drugs since, and, well... Here we are, offering up death's-door apologies to old friends at funerals."

"Don't blow smoke, Leno. You didn't come to apologize. You came because you wanted something from me."

"All right. Yes. But I did always have a soft spot for Geneva. She had the best advice. And I came to her funeral to connect with you, but also because I wanted to...I guess, accept my reality a little more. I'm still trying to get my mind around the fact that one day soon, I just...won't be here. Maybe not be anywhere at all. That scares me more than the old hellfire doctrine, I think. The idea of not being, anywhere, ever, lost in an eternal void of nothing."

I lick the whipped cream off the top of my drink. "I think you'll still be somewhere."

Leno leans forward, looking at me intently. "You believe that?"

I shift my weight in the chair. One of the problems with a short dress and no stockings is the bit where my legs stick to hard surfaces, and one of them comes loose now with an obscene sucking sound that I can only hope he doesn't think is a fart.

"Geneva believed it. And I think I do? She always talked

about her dearly dead as if they were gathered around, watching her live her life, offering suggestions. She said they were just right there, on the other side of reality. I argued that we couldn't see them. She argued back that we can't see gravity working, but it's obvious that it does. And I...want to believe Geneva is still Geneva. You know?"

"I do," he says, with that half smile, the one that used to make the girls squeal out loud when he did it from the stage. Now it looks sad and bent, as if it's already served its purpose and is ready to move on before he does. "But just because we wish it, that doesn't make it so."

I sigh because he's right, of course. There's no proof of an afterlife, and faith feels like a thin substitute for knowing right now.

I gesture at the demolished pastry on his plate. "Were you going to eat any of that?"

I'm a comfort food girl, and I could use more sugar than my coffee is providing.

He looks down at the mess he's made. "It looked good. But then it didn't. No appetite to speak of. Help yourself." He shoves the plate toward me, leans on his elbows, and says, "Plan a send-off party for me. Like the one Geneva wanted in the letter you read."

"Now?"

"No, silly. After. That's what you do, right? Parties, weddings. Your business card is on the bulletin board when you walk into this place. You've got an ad in the paper."

"No," I say. "Two reasons." I pick up a piece of his pastry and pop it into my mouth. Mmmmm. Danish, with just the perfect amount of sugar and grease. I slurp my drink, wipe my mouth, and go on. "Reason one. The family. The friends.

They're conditioned to funerals, not parties. So, they insist on the kind of event my family orchestrated today. Some people are open to a celebration of life, but most aren't going to be on board with a big party. Don't forget that I've met your mother."

I shiver a little at the memory of those cold blue eyes looking me over and finding me so very wanting.

"So let them," Leno says. "They can have their funeral. But the party happens anyway. I'll pay you. I'm not asking you to do this for free."

"Which brings us to reason two. I'm small townsville—not up to snuff with the sort of parties you're used to."

"How hard can it be? A band, a bar, some dancing and games."

"Small and local, then? Just Fox Valley? Old classmates, that sort of thing?"

"God, no. I want everybody here. My music associates. Hollywood people. The Paparazzi. I aim to go out in a blaze of glory."

"I'm not your girl for that. I don't have the connections to pull it off."

"But I do. We'll plan it together."

I eat some more of his discarded Danish, mulling. I'm good at my small-town events, but I have no idea how to throw the sort of glitter-and-glamor party he's looking for. I know my limitations, and crushing failure and public humiliation don't sound like fun to me. Neither does dealing with the fallout from Leno's family.

"I don't think so, Leno. It's not—I mean, I get it. I'd want that kind of send-off, too. But I'm not the right person for this."

"You are, though," he says. "You're the only person. You're brave. You read your grandma's letter at the funeral. You wore that dress instead of something mournful. You'll wear that dress to my party."

I snort, thinking about the kind of party he's talking about and me showing up in the daffodil-yellow sundress I bought at Target. "Leno. Come on. Be serious."

"I am serious. I don't have time not to be serious. Ten thousand."

"Ten thousand what?"

"What I'll pay you. To plan and execute my send-off party. And I'll put a bunch of money in an account to pay for catering and musicians and whatever. Ten K pure profit for you. What do you say?"

"My God. You're insane." I look at him wide-eyed, considering. Then I shake my head. "I can't."

"And my car. I'll throw in the car. Say yes."

"Leno—"

"Addy." His hand closes around mine on the table, the fingers thin, the skin dry and papery, the veins way too visible through translucent skin. "Do you know how amazing it is to be able to talk to somebody like this? My family is horrified when I joke even the tiniest bit about my death. Mom still insists that I'm going to get better. Owen—do you remember Owen?"

"We met once at a party. He was already in college when your family moved here. Never came home for the summers."

"Right. He worked summers at Dad's Chicago office. Anyway, he's temporarily in Fox Valley to 'support me' while I do the dying thing, but whenever I mention it, he just gets mad and tells me to shut up and stop talking about it, like I'm suffering from something embarrassing like a case of herpes."

"Which is exactly my point," I say. "Or at least one of my

points. How do you think they're going to react after you've died and they are grieving in their usual avoidant and angry way, and I pop up and say, 'Hey, guess what? Leno and I planned a big party, and I'm here to make that happen?'"

My coffee is melting, and I stop to fortify myself with a few good swallows.

"Not a problem," Leno says. "We'll tell the family ahead of time. I'll get Draco to draw up something legal and put money in an account for you to spend on venue and a band and food."

"Draco? Come on, now you're messing with me."

"Not Draco as in Malfoy. Draco as in the first Greek lawyer of record. Draco has lived in Fox Valley since the flood and has been the family lawyer ever since we moved here. And he's of Greek descent, I believe. Thus, Draco. Let's go see him now. We'll carpe diem and all that."

"Stop manipulating me," I say, wondering how the graveside service is going and how mad Mom is, or worse, hurt. I start to feel guilty, and then I remember how much Geneva did not want a funeral or public burial and that I'm actually honoring her wishes. What would Geneva want me to do about Leno?

"*Give the boy what he wants,*" her voice says in my ear. "*Maybe he didn't handle fame well, but what young kid does? He's not asking for the moon.*"

But then something else occurs to me. "You didn't know Geneva wanted an after-death party," I say slowly. "Not until I read the letter. So, what did you really come to the funeral to talk me into?"

"Shit," Leno says. "Should have known you'd put that together."

"Spill it, or I'm out of here."

"Fine," he says. "I'm going to die in five days, and I need..."

Whatever he needs is big because his voice trails off and he can't meet my eyes. He shifts his weight in the chair and wraps one hand around his empty coffee cup.

"Five days is awfully specific," I say, increasingly wary. "You have precognitive abilities now?"

"No, I'm using the Death with Dignity Act. I don't want to linger on like this, dying by inches. I want to choose my day and be done. And I want a party. You can help me with both."

"God, Leno." The shock of this hits me like a wall falling on my head. He's not talking about dying at some undetermined future date, close but still nebulous. Today is Thursday. Tuesday next week he'll be dead. I take a breath, keep my tone casual.

"You always were one for the dramatic exit. Your family is okay with this?"

He shifts his eyes to the table and picks at the last remaining flakes of Danish that I haven't eaten.

"Leno?"

"They don't know."

"So, you're just going to what, kill yourself in your childhood bedroom and let your mother find you? Surprise! I'm dead."

"Somebody is going to find me dead one day, Addy, no matter what. But no. I'm at the condo. I'll die there."

The condo is notorious. Leno bought it when the first album went gold so the band would have a place to hang out and have parties—which, by the way, I was never invited to. All the things my mother warned me about when it came to rock and roll happened there: drugs, drinking, sex. Possibly orgies. Maybe even devil worship, but I'm pretty sure that part was just Fox Valley gossip.

"You need to tell them, Leno. They're your family. They love you. Maybe they have things to say, or things they need to hear from you or—"

"See? This is why I need you. We can tell them together. About the party—and the death day. And you can be there with me when I end things, so I'm not—not alone—and so I don't lie around moldering and waiting for somebody to find me. And when I'm dead, you could call my mother and let her know."

"You really think I'm going to help you kill yourself and be the one to break the news to your family? Really?"

"Addy. I'm begging. You're the only one—"

"Hard no, Leno."

"To which part?"

I tick the items off on my fingers. "I will not help you tell your family that you've decided to off yourself. I will not help you do it. And I sure as hell am not going to be the one to call your mother to tell her that you're dead."

"I'm not that close to them," he says. "I only came home to die because New York doesn't have a right-to-die law. Do you have any idea how many hoops I've had to jump through to make this happen?"

"No, I don't, and I—"

"First, finding a doctor who is willing to participate isn't easy. Then, I had to make my request three times, twice verbally, once in writing. Oh, and I needed two doctors involved, not just one. I had to fill out a form and sign it in front of witnesses, and then finally, the doc wrote me my get-out-of-this-body-free card. I want to do it, but I don't want to do it alone. You are the only person I can think of who knows the real me."

"But I *don't* know you," I say harshly. "Even back then, I didn't really know you. I thought I did. I was wrong." I soften my voice when I see the misery in his eyes and add, "You must seriously want to die to go through all of that red tape."

"I don't *want* to die!" Leno flares. "But I don't want to be at the mercy of this fucking cancer. Everybody thinks I should patiently wait around until it decides to kill me. It's already stolen everything worth having. The pain is getting bad, and it's only going to get worse. I can't do music, can't do anything. Right now, I'm still in my condo, but what happens when I can't take care of myself? My mother certainly isn't going to play nurse, which means a hospice bed somewhere. So, yes. I'm going to end the nightmare. Be with me when I do it, Addy. I'll pay you another ten grand."

My heart squeezes tight, and I feel the burn of tears behind my eyes, but still. No.

"Obviously, you don't know me at all. There's not enough money in the world to make me do this. And you have to tell your family."

"If I beg, pitifully?"

"No."

"I bet your grandmother—"

"Don't even try that one. No."

He sighs dramatically. "Will you at least come with me to talk to Draco about the party? Please, Addy."

"No. No, no, no, and let me see...no. I'm going to finish my coffee, and then I'm going home to the post-funeral non-celebration for my grandmother. I hate being manipulated, Leno. I'm not planning your party. I'm certainly not helping you die. Do not ask me again."

CHAPTER 4

AN HOUR LATER, I'm sitting beside Leno, looking across the expanse of a polished and obviously expensive hardwood desk at Draco, aka Mr. Dawlish.

"Explain that to me again, if you would be so kind," Mr. Dawlish says. He looks like the movie version of a perfect British butler and has the accent to go with it. His words and manner are impeccably polite, but the way he folds his hands on the surface of the desk and tilts his head just off-center, eyebrows raised in an inquiring expression, clearly indicates his opinion that both Leno and I are idiots.

"Which part did you need to have explained?" Leno asks. "I think I made it fairly clear."

"I fear I missed the reasoning that makes this party scheme of yours anything other than a selfish whim."

"You mean the bit where I think dying sucks and I don't want a long-faced, lugubrious funeral?"

"I'm still hearing only the selfish part. What difference

does it make to you? You won't be there for it. Your friends and family will. Are you thinking about your mother at all?"

"Trust me. I'm thinking about her plenty. She's already got my funeral all planned, from the music to the flowers. Wouldn't be at all surprised if she's already ordered up a coffin."

"Your point?" the lawyer asks.

"My point is she's planning exactly the sort of event I'd rather die than participate in."

"I hardly think your participation will be called for. All you'll need to do is lie there and look...dead."

"Which is exactly the problem! I don't want a funeral, I don't want a casket, and I don't want everybody and their dog staring at my dead body. I want to be cremated. I want a rave. I want a huge 'Leno is dead' bash. Addy will plan it. I need you to write up a contract, all signed and official, between Addy and me, so Mom and Owen can't stop it. And I need money put in a party account to pay for food, musicians, and to secure a venue—"

"A venue?" I interrupt. "You do recall that we are throwing this shindig in the huge, sprawling metropolis of Fox Valley? We don't have venues. Also, maybe you really *should* consider the feelings of your family."

"The young woman has the sense that you lack," Mr. Dawlish says. "The media will be all over this. Influencers and reporters everywhere, harassing your family and friends. Having a party like this would really not be fair to your mother."

"Fair? There's nothing fair about any of this!" Leno bursts out. "In case nobody has noticed, I'm the one whose life is being cut short. I'm the one who is going to die. Mother will live to be a hundred. Owen will, too, and I'll be—"

"Do not say moldering," I cut in. "For the love of whatever comes beyond. Do. Not. Go. There."

He glares at me and enunciates clearly, "I will be moldering in the ground."

"Please," Mr. Dawlish says. "More to the point, do you not think your mother and brother will grieve you? Have you grown so selfish and shallow that this doesn't matter to you?"

"I can't afford to let it matter," Leno says. "Listen, Draco, I'm just trying to get through this the best I can. Of course, they will grieve. Hopefully, they'll even miss me. But I can't bear... I cannot abide the thought of being the object of a mass hysteria of weeping and wailing. People showing up only to gawk—a Matthew Perry sort of media frenzy where my tragic death is the news of the day."

"You don't think they are going to come gawk if you throw a party? Have you considered the feeding frenzy you'll be creating?" Draco asks.

"Yes, but I'll be controlling the narrative! Whether they think it's awesome or a travesty, they'll all be talking about the party. Not going on and on with bullshit like, 'He was taken too soon...poor tragic young man, his life cut short.' That's the part I can't... I just...can't."

For the first time since I stumbled over him in the church, Leno gives in to genuine emotion. His voice chokes off; his face crumples. "Oh, goddammit," he mutters and rolls his wheelchair out of the room, leaving the attorney and me looking at each other across the desk.

Mr. Dawlish passes his hands over his own eyes, and I see that he's no more immune to Leno's tears than I am. "I suppose there's no stopping him," he says after a silence. "But you should know that his family can be...formidable."

"I've met them," I say. "I have the good sense to be terrified."

"As you should be."

"Mr. Dawlish, I want you to know that—"

He smiles. "Draco. Please. Enough with the formalities. You are making me feel old."

I stare at him in discomfort and shift a little in my seat.

"Ah, I see," he says. "You feel you would be rude. But Draco is, in fact, my given name. Someone in every generation of my family carries it to remind us that our line extends backward into the eons of time."

"And your son?"

"Alas. I haven't one. Nor a daughter, either, before you suggest that she should be so afflicted. I fear the dragons will die out with me." His smile fades, and he sighs. "Speaking of dying—"

"And moldering," Leno says, rolling back into the room. "Draw up the contract. In the meantime, Addy, let me give you a small gesture of good faith."

He digs a money clip out of a zippered front pocket in the jacket he's wearing, peels off ten one-hundred-dollar bills, a sight I'm pretty sure I haven't seen before, and hands them to me. "That's not part of the ten thousand. It's extra. Consider it a signing bonus."

"Leno," Draco says quietly and with the sort of authority that is an automatic attention-getter. "If you must do this, you might consider telling your family soon rather than expecting Addison to break the news herself."

"Next stop," Leno says. "We're going there directly from here."

"Um," I say. "Sitting here. Will of my own. Conscious decision maker. Hard no to going to see your fam."

"I just tipped you a thousand bucks," Leno protests. "Can people not be bought anymore? We can tell them about the party and about my upcoming date with death while we're at it."

I've noticed that most clichés are threadbare for the same reasons as well-worn clothing. They are practical and serve a purpose. The age-old 'everybody has a price' is a case in point. I sit there, wondering if this is mine. Will I swallow this casual assumption that I'll do whatever Leno wants and help him run interference with his family? I certainly could use this money.

Rent is due. Again. The hike in electricity and rent and groceries and basically everything that happened after Covid has thrown my budget all out of kilter. Jezebel has started an ominous knocking sound, and I need new tires before next winter. On the other hand, the one thing I seem to have going for me so far in the life skills department is that I don't kowtow to anybody. I don't do guilt or obligation, and the only person who is the boss of me is...me.

I knew better than to come here with Leno, but I let sympathy carry me away. He'll keep on leading me along, one step at a time, like that *If You Give a Mouse a Cookie* book. If I go with him to talk to his family, we'll end up also telling them that he's going to end his life next Tuesday. And I'll end up picking up his prescription for him, and then, since I've already picked it up, I'll open the bottles...

No. I have to walk away now. I lay the bills down on the desk in front of me, neaten them up into a perfect stack, and get to my feet, leaving them there. "Funny how dying doesn't make somebody stop being a manipulative dick. It was nice meeting you, Draco. Don't waste your time preparing all of that paperwork."

"Oh, come on," Leno protests. "Don't be like that. I didn't mean—"

The door closes behind me on whatever lame-ass apology he was trying to offer.

CHAPTER 5

My family, along with Mom and Aunt Rachel's friends and frenemies, a handful of emotional vampires, and three widowers who are probably just hungry, are seated on folding chairs in the living room, consuming food from all the funeral casseroles that have been dropped off over the last week.

When I walk in, all voices stop and a deep silence descends. Every eye in the room is focused on me, some curious, some disappointed, a few obviously hostile. Some of the people in this room love me, but love has a tendency, I've noticed, to carry expectations and fuel anger. Especially over perceived betrayals. Especially when there is grief involved. Even Vic looks pissed off, and I can't really blame him. I did leave him to be Mom's sole support at the graveside. Which is fine, really, because all three of us know he's the only one she really wanted there anyway.

Groveling would only make things worse, so instead, I toss

a verbal hand grenade and brace myself for the detonation. "How was the graveside? Any food left? I'm starving."

Mom's face turns a congested sort of reddish-purple before she tries—and fails—to find release in a torrent of words. "How dare you be so...so..."

"Inconsiderate?" Vic supplies.

This releases the floodgates, and Mom is able to get on with her lecture. "Beyond inconsiderate! Your behavior at the funeral was bad enough. I thought I'd raised you better than this. Your grandmother loved you. I thought you cared about her. You two always seemed so close—but you couldn't even be bothered to show up to her grave."

Mom's voice breaks, and she dabs at her eyes with the tissue already clutched in her hand.

I shuffle my feet, hit with a wave of remorse. Not only has Mom just lost her own mother, but my behavior has now opened her up to gossip from her friends. Instead of respectfully and dutifully doing what was expected of me, not only by my mother but also by my brother and my entire social group, I told myself I was staging a protest for Geneva when, in reality, I was being manipulated by an asshole. A dying asshole, yes, but manipulation is manipulation.

Before I can open my mouth to apologize, Mom adds the final flourish.

"You're just like your father."

This is the lowest of low blows, and the worst part is that a tiny part of me knows she is right. Case in point, this nugget of fear doesn't inspire me to be a better person; it just fuels my contrariness. Despite the room full of people who will surely carry news of our altercation out into the wider world, I hurl myself onto a verbal battlefield, prepared to die a thousand wordy deaths before I surrender.

"Geneva didn't want to be buried. She wanted to be cremated and have her ashes scattered in the ocean or shot out of a cannon. She was really clear about not wanting a funeral or a coffin and definitely about not wanting to be buried, so excuse me for attempting to honor her last wishes."

Mom bristles. That might sound like a metaphor, but it isn't. Mom really can bristle. She gets all super-straight and extra-angular, and her eyebrows jut out, or at least they would if she hadn't over-plucked them in honor of the funeral. Even her hair seems to stand up at the roots.

"Funerals are for those who remain behind," she says with great dignity.

"And we want her body where we can visit it," Aunt Rachel adds, joining the fray. "So we can bring flowers and remember her."

"Well, I'd rather remember her alive instead of dead and buried," I retort.

Without warning, all the bristle goes out of Mom, and she sort of wilts. Then she sobs, a real sob this time. Now I really am sorry because I know she's hurting and I'm making it worse. I'm just not sorry for the things she thinks I should be sorry for.

I've taken precisely one step toward her chair, thinking maybe I should give her a hug, when Stephanie Markle exacts her revenge for my earlier dig about Rose.

"It's a pretty story, your respecting Geneva's wishes and all," she says. "But that's not really the truth of it, is it? You were at *Grounded* with that Leno Masterson character. Laughing! While your poor, dear grandmother was being lowered into the ground."

Damn, I expected gossip would catch up to me but not quite this fast. All eyes swivel toward me again, waiting for my response.

When there's a tap at the door, I nearly trip over my own feet in my hurry to answer it. But before I can get there, it opens of its own accord, and I see that this is not a reprieve but an ambush and that my mother has more or less summoned the devil by speaking his name.

My father knows how to make an entrance; I'll give him that. He poses on the doorstep as if it's a stage, playing the rich and successful movie star in his expensive suit and shiny shoes. The universe gets in on the action and lights him from behind, his hair gleaming silver in a well-aimed ray of sunlight.

"Sorry I'm late," he proclaims in a ringing voice. "Flights were a mess."

It's a great performance, but this is a hostile crowd. Dad strayed far from the church shortly after Vic and I were born. He strayed from his marriage vows not long thereafter. Most of his indiscretions were committed out of town during his travels with the off-Broadway productions he was part of, and Mom tolerated them until he had the nerve to carry on with a woman right here in Fox Valley and she could no longer ignore the truth.

"Oh, for pity's sake," Aunt Rachel says, after a long and very expressive silence. "I don't see why you bothered to come at all."

For possibly the first time in the course of history, I agree with my aunt. The only silver lining in Dad's arrival is that his entrance has topped mine and given everybody a bigger target for their animosity.

Oblivious to the hate, he turns to me. "Got a hug for your dad, Addison?"

I've exhausted my oppositional powers for the moment and move into his dramatically open arms. He smells expensive and foreign, and it's like hugging a stranger. He usually calls on birthdays and Christmas, but it's been a couple of years since I've seen him.

Vic gets to his feet and comes over.

"Hello, son," Dad says, but he's smart enough not to go for a hug.

"Richard," Vic replies.

There's a moment of awkward silence; then Dad steps farther into the room, where he pauses to inspect us both critically, as if he's in charge of a casting call. "So hard to believe the two of you actually looked alike when you were babies."

Which is true. Vic got Dad's physical genes—the fabulous facial structure and wavy, dark hair, those dreamboat hazel eyes with to-die-for lashes, and a long, lean physique that allows him to eat whatever he wants and still look like he goes to the gym every day, even though he doesn't. Me? I'm all flyaway carrot-colored hair—nothing so elegant as auburn going on here—with eyes that are sometimes brown and sometimes green, and a persistent chubbiness that is unfazed by any diet or exercise program I've ever thrown at it. Of course, I'm not exactly disciplined, so these attempts never last long.

Dad surveys us, beaming, and then, even though I'm the one who has dutifully hugged him and the one who still cares enough to call him Dad, he chooses to put me down right there in front of everybody. "I'm not sure that dress is entirely right for you, Addy."

"That is the dress *your daughter* wore to the funeral," Mom says. "After which, she went out for coffee with a movie star while the rest of us were at the cemetery." Her tone makes it amply clear that the apple hasn't fallen far from the tree and that my being with Leno instead of at the graveyard is equivalent in the sins department to all of Dad's philandering and neglect.

"He's not a movie star, he's a musician," I retort. "He was shaken up by the funeral and his own approaching death and asked if I'd talk with him a little. It seemed a good way to honor Geneva to offer comfort to someone who isn't far behind her. Since I wasn't going to the graveyard, I did that. Anybody else want to beat me up about where I was or what I'm wearing?"

Watching their faces, I can see that I've just declared open season on Addison. They are all delighted by the idea of beating up on me, and I can practically see them sharpening cutting remarks in their heads.

Vic, not for the first time in our lives, saves me. He turns the full beam of his considerable charm on all the ladies in the room. "Who wants some dessert? I happen to know there is a strawberry cheesecake in the fridge. Jeannie brought that, I believe, and we all know how delicious her desserts are."

"It was my mother's recipe," Jeannie says modestly.

"The one you made for Carolyn Ingram's wedding shower?" Aunt Rachel asks. "I've been meaning to ask you for the recipe."

Mom gets out of her chair. "I could use some dessert. Coffee, anybody?"

"I'll make coffee," Vic says. "I believe Stephanie also brought some of her fabulous apple pie. Didn't you, Stephanie?" He lets his hand rest, respectfully but not too respectfully, on Stephanie Markle's lower back, ushering her forward.

Everybody follows him like he's the Pied Piper, and I consider making a break for my car and getting out of here altogether, but the lure of cheesecake is strong.

My phone rings. It's an unknown caller, and I silence it. It rings again, same unknown number. Again, I hang up on it. And then a text message pops up.

> Unknown Number: So, today was bad timing. How about tomorrow?

I ignore it, but Leno's not one to give up easily. His mother spoiled him rotten to begin with. Add in years of groupies fawning all over him, and obviously, he's used to getting everything he wants. Well, this time he can go on wanting.

> Unknown Number: Come on, Addy. Don't be like that.

I add his number to my contacts so I'll know it's him if he calls again and be sure not to answer, then shove the phone into my purse and head for the kitchen.

Thanks to Leno, everybody got here before me. The space is jammed full of church ladies, plus Dad, Mom, Vic, Aunt Rachel and Uncle Newsom, and the three hungry widowers, all lined up for cheesecake. By the time I get there, nothing will be left but crumbs. I'm contemplating the logistics of absconding with the empty pan and licking it clean somewhere when my phone starts pinging again.

And, of course, I can't resist looking at it.

> Leno: Name your price.

> Addy: I missed out on the best cheesecake in the history of mankind because of you. Also, we were seen at Grounded, and everybody's mad. Also how did you get my number?

> Leno: At least you're not dying.

> Leno: It's on your business card.

> Leno: Don't suppose I could talk you into picking up my Leno-has-a-right-to-die prescription? It's ready, apparently. Too tired to go get it.

> Leno: Seriously. I need you.

Oh hell. I'm fairly impervious to the words "I love you," mostly because I've had enough experience to know how transient and often deceptive and manipulative those words can be. But *I need you*? That gets me every damned time.

Not this time. I'm out.

> Leno: I'll order you in all the cheesecake you want. We can fly it directly from the Cheesecake Factory.

> Leno: Really. I'm sorry. Come talk tonight? There's something else I really need to tell you. It's more important than anything else.

> Addy: No.

> Leno: Tomorrow then. At Grounded. Just to talk.

> Addy: ☺ No. Non. Nein. Nyet.

I catch a whiff of expensive cologne, and then Dad's voice says behind me, "Is that the movie star?"

"Rock star."

"You should go talk to him," Dad says.

For a fraction of a second, I believe maybe he's developed some compassion or empathy and is feeling sorry for a dying man or has wisdom to offer about how I should not be petty and should do the right thing.

A mistake which he quickly rectifies. "A connection like that could be invaluable for you and your business."

"Thanks, Dad, but my business is doing just fine."

"Is it, though? I saw that old wreck of yours parked in the driveway. You need a new vehicle with your business logo on the doors. You should expand out of Fox Valley. Get a loan, hire a team. You could work in Spokane, Seattle, Tri-Cities...maybe expand into Oregon and California. Networking is everything. Maybe this Leno person—"

"He's dying, Dad. Possibly not the best networking connection."

"Better make it quick," he says, with a smile that is disturbingly similar to Vic's, except for the way it's lacking humanity and warmth.

"Right," I say, edging away from him. "Thanks for the tip. I need to, um...wash dishes."

Crusty casserole dishes are soaking in the sink, dirty plates are stacked on the counter, and the dishwasher is already full and running. Mom is not a believer in paper plates—and not for reasons having to do with preserving forests or preventing global warming.

"Paper plates are not civilized," she always says, and maybe she has a point. Anyway, for possibly the first time ever in my life, I prefer to be stuck in the kitchen while everybody else wanders off to the living room to stuff themselves with dessert and snacks while reminiscing about Geneva.

And when the dishes are done, I slip past the living room and the few die-hard comforters still remaining, and tiptoe up the stairs to the room that has been Grandma Geneva's for the last six weeks, which was when she got too weak to be able to take care of herself at home.

I lie down on the bed that she died in and close my eyes, wanting more than anything to feel close to her, but the bed has been remade with new sheets and a new comforter and smells like fabric softener. Mom and Aunt Rachel have already either trashed or tucked away all the small belongings that were part of her dying. She's not here. She's not where they buried her. She's not anywhere.

"I miss you," I whisper, trying to sense something, anything, of Geneva still lingering. I hear the distant murmur of voices downstairs. A car driving by outside. The drone of a lawnmower from across the street. "I'm sorry I didn't do your party. I caved."

"You could do that Leno boy's party," Geneva's voice says in my head.

"God, not you too?" I respond out loud, just in case she can hear me.

"Just saying. Some dead person should get their last wish," imaginary Geneva says.

Right that minute, my phone pings. Leno again.

> Leno: I'm thinking Buena Vista. For the venue.

> Addy: I said no.

> Leno: I'm sorry I was a dick.

Addy: You're still being a dick.

Leno: Please.

Addy: What do you want?

Leno: Besides another fifty years? Wish list: pick up my pills from the pharmacy, plan my party, be there when I die...

Addy: Not a chance.

Leno: Okay, just pick up the pills? A loaf of bread, a bottle of wine, the prescription at the pharmacy...maybe they have cheesecake.

Addy: No.

Leno: Fine. But we really do need to talk about this other thing. If you won't meet me, I can call you now.

Addy: No.

Leno: I need you to do something nobody else can do.

Leno: It's not something I can text. In case somebody sees my phone.

Probably it's just guilt-fueled imagination, but I hear Geneva's voice again. *"Here's your chance, my girl. Why won't you do this for him?"*

"Because he's an asshole?" I say out loud. "Because I don't like being manipulated?"

"It costs you nothing to listen," the whisper says. And that's it. Nothing more.

Still, I feel a little closer to her. There's also that thing about being needed, combined with my curiosity and the thought of how guilty I'm going to feel after Leno's gone if I refuse to even listen to whatever deathbed confession he feels compelled to spill in my ears.

> Addy: Fine. I'll talk. No promises. Tomorrow. Grounded at 2.

> Leno: Deal. Will you pick up my meds?

> Addy: 😒 No.

FRIDAY

CHAPTER 6

I'M at a Leno and the Lonely concert in the high school auditorium with Vic and Britt and, weirdly, also Aunt Rachel and Dad, who are dancing together in the aisle. Everybody is in full evening dress, except for me. I'm wearing pajamas, my hair uncombed, my teeth unbrushed. I'm clutching a stack of books, my Intro to Chemistry *text right on top.*

The band starts to play "Live While You're Young," and Leno looks down off the stage directly at me and announces, "Addison Winters is going to take the solo on this one."

"Go on," Britt says, shoving me toward the aisle, but I can't. I'm not dressed properly and I can't sing anyway and...

My eyes fly open. I'm in bed. Bruno is doing his best meatloaf impression on my chest, and my phone is ringing. I'm still in my pajamas and my hair is still uncombed, but thank God nobody is expecting me to sing and I'm long done with chemistry classes.

Sure that it's Leno again, I answer without checking caller ID. "Would you stop harassing me?"

The voice on the other end is irritated, female, and definitely not Leno. "I need you, Addy. We need to go over things, right this minute. I've left you messages, but you don't answer."

"Lisa? What time is it?"

"This is an emergency, Addison. Meet me at *Grounded* in thirty minutes."

I nudge Bruno off of me and sit up, feeling dazed and hungover, which isn't fair because I never had a drop of anything stronger than funeral fruit punch yesterday.

"Lisa, wait. I can't possibly be there that soon."

"You promised me when I signed you to plan my wedding that I would be absolutely the most important thing in your life for the full three weeks leading up to the wedding. And it's in ten days. Ten days, Addy, do you hear me?"

I hear panic and a Bridezilla moment in the making, and I am so not in the right frame of mind for this. Still, I take a breath, sit up, and get my eyes open, thinking through what I need to do. Nearly every bride has a meltdown moment, and I know one sure remedy. Undivided attention, checklists, calm, competence, and reassurance.

A little strategic guilt can also be helpful. "I'm so sorry, but it was a long day yesterday, what with my grandmother's funeral and all," I tell her, making my voice sound as pathetic and exhausted as possible.

"Oh, Jeez, Addy—"

"Give me an hour to pull myself together. I'll meet you there at...better make it 11:30. Okay?"

"I'm sorry, Addy, about your grandma. I just—"

"I shouldn't have mentioned it." I add a little quaver to my voice, take a breath, and switch up to a bravely moving-on tone. "I'm all yours now, okay? Everything will be fine."

"All right," she says. "Eleven-thirty."

She hangs up, and I sit there, trying to get myself fully awake. Bruno yawns, stretches, and rolls over on his back, inviting me to pet his belly.

"Not falling for it," I tell him. I know from experience that if I succumb to the temptation of stroking that tempting and vulnerable expanse of fluffiness, my hand will be instantly trapped in teeth and claws while he shreds me with a series of kangaroo kicks.

He meows pathetically, then springs up into the air, coming down on all fours and sinking his teeth into a teddy bear that is nearly as big as he is. It's not his. Not mine, either, and it wasn't here when I went to bed last night. Bruno, who goes in and out through a cat door, has a very bad habit of stealing things he's taken a fancy to and bringing them home.

"You're going to have to give that back," I tell him, tugging at the bear's floppy feet.

Bruno growls and lays his ears back, holding on tight.

"Fine, have it your way, then." I get out of bed and cross the approximately twenty feet to the corner of my one-room apartment that is more or less—mostly less—a kitchen. As expected, the sound of a can of cat food opening brings Bruno running, all happy trills and purring, to rub around my legs for all the world as if he wasn't trying to kill me thirty seconds ago. While he's eating, I rescue the teddy bear and put it in a cupboard where it's safe. Later, I'll take a pic and add it to the "*Is this Yours?*" section I've created on the community bulletin board.

Right now, I need to get a move on. I shower and get dressed in a blazer, blouse, and a neatly pressed pair of slacks, a uniform designed to convey competence and calm, but I'm anything but. Leno is planning to meet me at two. What if he shows up while I'm still dealing with Lisa?

She's the owner of *Foxy Lady Hair and Nails*—gossip central in our town. If she sees me with Leno, the news will be disseminated through various rumor feeds—both in person and on social media—to the farthest corners of the earth.

I'll need to be totally on top of this meeting. Keep her focused, allay all concerns, and move her on. Quickly. The timing should be fine. An hour, two, tops, and I'll have her squared away. The spreadsheets are all on my laptop, but I take time to run off print copies and put them on a clipboard. I put the clipboard, my laptop, and a couple of the pens I ordered specifically for her event into a briefcase. It's helpful for an anxious bride to have physical evidence that everything is under control.

When I arrive at 11:25, she's already at a table and halfway through her drink. Apparently, she told Kathy I was coming because my macchiato and an apple turnover are also waiting on the table.

Lisa's eyes are red, as if she's been crying, and she's fidgeting with a pen and paper. Making her worry list, I suspect, which is fine. Everything is under control.

"Bad night?" I query, sliding onto a chair across from her. I gaze longingly at my drink. I need coffee and sugar, and yes, whipped cream, but the whole point of this meeting is to come across as competent, business-like, and in control. Sucking on a straw doesn't quite go with the image.

"The worst," she says. "I got to thinking about things. Did

you remember that I changed my mind about my bouquet? And can we even really get peach-colored roses? I dreamed the bridesmaids were all carrying these hideous purple roses that were awful with their dresses. And about the dresses—"

"Lisa. Breathe. Really, I mean it." I demonstrate with a slow, deep inhalation. "Come on, do it with me. In through the nose, out through the mouth."

It's nearly impossible not to go along with somebody inviting you to breathe. I get her to take three deep breaths, then an extra one for good measure, before I open my briefcase and hand her the clipboard to look over while I pull up files on my laptop.

One by one, I go through the items. The flowers I've ordered for the bridal bouquet, the bridesmaids and the floral arrangements. I assure her that I've checked in with Fox Valley Flowers and Gifts just two days ago, and Barb has ordered everything from the wholesaler and promised it will be here right on time. I remind her that the bridesmaids' dresses have all been fitted and are already hanging in my closet, where there's no danger of accidents befalling them. The tuxedos are rented, including the smaller one for her twelve-year-old son, Jackson. We go through the music, and I show her confirmation emails from the musicians and the check-in I did with them last week.

And on through the list and the plans. Marriage license, minister, vows, ring bearer, cars from the church to Buena Vista, the menu, the cake, the decorations for the wedding and the reception.

Lisa makes little checkmarks next to each item on the clipboard, but she looks increasingly agitated rather than reassured. Finally, she makes the final check mark and lays down the pen, drains the last of her skinny, sugar-free, why-bother-drinking-it latte, and gets to the real problem.

"Can I tell you something, Addy?"

"Like what a wonderful job I've done and you can't believe how organized things are?"

This fails to elicit even the smallest of smiles, so I know I'm about to hear what's really on her mind and that it's probably got nothing to do with the wedding arrangements. Brides—and grooms—confide in me. I carry secrets around that I half expect I'll be killed for one of these days.

I allow myself one fortifying sip of my drink, wondering what Lisa is about to tell me. Will it be garden variety pre-wedding jitters, concerns about Jackson having a stepfather, a last-minute cheating story, or something even more sinister and dark, like that she's discovered Brad is a serial killer and is afraid for her life?

She twists the diamond on her finger. "I think the real problem is I don't want to get married. Or, at least, not to Brad. Is that awful?"

Just jitters, then. I know what to do about this. Calm reassurance. Normalization. It's already after one and I need to move her on out of here before Leno shows up.

"It's not ideal," I say, "but you wouldn't be the first bride to get cold feet. Honestly, it comes with the territory." I give up on my professional image and slip into the role of girlfriend and confidante, which means I can finally take a real slurp of my own non-skinny drink. It's mostly melted but still delicious, and my brain cells are ecstatic to finally get the hit of sugar and caffeine they've been waiting for.

"Did you hear about Leno Masterson?" she asks, as if somehow reading my thoughts.

All of my complacency vanishes as I scan the room, my heart rate kicking up a notch. Is he here already? Did I miss him rolling in?

"What about him?"

"I thought I was going to marry *him* in high school," Lisa says.

"We all thought we were going to marry him in high school," I say, watching the door. "If that's what this is about, let it go now. All an illusion. You got cold feet. You started asking *what-if* questions, and then all of a sudden, there was Leno reminding you of the life you could have had."

She laughs, then sobs, then pulls a tissue out of her purse to blot her eyes and wipe her nose. "I can't believe he's dead. I can't believe that I..." Her voice breaks, and she buries her face in her hands.

Obviously, I've heard her wrong. I stare at her, my brain trying to make sense of her words. "He's not dead," I say. "Dying, maybe, but—"

Lisa raises her head and looks at me. Mascara has smeared under her eyes, but the tears have already stopped.

"Oh, he's definitely dead. I heard it from Cass Murphy first thing this morning when I was doing her hair. She heard it from Maureen. Mo cleans house for Sylvie Masterson, and she told Cass she went over to clean like she always does on Fridays. When she got there, she was turned away at the door —could hear Sylvie Masterson wailing inside somewhere, and Leno's brother came to the door and said that Leno had died during the night. He said they'd pay her for her time but asked that she please just go away."

"But he can't be dead," I repeat, caught in a loop of shock

and denial. Leno isn't scheduled to die for another four days. He's meeting me here in...twenty-five minutes.

"Maybe Cass got it, I don't know, confused?"

"How do you confuse something like that?" Lisa's mascara-smeared eyes narrow.

"Was it... How did he... Are they... How did he die?" I ask, doing a bad job of containing my shock. A surge of surprising sadness threatens to swamp me. Leno was a manipulative asshole, but he was a young and talented one. And, once upon a time, he was my friend.

"He had *cancer*," Lisa says, slowly and carefully, as if I'm a total imbecile.

"But he was fine yesterday. I mean, as fine as he could be when he is—*was*—dying. I expected he'd, like, linger, you know?" I figure Leno telling me about his right-to-die program was in confidence, so I keep that to myself.

Lisa is still looking at me like I've totally lost my mind.

"It's so hard to believe he's actually dead, you know?" I explain. "I mean, he was our age."

"Killing yourself like that, though," Lisa says. "That's the part I can't get around." Her eyes are still all teary, but she's got that fascinated expression on her face, the one people get when they're looking at some awful traffic accident or watching a horror movie. "Shannon said she heard that it was medically assisted suicide with a prescription and everything." She shivers. "Can you imagine? I could never do it."

My brain is spinning, spinning, and all I can think of is this: if Leno was planning on crossing the rainbow bridge last night, then why on earth was he so insistent on meeting me today?

"Could you?" Lisa asks, and I drag my mind back to her question.

"End my own life? I don't know," I say, pretending I'm pondering an answer while I'm really confronting another question that has just popped into my head.

What if he didn't die on purpose? What if somebody killed him?

The last two things Leno really wanted were to choose his own death and to have a big send-off party, and they were things I could have helped him with, well, the party anyway, and I got stubborn and said no. Typical for me, guilt morphs into anger, and anger into a need to do something to rectify all that is wrong in this world. Geneva didn't get her send-off party. Leno is going to get his.

It needs to be soon. The Sunday of Lisa's wedding would be perfect. And the only venue in town that could accommodate a send-off party for Leno is the venue we've booked for her reception. Buena Vista is Fox Valley's version of a country club. It features a banquet hall, extensive gardens, and a gorgeous view. It can accommodate three hundred guests inside, a couple hundred more if the weather's fair enough for outdoor tables.

For about twenty seconds, I balance on the edge of an ethical dilemma. I need Lisa's venue for Leno's party. I need the time and attention I'm going to have to lavish on her because frankly, pulling off the kind of bash Leno wanted in the amount of time allotted will test all of my resources and abilities.

With the release of one deep breath, I dive into the shark-infested waters of client manipulation.

"What are you thinking?" Lisa asks, which gives me the perfect opening.

"I guess I'm thinking about how short life is, how we should live it to the fullest, and how you never really know what other people are capable of, even when you think you do."

Her eyebrows go up, her face conveying the warning that she's still half Bridezilla and I'd be wise to watch my step. "Did you have a point?" she asks.

I lean forward, fix her with my most earnest and compelling gaze, and say, "Run for the border. Go into witness protection. Something. Anything."

Her face goes ashen. One hand flies up to cover her lips. "Oh my God. What do you know?" She's staring at me like a deer frozen in the headlights, and I realize, a little late, that I may have overstated my case and made it sound like Brad really is a serial killer.

"I don't know anything, honest. It's just a...feeling I have. Don't marry Brad, if you're having doubts. Call it off."

"But..." Her expression goes blank, as if all activity in her brain has ground to a hard stop, and she just sits there, looking like a panicked bunny, too scared to run.

"Breathe with me," I say. "Deep breath in through the nose, slow breath out through the mouth..."

She follows along as if on autopilot. After the third breath, she blinks and appears to actually see me again. "But my beautiful wedding. I can't give that up."

It's not Brad who immediately springs to mind, I notice. Not how much she loves him and wants to be with him. And she was awfully quick to believe that he'd done something terrible. Maybe I'm actually doing her a favor by talking her out of the wedding.

"You can always plan another one. Or, you know, use these plans next time. Aren't you worried this is going to turn into a not-so-beautiful divorce? Think about the effect of that on your kid. Trust me, I'm the child of divorce and the scars run deep."

I almost have her. I see it on her face, in her eyes, in her body language. She sees it. She knows it. She's almost there.

"Planning it was really the fun part, wasn't it?" I press. "Way more than the actual day. Trust me. Standing around all day, trying to look beautiful and virginal in a white dress that is not going to be comfortable..."

She gasps, as if she's just now remembered how to breathe without being coached, and comes back from suspended animation. Her brain is now in on the action, and I launch my best shot.

"Come on, Lisa. Be honest. Those misgivings you're having are more than cold feet. Brad is pretty to look at and he can be charming, but do you really want to be married to him? Maybe the real reason you feel so nostalgic about your time with Leno is because you feel a bit like you've settled."

"I will kill you if you repeat this," she says, lowering her voice and leaning closer, even though the closest occupied table is ten feet away, where Bill Greenway is plugged into headphones and a laptop and obviously not listening to a word we're saying. "I do sometimes wonder if I might have done better. Maybe I don't want to live in Fox Valley forever, you know? I want to expand my business. Open a second location, or several, even. Brad is not exactly...ambitious."

I know when to say nothing, and I just sit there quietly with a sympathetic look plastered on my face, letting her go the rest of the way on her own. Everybody knows Brad is a womanizer and a party guy, and rumor has it he was seen with Delia Greenberg just last week, maybe flirting but maybe something more. Lisa has to have heard the gossip.

"You're right about my kid, too," she says. "Brad and Jacky are always butting heads. Everybody keeps telling me that it just takes time, but Brad tells Jackson what to do; then Jackson yells things like, 'You're not my father.' He's started acting out in school, and the teachers think it might be stress about us getting married."

But then she looks down at her hands, at the ring she's been twisting and twisting on her finger. "I'd have to give it back." Tears fill her eyes. "And I do love it so much."

I lean toward her and touch the huge diamond with one finger gently, then let my hand settle on her wrist. "I always wondered where Brad found the money for a rock that size."

"Oh, God," she says. "Do you think it's a fake? Of course, he doesn't have money for a diamond like this. I should have seen it earlier, right? How could I be so stupid?"

"Oh, do you think that could really be true?" I keep my voice skeptical, a little alarmed by what I've set into motion. I'd only meant to remind her that Brad doesn't have a lot of money, that he probably is way in debt over that ring. But it's way too late to backpedal now.

She's on her feet, her voice rising. "Why would I want to be married to a man who would give me a fake diamond? I'm going to go tell him it's off right now. Would you please be a darling and cancel everything? Could you take care of notifying all the guests, too?"

"I'm on it. Consider it done."

"You're the best, Addy. I owe you big time." She hugs me, then stalks off in a way that means nothing good for Brad.

For a very short minute, I feel sorry for him and a little bit guilty, but I really have done them both a favor, young Jackson, too. Brad will never have the kind of money and prestige Lisa is looking for, so she'll nag him to death, and he'll go on cheating, and the poor kid will be caught in the middle. Brad may not have really tried to pass off a cubic zirconia as a diamond, but he deserves what's coming to him all the same.

And Leno? Leno was certainly no saint, but I am going to be sure that he gets the party he wanted. I won't cancel Buena Vista; I'll just change the reservation and get Lisa her refund.

If it's not too late to get Draco to give me the money.

CHAPTER 7

WHEN I TURN the key in the ignition, Jezebel actually starts for once, sending up only a single black puff of exhaust in protest. I check my phone before I start to drive and wish I hadn't. I've got text messages from a wide selection of clients and former classmates and eleven voicemails, one of which is from my mother. Knowing I'll be sorry, I listen.

"Addison? Why is that you never answer your phone when I call? Did you hear the news about that boy you were with yesterday during Mother's funeral? You know the one. The rock star. He killed himself last night. You were just talking to him! He must have said something. You should have gotten him some help. I know Pastor would have been more than happy to go over and pray with him. Well, anyway, your little visit to the café is in the local news and all over the internet, Rachel says. Call me."

I check Instagram, and sure enough—pictures of Leno and me at *Grounded* are all over my feed. One of them has been badly photoshopped to make it look like the two of us are holding hands and gazing into each other's eyes. Shit. That I didn't see coming.

I scroll through the text messages, all hungry for news. *What do you know about Leno? Did he tell you he was going to kill himself? Were you dating?*

The only one I respond to is from Britt: **You okay? Call me!**

More or less, I text back. **Call soon.**

If I call her now, she'll try to talk me out of what I'm going to do. I'll call her after I see Draco and get the go-ahead to plan this party. She and Vic will both have plenty to say about that, but it will be too late, the wheels already in motion.

"Mr. Dawlish is very busy," Charlene says when I walk into the office and ask to see Draco. She tries to look down her nose at me from behind the reception desk, but she's sitting and I'm standing, which means she has to look up. Her sleek updo and power suit are elegant and professional, but the effect is lost on me.

I remember the time she got gum stuck in her hair and she had to cut it out with scissors in the girls' restroom and the time she walked around for an hour with her dress tucked into the back of her pantyhose before somebody—me—finally told her. I would have told her sooner, only she was a mean girl that year, power-drunk after being chosen as part of Queen Bee Marisol's inner circle, and I very nearly didn't tell her at all.

"I'm sure he is," I say, smiling sweetly when what I want to do is reach over and pull the pins out of her hair. "Could you please tell him I'm here to discuss some concerns around Leno Masterson's estate? I'll just wait right here until he has a moment to spare."

I drop into a chair, cross one knee over the other, and dig in my bag for the bubblegum I keep around for moments such as this. It's not that I actually like the stuff; it's that it's so deliciously annoying. Especially given the whole Charlene gum-in-the-hair incident, which is a bonus.

When she looks up at me over her computer screen, trying to be all haughty and repressive, I grin at her and blow a bubble until it pops. As I peel it off of my face and shove it back into my mouth, her superior act vanishes. She glances toward the door, then back at me.

"Addy," she says, pleading now, "I've got important clients coming in just a few minutes. Out-of-town people. With money. Would you please leave?"

I snap my gum loudly. "Sooner you get me in to see Draco, sooner I'm done sullying your waiting room."

"Addy..."

"You know, I am kind of hungry," I say, considering. "I could step down the street and grab a tuna salad sandwich."

"Would you? Please?"

"Extra onions. And bring it here to eat while I wait..."

Charlene caves. "Oh, fine. I'll let him know you're here, if you promise to leave if he says he doesn't have time to see you."

"It's a deal."

She picks up the receiver and says, "Addy Winters is asking to see you. I told her you were—but she doesn't have an appointment and—but—yes, Mr. Dawlish. I will." She hangs up and glares at me. "He'll see you now."

"Thanks awfully, Charlene. You've been super helpful. Don't bother to get up. I know my way."

If she had a dagger on her and knew how to throw it, it would be quivering in the flesh between my shoulder blades as

I walk down the hallway. Draco's door is open, and he looks up from the paperwork he's frowning over as I walk in and plop down into a chair.

"Miss Winters. What can I do for you?"

"I thought we were on a first-name basis now, Draco."

He gives me a repressive look over the top of his glasses—he really does have that whole snooty butler thing down to a tee—and doesn't respond.

"Is he really dead?"

Draco blinks, takes off his glasses and wipes them with a soft cloth he pulls from his desk drawer, and then puts them back on and adjusts them.

"I'm afraid so," he says, finally. "Was that all? I really do have some important clients arriving at any minute."

"I just... Leno wanted to meet me today. He said he had something really important he needed to tell me."

Draco lifts both eyebrows and looks at me inquiringly. "You were one of the very few people aware in advance that he planned to take his own life. Surely, you are not surprised that he's actually done it."

"But he wasn't going to do it until Tuesday."

"Apparently, he changed his mind. Now, Miss Winters—"

"But he said what he wanted to tell me was super important. We made plans to meet at *Grounded*, even. Today. At two."

Draco sighs. "Well then. It must not have been so very important after all."

"He wanted me to pick up his prescription, though," I say, blundering along. "He said he was too tired to pick it up himself. So how did he... I mean, did you, maybe?" I let my voice rise at the end and my own eyebrows with it, hoping he'll take the hint and tell me how Leno actually died and whether he was alone.

Draco doesn't take the bait. "I was quite clear with Leno that I would not assist him with hastening his own death. Now, if there's nothing else I can help you with, I really—"

"There is, in fact, something you can help me with." I settle into a chair to indicate that I'm prepared to hang out until my business is concluded. "I've decided to throw Leno that party he wanted. I'll need access to the account he asked you to set up."

"My understanding, Miss Winters, was that you had refused to plan that party."

I smile at him brightly. "It's Addy. Please."

"Addy." He lowers his voice and leans toward me, taking on a fatherly tone. If he knew about my relationship with my own father, he'd know this is a mistake because all it does is alert me to the probability of incoming misdirection.

"May I say that you were wise to refuse that bit of folly and suggest that you let the idea die with Leno? His family will be most appreciative, and Leno, God rest his soul, will never know."

"I'll know."

Abandoning the attempt to sound fatherly and wise, Draco sniffs and leans back in his chair. "What brought about this change of heart, if I may ask?"

"It's because he's dead."

"That was always rather the point of this misguided party idea, was it not?"

To my dismay, tears blur my vision—real ones, not a display I've summoned for the purpose of persuasion.

Draco slides a box of tissues across the desk. "Leno's death is truly sad and unfortunate on all levels. But I'm afraid I don't see how throwing a party will bring him back."

"Well, of course, he's not coming back." My voice wobbles.

"Possibly you are feeling guilt now, as if perhaps your refusal to help with his party led him to give up hope and just end things immediately?" Draco suggests.

"No!" I stare at him in dismay. I hadn't even considered that possibility. "I was just wondering if maybe somebody else might have...hurried him along."

"If you're trying to imply that there was some nefarious action that ended Leno's life, that is morbid and also ridiculous. Leno was dying. If, for some obscure reason, somebody wanted him dead, they'd need only to wait either for the cancer to take him or for him to do the job himself. I'd suggest that you drop such thoughts, and I certainly recommend that you don't share your suppositions with others. Particularly the media."

He's hiding something. I'd stake one of Kathy's caramel macchiatos on it. But I don't push the issue, because his face has gone hard, his eyes cold, in a dangerous sort of way that makes me want to scoot my chair back a couple of inches.

Draco opens his desk drawer and withdraws a large manila envelope.

"I refuse to discuss the manner of Leno's death with you further. Regarding the misguided party, I do, unfortunately, have clear directives and last wishes from Leno on that matter. In hopes that you would change your mind, he set up an account for the party yesterday and left a debit card for you with me. You will find it—and the pin number—in this envelope, along with a checkbook. You are authorized to write checks on the account."

He lays the envelope on the table, then withdraws another from the drawer, this one white and business-sized, and lays it on top of the other. "This contains a check for the money he wanted to pay you to plan his party. And that, I fear, is the end of my involvement with your project. Good luck. I think you'll find you need it."

"Thanks, but I think I make my own luck," I say, even though I could definitely use a little luck on my side. I open both envelopes just to be sure that everything is as he says. The check is for forty-thousand dollars, double what Leno said he'd pay me. That's a year's profit for me.

"If we're done here, I do have some clients I'm expecting," Draco says.

This time, I allow myself to be dismissed.

He calls me back when I'm halfway to the door. "One last thing. I suppose I might as well also tell you now. Leno wanted you to have his car, and he wanted you to have it right away— before his will was probated."

"He what?"

"I believe he mentioned it to you."

"I didn't think he was serious."

"His brother, Owen, is aware; you'll have to coordinate getting the car from him. And then do remember to transfer the title. Good day, Miss Winters. Please close the door on your way out."

Dismissed, I do as he says without another word, not even stopping to harass Charlene as I pass by her desk.

Things that are too good to be true usually are, and I don't trust the check Draco gave me at all. I drive directly to the bank, which is unusually busy, and I stand in line for a good fifteen minutes, fidgeting, before Missy Havers finally calls me over to her window.

"God, what a day, Addy. Been asking myself all morning how I ended up back in this town doing this job. I had dreams, you know? Business or personal account?" she asks as I sign the check and slide it across the counter.

"Definitely business."

I see her eyes widen as she picks up the check. "Holy shinoly. Sorry. I'm not supposed to react, but...wow."

"I'm planning a party for him," I say casually, knowing she'll for sure tell her customers. I want the whole town to be buzzing about this party.

"I heard he died, though." She leans forward and whispers this, as if it's a big secret. "I heard he killed himself."

"Not sure how he died," I tell her. "You know how gossip is."

"But—you're not still planning a party, his being dead and all."

"It's a send-off party. It will be at Buena Vista. You're invited."

She rewards me with a glowing smile. "Wow, Addy. Thanks. I'll get this deposited... It will probably take a few days to clear, given that it's so much."

"Understood. One more thing while I'm here."

I want to make sure the debit card for the party fund actually works, so I make a $100 withdrawal and get Missy to check the balance: one hundred and ninety-nine thousand and nine-hundred dollars. Which ought to be enough to cover a party that Fox Valley will be talking about for years to come.

SATURDAY

CHAPTER 8

I SHOULD HAVE GONE with Leno to tell his family about the party. Now that he's dead I have nothing but bad choices. One, I could just let them find out what I'm doing through the rumor mill. Two, I could send them a party invitation. Three, I can break the news in person. I'm inclined to the first option, but given the way Sylvie Masterson holds herself aloof from the general population of Fox Valley, it's possible the gossip will never reach her. And sending an invitation seems beyond insensitive, possibly even passive-aggressive.

So, option three it is. I call Britt and ask her to come with me to be my wingwoman and moral support.

"Have you lost your ever-loving mind? I'd rather be thrown into a pit of poisonous snakes. At least they don't pretend they're not going to bite you."

"Britt—"

She hangs up on me.

I swing by *Baked by Brie* for a box of pastries—croissants, apple turnovers, and a couple of Danishes. I'll offer food as an icebreaker, then move on to heartfelt condolences, and then I'll bring up the party. Casually. Charmingly. And then I'll ask about the car. What could go wrong?

The Masterson house—known to the community as Masterson Manor—is nearly at the top of Fox Mountain. The mountain is really more of a glorified hill, but the road is still winding and curvy, with steep inclines that Jezebel takes exception to. She gasps and shudders, being dramatic as usual, but in the end, she gets me there.

The wrought-iron gate is open, and I drive between the stone pillars with the honest-to-God stone lions on them. A paved drive curves between emerald-green lawn, flowering shrubs, rockeries, and meticulously tended flower gardens. There's even a pond with a fountain. There are three garage doors, all closed, and I wonder whether my new Maserati is hidden behind one of them.

I grew up in a modest bungalow, and I have friends and clients who live in manufactured homes. Even Britt's family— her dad, a doctor, and her mom, a tax accountant—live in a house about half the size of this one.

Stepping stones lead between raised flower beds to an imposing front door with heavy brass fittings and stained-glass windows. The doorbell button is set inside a polished brass plate with a fancy monogrammed *M* on it, and when I press it, the resulting sound is like a pipe organ in a cathedral.

Sylvie Masterson opens the door herself. She's wearing a little black dress, complete with a diamond pendant and earrings. Her frosted blonde hair is smoothed into an elegant chignon; her makeup is flawless. She doesn't look at all like a woman mourning the death of her favorite son.

"Can I help you?" she asks, her tone and expression making it clear that what would be most helpful would be for me to turn around and walk away.

Instead, I paste a smile on my face and hold out the box of pastries. "I'm so sorry for your loss."

I hear footsteps and look up to see Leno's brother, Owen, crossing the high-ceilinged entryway. He's tall, maybe six-two. Unlike Sylvie, he's wearing normal clothes—a pair of comfortable jeans and a black T-shirt without any sort of slogan. Average features, brown hair, glasses. But behind those glasses is a pair of keen gray eyes, the irises rimmed in black, that are anything but ordinary.

He stops behind his mother, and both of them stand there, barring the door, glaring at me.

"I'm not sure if you remember me," I say, to fill an awkward silence. "I'm Addison Winters."

"I know who you are," Owen says. "And I suggest you take your pastries and get back in that..." his eyes scan Jezebel, widening slightly, "whatever that is."

"You have something against pastries?"

"I'm against taking advantage of a dying man," he retorts.

"Manners, Owen," Sylvie murmurs, her tone implying that one must humor the plebeian hordes. "How kind of you to bring us some...food."

"She's here for Leno's car." Owen's eyes drill through me as if he's got magical X-ray vision that can read my soul. "The pastries, however delightful, are only a ruse to get in the door."

His face is lean and tanned, with a mouth that might be generous when it's not all tight with outrage and possibly grief.

"Generally, us commoners down below bring food to the

bereaved as an expression of our sympathy, just to be clear. If you don't want them..."

Owen takes the box from me and lifts the lid. "It's you I'm objecting to, to be clear. Not the pastries. Per se."

I remind myself that these people just lost a son and brother. Also that I am here on a mission, and there are ways of responding that will be helpful and ways of responding that will be unhelpful. What comes out of my mouth, and especially the tone of delivery, is decidedly in the unhelpful camp.

"Would you care to tell me why you object to me, *per se?*"

"Multiple choice," Owen says. "You're a gold digger or a grief vampire or an opportunist. Possibly all of the above."

"What could you possibly do for Leno now?" Sylvie asks. "After...after..." Her eyes fill with tears. "Owen, would you, please?" she murmurs in a broken voice. She turns and taps across the entryway and down a hallway, back stiff, head high, never saying exactly what it is she wants Owen to do.

"You should leave," he says. "The car is still over at the condo. I'll arrange with you about it later—maybe after the funeral, if you're able to restrain yourself that long."

"Like I said, I didn't come about the car. I came here as a courtesy to tell you what I'm doing—what Leno *asked* me to do —so you don't find out about it in the papers or the tabloids or whatever. I don't give a flying falcon about the car. Keep it. Donate it. Whatever floats your boat."

"Oh, come on," he says. "You expect me to believe that? You could purchase a house in this town with what that car is worth. Also, you are driving...*that*." He gestures toward Jezebel.

"She can hear you," I say. "My car. And she'll take it out on me. So, if you're done insulting both of us, I'll be off. Enjoy your pastries. Have a nice day."

"Did you just tell me to have a nice day?" he retorts. "My brother just died."

"Which is not *my* fault, so maybe don't take it out on me. Also? Just to be clear, I didn't ask to be involved in Leno's plans. I didn't ask for the car. He harassed and badgered and manipulated me."

"Well, that does sound like Leno." He sighs and rubs his hand across his face. "What sort of scheme is my brother hatching this time?" As soon as the words leave his lips, he stiffens, sucking in a sharp breath.

I feel the kick of that accidental present tense in my own belly.

He looks suddenly older, wearier. There's a sag in his shoulders that wasn't there a minute ago. "I'm sorry," he says, in a voice now scraped and raw with unpracticed grief. "I made assumptions, and I was a jerk. Would you like to come in?"

"To be fair," I say, "the pastries *were* a ploy to get in the door."

An unexpected smile tugs at the corners of his lips. "I would expect no less," he says, stepping to the side and gesturing me in. "This way."

I follow him down a gleaming hardwood hallway and into a room that I immediately label "the parlor." It certainly bears no resemblance to the outdated wooden paneling, nondescript, beige-ish carpet, and worn furnishings of the living room at Mom's house.

This floor is the same burnished hardwood as the hallway. Furniture is arranged around pristine squares of carpet that are probably handwoven from unicorn tail hairs or something. There's another chandelier suspended from the ceiling, this one bigger than the one in the entryway. The windows, highlighted by flowing cream and white draperies, look out on a manicured lawn and a rose garden. The sofa and chairs are all understated earth tones and look like they're rarely sat on; for sure, nobody sprawls on them to read while munching from a bowl of potato chips.

On the walls, in place of the slightly crooked array of gap-toothed school photos that adorn Mom's living room, hang four huge portraits in ornate gold frames. Leno poses with a guitar in his hands, his red-gold hair artistically mussed, eyes smoldering. Owen leans on a mantelpiece, his eyes focused on something in the distance, lips just turning up into a half smile, as if something surprising and delightful has just caught his attention. The other two paintings are presumably the parents, although I'm willing to bet Leno's mother's nose was never that small, nor her mouth that generous. His father looks imposing and severe, though undeniably handsome.

"Ghastly, aren't they?" Owen says.

"They are very...um..." Words fail me, for once. "Did you actually have to stand there for, like, a whole day while the artist painted you?"

He snorts. "Thank God, no. He worked off a photograph, so the worst of the ordeal was the hour it took for the photographer to be happy. Still, they are the gift that just keeps giving."

I spin around at the sound of heels tapping in the hallway, fight-or-flight adrenaline kicking in again at the thought of a rematch with Leno's mother. Owen does the same maneuver, and I sense him going tense beside me as she enters the room.

"Oh," she says, her eyebrows lifting. "I heard voices and thought we had *company*."

"Addison was about to tell me about what Leno had

requested of her," Owen says. "I thought it best that we have the conversation inside."

I half expect Sylvie to suggest that he should take me along to the kitchen, given that people of my class are simply not entertained in the parlor. But instead, she says, "I think I'd better sit down, hadn't I?"

She does so, lowering herself gracefully to perch on the edge of an uncomfortable-looking chair. Owen gestures me toward another, equally uninviting, and I settle myself onto its unyielding surface.

"Well, let's have it then," Sylvie says.

"First," I say, feeling my way along, "I should apologize. Leno wanted me to come with him to tell you about this together, but I—"

"Dear God," she says. "You're not...with child?"

"What? No. Oh my God, no. No!" Next to that assumption, I figure what I have to say might come as a welcome relief, so I take a deep breath and just dive in. "It's only that he asked me to throw a big party for him."

"I'm a party planner," I add when they both gaze at me with looks of incomprehension.

"But he's passed now," his mother says. "Surely this is no longer relevant?"

"The party Leno wanted is for...after. Now, actually. Or, more accurately, Sunday next week. Only, he wasn't planning to die until Tuesday, so maybe it would have been better to have it sooner, only that's the only day I can actually get the venue..."

They're both staring again, but this time, the shock runs deeper, and I trail off under the sheer volume of their incomprehension.

Owen drops his head into his hands. "Oh, God. He tried to tell me," he says, his voice muffled.

His mother's tone sharpens. "You knew about this? That he was going to do—what he did?"

Owen raises his head. His face has gone pale, the faint lines around his mouth and eyes etched deeper.

"Perhaps you would be so kind as to fill me in," Sylvie says.

"It sounds like Addison knows more than I do," Owen says.

"Leno came back here to die because Washington has a right-to-die law," I say. "He got doctors to sign off on the paperwork, and they wrote him a prescription. He was planning to—hurry along his death. But not until Tuesday. He asked me to be there, but I said no, and now he's dead. Early."

Owen gets up from his chair and crosses the room to the window, where he stands with his back to us, looking out, one hand braced on the window frame.

"I should have been there," he says. "So he wouldn't have died alone."

His words—and the tone they are uttered in—knock the breath out of me like a blow to the solar plexus. I wrap my arms around my belly, holding myself together.

Owen draws a ragged breath, then says, turning back to face me, "You'd better tell us all about this party."

I blink back tears and take a minute to steady my voice. "He said he didn't want a funeral. He hired me to throw him a big send-off bash—music and dancing and drinks. He...paid me in advance."

Sylvie's beautiful face looks carved from ice, and her voice is cold enough to match. "That's entirely out of the question. Leno could be... Well, let's just say his glamorous lifestyle created a certain hunger for sensationalism. Details of the funeral have already been arranged. Everything is in order. So, please don't trouble yourself with this wild notion."

"He wanted the party very much," I say. "His last wish. I'll be doing what he asked me to do."

"This may be something you're not able to grasp," Sylvie says, "but Leno is no longer here. We, his family and friends, are left to deal as we may with his passing. And how we choose to grieve is no longer his concern. And certainly, it is not yours."

"That's nearly exactly what my mother said about my grandmother's wish to have a send-off party. So, we didn't. We had a funeral, even though she made her wishes very clear. I'm giving Leno what he wanted."

Sylvie rises to her feet with great dignity. "Have you ever dealt with the paparazzi? With the media whores and the influencers?"

"No, but—"

"That is a Pandora's box you do not wish to open. And you will not. I forbid it."

She glides out of the room more slowly than she entered it. Her shoulders and back are straight, her steps steady, head high, but she moves carefully, as if no longer trusting that the ground will hold her. She looks suddenly fragile, a being of dust held together by willpower and pride.

"This will end her," Owen murmurs, watching her.

"The party?"

"The manner of his death. The gossip. And yes, the party. What she would call a vulgar display of poor taste, I imagine."

"Hey, my parties are never in poor taste."

"Right. Let me guess. Music—as in some second-string cover band, dancing, and booze."

"Tasteful cover band, dancing, and booze," I quip, unable to maintain the tension in this room for another second. Either we're going to lighten up, or one or both of us will explode in a mushroom cloud of toxic emotional radiation.

Owen's lips twitch in what is nearly a smile, but it dies before it's ever born. "We weren't...close. It wouldn't have been easy to talk to me."

"You want to help with the party?" I ask.

"You're really something, you know that?"

"So I've been told."

"I don't suppose I could talk you out of the party. Mother isn't going to respond well."

"Maybe your brother's last wishes matter more than your mother's concern for social conventions," I say. "Or yours, for that matter."

"You should go."

At first, I think I've pissed him off, but looking up into his face, I see that I've hurt him with what I've said. Well, it's too late to take it back now, and besides, I meant it. I head for the door, feeling like a heel.

"I'll be in touch about the car," Owen says, following me.

"No hurry."

As I'm backing Jezebel out of the driveway, he remains standing in the open doorway, watching me.

CHAPTER 9

"I am not helping you with this insane party," Vic says.

"What makes you think that's what this is about? Maybe I just wanted to talk to you." I bend down to lick whipped cream off the top of my macchiato.

"You want to talk to me *about* something. Or, more likely, you being you, *into* something. And the thing on your mind right now is Leno Masterson and the ridiculous party he asked you to plan."

"Fine. I need somebody to be in charge of the drinks and the bar. By an amazing coincidence, my very own brilliant brother is the owner of *Raven Brews and Bites* and makes fabulous craft beer and has a liquor license."

"I don't do wine, I definitely don't do champagne, and you can stow the flattery."

"Are you telling me you're not brilliant? Or that you don't make fabulous beer?"

He flips me off, and I laugh.

"Seriously, Vic. I bet a lot of guests would love to try your signature brews. And you know where to get the other stuff. It will be good for business."

"Wonderful as that sounds, I don't have money in the budget right now to give away free drinks at a shindig of the magnitude I think you're planning."

"You'll be paid. For product and time. Leno left me an expense account."

Vic, who knows me better than anybody in the world, gives me *the look*. "How much money?"

"A lot."

"How much, Addy?"

"Two hundred grand. He wants a star-studded crowd."

Vic whistles. "Okay, that's more than your usual budget. But still. You know you can't just invite everybody in town and put out a local news spot or something. You'll need a head count, a guest list, attendance by invite only. The people you're talking about have expensive tastes."

"I know these things," I retort. "And I also know I'm going to need help. Which is why I'm actually, you know, asking my one and only brother."

"If you're determined to proceed on this course, I'll help you," Vic concedes, as I knew he would. It's not just that he's been trying to get his brewpub off the ground for a couple of years now and this will give him some visibility. Vic always comes through for me in the end, even if he feels the need to lecture me first.

"I'm going to need coffee for this conversation," he says. "Who else did you summon to this meeting of the minds?"

"The usual suspects," I say evasively. I deliberately texted him an earlier meeting time than I did the others so I could get him on board first. "Want me to get you something?"

"I'll get it," he says, already heading for the counter.

I watch Kathy's face light up as he bends his head toward her and says something I can't hear. She laughs, looking at him in a way that doesn't make me jealous, exactly, but...yes. Fine. I'm jealous. She's my special barista, and now she's flirting with Vic.

Here's the thing about Vic. Starting in the womb, he's had the best of everything. He was nearly a whole pound bigger than me when we were born. As the doctor told my mother, and she later explained to us, one twin often gets more of the resources. Vic also got our father's looks, and some recessive gene in the pool gave him a marvelous personality to go with it. In addition to the looks and charm —maybe because of them—he also got the larger share of our mother's love.

I adore him, despite his perfection and the way he can do no wrong, ever, and... Oh, all right, yes. I'm also jealous of my brother. But I would die for him, if it came down to it.

My attention is drawn from Vic and Kathy by the grand entrance of my father. He's wearing dark glasses, even though the day is cloudy and it's dim in here. A ball cap shades his face. His branded polo shirt and designer jeans shout that he is somebody special who is not from here—even though he actually grew up in Fox Valley and lived here most of his life.

He stays there in the doorway long enough for all the patrons to notice him before he removes the sunglasses, raises a hand, and calls out to Vic, "Son, get me a latte while you're at it, would you?"

Vic glares daggers, not at Dad, but at me. I return his gaze and shrug. If I'd told him I'd invited Dad, he wouldn't have come.

"The usual, Mr. Winters?" Kathy sounds a little breathless and looks starstruck, even though Dad is sixty and only a small-time star. I mean, he was in one B-rated movie. The movie came to the theater in Fox Valley, and everybody saw it, so now, to them, I guess he kind of is a star.

"You remember my drink?" Dad calls across the room to Kathy, moving forward to a spot where there is better lighting.

"Brown sugar and cinnamon," Kathy says. "Grande, three shots. Coming right up."

Dad sits down across from me, and I already regret inviting him to this planning session. "Always good to see my favorite daughter," Dad says. "You're looking well, Addy."

"Knock it off. Flattery doesn't work on me."

Vic returns with a drink in each hand. He thumps the latte down onto the table just hard enough to make a point without actually smashing the cup or spilling anything because he is Vic and this sort of thing works for him.

"What's Richard doing here?" he demands. Vic hasn't used the word Dad since the day our father left us. He stops short of the disrespect of calling him Dick, but he also never uses Rich, which is the version our father has chosen.

"I need you both if I'm going to pull this party off," I say. "Sit down, Vic. Please."

Vic hesitates and then finally takes the chair next to Dad instead of beside me. I figure he doesn't want to have to look at Dad and he does want to glare at me, so he's chosen proximity as the lesser of two evils.

"Well?" he says. "We're waiting."

I take a nice, long, frosty slurp of my perfect drink. "Wait one minute. We've got another person. She should be here in—"

The door opens, and Britt glides in.

Britt has been my BFF since middle school. Both of us were forever in detention. She was always questioning the teachers, pointing out errors, and refusing to accept anything presented without rationale and reason, a characteristic that was often interpreted as insolence. I was in detention because I'm me—unable to keep my mouth shut or my emotions under control.

Then we were roommates at Washington State University, where she excelled in computer science while I muddled my way through an English degree because I like to read and couldn't think of anything else I wanted to do. Vic took pre-law and aced it, naturally, with a 4.0. And then the three of us went separate ways for a while. Britt landed a high-powered tech job in Silicon Valley. Vic, despite his stellar grades, decided he didn't want to be a lawyer after all. He'd been playing around with making his own beer, which was hugely popular at parties (okay, so he isn't always perfect, but he is always popular). He landed a scholarship to study brewing at Central College and spent a couple of years in Ellensburg getting a certification before coming home to start building his own business.

My English degree didn't really prepare me for any sort of real-world job, but my involvement in a ton of social clubs paid off. I came home and launched a party-planning business, taking on Fox Valley's weddings, retirement parties, birthday parties, and the occasional business event.

Fox Valley has a way of sucking escapees back in, and now, here the three of us are again. Vic, with his very own start-up brewpub, and Britt for less positive reasons. Her dad has cancer, and she quit her job to come home to help her parents.

"What's happening?" she asks, sliding in beside me and giving me a quick hug before turning her attention to the men across the table. "Vic. Mr. Winters."

"Call me Rich, please," Dad says. "Mr. Winters makes me feel old." He flashes a smile that makes me roll my eyes because she's my friend and obviously my age. The expression "old enough to be her father" is glaringly obvious.

"You look fabulous," he adds, which is true.

Britt is lithe and lean and graceful. Her skin is smooth and always looks tanned and sun-kissed, even in winter. Her black hair is thick and glossy and wavy, and her amber eyes are dramatic, ever so slightly tilted under perfectly arched brows that never need plucking.

Dad reaches his hand across the table for hers, and when she reaches out to shake, he lifts it to his lips, instead.

I want to gag, but instead, of course, because I am always so graceful, I choke on a mouthful of coffee and spew it everywhere. This, at least, has the desired effect of making Dad back off, and since I'm not trying to impress anybody, it really doesn't matter. While I cough, Dad looks vaguely disgusted, and Vic and Britt grab napkins to start sopping up my mess. I can't help thinking, not for the first time, how much better they all did than me in terms of intelligence, charm, and looks.

But it's all right, really. I wasted a couple of years in my teens wallowing in the victim swamp, and I didn't like it there. I love my party-planner business and my life in general, and I love Vic and Britt. As for Dad, well, he's Dad. Family.

"Dearly beloved, we are gathered together," I begin as soon as I can speak again.

Vic shakes his head.

I add, "What? Too soon? Right. Okay. Here's the thing. I have a huge, glamorous, star-studded party to plan—the biggest of my life, and I need your help.

Silence follows. Dad looks bewildered, as he always does, by the idea that he would do anything out of the goodness of his heart. Vic is already on board but still frowns, most likely because he's just figured out I'm involving Dad.

Britt shakes her head with emphasis. "Nuh-uh. If this is about Leno Masterson, count me out. Let me get my drink. BRB." The words trail behind her, as she's already out of the booth and halfway to the register.

"I don't know," Dad says. "I was planning on heading home tomorrow."

"I'll pay you."

"But maybe I can stick around." It might be the offer of money that has swayed him, but from the way he's watching Britt, there might be other reasons involved.

Vic is watching her, too. He had a major crush on her the last year of high school, and her rejection of his advances was harsh and bruising to his ego. It created an awkwardness in our three-way friendship for a while, but somewhere along the line, they seemed to have figured it out. I thought he was over her, but from the expression on his face now, I'm not so sure.

"Would the two of you please stop ogling my friend? She's my age, Dad."

"Nothing wrong with looking at a beautiful woman."

"If you could only just look, that might be true," Vic says. "But you're not very good at just looking, are you?"

Dad's gaze locks with Vic's, the air between them crackling with an energy I can practically see. To my surprise, it's Dad who looks away, and a flush rises to his face. If I didn't know him better, I'd think it looks like shame, but I dismiss that idea. He's not capable of that emotion.

He swallows, finds a smile, and turns his attention back to me. "Tell me more about this party."

"Stars," I say. "Influencers. High-powered media. All the right people, here in Fox Valley."

"And what is it you want from me?"

I give him my best adoring look. "Two things. Help me decide who should be invited, and then help me get them here. You're the only person I know with those connections."

"What's the occasion?" he asks, hedging his bets. "They won't come just because you've decided to have a party."

"Wait for Britt so I can tell you all at once."

We wait in an awkward silence, Vic fuming, Dad scheming, me ignoring both of them.

It seems like an hour before Britt slides back in beside me. I know what she's got in that cup—tea. Probably green, no sugar or even honey.

"Before we talk about this party that I'm not, under any circumstance, helping you with," she says, "how did it go with the Ice Queen?"

"She accused me of being pregnant with Leno's child. Owen called me a gold digger. They weren't exactly enamored by the idea of Leno's party. And they didn't even know he was planning the death-with-dignity thing."

"So, you're going to come to your senses and not do it, right?" Britt says.

"Did you get the car?" Vic asks.

"You're pregnant?" Dad exclaims way too loudly.

Several heads turn in our direction.

"No, I am not pregnant," I say, loud enough to hopefully stop that rumor in its tracks. Then I lower my voice again so only my people can hear. "I did not yet get the car. And I'm absolutely throwing the party. And Britt, you know you're going to help."

"I don't think so," she says.

"What's your thing with Sylvie Masterson?" I ask. "I mean, yes, she's an ice queen and condescending and obnoxious, but so what?"

"Well, Sylvie did throw a fit about Leno dating the colored girl," Vic says. "Wasn't that what she called you, Britt?"

I hear his words but can't seem to make sense of them.

Britt is suddenly intensely focused on lining her cup up perfectly with some invisible mark on the table. A flush rises to her cheeks. Her eyes dart upward to meet mine and then skitter away again.

"What are you talking about?" I ask after a silence that seems to last for an eternity. My lips feel stiff and strange, like they don't belong to me. My macchiato sloshes uneasily in my stomach.

Britt continues to be obsessed with finding the perfect alignment for her cup.

"Oh, hell. You don't know," Vic says.

"What don't I know?"

Obviously, I see where this is going. I'm not stupid. I just can't believe it. Britt wouldn't have, not knowing my history with Leno. Besides, we've always told each other everything. Or at least I thought we did.

"Britt?"

She sighs deeply and finally meets my gaze. "It was the summer after we graduated. You went with your grandma on that cross-country trip, remember? Leno and the band were in town, practicing their stuff, getting ready for a tour. And he... asked me out a few times."

"And you didn't tell me this? We talked like every day."

"I didn't tell you because I knew you'd feel... Oh, God. I don't know. I was seventeen. Life was complicated."

"And you knew." I look at Vic, who has begun fidgeting with his own drink. "And you didn't tell me, either."

"Figured if she wanted you to know, she would have told you."

I sit there, looking from my twin to my best friend, both of whom are avoiding my gaze, feeling what I thought I knew about the world shift around me. It occurs to me that you never really know somebody, that we all have secrets we choose to keep to ourselves for whatever reason.

"I thought Leno and Spiro were a thing," I say bitterly.

"Spiro had a thing with all the boys in the band, it turns out," Britt says. "So Leno had a revenge fling with me."

"Who is this Leno person?" Dad asks.

"Was," Vic says. "Not is. He's dead. Addy is planning a huge 'Leno is dead' party."

"Was he a celebrity?"

"Leno went to school with us," Vic explains, since Britt and I are still not talking. "Moved into town in, what, ninth grade? He and Addy were buds until that Spiro chick joined the band. Then overnight, Leno was a rock star and stopped talking to Addy and started all hot and heavy with Spiro. That about sum it up, Addles?"

"Wait," Dad says, the light dawning. "This the guy you were texting with, Addy? His band—what was it?"

"Leno and the Lonely," Vic says.

93

"Right. They were featured in *Rolling Stone* a couple of years ago. Sell-out concerts in the US and Europe. Didn't one of their albums go platinum?" Dad's all in now. He likes famous people. "So, he dumped you when he got famous?"

"There was no dumping. I went to school one day, and suddenly I was utterly beneath his notice. Unlike certain people at this table who dated him."

"Nobody is dating him now," Britt says.

She has a point, but still, I feel dizzy and disoriented, as if the reality around me has suddenly altered. Britt was there the day I walked up to Leno in the hallway, fully expecting the glow of his new status as the coolest kid in school to spill over onto chubby, weird-girl me. He'd looked at me with a blankness in his eyes, as if he'd never seen me before. As if we hadn't spent hours together in the library, studying. Or on the phone, commiserating about being misfits at school, about unfair teachers and demanding mothers and absent fathers.

And then he'd laughed and wrapped his arm around the waist of the new girl standing next to him—an edgy girl I'd never seen before, with a mohawk and facial piercings and tattoos on her long, smoothly muscled arms.

"Who is this chick?" she'd asked, with absolute utter disdain.

"She's nobody," Leno said. "Come on, Spiro, I'll show you where the classroom is."

Britt knew how much that moment marked me. It's taken me years to claw my way back to some semblance of confidence. And she dated him anyway?

"How'd he die?" Dad asks.

"Killed himself, I heard," Vic says.

"He had cancer," Britt adds. "He did a right-to-die thing, didn't he, Addy?"

I feel numb, a little shocky, but I don't want to let on how deeply I'm hurt. I suck up enough of my drink to give me a brain-freeze moment, and the pain steadies me.

"That was his plan," I say. "But here's the thing. He scheduled his date-with-death for Tuesday. And the night before he died, he was texting me and asking me to pick up the prescription he planned to kill himself with, still on Tuesday. And he wanted to meet me at *Grounded* to tell me something he said was really important."

"Maybe somebody killed him," Dad says.

"Why would you even go there?" Vic asks. "You're as bad as Addy."

Which isn't fair because I haven't voiced any of my suspicions yet. But then, Vic being Vic, he probably knows what I'm thinking.

"When you reach a certain level of notoriety, you have crazy fans and jealous rivals. You have to always be on alert," Dad says, as if he, personally, has reached this dangerous pinnacle of success. "Bodyguards. Always watching for danger." He delivers these lines as if they're scripted, partly to us, partly to the people at the other tables, to see if anybody else is noting the burden of fame that he carries.

"On the other hand, he did have cancer," Britt reminds him. "Maybe something ruptured or bled or he had a blood clot in his brain."

"Or he overdosed on something else," Vic says.

"Or somebody killed him," Dad says.

"Why?" Vic asks. "I mean, since he was dying anyway, why would somebody want to murder him?"

"Money," Dad says. "Murder is always about money."

"Or revenge," I add, remembering certain dark thoughts my teenage self had after Leno cast me off. "Or a crime of passion. Alex says murder is always some variation of those things."

"Could we skip the murder discussion, no matter how fascinating, and get back to the party planning thing?" Vic says. "I've got a business to run."

"But this Leno person is dead," Dad says. "A little late for party planning, isn't it?"

"I already told you, count me out," Britt says. And then, "Do you really think somebody could have killed him?"

Vic rolls his eyes. "I'm in a lunatic asylum."

I raise my right hand and wave it. "If I could speak?"

He makes an exaggerated sweeping gesture with one arm that I interpret as, "By all means, please do explain."

Dad just looks at me. Britt sips her tea.

At least they are quiet and possibly listening, so I dive in and give it my best pitch. "Dad, as the others already know, Leno hired me *before* he died to throw a party for *after* he died. His last wish was to have this party. You're always telling me I'm wasting my life, that I should do something bigger and aim higher. Well, this is my chance for that, and you could help me for once."

To my surprise, he doesn't try to talk over me or jump in the second I'm finished.

I turn to Britt. "Obviously, I don't know what your issues are with the Mastersons, and frankly, I don't care." This last bit is an outright lie, and everybody at this table, except for Dad, knows it, but they'll let me get away with it because nobody wants to talk about the giant woolly mammoth in the room.

"You have skills that could make the difference between this thing being a big success or...or...not." I pause for breath and also to steady my voice because I'm on the brink of tears and I will not cry in front of her. Not now. Maybe never again.

"Is this charity? Or are you getting paid somehow?" Dad latches onto a point more salient than my emotions.

"I'll help," Britt says. "Because, believe it or not, I love you. But I want zero contact with the Ice Queen."

"I've already committed," Vic says.

Which leaves Dad. I look him directly in the eyes and launch the money rocket. "Leno paid me forty grand. And he gave me his car. And there's a two hundred thousand dollar budget."

"If he is—was—throwing around that kind of money," Dad says, "Somebody probably did kill him."

"Could we please not keep talking like he was murdered?" Vic says. "If there were any real grounds for suspicion, then the law would be involved."

"By the law, I assume you mean Alex," I say.

"Speak of the devil," Britt says, and I look up to see my former boyfriend heading for our table.

He's in uniform, not plainclothes, and I very much doubt this is a social call.

"Hey, Alex." I wave, manufacturing a smile that I hope doesn't look as fake as it feels. "How's it going?"

"Addison," he says, without a hint of warmth, reminding me that I need to make better life choices.

First, if you live in a small town, don't date somebody in local law enforcement. Second, if you do date them, do not break up with them. Marry them. Become a Stepford wife if you have to.

"I'm here in an official capacity," he says stiffly.

"Doesn't mean you couldn't have a cup of coffee. Maybe a donut," Vic says. "Or two. Pull up a chair." He never did like Alex, starting somewhere in middle school. "You do like donuts, don't you?"

I kick him under the table.

"I'm here about Leno Masterson," Alex says, glaring at me, even though I'm not the one who made the donut quip.

My hand flies to my mouth. "So, he really was murdered, then?"

"What? No, he was not murdered. As I know you know, he was dying of cancer. He died alone in his condo in a gated community, and murder is not a consideration. I'm here at the request of his family. They said you were at the house harassing them this morning."

"I was not harassing anybody. I took them pastries and told them I'm throwing a goodbye party for Leno."

"Even if she was harassing them, why would they call you?" Britt asks. "You're sort of above all that, aren't you, with that whole detective badge and all?"

Alex doesn't answer her, and I know why. He never would have been assigned to this; he volunteered because it gives him a chance to put me in my place.

"Leave the family alone," he orders. "Don't go to the house again. And they do not want you throwing an after-death party."

"Leno hired me to do the party. His family really has nothing to say about it."

"Drop it, Addison. Don't make me arrest you," Alex says. There's a heat in his eyes that makes me want to shrink smaller and wish I was wearing a big shapeless sweater or maybe a parka. Invisibility would be nice.

"I think she'd have to break a law first before you can arrest her," Vic says conversationally. "Unless this is some sort of role-playing game, in which case, please don't play it in front of me. Because, ew."

"Did they actually file a restraining order?" Britt asks.

"Nothing has been filed. Yet."

"Because there are no grounds for filing one. Also, Addy would actually be in breach of faith if she didn't go ahead with the party, given that she's accepted payment."

"Maybe the family is protesting too much?" Dad suggests. "I mean, guy with money like that? Family could have totally killed him."

"There's absolutely no reason to believe—"

"Well, of course not," Dad says. "It's not like the family is going to call in the cops and say, 'Hey, Officer, look at all of this evidence that we offed our loved one.' Did you investigate at all?"

Alex flushes. His jaw goes tight, and his fingers twitch. "Mr. Winters, I will not discuss his death with you. Addison, you will leave the family alone. I'd advise you not to throw this party—"

"Is that an official law enforcement advisement?" Britt asks. "Or a personal recommendation?"

"The party is happening," I say, wondering, not for the first time, what I ever saw in Alex. I mean, I know what I saw in him —he's cute, he's got a nice, tight ass, he works out at the gym. He's also good in bed and looks super sexy in uniform. But still. Personality is kind of important, and he's controlling and demanding and likes to tell me what to do.

"You sure you don't want a donut?" Vic asks.

The flush on Alex's face darkens. His jaw clamps tighter and tighter until I brace myself for the sound of cracking teeth. "Don't say I didn't warn you," he says, then turns and stalks out.

"Damn, I'd hate to be anybody who is speeding right now," Britt says. "That dude's on a power trip."

"Tell me about it." I slump back in my chair, wondering for a minute if maybe I have taken on more than I can handle.

The logistics of the party are complicated enough without adding in potential legal issues and the opposition of powerful people. Not to mention Dad. And now this awkwardness with Britt.

"Don't look like that, Addles," Vic says. "They don't have a legal leg to stand on. And don't let Alex get to you. Never could stand that guy. Let's talk party. I've got to get moving."

"Me too," Britt says. "Mom needs some time out of the house. I promised to sit with Dad."

"Here's what I need," I say. "First thing, I guess I need an invite list, so I know what to tell the caterer, so Vic knows what he needs to do about drinks, and so Britt can send out invitations and do a press release."

"And how are we deciding that?" Britt asks.

"That's the part where I'm really kind of stuck," I admit. "I was thinking you might help with that, Dad. You know some people who know some people..."

"But these need to be Leno's people, not Dad's people," Vic objects.

"I wonder if Owen might help," I muse.

"Leaving the Mastersons alone, remember?" Vic says. "That includes Owen."

"Don't worry, I've got this," Dad says. "I bet my agent can hook us up." He pulls out his cell phone and makes a point of showing it to all of us. "If you haven't upgraded to iPhone 16 yet, do it," he says, as if all of us sitting here at the table have that kind of money. Then he makes a point of looking thoughtful as he scrolls his contacts. Then he makes a call.

"Mavis," he says. "How's my favorite agent?"

"Mavis?" Vic mutters. "Is anybody still allowed to be called that?"

Dad is oblivious. He's turned slightly so that his profile is visible to anybody else in the café who might be interested.

"Actually, hon, I was just hoping you could hook me up with a phone number. I'm putting together a little event. Might you be able to put me in touch with whoever is representing Leno Masterson? Yes, that's the guy. Yes, he's dead. You can? You're a doll! I'll wait for your call."

He hits end and beams at us.

"When?" I ask.

He looks at me like I'm speaking a foreign language.

"When will she get back to us?"

"You can't rush these things, Addison. She's a busy woman with important clients. She said she'd ask around."

"We don't have time for her to ask around. We need to make the guest list right away so we can start deciding who to invite and how many reporters and influencers to include."

"Maybe we ask one of the other band members," Vic suggests. "Anybody still in touch with Sig or Jax?"

"Are you kidding? Neither of them knew we existed when we shared a classroom," I say. "They were as bad as Leno. Unless you were dating them, too, Britt?"

She gives me the middle finger.

"Pretty sure the whole band will have unlisted numbers and people to run interference between them and fans. And as for Spiro?" I just shrug, but we all know what I mean.

Spiro, Leno and the Lonely's bad-ass female drummer, wasn't on good terms with anybody.

"There was that other kid," Vic says. "The drummer before Spiro."

The kid he's talking about sat behind me in English class. He was tall and awkward and had a bad case of acne. Even his brief affiliation with Leno and the band didn't redeem him socially. He totally fell off the radar about the time Spiro showed up and the band got famous.

"Robbie?" I ask tentatively.

"Rodney, I think," Vic counters.

Britt shakes her head. "Not even close. His name is Gary Carruthers. His family moved to Florida, which is why the band auditioned and brought in Spiro."

"Huh. I always thought they sidelined him because he was weird."

"You were weird," Britt reminds me. "I was weird. And no. Gary moved. Then they auditioned."

"Does it matter?" Vic tries to round us up and get us back on track. "I don't suppose anybody here has a phone number for Gary Carruthers. And even if you did, he's not still part of the—"

"Gar?" Britt has been playing with her phone while we argue, apparently finding and dialing because she's already hit pay dirt.

"Yeah, it's Britt. Yes, we totally should get together, but I'm back in Fox Valley. Long story. Anyway...yeah, super sad about Leno. That's why I'm calling, actually. Leno wanted a big after-death send-off party, and we need some help creating a guest list. Don't suppose you're still in touch with the band members? Wait, really? Cool! That would be awesome."

She sets down the phone and looks across the table at us. "What?"

"You're BFFs with Gary Carruthers," I say, wondering what else there is about Britt that I don't know.

"We had a thing for a bit. We were in a production together in L.A. He keeps tabs on all the band members—apparently they were involved in a movie he was in."

"Gary Carruthers was in a movie?" Vic, this time.

"He's an actor now. Bit parts in B-list movies so far, but people are noticing him. Fantastic dancer. Anyway, he's texting me Spiro's phone number. Get this—Spiro's here in Fox Valley. Came up a week ago to go over some band legacy stuff with Leno and has apparently not left yet. She's staying in his condo."

"There's your murderer," Dad says.

Vic is tapping on his phone. I grab it out of his hand and see that he's Googling Gary and that Gary is no longer gangly or pimply.

"Damn, that boy grew up fine," I say.

"Give me my phone." Vic lunges for it, and I let him have it instead of trying to play keep away.

"So, you're dating old Gary then?" he asks Britt, trying to sound casual.

"Just friends."

"Sounded pretty chummy."

"It was a production thing. When the play was over, we drifted apart. It happens. Tell him, Mr. Winters."

And then we're forced to listen to Dad tell us about the

women he's connected with on the set or on the stage, which wasn't fair of Britt at all because Vic was the one being a jealous jerk about the whole thing, and I shouldn't have to suffer for his mistakes. Britt's phone pings while Dad is rhapsodizing about the physical attributes of some woman who is probably younger than I am.

"There we go," Britt says. "Gary texted me Spiro's number, and he's texted her to let her know you'll be calling. Here, I'm sending you the number and the address."

My phone pings, and sure enough, there's Spiro's phone number. I stare at it, my brain spinning in a whole new direction. "Wait," I say, slowly. "Didn't Alex say Leno died in his condo?"

"Yes, so?" Vic asks.

"If Spiro was staying there—"

"Oh my God, give it a rest," Vic says. "Spiro didn't murder Leno. What's the party venue?"

"I've got Buena Vista."

"How did you manage that?" Britt asks. "That place is usually booked solid a year in advance."

"Well, Lisa sort of called off her wedding, so—"

"You didn't," Vic says.

"I didn't what?"

"You persuaded your client to call off her wedding so you could have the venue for this party," he says. His tone is almost admiring.

"She had a change of heart. Do you think she should have married Brad? I wasn't about to persuade her otherwise."

"If you don't need me to help with the guest list, what do you need me to do?" Dad asks a little pathetically.

Vic quirks an eyebrow. "Yes, Addy. Please do tell us what you've got planned for Richard."

What he means is that it better be very good to be worth the price of us having to endure our father's presence for an extended period. Not to mention the backlash from Mom if she finds out he's staying in town on account of me.

"I need you at the party. To charm and schmooze." I take a breath and throw out the lure I know he can't resist. "And I need you to manage the media and the influencers and all that."

You can practically see the shot go home. Dad could never resist a camera, probably not even to save his soul. To ask him to run interference with people who might just turn around and take a snap of him is like setting a kid loose in a candy store.

"Why do I feel like we've just launched World War III?" Vic makes a gesture like a bomb exploding. "Kaboom!"

Dad's face looks like a kid at Christmas, and he's gazing off into the middle distance, daydreaming about the glory to come, I'm sure.

"I'll make a spreadsheet," I say.

"Oh, heavens, defend us," Vic says. "Not one of your infamous spreadsheets."

"How else are we going to organize things? And I'll give you all some check-in points and timelines. It's going to be a super-tight turnaround, but I believe we can pull this off."

SUNDAY

CHAPTER 10

WHAT HAPPENS in a medical clinic is supposed to stay in the clinic, but nothing in the universe—including the HIPAA law that rigidly governs confidentiality—is powerful enough to stop small-town gossip.

My old classmate, Millie, is one of the worst offenders. As a receptionist, she's not privy to all the medical details, but she's got big ears and a brain that stores away every overheard conversation, every little gem of gossip that she picks up in the waiting room, in the hallways, even in the restroom. As luck would have it, she's home, bored, and delighted by my invitation to meet me at *The Raven* for drinks and a good gossip session.

I, of course, have ulterior motives. I want to know how Leno died, and I'm sure Millie has intel. I'm hoping that under the influence of some good gossip—aided by a couple of frosty mugs of Vic's finest—she'll tell me anything she knows about Leno.

"Damn, these nachos look amazing." I survey the platter that has just been delivered to our table and select a chip dripping in melted cheese and loaded with olives and ground beef. I transfer it to my own plate as if it is absolutely the most important thing on my mind. As I spoon sour cream and guacamole onto it, I add, casually, as if it's an afterthought, "So sad about Leno Masterson, isn't it?"

"Oh my God." Millie sets down her glass, already almost empty, and shakes her head. "Can you believe it? He was our age."

"First of our classmates to go," I say before biting into the spicy, gooey goodness that is a *Raven* nacho.

Vic's got the brewpub food menu down. Not healthy by a long shot, but it all pairs perfectly with his craft brews. My drink, sadly, is nearly untouched. I know my limits, and I'm on a mission.

"Let me get you another drink." I wave my hand at Rosa, who is looking our way, and point at Millie.

"Leno's not the first, though. You've forgotten Nancy," Millie says, nibbling at an almost dry chip. She is always on a diet, which means more food for me. Also, more drinks on an almost empty stomach for her, so win-win.

"Does Nancy count, though?" I take a swallow of my dark amber ale, savoring the rich, complex flavor, then grab another nacho. "Nancy left town in what, seventh grade?"

"Still a classmate. They aren't even sure if it was an accident. Did you know? She wasn't wearing a seatbelt. She'd been drinking. Drove right into a tree." She shivers, an expression of fascinated horror on her face. "Lou thinks she tried to kill herself. Nancy, I mean."

"Leno, though," I say, steering the conversation back to

where I want it. "So awful. I'd take the car-into-a-tree scenario over going out with cancer."

Conflicting emotions chase each other across Millie's face, but the struggle is mercifully brief. She leans forward and says breathlessly, "Can you keep a secret? I'm not supposed to tell you this, but..."

"Millie, I'm a vault of secrets. It's part of my job description." I mime zipping my lips and throwing away the key.

"Okay, but you can't tell anybody I told you this. Leno was all set up to use the Death with Dignity Act."

I gasp, as if I'm shocked by this bit of news, and lean closer. "For real? I heard he killed himself. But you're saying it wasn't really suicide?"

"Technically, Death with Dignity isn't considered suicide, but it still is. Don't you think? I mean, legal or not, you're ending your own life."

Rosa arrives at our table, new glass in hand. She glances around the room to make sure she can spare a minute and slides into the booth beside me. "Is this about Leno Masterson? Spill it. I've been dying of curiosity."

Neither Millie's meager willpower nor her scruples stand a chance against an eager audience of two. I make myself a note to persuade Vic to give Rosa a raise.

I take a sip of my drink. "This stuff is amazing, isn't it? Vic's brews get better every time, don't they? Cheers." I hold my glass out toward Millie, and she lifts her own to tap against it, then takes a nice big swallow.

Rosa asks, "So that's what happened with Leno? He really did it himself?"

"He did," Millie says, slurring her words. "I was one of the witnesses for his Death with Dignity paperwork. Doc Marten wrote the prescriptions for him. Three of them. Three different meds to ensure that it works." She pauses for full dramatic effect, which I make sure to give her. Elbows on the table, leaning forward, my mouth gaping, eyes wide.

"I might do it that way if it were me," Rosa muses. "Take some pills and go to sleep."

Millie looks conflicted, and I'm pretty sure she's holding something back.

"I can't imagine how suicidal people do it, ever," Rosa continues. "But pills seem like the easiest way to go."

A guy has walked in and is standing at the bar, looking around for service, and she slides reluctantly out of the booth. "Coming!" she sings out to the waiting patron. "You'd better fill me in later," she says.

"Cross my heart!" I eat another nacho while Rosa makes her way through the other tables back to the bar.

Millie drinks, then leans a little closer to me across the table. "So, here's the weird part. I heard Dr. Marten talking to Dr. Kennedy, and he said Leno never even picked up the prescription after all of that trouble they went to. Dr. Marten doesn't like the right-to-die law in the first place, and he said maybe the next time somebody asks him, he'll just say no. And then Dr. Kennedy said he heard that Leno overdosed on his morphine instead. And then Dr. Marten said it must have been an accident because if you'd gone to all the trouble to get a prescription that was pretty much guaranteed to work, why wouldn't you use it?"

Millie nibbles at a chip and takes another drink.

Then, all big eyes, says, "It is weird, right? And I mean, it could have been an accident with the morphine, but what if he didn't do it himself? I mean—I saw this episode of *Bizarre*

Murders where this person with muscular dystrophy died sort of unexpectedly—I mean, it wasn't cancer like Leno, but still—and everybody just figured the disease progressed faster than they'd all thought. Only the guy was rich, like Leno, and somebody wanted him dead faster for the insurance money. It was the guy's brother, if you can believe it. All he had to do was wait a few days, a month at the most, but he had gambling debts or something, so he just decided to speed things up. And then, when the cops actually caught him and proved what he'd done, the guy said, 'He was going to die anyway. I figured he might as well die now to save me rather than both of us be dead.'"

She pauses for breath. Tears are pouring down her cheeks on behalf of this guy she's never met, which tells me maybe she's had more than enough to drink.

I pat her hand consolingly. "Mills, you don't happen to know who was working the ambulance on the Masterson call out, do you?"

She shakes her head, which is obviously a mistake, because she lays both hands flat on the table and her face goes a little bit green.

"You okay?"

"Just...the room is spinning," she whispers.

"Come on, Millie," I say. "Let me drive you home."

My phone pings with a text, and my heart rate kicks up as I read it.

Spiro. Got your message. Can meet here at the condo in 30 minutes.

Addy: Fab! I'm in the middle of something. Make it an hour?

Spiro: Now or never

Addy: Perfect! See you then.

But it's not perfect at all. I need to get Millie home first, and I need some time to think about the best way to approach Spiro. Yes, I want her to help with the party. But I also want to find out what she knows about how Leno died. If he was murdered and if she killed him, then I might be able to prove that.

Not that I want Leno to have been murdered, of course. And not that I hold a high school grudge against Spiro or... Oh, all right. That's a lie I can't tell even to myself. Yes. I hold a grudge. Seeing her locked up would be immensely satisfying.

"I'm sad," Millie says, peering into her empty glass. "I want another drink."

"Not a good idea." I get to my feet and hold out a hand. "You've got work in the morning, right? Trust me. You don't want a hangover on a workday."

I'm pretty sure it's too late to save her from a hangover, but since it's my fault that she's plastered, the least I can do is get her home safely.

Rosa reappears at our table as if summoned. "You didn't finish your drink. Or your nachos. And you need to spill the gossip."

I look down at the food with regret. "Sadly, we do need to go. Promise to come back for a chat later, though."

"I'll package them up for you," Rosa says. "Just heat them in a pan in the oven for a few minutes when you're ready, and they'll be better than ever."

"Whoa," Millie says, staggering up onto her feet. "When did the room start spinning?"

"Before you finished that last drink. Come on." I put an arm around her and get her moving. Rosa appears with a foil-wrapped package and I balance that in my other hand.

Outside, the air is cool, the spring afternoon moving toward evening. Jezebel is cantankerous but consents to start, which is good. What is not good is my passenger puking halfway home. How somebody who didn't actually eat more than three dry chips can have that volume of stomach contents is a mystery. Also, while Vic's beer smelled wonderful in the glass, recycled it produces a next-level stench.

"I'm sorry," Millie wails, sobbing. "I tried to open the window, but it wouldn't."

Of course it wouldn't. Jezebel decided a couple of years back that she didn't like the windows to open, and the only one that still works is mine. I tried to get them repaired, but neither an overhaul of the electronics nor the installation of new windows resolved the issue. Stephen King's *Christine* has got nothing on Jezebel.

So, we drive with my window wide open, and by the time we get to Millie's place I'm shivering and my hair is a tangled mass.

I help her inside, taking the key from her after three failed attempts and getting the door open to the tune of loud and frantic yapping from a little dog on the other side. In addition to the barking, I can hear it leaping rhythmically up against the door. Thud. Nails scratching down through the wood. *Thud. Screech. Thud. Screech.*

When I finally get the door open, it bares its teeth and alternates the yapping with ferocious growls, running circles around us as I escort his mistress to the couch. I am not going to go so far as to help Millie take off her clothes and get into bed. It's not like I held her down and poured beer down her throat. She closes her eyes and lies still. I don't think I need to worry about alcohol poisoning, but I check her breathing and her pulse, just to be sure. All regular. She'll be fine.

The dog pursues me to the door, making little running lunges and then backing away, yapping non-stop. His whole body is vibrating in that nervous-energy way small dogs have, but he's still putting his whole heart and doggy soul into this guard dog routine.

"Look, buddy," I say. "Lay off. You're nothing more than a rat with fur. You try to bite me and I'll send you flying. Do we understand each other?"

I'm bluffing, and I'm pretty sure he knows it, but he stops barking. Tilts his head to one side, sharp little rat-nose wiggling, then advances toward me, lifts a leg, and proceeds to pee on my foot.

"Hey!" I step back, but it's too late. I've been watered. I also smell faintly of vomit.

Unfortunately, there is no time to go home for a shower and change of clothes.

CHAPTER 11

LENO'S CONDO is in Fox Valley's one and only gated community. I've never been there, but this is Fox Valley, so of course I know where it is. Up Wynne Mountain, on the other side of the valley from Fox Mountain—just high enough to offer a spectacular view without being too far from town. The road is steep and narrow, with a couple of dangerously tight curves.

Much as I'm in a hurry, I slow for Suicide Corner. Two white crosses on the shoulder are draped in flowers, serving as a reminder of the most recent traffic fatalities that have happened here. In both instances, the cars took the corner too fast, got their wheels caught in the soft gravel of the shoulder, and went over the edge in one of those epic rollovers movies are fond of.

There's no reason to believe the victims were trying to kill themselves. We call it Suicide Corner because taking it at high speeds or trying to navigate it in snow or fog is asking to die. There's now a guardrail, and that section of the shoulder has been paved so the danger of going over seems small and far away, but I'm still not taking chances.

As soon as the road straightens, I go back to encouraging Jezebel along with my foot almost to the floor as she gasps and shudders her way up the steep incline.

Finally, I turn off the road into Valley View Estates with a sigh of relief. "You did great," I say, patting the steering wheel. "Going back will be easy. And then I promise to get you all cleaned up."

We stop at the closed gate, and the window of the little booth opens. "I'll have to call up and get permission to let you in," the security guard says.

"Come on, Jen. You know me."

"Exactly. And I happen to like my job."

Apparently, Jen Chivers can hold a grudge. I got us both a long stretch in detention once when we were in middle school, along with a kid named Cal. Vic and Britt had been smart enough to say no to my bright idea that we could sneak off campus and run to the corner store for ice cream during lunch break. They were right, of course. The break wasn't long enough, for one thing, plus Mr. Myers, the store owner, turned us in. Jen wouldn't hang out with me after that. She said her mother forbade it, and at the time, I believed her.

Jen calls a number, waits while it rings, and says, in very official tones, "I have an Addison Winters here who claims to have an appointment. Oh, she does? All right. Thank you."

She hangs up the phone and turns back to me.

"You can go in," she says, repressively. "But she says you're late. Park that...thing in a visitor space. Numbered spaces are for residents only."

"Yes, Officer," I say, which I immediately regret since she's the one womanning the gate, and she could still totally decide not to let me in. But the barrier lifts and I drive through and then circle the parking lot a couple of times, looking for a visitor spot that will accommodate Jezebel.

And then, even though I'm late, I sit there for a minute, trying to pull myself together. The moment of Leno's betrayal has been playing on auto-repeat all the way up here. I can still hear his voice saying, "She's nobody." Can see the contempt on Spiro's face. And now here I am, meeting her again, and of course, I smell of vomit and dog pee, and my hair is a wild rat's nest, thanks to driving with the window open. I'm gonna need half a bottle of conditioner and some detangling lotion to get this mess sorted, so I just find a hair elastic in my bag and pull it up into a messy bun.

Fortunately, I keep a pair of sandals in the car, so I slip off shoes and socks and wipe my foot down with one of the disinfectant wipes I've carried with me ever since Covid first hit.

"I am a competent, powerhouse party planner," I say to my image in the mirror, but there's no magical transformation. I'm still a very disheveled me. So I quote Geneva instead: "Be yourself and go with your gifts."

Better. Maybe my less-than-polished appearance will put Spiro at ease. There's absolutely zero chance of her feeling threatened by me, so she won't be on her guard and it will be easier to get her talking. I take a deep breath, set my shoulders, and walk to the sheltered entryway. There are a couple of wood and wrought-iron benches, half a dozen flower baskets, and a sign that reads, "No parking. Unloading zone only." The doors are locked, and I press the buzzer.

"Who is it?" The voice coming through the intercom is definitely Spiro's.

"It's Addison Winters."

The door clicks, and I walk into a lobby that isn't even on the same planet as the one in my building. It's spacious, and the floor is neither cheap carpet nor battered linoleum but tile —possibly marble. I take the stairs up to the third floor and make my way to number 304, all the while repeating under my breath, "I will be cool. I will be calm. I will be myself."

There are only four units per floor, but the hallway is still pretty damn long. When I reach 304, Spiro is standing in the doorway. She's got a couple of inches of height on me and considerably fewer pounds. The mohawk has been replaced by straight black hair, long enough to reach the middle of her back. She's got full tattoo sleeves in color. Even though she's barefoot, wearing a tank top and low-slung jeans, she still has a presence that says, "I'm important. I'm special. I'm cool."

"Oh my God!" I squeal, like I'm a freaking teenage fangirl. "It's so amazing to be meeting with you! I can't believe we actually were in high school together! Do you remember me?"

Her nostrils quiver, and I wonder if she smells vomit. "Gary said this was about a celebrity bash for Leno."

"Right, of course, sorry. It's just that I'm so excited. Do you... Would you... I brought a CD, and I wondered if you'd sign—"

"Look, if you're just here to fangirl, then you need to go." She starts closing the door, and I step forward so I'm in the way of it.

"Sorry, sorry. Leno hired me to throw him a dynamite send-off, but I can't do it without your help."

She looks me over, obviously unimpressed, but at least she doesn't slam my foot in the door. "Why you?"

"Because I'm the only party planner in Fox Valley?"

"Go figure," she says. "Well, you might as well come in."

She leads the way down a short hallway, which opens into an open area floor plan. You could fit my whole apartment in here five times, maybe six. The kitchen is sleek and modern, with a stainless fridge and stove. The countertops are granite. There's a full-sized espresso maker.

A large area rug, obviously expensive and possibly Persian, defines the living room, which is furnished with comfortable-looking leather couches and an adjustable standing desk. A mural, mostly of Leno, with the band blurred in the background, takes up an entire wall.

"Wow," I say as I sidestep past her and walk over to examine the painting. "Hard to believe he's not still with us, isn't it?" I spin around and take in the entire room.

Windows on the adjacent wall offer a panoramic view of the valley. The opposite wall is mirrored, reflecting Leno and the outdoors and creating an illusion of a much bigger space. It also reflects me and that is not confidence inspiring.

"How can I help you?" Spiro asks.

"Mind if I sit down?" I don't wait for her response, sinking into the buttery softness of a luxury leather sofa. I've sat on leather couches before, but not like this. It feels so amazing that it's all I can do to keep from patting it, as if it's still alive and sentient and I can express my appreciation.

"Of course, you and Leno being so tight and all, you know how important this party was to him," I say. "I really want to pull it off, to make it everything he dreamed of."

She makes a noncommittal sound, but at least she sits down across from me.

"Here's the thing. I've got the venue secured, and my colleague is creating a press release and designing invitations."

I pause, thinking about Britt, hoping this is actually true. Then I take a breath and keep going. "But we'd love to have some help with the guest list, make sure we invite the people who were close to Leno and also any big names in the music business who should be there—reporters, influencers, that sort of thing."

"Of course." She folds her long legs up under her and raises an eyebrow, not volunteering anything.

"We didn't get to talk much," I say. "He was going to tell me more, but then, well—he wound up dead."

I leave that hanging, hoping she'll volunteer something about Leno's death, but she just sits there, with silence stretching between us.

When it becomes obvious she's planning to wait me out, I offer what I hope is a disarming smile and start the conversation myself.

"Leno wanted good music, dancing, food and drinks and fun. No sad speeches or celebration of life stuff. And he wanted it to be the sort of event that would create a buzz and give people something to talk about other than the cancer and the way he was planning—the way he died."

"You've got a problem right off the top," she says.

"Right. The guest list. Which is why I'm here."

She waves her hand dismissively. "That part's easy. Your problem is that you'll never get a decent band. Anybody that's any good is already booked. A bad band is worse than nothing. You might get a decent DJ, I suppose."

"I don't want a DJ. Do you have any ideas?"

She shrugs a narrow shoulder. "Solo acts, maybe. Some of the people he knew might do it just because it's Leno."

I stare at her, processing a sudden, brilliant, out-of-the-blue idea. It's perfect—if I can get Spiro on board. It's a big if, and getting to yes is going to require serious motivational finesse.

"What?" she says. "You look like you're having a seizure or something."

I sigh. "I had an idea for a band and got all excited for a minute. But it would never work. Let's just talk about the guest list, shall we? And then I'll poke around to see who I might get to play. We've got a local country band that's pretty good—the Fox Valley Boys. They might do it on short notice if I pay them enough."

"What was your terrible idea?" she asks. "Humor me. Curiosity killed the cat and all that."

"Oh, I'm almost embarrassed to say..."

She glares.

I shrug. "I had this thought that we could get Leno and the Lonely back together one last time as a tribute to Leno. But of course, it would never work, right? I mean, without Leno, you've only got *the Lonely*. He practically was the band."

Perfect. If looks could kill, I'd be dead. Spiro's practically vibrating with damaged ego. I keep going.

"I mean, you are like, the hottest, most kick-ass drummer ever, but still. Without Leno..." I lift my hands and let them fall helplessly into my lap.

"I don't know about that," she says coldly. "The rest of us are pretty fine musicians. All of us sing harmonies on every song. We could totally do it if we wanted to."

"Well, if you don't want to, of course, I understand. This will be a huge media event. We'll be reaching out to *Rolling Stone Magazine*—my PR person has a contact on their staff. It would probably be best not to put yourselves out there if you're not quite up to what Leno's fans expect..."

And then, letting my voice trail off, gazing out the window into nothing, I add, "I wonder if Gary might put together a tribute band and do a song or two..."

She snorts, tossing her head scornfully. "Gary can't drum his way out of a paper bag."

"Well, not everybody can be you," I say. "But it would be amazing to have some of the band's music at the party."

"I can't confirm absolutely for certain, but tentatively, and as far as I'm concerned, the band will play at the party," Spiro says. "I'll call Sig and Jax to double-check."

"When do you think you could tell me for sure? If we can include that info in the press release and the invites, that would be awesome."

"I'll call you tonight. Don't you worry. We'll make it happen. For Leno." The last words feel tacked on, but I don't really care what her motivations are as long as I get what I need. "Okay. Now, about that guest list."

I get out my notepad and a pen, and she scrolls through the contacts in her phone and gives me names, phone numbers, and the occasional email. This is pure contact gold. If I can get even a handful of these people to RSVP that they're coming, then getting the media on board will be a breeze.

When we're done, I put away my notepad, look up at her, and say, "Could I ask you a question? It's about Leno."

She's relaxed a little while we've been discussing guests but immediately goes wary. "I won't promise to answer," she says.

"Were you...was he alone when he died?"

"What does that matter to you and your party?"

"It's just... He really didn't want to die alone. I mean, when he talked to me about the party, he even asked me to be there with him when he...did it. So I was just wondering if he was alone or if maybe you were with him."

Spiro bounces up onto her feet, glaring down at me with so much intensity that I brace myself in case she tries to hit me or try to strangle me or something. "No, I was not here, and no, I didn't help him. I would have fucking stopped him if I knew what he was doing."

"So, the rumors are true? He did kill himself, then?"

"You need to go now."

She looms over me in a way that persuades me to stop asking questions. I get up from my comfy chair and make my way toward the door, Spiro right behind me.

"I'm sorry," I say, my hand on the doorknob. "I certainly didn't mean any offense. Will you still ask the band?"

"I'll ask. I'll call you."

She slams the door behind me, and I walk out to the car in a cloud of questions. Spiro knows something she didn't want to tell me, but what? She could be lying. Maybe she was with him but doesn't want anybody to know. Or maybe she had a reason to want him dead.

CHAPTER 12

I'VE JUST PULLED into the parking lot outside my apartment, my mind alternately replaying my conversation with Spiro and running ahead to the bliss of a hot shower, warmed over nachos, and a glass of wine, when my phone buzzes with an incoming text. Probably Vic, wondering how things went with Spiro. Maybe even Britt. Or Spiro, already texting to confirm that the other band members have agreed to play the party.

But when I persuade the phone that I am not, in fact, driving, and it lets me see the message, it's from the last person I could possibly have expected.

> Leno: Could we meet? The Raven. Thirty minutes?

> Leno: Are you there?

My heart is racing, my hands shaking. Do I really want to respond to a message from beyond the grave?

Curiosity wins.

> Addy: Maybe?

> Leno: So can we? Meet?

> Addy: That would be easier were you not dead.

> Leno: Sorry, what?

> Addy: The rumors of your death have been highly exaggerated?

> Leno: Oh. Oh God. This is Leno's chat.

> Addy: Right. Glad we cleared that up.

> Addy: If this is a joke, it isn't funny.

My phone rings. I startle and drop it, then fumble for it frantically. If it really is Leno, taking a phone call is better than an in-person visitation.

"Addy. Hi. I'm really sorry about that. I was on Leno's laptop, and when I messaged you, of course it would say it was from him. I wasn't thinking. What a thing to do."

Not Leno. That's all I can think. I'm not hallucinating, and I'm not being haunted. I don't say anything. I just sit there listening to my own raspy breathing, my heart continuing to pound a rapid rhythm in my ears.

"Addy? It's actually Owen."

"I know who you are. But I have no idea what you could possibly want."

"Just to talk. Meet me at *The Raven*."

"I had a visit from the police. I don't think I'm supposed to talk to you."

"Sorry about that. That was my mother with the police. She can be...well... Obviously, I'm not inviting you back up to the house. Thus, *The Raven*. Or I could come to your apartment, if you'd rather?"

I would definitely not rather.

"You implied that I was trying to manipulate your brother for his money," I say.

"And you implied that I was the worst brother in the world."

"Look, I'm sorry Leno died," I say. "I'm sure it's all very difficult for you. But I'm not sure talking is a good idea."

"I'm bringing the car," he says. "If you want it, come and get it." And then he hangs up.

Seriously? What is up with this guy? I fling my phone into Jezebel's passenger seat. It skitters over the slick vinyl surface and right over the edge, between the door and the seat. If I'm lucky, it will have stopped there, and all I need to do to retrieve it is open the door.

But if I know Jezebel, and I do, the phone will have slid down into a black hole of nothingness where lost items have hung out for years. With a sigh, I turn off the ignition and go into the apartment for a roll of paper towels, a trash bag, and the pet-mess cleaner I use when Bruno coughs up a hairball and set to work cleaning up after Millie before conducting a search for the phone.

The orange scent from the cleaning solution is overpowering in close quarters, but relatively speaking, it's a definite improvement. It will have to be good enough for now. I'll get to the carwash and scrub the floor mat properly tomorrow. Right now, I need to find my phone.

Aided by the flashlight I always carry in my bag, I begin

delving into the depths under Jezebel's passenger seat. I recover enough loose change to buy my next coffee, a handful of paperclips—even though I never actually look at paperwork in the car, and if I did who paperclips things anymore?—the earbuds I lost two years ago, and a couple of plastic water bottles. Still no phone.

It's clear that the only way to find the damned thing will be to have somebody call it, and I can't ask anybody to call it because I can't text or call them to ask them to call me. Which means I don't even know exactly what time it is, since Jezebel's dash display clock gave up years ago and perpetually reads 4:44. It occurs to me to just ghost Owen. To go sensibly into the house, message Vic from my computer and ask him for help. Then shower, eat nachos, have a drink, and go to bed, like I'd planned.

But I'm full of questions, and Owen possibly has answers. Also, I do want that Maserati. I'm definitely going to *The Raven*. If Jezebel will consent to take me. She was running just fine— for her—before Owen called. Now, she coughs pathetically, pretending she's dying. She's just trying to play on my sympathy and remind me where my loyalties lie. It wasn't a good idea to talk about the Maserati in her hearing.

"I will always love you," I say, turning the key again with the same result.

"No fancy sports car could ever replace you," I say, and this time, she sputters and pretends to start, then dies again.

"You and me forever, baby," I say, and she groans pitifully, but then the engine coughs and turns over.

As I look in my rearview mirror, ominous black smoke is swirling behind me, but I ignore both that and the clanking sound Jezebel is making and head for my destination, fingers crossed that we don't have to stop at any intersections because I really don't want to break down in the middle of town.

Fortunately, there are only two stoplights in Fox Valley and both of them are green, so I don't have to risk stopping and never getting going again. Jezebel backfires once, loudly enough that I flinch and duck, inborn instinct taking over, although the probability of a gunman letting loose in our little town is small. Just as I'm turning into *The Raven's* parking lot, Jezebel belches out one last cloud of black smoke and falls silent. Her weight and momentum keep us rolling for a few more feet, me fighting with the steering wheel, which suddenly weighs a hundred pounds. I'm starting to hope I can hit an empty parking spot when we roll gently to a stop, blocking in three vehicles.

One of them is the Maserati. Perfect, Jezebel. Way to win friends and influence people. I sit there for a minute, trying to come up with a plan. Even if I had access to my phone, Fox Valley's one-and-only towing service is operated by Brad, Lisa's former fiancé. Not a good thing, given Jezebel's proclivity for breaking down in inconvenient places.

Owen is waiting inside at a two-top, a still foaming glass in front of him. Either he hasn't been waiting long, he doesn't like the taste, or maybe he's ordered the drink to help him blend in.

If that's the case, it isn't working. I'm not sure what it is that makes him stand out from the rest of the evening crowd. He's casually dressed in jeans and a black T-shirt, and there's nothing about his hair or his face that screams "not from here." He's not the only person drinking at a table alone. He's not the most striking or the most handsome or the most anything, but still. If this was a scene from a movie, he'd have special lighting, there'd be a close-up shot, a change in the music, and we'd all know he was important to the story.

It takes me a few minutes to make my way over to him because I know everybody and everybody knows me.

"Sorry about Geneva," Jack Connelly says, laying a trembling hand on my arm.

I remind myself to have a word with Vic about cutting Jack off sooner. He's getting too old for this routine. His eyes are watery, his nose red, and he's gotten way too thin. He's been a functional alcoholic for years, but there comes a point, I know, where his body will betray him and the functional bit will go right out the window.

"You were in love with her, Jack, weren't you?" Gerry says. "Back in the day."

"Forget back in the day," Tilda jibes, but gently. "He had a thing for her right up until the day she died, though here he is married to me."

I smile at her. "And lucky he is, too. Bet he even knows it."

By the time I reach Owen's table, he still hasn't made much progress on his drink. "Did you get that for me?" I ask, reaching for it.

His hand curls around the glass, unconsciously possessive, and I can't help smiling. Score one for Vic.

"Get your own," he says, his lips tucking up at the corners into an almost smile, and I move past him and up to the bar.

"Addy! What will it be?"

Rosa's not surprised to see me back here again. I don't have an actual office, and there aren't a lot of places to meet with clients. So, it's *Grounded* earlier in the day, *The Raven* in the evening. Vic gives me not just the family rate but the twin rate, which means my food and drinks are free, although I always pay for my clients.

I look at the blackboard where the names of the new offerings are written, tempted. I didn't get to finish my drink when I was here with Millie. But then I think about that powerful sports car waiting for me in the parking lot and the man waiting for me at a table, and I opt for a clear head. I can drink later.

"Give me a kombucha, would you?"

"Sure thing." She leans closer and drops her voice, her brown eyes full of curiosity and questions. "That guy over there already paid for your drink."

"But my drinks are already free."

She dimples. "He doesn't know that. Spill. Who is he?"

"Leno Masterson's big brother."

"Dios mio," she says, crossing herself. "The guy who killed himself? You sure you don't want a real drink?"

"I'm sure."

"Wise, very wise. I have a feeling you need your wits about you for that one." She turns and fills a mug with fizzing kombucha and brings it back to me. "Luck," she says.

I open my mouth to explain that this is just a business meeting, not a date, and then close it. It's already too late to stop the gossip. Every eye in this room is taking note of the fact that I'm having a drink with a stranger. Probably, they also know Owen's identity and that I was having coffee with his dead brother while my grandmother was being put in the ground. Phones will come out. Photos will be taken and posted.

Well, if they want to talk, there's nothing I can do about it. I hold my head high and saunter. Owen watches me cross the floor. Watches me settle into a seat. Watches me take a big gulp of my drink—no need for him to know it isn't actually alcoholic. I smile at him and bat my eyelashes. "I'm here."

"I noticed. Pretty sure everybody noticed."

"So, do you have something for me?"

"Not so fast." He takes a deep swallow of his drink, then wipes his mouth with the back of his hand. "Could we just talk for a minute?"

"Why not?"

But he doesn't seem to be in any hurry to dive in, and I resist the impulse to let the silence lure me into being the first to speak. I wait. And drink. And sneak glances at him whenever I think he's not looking, wondering if he remembers the time we met.

BRITT and I are a little drunk with the freedom of our first semester of college. No parents breathing down our necks, waiting up when we're out late and lecturing us about our futures. When there's a Leno and the Lonely concert in Seattle, Britt somehow manages to score not only front-row seats but a backstage pass and an invite to a private after-party. She says she won them in a contest, and I believe her.

Despite my history with Leno, I'm not about to pass up a free concert or a rock star after-party. As for meeting the band backstage, I have no desire to talk to Leno, and when I remind Britt of the Grand Canyon-size grudge I'm holding against him, she says, "Fine. Who wants to watch a bunch of groupies getting their boobs signed, anyway? Let's just get to the party."

The band, of course, arrives late, and I've already got a couple of drinks on board and am overheated and out of breath from dancing by the time Leno, in his rock-god persona, graces us with his lordly presence. I turn to say something snarky to Britt, but she has turned toward the band like a sunflower to the sun. And then Leno makes a royal procession through the crowd, grabs her hand, and drags her out onto the dance floor.

She glances back at me over her shoulder, her lips moving in a single word. I can't hear her over the music and laughter, but I'm pretty sure she says, "Sorry." She doesn't look sorry. I watch them go with a stab of betrayal, even though I know that my thing with Leno doesn't really have to be hers and that most people in this room would be elated by being chosen by the star of the show. I should be happy for her.

I'm not.

Feeling abandoned and sorry for myself, I isolate myself in a corner with a drink, recounting a tale of all the ways I am an unloved social outcast. And then, a tall, dark-haired man walks past a nearby cluster of groupies, all giggling and barely dressed, arriving in front of me as if I am his actual destination.

"You look rather pensive for the middle of a party," he says. "Tell me what you're thinking and I'll buy you a drink."

"Trust me, you don't want to know what I'm thinking."

"Try me."

I only half glance at him, unable to tear my attention away from Britt. Laughing. Leaning in close to Leno, who made it clear, in public, that I was absolutely nothing and nobody and scarred me for life.

When I still don't answer, the dark-haired man says, "You know, I'm an alien from outer space with magical powers who can kill people with my thoughts."

"Mmmm, interesting," I murmur before I realize what he's

actually said. Startled, I turn my head and find myself gazing into a pair of keen, strikingly gorgeous gray eyes. And then the rest of his face comes into focus—lean, clean-shaven. Strong chin, sensitive lips, curved into a smile that is equal parts rueful and mischievous.

"Prove it," I say. "Who will your victim be?"

His eyes scan the room and linger in the vicinity of Leno and Britt. "Truth time," he says. "You'd rather be dancing with Leno."

"Who doesn't want to dance with Leno?" It's a rhetorical question. Bitter and ironic because, obviously, I don't.

"You're right, of course," my companion says. "The whole world wants to dance with my brother."

He dips his head in a small nod, then turns and walks away. Not to get me a drink. Not to dance with another girl. He moves through the crowd and out the door.

And that was the time I met Owen.

"Can you still kill people with your mind?" I ask, now, half hoping he doesn't remember.

"Once you have the power, it's yours forever," he says. A light comes on behind his eyes, his lips turn upward ever so slightly at the corners, and I think he's actually going to smile. Then the light fades, and his jaw tightens. He drains half of his mug, then slams it down on the table. "Let's talk about this party Leno asked for."

I feel like I'm under a spell of compulsion; I can't look away, can't think clearly. "We already had that conversation," I say after a couple of eons of time pass by. "It didn't end well. Insults exchanged. Police contacted."

"To be fair, your whole party thing was a bit of a shock. And I did think you were a gold digger."

"And what-oh-what might have changed your mind about that?"

"Leno left me the password for his computer. I read through your text messages, which is why I was texting you as him, not me. Again, sorry about that."

Of course he read through Leno's messages. If something unimaginable and awful were to happen to Vic, I'd comb through every inch of his life, every document, every message, searching out every last crumb of every last interaction he had with anybody. Privacy be damned.

"And?" I ask.

"And it's obvious he was the instigator. It's also obvious how much he wanted this party."

"And?"

He sighs. "Going to make me say it, I see. All right then. I'm sorry I thought you were taking advantage of him when it was clearly the opposite. Not to speak ill of my beloved dead, but he was very good at manipulating people."

"You think?"

"You don't have to do it, though," Owen says. "The party. He got everything he wanted while he was alive, so maybe—"

"Except keeping on living," I interrupt. "He didn't get that."

Owen's eyes go dark. He runs a hand through his hair. Lifts his glass to his lips but then sets it down again without drinking. "No. He didn't get that."

"I'm doing the party."

"I'm asking you not to."

"You don't have to go. What harm is it going to do you?"

"Do you know anything about media? How far some reporters and influencers will go to chase a story? They are already all over this, in case you haven't noticed. They've been up to the house, trying to get past the gate and talk to Mother. It will only get worse if you feed it." He runs both hands over his head and then leaves them there, clutching, as if pulling his hair will provide more space in his brain. "Keep the money and the car. Let the party go. Leno will never know you didn't do it."

"I'll know. And I'm counting on the media to get the party buzzing, so yay!"

"You know they've got some stuff about you and Leno already?"

"Seen it. Good for the party."

He groans. "This is going to be an unmitigated disaster." He releases his hair and lays both palms flat on the table. "Is there nothing I can say to make you see reason?"

"Sorry, but no."

"And if I said I won't turn over the car unless you call off the party?"

I shrug.

"You do realize how much money the Maserati is worth? You could sell it."

"What can I say? I'm a really bad gold digger but an excellent party planner."

"God." He empties his glass in one long swallow. "Mother will absolutely lose it over this. Well, maybe we can hide out at Leno's condo until after your party is over. More layers of protection with the manned gatehouse."

My mind boggles at the image of Sylvie Masterson sharing a small-ish space with Spiro. "Is there room for you all?" I ask.

Owen stares at me again, this time like I'm speaking a foreign language. A dead one. "Mother and I are not precisely besties, but I imagine we can co-exist in a two-bedroom condo for a few days."

"Only, you know, Spiro is in one of those bedrooms. Unless you and Spiro are a thing, there's not going to be enough beds."

Owen's gray eyes narrow. His right hand, open on the table, clenches into a fist. "You have got to be kidding me. When did the vulture roll in?"

Okay, good to know. Owen is not sleeping with Spiro. "She's been in town since last week. They were discussing band business or something. You didn't know?"

"No," he says. "I didn't know." He shoves back his chair, gets to his feet, and heads for the door without another word.

"Where are you going?" I shout after him.

He doesn't answer. Maybe he doesn't hear me over the clamor of voices and laughter and music. Or maybe he just doesn't want to reply.

Why, I wonder, does Spiro being in town bother him so much? No need to follow him to ask my question because, even though he doesn't know it yet, Owen isn't going anywhere.

CHAPTER 13

I SWILL kombucha and count the seconds while I wait. Owen is back before I get to forty-five.

"Forget something?" I ask, looking up at him, all innocent eyes and surprise.

"Are you always like this?" he demands.

"Like what exactly?"

He glowers silently.

"Ohhhh." I finish off my kombucha and smile sweetly. "The parking situation, you mean."

"Yes. The parking situation. I need you to move that junk heap out of the way."

"I can try. But only if you tell me what your problem is with Spiro." I set down my glass and get to my feet, which puts my eyes level with Owen's chest. I can't help noticing that it's a good, broad chest, with all indications that it's nicely muscled beneath that T-shirt. I tip my head back so I can look into his face, wondering how I ever thought it was ordinary. Those eyes. That chiseled jaw, the sensitive lips...

"Fine," he snarls. "Move your junk heap and I'll tell you some things about Spiro."

His sudden capitulation leaves me off balance, as if I've been playing tug of war and the guy on the other end of the rope suddenly let go. I feel myself tilting toward him and have to look away to steady myself by taking in the familiar surroundings. Vic stands behind the counter, watching, eyebrows raised in a way that means, "Just ask if you need me."

I shake my head slightly and turn back to Owen. "Deal." I hold out my hand, and after a too-long and awkward interval, he reaches out to grasp it in his.

A strong hand. Warm. Neatly cut fingernails. Calluses on both palm and fingertips. He shakes once, then releases me and leads the way outside.

It's mostly dark, the parking lot lit only by a couple of streetlights. Jezebel, parked right where she shouldn't be, looms large. I get in and turn the key, but absolutely nothing happens, except for a tiny click that is extraordinarily loud in the silence.

Owen bends down to peer through my open window, and I cringe. All the crap I found under the passenger seat is still sitting there, as if I hoard weird, random objects and drive around with them. His nose wrinkles. His gaze travels from the collection of junk on the seat to me. His eyebrows go up, one of them higher than the other. He sniffs tentatively, and his nose wrinkles. "I don't think I want to know, and yet I can't help guessing."

"And what is your guess?"

"I'm going with a gigantic drunken squirrel nesting in your

car," he says. "With a passion for oranges and beer. Are you going to move?"

"That is up to Jezebel, I'm afraid, and I think it's improbable."

"And Jezebel is?"

"The car on which you are leaning. She doesn't like leaners." I turn the key in the ignition again. Nothing. I shrug, turning both hands palms up to demonstrate clearly my helplessness in this situation.

"Maybe you could call a tow truck?"

"Yeah, about that... I can't."

"The town does have a tow operation, yes? I mean, I haven't actually lived here for any length of time, but surely?"

"We do. But it's Brad."

"And Brad is what? Incompetent? Expensive?"

"Just trust me. Brad is not going to come and tow my car. Not tonight. Not ever. You could call him and he might come out, but don't tell him my name."

"What's the number?" Owen asks, looking at me like I've lost my mind entirely, and honestly, I can't say that I blame him.

"Lost my phone. You'll have to look it up."

He does. The phone rings once, and I can hear Brad's voice come on. "This is Brad. Sorry, call me back in the morning. Don't bother leaving a message. Beep beep beep."

Owen's eyes meet mine again.

I shrug.

"That wasn't a recorded message."

"It was not."

"There were voices in the background. And music. And he made the beeping noises himself."

"He's drinking," I say. "His fiancée just called off the wedding, so you can't really blame him."

"Why do I feel like you have something to do with that?"

"No comment."

"Winning friends and influencing people seems to be your talent. Fine. I guess we are moving this beast ourselves."

It's my turn to lift my eyebrows.

"Put it in neutral," he says. "I'll push."

"Her, not it," I mutter. "But if you say so." I shift into neutral.

Owen moves around behind the car. I watch him in the rearview mirror as he presses his hands against the trunk and leans forward. I see the muscles bunch in his biceps, the cords strain in his neck. A vein pops out on his forehead as his face goes red with effort.

Jezebel doesn't budge.

He straightens up. "Have you got her in neutral? You do know what that is, right?"

"The one that isn't D or R or a number?"

"Foot off the brake?"

I open the door and get out. "Let me go in and get some help. One person can't move her, unless he's like a bodybuilder or something."

"And you couldn't have said that earlier?"

"Wanted to see how strong you are."

"I'm surprised, frankly, that you still live and breathe," he mutters. Then, louder, "Let's see if the two of us can do it first. Ready? One, two, three, push!"

This time, I add my weight to his, bracing my hands on the frame of the open door. Jezebel grudgingly rolls a few inches forward.

"Again!" Owen shouts, and this time, she permits herself to be rolled across the parking lot to a place where she's still in the way but no longer blocking in cars. Owen bends over, hands braced on his thighs, breathing hard. After a long moment, he straightens up and levels a stormy gaze at me. "If I weren't about to turn over a high-performance vehicle into your care and keeping, how were you planning to get home?"

I shrug. "Wait for Vic to get off work so he can drive me home."

"And Vic is? Husband, boyfriend?"

I'd forgotten that Owen isn't from here and wouldn't know that very basic thing about me. "Twin," I say. "Owns *The Raven*. Want to tell me why you were leaving and taking my new car with you?"

"I need to talk to Spiro."

I follow his gaze as it travels from me to Jezebel's hulking presence to the Maserati, and I have an idea. The sad truth is that I have no idea how to operate a high-performance vehicle, as he puts it. I certainly don't want to be trying to figure out how everything works while he watches me. I need some time with the owner's manual. Or better, Vic. By daylight. But maybe this will work.

"How were *you* going to get home after you turned over my new car?" I ask.

"I had thought perhaps you might drive me. And I could mansplain to you on the way how to drive it, just on the off chance that you haven't driven a Maserati before."

"How about this?" I suggest, with as much nonchalance as I can muster, as if I'm making a huge concession. "You drive on up to have this super-urgent convo with Spiro, and I ride along.

You can explain as we go. When you're done, I'll drive you home."

He hesitates.

"I'm waiting to hear from her anyway," I say, "Only I lost my phone. This would give me a chance to check in."

"What kind of business do you have with Spiro?" he demands, as if he has a right to know.

"Party stuff. Nothing you'd be interested in."

"Your guest list."

"Well, that and whether the band is going to play, or—"

"You have got to be kidding me."

I give him my most annoying smirk.

"You're not kidding me. Get in. We'll discuss this on the way up there."

He gets in the driver's side and slams the door, and I make a dash for the passenger side before he changes his mind and leaves without me.

The seat is plush leather, buttery soft, with lumbar support. It even smells good—not like new-car or air fresh-ener, definitely not like vomit and oranges, but like leather and...Owen. A subtle dusky scent of shampoo and aftershave and probably anger pheromones.

It also feels dangerous, a wild creature that might turn on me at any minute. I remember a guy I knew in college who sold a motorbike after driving it only three times. "It wanted to kill me," he'd said. Leno's car feels like it might be contemplating homicide.

"Just a machine," I can hear Vic scoffing. *"Cars don't have souls, Addy. Or wills of their own."*

"Have you seen Christine?"

Imaginary Vic rolls his eyes. "You do know none of that was real? The car wasn't driving itself. The people were actors. Nobody was harmed in the making of that movie."

Despite whatever it is that has gotten his shorts in a bunch, Owen actually holds to his end of the bargain. "I assume you've never driven one of these. Don't want to explain anything you already know."

I snort. "Maseratis on every street corner around here."

He just looks at me.

I sigh. "Listen, Jezebel is the only car I've ever owned. It's safe to assume I know nothing other than how the steering wheel works. And maybe the gas and brake pedals."

"Okay. This is a keyless start. If the fob is in the car, all you have to do is push the start button. This is the fob. I guess I might as well hand it over now."

He holds out a keyring attached to a black oblong plastic bit that looks just like what Vic, Britt, and all of my friends have for locking and unlocking their doors. Jezebel frowns upon such modern madness—with her, it's a key in the lock or nothing.

Owen pushes a button to the right of the steering column, and immediately, the engine begins to purr. Dangerous. Jungle cat, not a house cat.

"What's her name?" I ask. "Or his. Feels more him than her for some reason."

"Of whom would we be speaking?" Owen shifts into reverse and begins backing out of the space.

Britt's car has a backup camera, but nothing so high-def as this one. The dashboard makes me dizzy with all the lights and colors. There's even a touch computer screen.

"This car."

"Maserati," he says.

"No, not like that. Like, my car's name is Jezebel."

"If Leno named his car, he didn't confide in me. But then, as you've noticed, we weren't exactly close."

"Maybe Bob, then." Clearly, this is not the right name for this car, but it makes me feel a little better to call it something ordinary because what really comes to mind, right after Christine, is Hannibal.

"Aren't cars generally given girl names?" he asks.

"Are you sexist?"

I can't be certain in the half-dark, but I'm pretty sure he rolls his eyes. I shut up and survey the lights and gauges on the dash, wondering how Leno might have felt the last time he drove this car. Being able to still direct this kind of power, even while knowing there's a wheelchair in the trunk. Was he thinking about death? The party?

"So, tell me about Spiro."

We've already left the lights and traffic of town, such as they are, behind us and are winding up the mountainside. It's full-on dark outside, and all I can see of his face is his profile, but it's obvious he's still wound up tight.

"Spiro is hungry for power and prestige and money. She's Leno's full partner. Her name is on all the bank accounts. With him out of the way, she's queen. Finally."

"You don't think she would have... I mean, he did do it himself, right? The morphine or whatever."

"Wouldn't put it past her to have helped him along."

"She said she wasn't there when he did it."

"Spiro lies. And patience is not one of her virtues, if she has any." He glances over at me. "You had the thought, too, apparently. That she might have done something. That he didn't do this himself."

"I did think she might have helped him. Which would actually be good, wouldn't it? He was scared of dying alone."

Owen's hands tighten on the steering wheel, and he steps on the gas. We're going way too fast for this road in the dark.

"I should have been there," he says.

"She said she wasn't there. She said she would have stopped him. Slow down a little, would you? Suicide Corner is just up ahead."

He doesn't slow down; if anything we're accelerating.

"Spiro would do anything for money and fame. Trust me."

"Seriously, Owen. Slow the fuck down."

He doesn't. Headlights suddenly glare in the rearview as another vehicle rounds a corner behind us, not just bright but on high beam. We're moving fast, but they're gaining.

"Jeez, buddy—" Owen says.

I fist both hands around the edges of my seat and suck in a breath as the lights illuminate the interior of the car with a blinding brightness. I look over my shoulder but can't make out anything against the glare. The lights swerve out into the other lane, double-yellow line be damned. They'll never make it past us before we reach the corner. And if someone is coming from the other direction, we're all going to die.

But the vehicle hangs back right on our tail.

"What the hell are they doing?" I squeak.

Owen slows way down, but still, the other vehicle doesn't pass. Again, I look over my shoulder. A pickup truck, I think. Maybe an SUV. Just as we reach the corner, a jolt flings me forward against my seatbelt. The Maserati skids toward the shoulder. My entire body clenches as I wait for the screech of metal against the guardrail, for momentum to propel us up and over, for the plummet down into certain death.

But Owen pulls us out of the skid, gets us back onto the road, heading in the right direction. I take a breath, thinking it's over, that the idiot driver, obviously high or drunk or otherwise impaired, has sobered up enough to back the hell off, but then there's another jolt, and this time Owen can't save us.

A scream tears my throat, and I make a bizarre wish that it isn't the last sound I'm ever going to make. I feel the tires sinking into something soft. I tilt sideways, my body involuntarily leaning against the door, but then we stop. My brain tries to feed me information.

We're in the ditch. The guardrail and the chasm must be behind us. But we're still not safe.

The vehicle behind us has also stopped, lighting us up in a harsh white glow. I've read enough thrillers and watched enough movies to know what happens next. They'll pop out of their vehicle, carrying guns, and finish us off quickly with a professional round to the head. Unless they want to torture us first.

"Get down," Owen says, obviously entertaining the same idea.

I duck behind the dashboard, holding my breath, praying at least the coming death will be quick, even as I'm wondering who could possibly want to kill me. I can hear the rumbling motor of the truck behind us. Will I hear the footsteps, or is our own engine too loud? Which comes first—the sound of a gun being fired or being dead as the bullet tears through my brain?

Then I hear another vehicle approaching, and I turn my head to peek up over the dash to see headlights coming toward us. Owen turns on the flashers, and the oncoming vehicle slows. Behind us, I hear the crunch of tires. The headlights retreat, and I dare to turn around in time to see a black pickup doing a three-point turn. It peels off with a squeal of tires and the acrid stink of burning rubber.

The new vehicle, another pickup, drives on by, and I think it's going to keep going, but then it turns around and drives up behind us. I bury my head in my arms and stay down. Half the population of Fox Valley drives pickups, so it's irrational to believe this is yet another murderous attempt, but terror isn't conducive to logic.

Even with my head buried in my arms, I can see the glare of headlights. I hear the click, click, click of the flashers. Owen's breathing and my own. When he sits up and rolls down the window, I want to tell him to stop, but what difference does it make, really? If somebody wants to shoot us, a little window glass isn't going to stop them.

My whole body is trembling. I'm breathing in great, sobbing gasps. Owen's hand settles on my head, gently stroking my hair. "It's okay, Addy. It's over," he murmurs. "It's okay. We're okay."

"You in trouble here?" a familiar voice asks through the open window.

I uncurl and look up to see Henry Grabel's worried face peering in at us.

"Addison? What are you doing out here at this time of night?" He says it like it's midnight and I'm a teenager out past curfew, and I see him eyeing Owen and probably jumping to all sorts of wrong conclusions.

"Pickup truck ran us off the road," Owen explains. "They drove off when they saw you coming."

"Assholes," Henry says, which is very strong language for him, proof of the strength of his own emotions. "Probably drunk."

They weren't, though, I think. The driver was very much in control. Two words keep blinking inside my head in neon lights: ON PURPOSE.

Owen opens the door and scrambles out. "How bad is it?"

I think about getting out to join them as they move around the car, examining it with a flashlight, but it feels like too much trouble. If I take off my seat belt and open the door, I'm going to tumble right out into the ditch. Exhaustion floods through me as the terror ebbs. I'm cold. I can't stop shaking, and I'm afraid my legs won't hold me.

"Left rear fender damage," Henry says. "They actually hit you?"

"It was deliberate," Owen says.

"Thought only cops did that maneuver," Henry says.

"Apparently not."

"Got yourself some enemies?"

"None that I know of," Owen says. "Maybe they were after Addy."

This is ridiculous enough to surprise a snort laugh out of me. Who would want to kill me? I know I can be annoying, but whoever did this was well beyond annoyed. I start digging for my phone in my bag to call the situation in, and then remember, again, that a) my phone is lost, and b) this is a cellphone dead zone anyway, and nobody is calling.

"No cell service here," Henry says, echoing my thoughts. "We'll get you out of the ditch and on your way. As soon as you're in town, you'll need to call your insurance company and the cops. What a beautiful car." His voice has taken on the tone men fall into when worshipping high-performance vehicles.

I let my eyes drift closed, accepting the probability that we'll be here for a while.

"It's not going to just drive out," Owen says. "I tried that."

"Never go anywhere without a tow rope," Henry says. "Just a little yank and you'll be right as rain."

"Better take some pics for the insurance company before we move it," Owen says.

I hear his footsteps moving around the car, see the bright white glow as the flash goes off from all sides of the car. Then Henry turns his truck around and backs it up on the shoulder, and I watch the two of them in the headlight beams as they hook up the tow rope.

"You okay?" Owen asks, climbing in beside me.

"Define okay." I hate that my voice trembles, but I notice that Owen's hands, resting on the steering wheel, are also shaking, which makes me feel a little better.

"Sorry your car got damaged before you even got to drive it," he says.

I shrug, summoning up bravado. "At least I don't have to pay for the damages."

He laughs and starts the car. Then he rolls down his window so he can shout at Henry, "Ready whenever you are."

Henry gives him a thumbs-up and gets into his truck.

Owen shifts into first, and Henry's truck rolls forward. There's a jolt as the towline goes tight and Owen steps on the gas. The wheels spin, sending up gravel on my side. But then we're moving, up and out, the tires are rolling on pavement, and I have a wild desire to jump out of the car and kiss the ground.

Henry gets out of his truck and detaches the tow rope. Then, to my surprise, he comes around to my side. I roll down the window and look up into his familiar, weather-worn face. "You can ride with me, if you'd rather. I'll drop you home."

I consider it. "Are we still going to Spiro's?" I ask Owen.

"That can wait. Actually, if you wouldn't mind..."

"What?"

"I don't want to upset my mother with all this. Could we call the cops and the insurance people from your place? And I'll get a ride from there."

"Sounds like a plan," Henry says. "I'll follow you in just to make sure you get there safely."

"Thank you, sir," Owen says. "Don't know what we'd have done without you."

Thinking about what might have happened without Henry sets me shaking again, harder than ever. We'd be hanging out with Leno and Geneva; that's what we'd be doing. And I'm so not ready for that yet.

"Glad I came along right then," Henry says. Then he turns and hobbles toward his truck, his right leg hitching a little, the way it's done as long as I've known him.

CHAPTER 14

OWEN TURNS the car around and heads back down toward town. Neither of us says anything. I give him directions to my apartment, and he parks the Maserati in the lot.

"Well?" he says when I continue to just sit there, not even taking off my seat belt.

I've never been bothered that the parking lot at my building isn't particularly well lit. This is Fox Valley. Everybody in my building knows each other. Strangers are rare and watched with suspicion. I've never in my life feared the dark, not even as a child. Now, the thought of getting out of the car and walking through the shadows feels daunting. What if somebody is lurking behind one of the cars, ready to ambush me? My brain is full of images of guns and knives, rape and murder and pillaging.

Fortunately, when it comes to fight or flight, though, I'm more of a fight kind of girl, and my inborn contrary streak takes over. I am going to do this party for Leno. If somebody killed him, I'm going to figure out who. And if somebody is trying to kill me—well, I don't know what I'm going to do about that, but I'm not going to hide in a corner.

I get out of the car and slam the door, daring any waiting danger to come and get me.

As it turns out, there actually is somebody lurking in the parking lot, leaning up against a car two spots down.

"Upgrading?" Carmen inquires, slowly peeling away from her car and coming over to investigate.

"New blend?" I sniff, tentatively, at the smoke wafting in my direction.

Carmen is a licensed grower and creates her product line with as much passion and creativity as Vic puts into his craft beer. Some of Carmen's blends have knocked me on my not-inconsiderable ass, and one kept me awake until morning communing with my plants.

She saunters around the Maserati, looking it over, then leans up against the trunk and asks, "How does Jezebel feel about this?"

"Jezebel is dead."

"God rest her soul," Carmen intones solemnly. "Does the driver come with the car?"

"This is Owen. Owen, this is Carmen, one of my neighbors."

"Neighbor, supplier, and feline probation officer," she says, shifting her pipe to her left hand and holding out her right.

"Unusual list of creds." Owen shakes her hand, then inhales deeply and makes a little humming sound. "And suddenly, I'm sixteen again. What is that?"

"Proprietary blend," she says. "Sold only through my official shop, of course. One hundred percent in compliance with the law, unlike that felonious cat of Addy's."

I groan. "What's Bruno done now?"

"Let me just say you'll want to avoid Blake for the foreseeable future." She tips her head back to look up at the stars, the silver rings in her eyebrow and lip shimmering in the glow of the streetlight.

"Can I have a hit?" I reach out my hand for the pipe. Trouble with my cat is one straw too many, and the invitation to relax into a fuzzy, warm glow is strong.

Carmen, always willing to share, hands it over, and I take a big hit, sucking the smoke deep into my lungs, holding it, ignoring the harshness in my throat, the burn deep in my chest, until I can no longer repress a cough.

"Easy there," Carmen says. "This stuff mandates a tolerance I don't think you've got."

"Lay it on me. I have had a hell of a day."

"One more, but go easy," she advises.

I take another big lungful, and Carmen laughs as my body goes soft. I drape myself backward against the car, feeling every curve of it against every curve of me.

"You want a hit?" she asks Owen.

"I think one of us should be able to talk rationally to the cops," he says.

I'm already behind a big enough cushion not to trust my perceptions, but I think he sounds more wistful than censorious.

"Did you miss the part about me being legal?" Carmen asks.

"Not about you," he says. "If you'll please excuse me for a minute?" He pulls his phone out of his pocket and makes a call.

I listen, blissfully hazy, as he explains what happened and gives my address.

"What's your apartment number?" he asks.

His voice is far away, and I'm fascinated by the streetlights, opening and closing my eyes, squinting, amazed by the way rays and bands form and dissolve, stretch and thin and glow.

Carmen fills him in. When he hangs up, she says, "Addy's got about zero tolerance, and that was a lot. Need help getting her inside?"

"That would be great," Owen says.

Carmen grabs one of my hands. "Somebody legit tried to kill you?"

"Certainly seemed that way," Owen says. "Although it's possible it wasn't us they were trying to kill. Come on, Addy, let's go."

He takes my other hand, and I let the two of them tug me away from the car. It feels good to allow other people to make decisions for me while I float between them. I like the sensation of Owen's hand holding mine and his solid masculinity beside me. And I like having Carmen there, too, a known and trustworthy ally.

My body feels warm and melty, like butter. Mmmm, butter. On toast. Biscuits would be better, but I don't feel capable of making biscuits. What a weird word that is. Biscuits. What is the *U* doing in there? Shouldn't the *C* be a *K*? And why do English people call cookies biscuits anyway?

Bruno is waiting outside the door, hunched over something protectively.

"Not in the mood," I say. The words string themselves out,

too slowly, the oos multiplying into many more than two. "What you got there, anyway?"

"Don't say I didn't warn you," Carmen says as I nudge my protesting cat out of the way with one foot.

He immediately starts purring and wrapping himself around my ankles. When he moves on to Owen's, I take advantage of the moment of distraction to pick up his most recent prize.

It's a necktie. Not just any tie, either, but Blake's beloved Playboy Bunny tie, the one he wears to every community gathering like a badge of honor, telling us all about the time he actually went to Playboy Manor, met Heffner, and was gifted this tie by the man himself. It's no longer in very good shape. Even from a fuzzy distance, I wince a little at the long rents in the naked woman's thighs. Her head has been nearly separated from her body.

"That is terrifying," Owen says.

Bruno pounces on the tie again, and rather than try to get it away from him, I just pick him up and let him carry it. Fortunately, I don't have to dig in my bag for a key because Carmen and I have keys to each other's apartments. In the very rare case that I'm away, she feeds Bruno, and if she's gone, I water her plants—houseplants only, to be clear. She's got employees to manage her grow operation, which is not here at the apartment complex.

"We should maybe try to sober her up a little?" Owen says as the door swings open.

The contrast between my apartment and the Masterson mansion, or even Leno's condo, goes a long way toward reversing my lovely buzz. The tiny space, with its threadbare beige carpet and scarred paint, seems particularly shabby with

Owen at my side. At least it's clean. The bed made, dishes washed, but it still looks cluttered. What was I thinking, agreeing to bring him into this space?

But Carmen takes charge, and things are better, at least marginally, in a matter of minutes.

"We need to feed you," she says. "What have you got that's easy?" She heads for the fridge while Owen goes to the sink and starts running water.

"Cupboard to the right," Carmen says, as if there is an abundance of cupboards rather than just the one.

Owen finds a glass and fills it with cold water. "Drink up," he says. "It'll help."

"Oooh, are these *Raven* nachos?" Carmen retreats out of the fridge with a foil-wrapped package. So much has happened since today's first visit to *The Raven* that I'd actually forgotten my precious leftovers. Now, I'm starving. My mouth is watering.

"Hands off. Those are mine."

"Chill, Chica, I've got you. Maybe just one?"

I cross the room and grab for the package. She laughs and pretends to fight me for them, grabbing one chip with congealed, melted cheese and shoving it into her mouth. "We could warm those up."

"Don't bother. There won't be time." I plop down at the table and tuck into the nachos, washing each bite down with icy-cold water. There is something grounding about cheese and chips, even soggy ones, the sting of jalapeño, and the creamy smoothness of guacamole. My feet on the floor. My cat attacking the naked-woman tie...

Okay. That bit is still surreal, as is having Owen in my apartment with Carmen. And when there's a knock on the door and Carmen opens it to reveal Alex standing there, the sense of weirdness and disconnect rockets into the stratosphere.

This is not the first time Alex has been in my apartment, of course. He spent nights here. We've been naked together in all the chairs, on the couch, and obviously in the bed. Now he swaggers in as if he owns the place, hand on his duty belt in a total power play. His eyes skewer Owen. "You the one who called in an accident?"

"That's right," Owen says, unphased by Alex's posturing. "I'm Owen Masterson. I was—"

"Brother of Leno Masterson, is that right? Died what, two days ago now?"

"Yes, and—"

"Last I heard, you wanted a restraining order on Addison and she was thinking maybe you murdered your brother."

Owen turns to me. "That was Mom with the order. You think I murdered Leno? Really?"

"Technically, that was Dad."

It's all too much for my THC-infused brain. Owen, Alex, and Carmen all together in my apartment, the cat growling over that obscenely horrid tie, the events of the last few days. Laughing is absolutely the worst thing I could do at the moment, but it bursts out of me, and there's not a thing I can do to hold it back. I can't breathe. Tears pour down my face, and I clutch at my belly as I whoop and gasp in a paroxysm that is half laughter, half weeping.

"What's wrong with her?" Alex asks. He sniffs the air, nostrils flaring like a hound on the trail, and turns his gaze to Carmen. "She's high. You got her high."

"It's legal," Carmen says.

"Just because you have a grow license doesn't make it legal," Alex says. "Been a lot more drugs in the valley lately."

"Don't look at me," Carmen says. "I already told you to keep your eyes on that new tattoo parlor. Perfectly legal for me to share with a friend."

"If I might?" Owen asks. "We were nearly killed tonight, which is the reason you're here. If we could focus on that?"

"I'll focus on what I choose to focus on. I'm the investigating officer here." Alex turns to me. "Let's start with where the two of you were going in that fancy car at..." he pauses to check his watch, "almost midnight on a Sunday?"

"Closer to ten when it happened," Owen says. "Perhaps we could talk about the people who tried to kill us?"

"Alex is just pissy because he thinks you're moving in on his girl," Carmen explains. She gets out her phone, taps it a few times, and points it at Alex.

"What are you doing?" he demands.

"Filming you. Just to make sure your feelings of rejection don't interfere with the law."

"You're dating this guy?" Owen asks, turning to me.

I hold up a finger, indicating that they should all wait for a minute and take a long drink from my glass. Then I get up, cross to the sink, and splash cold water over my face. The sensory shock breaks me out of my fit and I'm able to take a deep breath and turn to face them, my back to the counter.

"Was dating," I clarify. "*Was*."

"She broke up with him," Carmen says, gleefully recording Alex's expression for posterity.

"Put that thing away," he growls.

"Going to make me? Violence? Illicit arrest?" She's outright taunting him now, which isn't going to help at all.

Good thing my brain is starting to come back on track. "Alex. I am not dating Owen. Owen, I am not dating Alex. Owen is...helping me plan the party for Leno. We were on our way to consult with a possible band for the party."

"At this time of night?"

"There's not a curfew, Alex. A vehicle came up from behind us and rammed the rear end."

"You're sure this was deliberate?"

"It was a PIT maneuver," Owen says, looking Alex over as if he suspects him. "Happened right on a dangerous corner. Anybody in this town trained in that technique besides cops?"

"Look here," Alex says. "If you're implying—"

"Nobody is implying anything," I interrupt. "It's a perfectly valid question, Alex. Look. How about we all sit down, and we'll give you an organized statement."

"I can stand," Alex says, just to be ornery.

"But it would be so much easier for taking notes, wouldn't it?" I pull out one of my two kitchen chairs for him.

Carmen flops onto the couch, still filming, and Owen crosses the room and settles into my armchair. Bruno, dragging the tie, leaps up into his lap and settles down, purring. Owen looks startled, possibly more by the tie than the cat, but he begins gently stroking Bruno's fur.

"Now," I say, sitting down in the second of the two chairs at the tiny table. "How about we start over, Detective?"

Alex straightens his shoulders at the reminder of his rank and grudgingly sits at the table, sets his notebook and pen down in front of him, and turns to a blank page. "So," he says. "Maybe just tell me what happened. Who was driving?"

"I was," Owen says. "I saw headlights in my rearview mirror, coming fast. The vehicle swerved into the other lane, as if they were going to pass, but then hung back just on my bumper. They rammed us twice. The first time, I was able to recover, but the second put us in the ditch."

Alex has lost that jealous-lover look and morphed into cop mode. He taps his fingers on the table, staring down at the paper and the pen, forehead furrowed in actual thought.

"It was a pickup truck," Owen says. "Black or at least dark colored. They stopped when we were in the ditch. I thought they were going to get out and come over to the car, but then some guy came along from the other direction and they peeled off."

"Henry Grable," I supply. "In case you want to verify the details."

"License plate?" Alex asks.

"Headlights were blinding. I couldn't see it."

"Addy?"

"Hmmm?"

"Did you catch the license plate?"

"Lights were too bright to see anything."

"Make, model, and license plate number of the car the two of you were in," Alex says. "And your driver's license and registration."

"We're the victims here," I remind him.

"Standard procedure in an accident, Addison," Alex says.

"But this wasn't an accident! They were trying to kill us."

Owen gives him the make and model of the car. "I'll have to go look at the plates. I haven't memorized them."

"You don't know your own plates?"

"It's not my car," Owen says.

Alex looks up sharply. "Whose car is it?"

"Mine," I say, at precisely the same time as Owen says, "Leno's."

Alex looks from one of us to the other, eyebrows raised, and I clarify. "Leno gave it to me. Owen was showing me how to drive it."

Owen's gaze flashes to mine. Our eyes lock and hold just long enough for me to catch what looks like fear before he turns away. I suck in a breath as a host of incoherent thoughts and impressions suddenly converge and clarify.

"Either of you have enemies?" Alex asks. "People who might want to kill you?"

"Besides you?" I quip to make myself feel better.

He glares, and I grin at him, then shrug. "No recent death threats. Owen?"

"Me either," he says, looking down at the cat.

"Hear me out," I say slowly. "What if whoever did this somehow missed the memo that Leno is already dead?"

Now, all of them stare at me. Alex, as if I'm stupid. Carmen with a touch of wonder, as if whatever I smoked has had an unexpected effect.

Owen, on the other hand, looks like he's been sucker punched. His face goes dead white, and his hands stop mid-stroke. Bruno headbutts him to remind him of the important things in life. "You think they were after Leno?" he asks slowly. "I suppose it makes more sense than somebody trying to kill either of us. But surely everybody knows by now that he's dead."

"It's possible somebody might have missed it if they don't watch the news and aren't on social media," Alex says, actually considering the idea. "Was Leno mixed up in something criminal?"

"Nothing that I know of," Owen says, running both hands through his hair. "Ow! Watch your claws, you little beast."

"If he's in your lap, you're supposed to pet him," I say. "He has rules and expectations."

"I think we can rule out anybody seriously going after Addison," Alex says.

"Brad might have it in for me. I did encourage Lisa to break things off with him."

"Or maybe it was you, Alex," Carmen says. "A crime of passion, thinking she was dating Owen and all."

"That's ridiculous, Carmen, and you know it."

She shrugs. "Still. Maybe somebody else should take over this investigation."

"I was in the bullpen writing up notes when it happened," Alex says. "And Pete was there. I don't own a pickup truck. Also, Addy is free to date whomever she likes. I certainly don't care." Maybe he realizes that he's protesting too much because he stops, clears his throat, and turns back to Owen. "What is it that you do?"

"Family business," Owen says.

"As in Masterson Enterprises? Heard some rumblings about some trouble there, didn't I?" Alex asks. "Money laundering. Shady real estate. All kinds of rumors but nothing proven."

"Five years ago. Before my father died."

"And now you're running the company. Maybe some disgruntled victims, I mean customers, from back then coming after you? Or some business partners, even."

I've got to hand it to Alex. He's not as dense as he appears to be, and sometimes, he can latch onto relevant bits of information.

"I live in Chicago. If anybody wanted to take me out, there would be plenty of opportunity to do it there."

"And you're in town, why?" Alex asks.

"Because my brother is dead?"

"But you've been here since before he died, is that right?"

"I came to support my mother and my brother during this difficult time," Owen replies.

"Right," Alex says. "And you have absolutely no idea why a black pickup truck, make, model, and license plate unknown, with a driver who can do a controlled PIT maneuver on a tight corner targeted your brother's car."

"No idea whatsoever."

"Maybe they were gunning for you," Alex says. "Maybe they were after somebody who is already dead. A lot of maybes."

"Henry might have noticed something about the other vehicle," I offer.

Alex shoves back his chair and gets to his feet. "Possible. I'll be talking to him."

"Alex, in light of this, could you maybe look into Leno's death?" I suggest. "I mean—just say that whoever was driving that truck didn't know he was dead. Maybe they weren't the only one and somebody beat them to it."

"There's no evidence he was murdered," Alex says. "He had planned on ending his own life. He had cancer. The coroner has already ruled it natural causes as the Death With Dignity Act mandates."

"But he didn't even pick up his prescription," I protest. "Maybe at least do an autopsy?"

"I don't know how you know that, but I'm not discussing this with you, Addy. I'll look into who ran you off the road tonight, but I'm not going down one of your rabbit holes. Good night, Addison. Carmen." And with that, he's gone, the door closed behind him.

We all breathe in and out as if we're one symbiotic organism responding to the exit of a threat.

"Well, I'm headed home." Carmen gives me a hug. "Bang on the wall if you need me. I'm sorry about your brother, Owen, but he was suffering."

"You knew him?" Owen asks.

Of course she did. Pot is a mainstay for cancer sufferers—it calms anxiety and nausea, stimulates appetite, helps with pain. Somebody like Leno would have sought her out, and Carmen being Carmen, she probably created a special blend for him. But her professional discretion is top shelf, and she just says, "Come by the shop sometime, Owen, and I'll hook you up at a discount."

The door closes behind her, too, which leaves me, Owen, and Bruno, who has fallen asleep in his lap now that he's resumed the gentle stroking. I watch his hand, remembering the warmth of it on my own hair. His murmured reassurances. Whatever he's hiding, and he is hiding something, Owen's not a murderer.

I don't think.

He closes his eyes and lets his head lean against the back of the chair.

"I guess we need to get you home," I say, or mean to, anyway, the words distorted by a jaw-splitting yawn.

Owen opens his eyes. "Don't take this wrong, but I think maybe you shouldn't be driving tonight, especially not a car you've never driven before. Is there a way to remove this cat without getting mauled?"

"I've got him." My fingers graze Owen's thighs as I scoop up the drowsy bundle of fur and potential claws. I'm struck by a completely irrational desire to sit in his now vacant lap, to rest my head against his chest.

Not good, Addy. Not safe.

I retreat to the opposite side of the room. "You can take the car if you want, but I'm not sure either of us should be driving it. I mean, what if whoever it was tries again?"

"You've got a point," Owen says. "I'll get an Uber."

"At this time of night? In Fox Valley?"

"Might get lucky," he says, tapping at his phone. "Wow. Actually scored. They'll be here in a few, so I'll just go down and wait in the parking lot." He gingerly picks up the tie, left behind in his lap, between thumb and forefinger. "Yours?"

"A neighbor's. My cat steals things on the regular."

"A criminal feline. Sounds about right." But he smiles as he says it, draping the tie over the arm of the chair.

At the door, he turns and cups my cheek in one warm hand, gray eyes looking directly into mine. "Be careful, Addy, will you?"

And then he, too, is gone, but the warmth of his hand still lingers.

Bruno, wide awake again, demands to be fed something other than kibble. I tend to him. Take a long, blissfully steamy shower and comb the tangles out of my hair.

And then I get out my laptop and FaceTime Vic.

"What time is it, even?" His face is shadowed, barely lit by his phone, but I can see his hair standing up every which way and the dark stubble on his jaw. He's lying down, surrounded by blankets and pillows. "Some people are trying to sleep. Also, where the hell have you been? You didn't answer when I tried to call you at a reasonable hour."

"Some people should put their device on silent if they don't want to be bothered at night," I evade.

"Ha," he says. "You're on the emergency list, so you come through anyway."

It's true, and I'm immediately sorry. Vic really does have me on his emergency list, and he once got dressed and picked me up from a party at 3 am with hardly any bitching.

"Care to explain why you've summoned me at this hour, Addy?" Vic's phone shifts to a view of the ceiling, and when he comes back on screen, he's wearing a T-shirt and walking the phone out of the bedroom and into his kitchen.

"It's about Leno Masterson."

"He's dead. You think somebody killed him. This does not warrant a middle-of-the- night call."

Bruno climbs up into my lap, the tie once more dangling from his jaws. He retrieved it while I was fixing a cup of cocoa and is so happy with his new toy I haven't had the heart to take it away from him again.

Vic's eyes widen, and he leans in toward the camera. "What does that creature have now?"

"Never mind the cat. Here's the thing. Somebody might have tried to kill Leno again tonight, only they couldn't, of course, because he was already dead."

"You're baked," Vic says.

"Vic, listen. Owen and I nearly got killed tonight. For a minute, I actually thought it was me they were after, but I think it might have been Leno. Or Owen. He's hiding something."

"What did you smoke?" Vic persists, ignoring my completely valid point. "I can smell it from here."

"I might have tried a little something Carmen has going—"

"Dear God," Vic says. "Is this going to be like that night you woke me up to ask whether I could hear your plants breathing? And told me to check whether mine were transplanting themselves."

"Vic, seriously—"

"Go to sleep, Addy," Vic says.

"Somebody in a pickup truck tried to run me and Owen off the road—"

"Accidents happen, Addy," Vic says. "Whatever Carmen has designed this time made you paranoid. In the morning, you'll see how bizarre this is."

I stop trying to defend myself and just keep talking. "A pickup truck hit us from behind twice, up by Suicide Corner, but we ended up in the ditch on the other side, not in the ravine. Henry Grable came along and saved us, and then we came here to my place. Then we had to call it in, and Alex came over..."

Vic is finally listening, with his mouth literally hanging open.

"And even Alex thinks maybe there's something to the idea that maybe someone didn't know Leno was dead already and thought he was driving, but he says there's no evidence, so he's not going to do anything about it."

"Are you okay?" Victor asks. "Also, oh my God. Does Mom know? Because if she finds out from Henry and not you..." He lets his voice trail away so I can imagine fully the wrath that will descend upon my head.

"I couldn't call anybody. My phone is in Jezebel somewhere."

"And Jezebel is at *The Raven*," Vic says. "I kept trying to call you, and you kept not answering. I thought maybe you and Owen were...occupied."

"We were occupied with trying not to be killed."

"I was surprised you went off with him, honestly," Vic says. "But it didn't look like he was holding a gun on you or anything, so I didn't intervene. Britt had a fit when I told her."

"Britt doesn't get to have fits about anything I do ever again."

"Addy, you have to talk to her. She feels awful."

"Yeah? And how do you think I feel? I can't believe you didn't tell me about her and Leno. You're both traitors."

"And yet you're talking to me," Vic says.

He has a point, I suppose, but not talking to Vic is like not talking to myself, and that's not ever going to happen, no matter what. I shift the conversation back to the reason I called. "Owen was showing me how to drive the Maserati. Also, we were going out to the condo to talk to Spiro because Owen thinks maybe she helped Leno do the thing."

"Addy—"

"Look, can't you see how suspicious this all is? Haven't you ever watched *The First Seventy-Two Hours?* Somebody killed him, and they're getting away with it!"

"What exactly do you want me to do?" Vic mutters into his hands.

It's hard to understand him, but I lived with him all through his talking with his mouth full stage, when he had braces, and the time he broke his jaw and had it wired shut. I've got this.

"I want you to help me find out how he died."

"You're not going to drop it, are you?" he says, resigned.

"I can't, Vic."

"Fine," he says. "Sleep off whatever you've been smoking, and if you're still sure in the morning, I'll help you. Are all of your doors and windows locked?"

"Yes."

"Go to sleep. We'll make a plan in the morning."

And then the only person I am looking at on my screen is me.

MONDAY

CHAPTER 15

I WAKE TO A RHYTHMIC, insistent banging. It takes a minute for me to realize somebody is knocking on my door. It takes another minute to get my eyes open, dislodge Bruno, and roll over. Light is flooding in around the blinds, creating bars on the floor. My head is both heavy and light, and reality still feels askew.

More knocking. I drag myself out of bed, grab my bathrobe, and shuffle to the door, making sure to look through the peephole before I open it.

"You could have used your key," I croak, getting the door open, squinting into the bright light.

"Didn't want to scare you. Figured you might be jumpy after last night." Vic holds out my phone. "I retrieved this for you."

"How did you find it?"

"I called it. And used a flashlight. Couldn't even fit my

hand in to where it was slotted and had to poke it with a stick—"

My arms around his neck cut into the rest of the explanation.

Vic hugs me back. "You okay?"

I just nod against his chest, not at all sure I'm okay. "Thanks for bringing my phone."

"I was gonna bring your car, but I couldn't get her started."

"I think she's dead this time," I say, a tiny quaver sneaking into my voice. I swallow it back and pull out of the hug. "Good thing I have a new car."

"Which, by the way, you can't continue to leave in the parking lot." Vic crosses to the window and opens the blinds. "You'd better come look."

"Oh, no. Did something else happen to it? It's not even in my name yet, and it's already been damaged—"

"It's fine," Vic says. "For now. Just come here."

I pad across the room in my bare feet to look at a crowd of people milling around in the parking lot. Okay, not a crowd exactly, just the guys who live in Units 10 and 12, Eva from Unit 7, and a handful of kids.

"What am I going to do with it?"

"Take it to Mom's and put it in her garage. Make an appointment to get that rear damage repaired. Then, sell it fast before something else happens to it. Or someone steals it." He's right, of course; selling the Maserati is the practical option.

I sink down, right there in the middle of the floor and go into my version of what Britt calls child's pose. In my case, it's more like just wilting forward from a seated posture, hair hanging down to cover my face.

"You need coffee," Vic says. "I can make you some."

I sit up so I can look at him properly. "Since when did you get all nurturing?"

"Since maybe somebody tried to kill you? Also, you just lost Geneva—"

"You lost her, too."

"But the two of you were extra close. And then Richard showed up, Leno died, and now this. I just think maybe you need to—"

"Don't start!" I've been relaxing into the warm fuzzy feeling of being understood and maybe nurtured, just a little, but now I suspect ulterior motives. "You think I've gone off the rails about Leno because of Geneva, you want me to call off the party, and you're not really going to help me figure out who killed him."

"I am, actually, going to help you. What I was going to say is that you've been through a lot and taken a lot of hits. So, maybe you need to talk about it. After coffee. And food." He opens my fridge, then my cupboards, and shakes his head. "You don't even have coffee. Or anything that qualifies as food, for that matter. How about you get dressed and we go to *Grounded* for coffee and—I was going to say breakfast, but let's call it lunch?"

"Brunch," I say. "That's what the cool kids call it." And then I get up and lean into him as he puts his arm around me.

"What will I drive, Vic? If we can't get Jezebel started and I have to garage the Maserati?"

"Coffee. Food. And then maybe we'll get a mechanic to look at your car, okay? Worst case, you rent one for a few days."

"Okay." But it's not, and apparently, I'm not. All at once, I'm sobbing and can't make myself stop.

I'm sad about Jezebel, awful as she is. I miss Geneva, and I'm so sorry I didn't give her the party she wanted. And what happened to Leno is awful—first the cancer, and then either killing himself or getting murdered. That makes me think of Owen, how I would feel if Vic died, and how guilty I feel about suspecting Owen because, obviously, he's grieving and wouldn't have killed his brother. And then I think about Britt and how she's the one I would normally be telling all of this to, but now I can't.

Vic pats my back, but I sense him getting restless—he doesn't do emotions any more than I do, and although he came over here specifically to comfort me, he's probably had enough already.

After a minute, he pulls away. "Come on, Addle Brains. Let's go. Coffee, food, strategy. And then I actually need to go to work. Mop up."

He tosses a box of tissues at me. I don't see it coming, and it hits me in the head and bounces, which jars me out of my moment.

I crawl across the floor for the tissues, grab a handful, then throw the box back at Vic, who easily evades it. My phone pings, and before I can stop him, he picks it up to check who's messaging me.

"What if that's private?" I demand, wiping my eyes and blowing my nose.

"Like you'd keep secrets from me," he says. "It's Britt." And then he proceeds to text something back.

"What are you doing?"

"Telling her to meet at *Grounded*."

"What the hell, Vic? I don't want to talk to her."

"You're going to talk to her, and you're going to do it this morning. This is ridiculous."

"Give me my phone!"

"What, this?" He holds it out of reach above my head as if we're ten again.

I lunge at him. He evades. I try again, and he gets me in a headlock with his free arm.

"Are you going to get dressed?"

I struggle, but he's stronger. "Give me my phone."

"You get it when we're in the car and on the way."

I stop fighting. We're going to *Grounded*. Britt will be there. Vic will make us talk. I might as well accept the inevitable.

VIC INSISTS on taking what I'm now thinking of as THE CAR in capital letters and leaving his Jeep in the parking lot. "This way, we can keep an eye on it," he says. "I'm driving."

Secretly, I'm relieved to let him. He, of course, has no difficulty with any of the technology and makes little crooning noises over the control panel, the seats, the steering, and especially the sound of the engine. He's right. I really need to sell this car as soon as possible.

I've seen the ads featuring women driving cars like this, so I know I'm supposed to be tall and thin with dramatically beautiful features and sculpted hair. I should be clad in black leather and stilettos. Whereas here I am with my frizz gathered into a messy bun, wearing baggy jeans and an old T-shirt. I'm not crazy about the attention we're drawing, all the admiring eyes that follow the car, the thumbs up, the waves.

I check my phone while Vic drives: a couple of non-urgent

messages from clients and a voicemail from Mom, which I'll listen to later. And the text from Britt.

> Britt: I know you're not talking to me, but I have intel on Leno if you want it.

And then Vic's response, pretending to be me:

> Addy: Of course I want it. Sorry for overreacting. Meet you at Grounded in 30?

"You apologized for me? What the hell, Vic? I have a right to be hurt by what she did, and you have no business—"

"I don't want to spend the next forty years listening to the two of you telling the story about how the other one screwed you over. She's your friend. She hurt you. Tell her that. She'll say she's sorry. Forgive her and let it go. You going to let a dead asshole come between you and Britt, for real?"

Of course, what he says makes logical sense. My brain is nodding in agreement, but my emotions are all tangled up in hurt and anger and I'm not remotely ready to let this go.

Vic parks at an angle, taking up two spaces. "You don't want door dings," he explains.

"Door dings seem to be the least of my worries," I mutter, thinking about the damage already done to the car's rear end, but Vic doesn't hear me. He's already striding into the coffee shop, not bothering to hold the door for me.

Kathy waves and smiles, and I know at least there will be a perfect cup of coffee in this awful day. Vic will even pay for it. I head directly for the table in the back corner where Britt is waiting. Nobody ever uses that table if there's another one available. The legs are uneven, and it wobbles. It's also right under both the air vent and the speaker, so you get blasted by cold air and easy-listening jazz while trying to prevent your drink from spilling every time you make a careless move.

We've always made a point of sitting here when we want a private confab with less chance of being overheard. The table rocks when I drop into a chair and Britt grabs her cup to keep it out of danger. And then we sit there in awkward silence, Britt clutching her tea like a talisman, me drumming my fingers on the table.

It feels like an age and a half before Vic comes back and starts unloading a tray. My macchiato, his Americano. A bagel and cream cheese, his. An apple turnover, mine. An egg white and spinach something or other, a bland, disgusting, tasteless mess, obviously for Britt.

"Perfect," she says, half breathless, as if he's fetched caviar, truffles, and a bottle of chilled champagne.

"Thanks, Vic." I wave at Kathy to express my appreciation. I take a long, freezing slurp through my straw, waiting for the resulting brain freeze to settle while sneaking glances at Britt.

"What's the intel?" Vic asks, wisely deciding to start there rather than our friendship problem.

Britt leans forward and lowers her voice. The table rocks, and Vic and I both lift our drinks.

"I might possibly have hacked into Julie Crandall's computer," Britt says.

Vic presses both hands over his ears. "Stop right there. I didn't hear you say that."

"Shhhh..." Britt admonishes as heads turn in our direction.

"Some things you just can't unsee, right?" I say loudly. "I mean, can I now wash my eyeballs out with soap?"

We keep quiet until everybody gets tired of waiting for more and returns to their interrupted conversations.

"Nice recovery," Britt says, the sarcasm coming through loud and clear. She taps a finger on Vic's forearm. "Pretend you're playing poker and keep quiet."

"Anything but that," I say. "Have you seen his poker face?"

"Right. Well, at least keep your mouth shut, would you? Now, where was I?"

"The part where you illegally hacked into the coroner's computer," Vic stage whispers.

"Don't say it like that," Britt says. "That sounds terribly felonious. Just Julie's computer. Julie, who we went to school with."

"Who also happens to be the coroner," Vic says.

"But..." My brain feels like Owen's drunken squirrel is staggering around, looking for forgotten nut stashes. I take a long, icy drink of sugar and caffeine to clear my head. "Why would you do that?"

"Because it's the Mastersons," she says. "The whole family is trouble, Addy. And you're determined to be mixed up with them. So, I wanted to be able to tell you that there's absolutely nothing weird going on."

"Except for the part where somebody tried to kill me and Owen last night," I say. "That's going on."

Her eyes go wide. "What do you mean somebody tried to kill you? And why am I just hearing about this now?"

"Somebody rear-ended the Maserati last night," Vic says. "Addy is sure it was deliberate."

"Somebody rear-ended the Maserati twice," I clarify. "On Suicide Corner. And then parked right behind us and took off when Henry stopped to help. So, yes, I'm sure it was deliberate."

"Oh my God," Britt says. "You did get the cops involved, I hope."

"Alex is 'looking into it.' But he about lost his shit about me driving around with Owen, and I'm not sure if he's looking for evidence in the right places."

"I did tell you to steer clear of that family."

Here comes the lecture. I take the plastic cap off my drink so I can lick the whipped cream and appear lackadaisical.

"You do know that if you want Addy to do something, you should tell her the opposite," Vic says.

"I can't believe you didn't call me," Britt whispers. "I mean, you could have died." Her voice wobbles, and her eyes well up with tears.

"I lost my phone," I say lamely. We both know I could have FaceTimed her from my laptop.

"Right," she says. She blinks the tears back and takes a sip of her tea. "I see you found it."

"Vic found it."

"Whatever." She takes a breath, and when she starts talking again, her voice is all professional sounding, like she's giving a presentation at a meeting. "So, here's what I found out. The official cause of death is cancer."

"All the gossip is that he killed himself," I say.

"According to the right-to-die laws, if somebody has done the paperwork and then ends their own life, the cause of death is still listed as whatever the underlying condition is that was going to kill the person. Natural causes. Cancer, in Leno's case. That way, there's no hassle with life insurance, that sort of thing."

"But he never picked up his prescription," I say, still not ready to concede.

"And I do agree that is weird. Julie also noted that he had obtained a prescription for a lethal cocktail from his doctor—my words, not hers—but hadn't picked it up. But she didn't see that as strange enough to change her ruling."

"So, there you have it," Vic says. "He un-alived himself, Addy. And Britt risked her freedom and professional reputation to do something for you. So, let go of your murder theory, kiss and make up, and let's plan this ridiculous party."

"I still don't believe it," I say. "It feels wrong. How did he die? Why didn't he stick with his plan? If he didn't take the prescription that he worked so hard to get, then how did he kill himself?"

"Alex won't tell you?" Vic asks.

I give him a withering glare. "Do you even need to ask?"

"Somebody maybe should have a conversation with Perch," Britt says. "If you want an insider's look at the death scene."

"And we would want to do that...why?" I can't think of a single reason anybody would want to talk to Perch, ever.

"He's an EMT, right? And according to my...research...he was one of the responders after Leno's death. The other responder was some guy named Barry Heywood, moved here from Richland a few months back. He's not likely to tell us anything, but Perch might talk."

We all exchange surreptitious glances, then get busy with our drinks.

"I'd volunteer," Britt says, "but I don't think that whole white supremacist thing he had going on in high school has mellowed any, so I doubt I'd get far."

I shudder. "Don't think he likes women much, no matter what color they are." Perch was a consummate asshole in high school, and I had enough encounters with him to do me for the next couple of lifetimes.

"He likes women fine if they don't talk and let him have his masterly way with them," Vic says. And then he realizes where this is leading and shakes his head. "No, thank you, ladies, but I'm out. I had him bounced from *The Raven* a couple of months back. Pretty sure he's holding a grudge."

"What is a guy so full of the milk of human kindness doing working as an EMT anyway?" Britt asks.

"Maybe he likes to watch people suffer. Fine. I guess I'll try talking to him."

But just at that moment, opportunity walks through the door in the shape of my father.

"Richard," Vic says.

"Dad," I say at the same time.

Our eyes meet. We both smile.

CHAPTER 16

DAD FREEZES like a deer in the headlights when he sees us all sitting there. He blinks once, twice. Then he shifts into an elaborate pantomime of "man walks into café, only to remember he's forgotten something important elsewhere and must leave without coffee, much to his regret." He looks at his watch. Glances back over his shoulder. Shakes his head sadly at his own foolishness.

"Jesus, he's a terrible actor," Vic groans.

"Why, though?" Britt asks. "I mean, obviously, he knows we saw him."

"I suspect when your offspring, who generally greet your arrival with indifference or outright loathing, suddenly look happy to see you, even Richard might wonder what's up," Vic says.

I wave both arms over my head and call out, "Dad. Hey, Dad! We're over here!"

Even Vic waves and smiles.

Dad hesitates, obviously still considering making a run for it, but his desire to appear cool and in control in the eyes of his adoring public wins out. He acts startled to see us, then fakes a smile and heads for our table. "I almost didn't see you here, all tucked away in the back," he says.

I suck up a huge swallow of my drink, using the resulting brain freeze to get my face under control. Vic leans back and channels his usual insolence toward our father.

Britt, who was brought up to be polite to her elders, pats the chair beside her and says, "Hi, Mr. Winters. Come and join us."

"Thank you, Bella." He lowers himself gracefully onto the chair beside her while his gaze scans the room to see who all might be watching his performance.

"It's Britt," Vic corrects. If he were a dog, the fur would be standing up along his spine and he'd be growling.

"Oh, I knew it was something with a *B*," Dad says easily. He flashes a smile at her—the one reserved for women he thinks are attractive, his eyes traveling her body, lingering on her cleavage. He lays his arm along the back of her chair.

"What brings you to the café, Richard?" my brother asks.

"Needed a little caffeine," Dad says. "But I can't stay long. What are you three up to?"

"Planning Leno's party," I say. "We've got leads on some huge names!"

Dad's fingers are brushing Britt's shoulder now. She sends me a look, half-panicked, half-laughing.

I call him on his behavior before Vic can lunge across the table and grab him by the throat. "Dad."

He shifts his gaze up from Britt's cleavage to me. "Hmm?"

"Britt and I had play dates when we were toddlers."

He dons his best bewildered, innocent expression, but at least his hand moves back to the table.

"This is going to be big time," I tell him, adding adrenaline to my average level of enthusiasm. "Guess who we've got for a band!"

He holds up his hand. "Can't wait to hear, but before we talk business, son, would you maybe go get me a latte and a muffin? One of those apple cinnamon ones would be great."

Vic opens his mouth to tell our father where he can put both coffee and muffin, but it's my turn to employ an elbow. He gasps slightly, face reddening.

"Why don't I do that?"

"Did you see that car out in the parking lot?" Dad asks, as Vic gets up and heads for the counter.

"Which car would that be, *Mr.* Winters?" Britt puts a little extra emphasis on the mister, making a point.

"Call me Rich," he says. "You're making me feel old."

"You are old, Dad," I remind him.

"All relative," he says. "I know girls might not notice cars, but you have to have seen it. Exotic sports car... Unfortunate bit of damage to the rear end."

"Oh, you mean the Maserati?" I ask, aiming for off-handed and blasé. "If you're trying to figure out who in here owns it, she's sitting right here at this table."

He surveys Britt with a whole new level of interest.

"Over here," I say. "Dad, it's my car." I can see the gears spinning in his brain, failing to connect.

Vic, sliding back in beside me, sees it too. "Confusion doesn't look good on you, Richard. Here's your muffin. Coffee's being made. What's up?"

"We were just talking about the Maserati." I slurp my

drink, which is sadly almost gone, in the most annoying way possible, before adding, "Dad's having trouble processing."

"You drive that abysmal old junk heap—"

"The one I bought for myself with the proceeds from my high school job? The one that Britt's dad helped me pick out because you weren't—"

Vic's elbow comes into play, and I wheeze without finishing the accusation while my brother carries on smoothly. "The Maserati does, in fact, belong to Addy. So, about the band for the party. Tell him, Addy."

"Best thing ever," I say in a half-strangled voice. "The band for the party is Leno and the Lonely!"

"But Leno is dead," Dad says. "The chap we're having the party for, yes? He hasn't had a sudden resurrection?"

Ignoring the abrupt switch to an abysmal British accent, I summon up a lifetime's store of patience and explain. "Leno is still dead. But I talked to Spiro, the drummer and also the band's new leader, and she's agreed they'll do it."

This isn't strictly true, as I haven't yet had confirmation from her, but I'm going with it.

"Which is huge," Britt supplies. "We'll share that in the media release going out today. This party is going to get so much attention."

"But wasn't this Leno person the lead singer?" Dad asks. "How does that work out? You don't want a band that is anything less than fabulous. I talked to my friend Antonia last night, and she knows of a band that might be available. *Captured*. She said she'd ask—"

Vic cuts him off. "You know, I don't think we should have Richard do that thing we were talking about. It's too risky."

"What thing?" Dad sits up a little straighter, taking the bait.

"It's way too dangerous, Mr. W.," Britt says, and I swear to God she leans toward him, glancing up through lowered eyelashes. "I think we'd better let Vic do it. He's younger and—"

"For God's sake," Dad exclaims. "I'm not so old as all that. Certainly not dead yet. Tell me what you all are up to."

"Well," I say, making the table rock as I lean forward and lower my voice to a stage whisper. "We think maybe Leno really was murdered, and the local law enforcement isn't exactly up to the task of finding the killer."

"So, you're investigating?" His eyes light up, and he actually forgets to leer at Britt. If there's anything Dad likes next to attention and women, it's...more attention and women. And what better way to acquire both than to play the hero in some sort of caper?

"You have to keep it a secret," Britt coos, gazing up at him as if he's the most attractive man on the face of the planet.

He adjusts his posture and his expression, taking on what he probably thinks of as a James Bond persona. "Well, of course."

"It's a tough role," Britt says. "We need somebody to go have a few drinks at Charlie's, get friendly with a guy who is a total asshole, and find out what he knows. We know you're a brilliant actor, but this requires—"

"That sounds right in my skill set," Dad says. "I'm great at reading people."

Vic goes into some sort of spasm. Dad has never been able to read any of us. Unless, of course, he does and just doesn't care to impress. Which is possible.

"Here's the thing." I lean forward and lower my voice. As if it hears my wishes, the music blaring from the speakers switches to an instrumental number that could be from the soundtrack of a spy flick. "We want to know all about the crime scene."

"The guy we want to get info from was the ambulance driver who responded to the condo," Vic adds. "He goes by Perch, but—"

"Perch like the fish?" Dad asks.

"Perch like the giant Percheron horse," Britt says.

Dad smirks, and I'm pretty sure his mind has gone directly to the gutter.

"Because he's a big guy in general and not because he's hung like anything in particular, okay?" I tell him.

"Eww," Vic says. "Now, I cannot unsee that implication."

We all snort-laugh like we're middle schoolers, even Dad, and I realize with an unexpected pang of regret that this might be the first time in my life I've actually laughed with him instead of at him. It's certainly the first time we've worked together on anything.

"Perch's given name is Walter Briggs," I say. "We want any information possible about the body and the bedroom. Did Leno leave a suicide note? Was there an empty prescription bottle? Blood everywhere? That sort of thing."

"I'm on it," Dad says. "And I'll find this Perch guy hanging out at Charlie's?"

"He's a regular," Vic says.

Dad sets down his drink and gets to his feet. "Don't you worry, I've got this."

"It's way early," Vic protests. "He won't be there before probably six or so. And if he's on shift, he won't be there at all."

"He's not on shift," Britt says. "Today's his day off."

"Do I want to know how you know that?" Vic asks.

"You do not."

"I've got clothes to buy," Dad says. "I can't hang out at Charlie's and buddy up to your guy in these threads, can I? Don't you worry about a thing. I've got this." He bends his elbow and brings his hand toward his forehead in a gesture that is almost a military salute, turns on his heel, and marches out.

"Dear Lord, what have we unleashed?" Vic asks as we all watch him go.

"I hope he doesn't get hurt," Britt says.

"I hope he doesn't spill the secret that we think Leno might have been murdered," I say. "Well, the cat's out of the bag, in any case."

"Feral cat," Vic says. "Paper bag."

I suck on my straw. The only result is air and a loud, obnoxious noise. My drink is gone.

Caught up in the challenge of manipulating Dad, I'd forgotten about the rift between Britt and me, falling easily into our familiar patterns. But now here we are again, sitting across from each other with so much still unsaid between us. I can feel her not looking at me, the way I'm not looking at her, the tension so tight I could reach out and pluck it like a guitar string.

"Oh, for God's sake," Vic finally says. "I'm going to drag you both into Mom's living room and tell her what's going on."

"So she can starve us into making up?" I ask.

"That's right. No dinner until you work it out," Vic says.

We both laugh, and that eases the tension enough to let me make an attempt at, if not our old trust, at least a truce.

"Thanks for what you did, looking into the coroner's ruling," I say.

"I wanted to help," Britt answers. "Wait. That's not quite right. I don't want to help with anything Masterson-related, but I—want to be in. I can write up a press release, if you want. And get it out there. Design some electronic invitations."

"Did you confirm with Spiro?" Vic asks.

"Not yet."

"Before Britt launches the press release, we need a contract with the band," he says. "I'll draw it up as soon as I'm back at my office. Get Spiro to sign it—in person with a witness. None of that electronic signature bullshit for this. Understand?"

"I do," I say. "I will. Only, Jezebel is broken, remember? How am I getting around?"

They both stare at me like I've sprouted antennae. "Seems to me like if I had a Maserati just sitting around, I might drive it," Vic says after a long silence.

"You told me to park it and rent a car." A cold finger of fear pokes at the base of my spine, and I shiver. "That car hates me. Also, what if somebody tries to kill me again?"

"Nobody was trying to kill you."

"Okay, what if somebody tries to kill Leno again without realizing he's not driving?"

"They've got to know by now that Leno is dead; the news feeds have picked it up."

"All over my Instagram, too," Britt says. "And TikTok."

This fails to make me feel better. "What if it really is me they're after?"

"It's not."

"But what if it is, though? Maybe they think he told me something, the thing they wanted to kill him for."

"Stay in town where there are people. Get Spiro to meet you at *The Raven* in, say, two hours? Get the contract signed, then Britt will send out the press release and the invites, and we'll be in business. Okay?"

"I'm on it," Britt says.

I just sit and look at him.

"Alternately, it's not too late to call this off," Vic says. "The party. And digging into Leno's death."

"Too late to call Dad off." My voice starts out a little choked but gets stronger as I talk. "And I am throwing the party."

"Well, then." Vic shoves back his chair. "Let's go."

"Where are we going?"

"You are driving me over to *The Raven*."

"Why don't we go home and get your car?"

"Because I have a meeting to get to in about ten minutes." He smiles at Britt. "See you later?"

"For sure."

She and I exchange a half smile, and I walk away without my usual certainty that I, too, will see her later.

The Maserati crouches in the parking lot, radiating superiority and hostility. "Maybe you should drive," I say casually. "Given that you're in a hurry and have a meeting."

"It's just a car, Addles. It doesn't hate you." Vic gets into the passenger side.

I hate when he gets bossy, but I also don't want to admit to my insecurity. I feel like I'm letting all women down by allowing myself to be intimidated, but the truth is, I'm more comfortable with Jezebel's retro-ness. All the dials and lights and computerized options on the Maserati's dashboard are nearly as frightening as the idea that somebody might try to smash into us again.

Damned if I'm going to admit to any of that, though, so I get into the driver's seat. "Don't tell me," I say when Vic opens his mouth to start mansplaining, even though I would actually like nothing better than to be mansplained to—just this once. I've watched both Owen and Vic drive this car. I ought to be able to manage the basics.

I press the start button, and the engine revs to life. The gas and brake pedals are right where they belong, and the shifting is fairly self-explanatory. All the rest of those intimidating lights and dials, and even how to use the backup camera, can all wait for later.

The horsepower is another thing entirely. I shift into reverse, put my foot on the gas, and zoom backward way too fast. I manage to get my foot on the brake just in time to avoid more rear-end damage, and then sit there, frozen, breathing hard.

"This car isn't Jezebel," Vic says, as if I haven't maybe noticed that for myself. "Maybe I really should—"

"Just shut up."

Surprisingly, he does. I shift into drive and feather my foot on the gas pedal. This time, I manage to proceed across the parking lot at the speed of a turtle. Gradually, I gain some confidence, and the rest of the drive goes so smoothly that I'm feeling equally proud of myself and annoyed with Vic by the time we approach *The Raven*.

He's managed to refrain from offering driving pointers but has felt compelled to tell me that the fuel indicator shows a quarter of a tank. Not only should I get gas, but I should remember to get premium. I need to get the title changed and notify my insurance company. He's also pointed out that I'll be paying a hell of a lot more for both gas and insurance, and I really need to get this car fixed and sold before it costs me more than I'm going to make from selling it.

He can't help himself, I know. My irritation stems from the fact that I actually would not have thought to do any of these things if he hadn't told me to.

Both my pride and my irritation vanish when I pull into the parking lot. There's a tow truck backed up in front of Jezebel. Brad stands behind her, one hand resting on her trunk, watching us drive in.

CHAPTER 17

"What is Brad doing here, Victor?"

"Just park the car."

I glare at my traitorous brother. "You called him? How could you?"

"Addy, I know you love that car, but it can't live in my parking lot. You need to either get it repaired or junk it."

"And you couldn't tell me? Maybe I have stuff in there that I want to get out of it before it gets towed away."

"I rescued your phone for you. And that little heap of detritus on the passenger seat didn't really look worth salvaging." He quirks an eyebrow at me, his superior look, and I wish we were still ten so I could get away with punching him.

"Go have your meeting," I say instead. There's no point explaining what he should have understood already—that I'm sad about Jezebel's probable demise and that I'd rather not be face-to-face with Brad.

He opens the door, puts one leg out, and then stops. "Let me know what time you're bringing Spiro by."

"Will do."

"All right. Be safe." He waves at Brad and vanishes into *The Raven*, leaving me alone to face my consequences.

Brad saunters over to my door and stands there, winding his hand around and around in a gesture I assume means he wants me to roll down the window.

I don't even know where the control for the window is. Rather than hunt for it while he watches, giving him ammunition he can use to mock my stupidity later, I opt for opening the door instead.

"Where do you want me to tow her?" he asks, for all the world as if I haven't just opened a door into him or interfered with his marriage to Lisa by basically calling him a cheapskate.

When he fails to either shout at me or beat me up, I walk over to Jezebel and pat her hood. "I don't know, Brad. I think she might be done for."

"Hard to let them go, isn't it?" he asks. "You spend more time with your car than your people. I promise to treat her with respect, if that helps any."

"I've had her for a long time. It would be good to know if she's fixable, I guess?"

"Whatever you need," he says. "I owe you."

Here we go. This is the moment when he'll threaten me.

But he's...smiling. "You," he says, "are a lifesaver."

"I'm sorry—I'm what?"

"God, when I asked Lisa to marry me, I really thought I was in love with her, you know? But she's kind of a bitch. Not just to me, but to her kid, right? Jackson's a good kid, doesn't deserve that shit, but I can't say anything; I'm not his daddy. But once you're engaged in this town, breaking it off is just as bad as getting divorced, as far as public opinion goes. As for Lisa— well, no wrath like a woman scorned, am I right? Anyway— you got me out, so I figure I owe you. I could take your car back to my place and poke around a bit, see if I can get her running."

"You would do that?"

"Sure thing, Addy. No problem." He shifts his attention to the Maserati and lets out a wolf whistle, as if she's a curvy woman walking down the street. "Nice wheels. Heard Leno passed them on to you. Shame about that rear panel, though."

"Pickup truck ran right into us," I say. "Up on Suicide Corner. Could have been a lot worse."

He bends down and runs a hand over the damaged area. "Should be able to be repaired, good as new. Course, you'll probably have to take it to a dealer in Seattle somewhere. What sort of asshole would do that to a set of wheels like this is what I want to know?"

All of a sudden, I understand Brad a whole lot better. He's much more worried about the car than the possible death of the passengers. And for some weird reason, this makes me feel better about everything.

"Want me to help you set that up?" he asks. "An appointment, I mean?"

"I'd love that, Brad. Thanks. And thanks for checking into the old car while you're at it."

"No problem at all." He grins at me again, hitches up his jeans, and goes back to securing Jezebel for towing.

I watch until Brad has done his work and towed Jezebel out of the parking lot and off down the street before I get back into the Maserati, which feels every bit as hostile as it did before.

"Listen, car," I tell it. "We're going to need to work together, you and me. We don't have to like each other, even. Just cooperate. I promise to get you to a more fitting owner as soon as I can, okay?"

The oppressive feeling is marginally less. "I'm sorry you got damaged," I tell him. "That wasn't my fault, you understand, and I'll get you fixed as soon as I can, too. How about a bath in the meantime? And a full tank of gas? We'll spend a couple of hours just getting acquainted."

Of course, I have more on my mind than hanging out with the Maserati. I'm only a casual caretaker, not about to get attached. I'm definitely going to sell it. Still, that's no reason I shouldn't name it—not it, *him*. Jezebel is a her. This is definitely a him. And if I'm going to be temporarily taking care of him, I might as well understand how he works and we can be friendly. Using his name is a good start.

"So, what is your name? I'm sorry I called you Bob earlier. Obviously, that's not it. It's actually Hannibal, am I right?" I press the starter button, and he rumbles into life. Tentatively, I pat the steering wheel. "Let me make a phone call, and then we'll go get you some gas."

My phone pairs automatically with the car system, and when Spiro answers, her voice sounds like she's right there in the passenger seat.

"Spiro, hi. This is Addison Winters."

"Addison! I heard what happened last night. Are you okay?"

"I'm fine," I say brightly. "What did you hear?"

"Only that you and Owen were run off the road by some maniac. How terrifying. And how sad for Leno's little car."

Leno's little car isn't sad, I think. Resentful, maybe. Pissed off, absolutely.

"I'm calling to see if we can confirm the band?"

"Talked to the boys and we are a go for that concert."

"Excellent news, Spiro! We've got a press release ready to roll. You and the band are front and center."

"You should get that right out there if you want anybody to show up. People have to travel; they've already got plans."

"Absolutely. First thing, I just need your signature on a contract."

She's silent for one breath, two, then says, "My word not good enough for you? Given that we're not being paid, a contract seems excessive."

"Oh, I absolutely agree. My business manager is a real stickler, though, you know? And the company lawyer is adamant that we have a booking contract for every band. Helps to avoid misunderstandings and make sure we're all crystal clear on expectations, that sort of thing."

She sighs, sounding heavily put upon. "Oh, fine. Bring it on over. I'll sign."

"You know—after what happened last night, I've got a case of nerves about Suicide Corner. Any chance I could sweet talk you into meeting me down here somewhere? I'll buy you a drink, lunch, whatever."

Then I hold my breath while she thinks about it. "Oh, all right. I need to grab a couple of things from Safeway, anyway. Where?"

"I was thinking *The Raven*. It's a brewpub. We can have a drink and sign everything."

"I'll be there," she says. "One hour?"

"Perfect."

I text Vic to let him know the plan, and then, before I set out to make peace with Hannibal, I text Owen, too.

> Addy: Found my phone. Hope you're okay?

> Addy: Meeting with Spiro in an hour at The Raven, if you still want to talk to her.

And then, on second thought, I delete that second message without sending it. I feel a tiny bit guilty—there's something about almost dying together that creates a sense of loyalty, but I need to get that contract signed and Owen is not going to be conducive to making that happen.

As I pull into the gas station, I realize I have no idea which side the gas tank is on. Everybody is staring at the car—and me —and if I get out to look for the gas tank, there will be laughter and scorn reflecting badly on women drivers everywhere and me in particular. So, instead, I just go inside and buy a bag of chips and a Monster.

The gangly kid behind the counter is all big eyes and questions. "Whose car is that? What happened to it? How fast does it go?"

None of which is surprising, but another good reason to ditch Hannibal as quickly as possible. I give generic answers. "Mine, hit-and-run accident, don't know yet." As soon as I've paid, I grab my snacks and flee. I meant to saunter casually around the car and look for the gas tank, but there are three guys standing there, looking lovestruck, so I just get in, smiling enigmatically in response to their comments, and drive off.

I park on a quiet side street to conduct my gas tank reconnaissance. Then I spend five minutes looking for the lever that will unlatch the thing before it occurs to me that there might possibly be a manual in the glove box. Wonder of wonders, there is, and it only takes a minute to learn that there is no lever. All I have to do is push on the little door and then pull it open. I test this out to make sure it's really that simple.

I'm about to drive off when it occurs to me that Leno's car could contain clues to his murder. Maybe he even left me some sort of hint. Why else would he want to give me his car? Why did I not think of this sooner? My pulse surges with excitement and anticipation.

"What do you know that you're not telling, Hannibal?"

Nothing but maintenance records and registration in the glove box. Chewing gum and a package of disposable masks in the console. All very ordinary and disappointing. Leno hasn't even left receipts, change, or empty coffee cups.

Note to self: before I do anything permanent with Jezebel, I definitely need to clean out her glove box, which is stuffed with receipts, notes, snacks, and who knows what else going back over twelve years.

I drive across town to a different gas station, pull up to the pump, get the tank open, and fill up with premium, watching the numbers on the pump in silent horror. Vic was right. The car is going to cost me a fortune in gas alone.

My next stop is the carwash. I go to the wash-your-own car version, not the automated one, remembering Vic saying at some point that those brushes scratch up a paint finish. When I'm done, I've still got some time, so I pull up to the vacuum and do the interior, even though it doesn't really need it.

Thinking about Jezebel and how she collects things under the seats, it occurs to me that maybe Hannibal has similar propensities. Thanks to my handy owner's manual, I find the controls to move the driver's seat and get down on my knees where I can peer under it. Either Hannibal doesn't collect things, or Leno was way neater than me because I find one small dust bunny and that's it.

Still, I check under the passenger seat, just to be thorough, and am rewarded for my efforts by the glint of something silver. Probably just the pop top from a can of soda, I tell myself as I reach for it, but my fingers close around a ring. When I fish it out, I see that it's not just any ring —it's a Fox Valley class ring from my graduating year. Not one of the cheap, silver-plated ones with fake stones, like the one I bought and then lost within a couple of months, either. This one is real silver. The blue stone is a genuine sapphire. I'm pretty sure Leno hasn't been wearing a Fox Valley class ring, and I only know one person who had one like this.

For a long moment, I sit there with my cold hand fisted so tightly around the ring that the stone bites into my palm. Then I slide it onto my finger for safekeeping. As I head for *The Raven* and my appointment with Spiro, I'm shivering with the shock of betrayed trust and the uneasy sense that everything I thought I knew about the world and the people in it is wrong.

⁂

I'M LATE, and Spiro is there ahead of me, but fortunately, Vic has got me covered. The two of them are sitting at one of the high tables by the window, and I can tell right away that she's responding to the famous Victor Winters charm. She's laughing, one arm resting on the table, her hand loosely curled around a glass that is still three-quarters full. Either I'm not *that* late, or it's her second glass. Either way, Vic has obviously done a better job of loosening her up than I would have done.

When I walk over, he looks up casually and drawls, "We were about to send out a search party." All of a sudden he sounds like he was raised in the South instead of right here in Fox Valley. I assume there's something about Southern charm that he thinks will appeal to Spiro.

I slide onto a stool beside him. "Sorry I'm late. Just getting acquainted with Han—with the Maserati."

"No worries. I was just getting acquainted with your attorney." Spiro smiles at Vic, and he smiles back, both of them apparently oblivious to the contract and the pen lying between them on the table.

Vic isn't actually a lawyer, of course, but Spiro doesn't need to know that.

"So, are you all right after last night?" she asks. "I hate that corner. I can't even imagine somebody running me off the road right there."

I grab Vic's glass and take a big swallow. "A little sore, but I'm fine. How did you hear about it, anyway?"

"It's all over the news," she says. "You didn't know?"

"Guess I didn't check my feeds this morning," I say, as if I check feeds regularly.

The truth is, I never look at the news if I can help it. Anything I need to know about local events will come through the gossip mill, and anything else will pop up on Instagram. Barring that, Mom and Aunt Rachel keep their fingers on the pulse of all national and international disasters, real or imagined, and feel compelled to keep me updated.

"You know what I think?" Spiro chugs the rest of her drink and waits.

I know my role and gasp out a wide-eyed, star-struck, "Tell me."

"Somebody was out to get Owen. You were an unintended casualty. Or complication, depending on how you look at it."

Of course, I've already had this thought, but I keep playing along.

"What? Why?"

"Crime is almost always about money, isn't it?" she asks.

"I don't follow you."

Spiro picks up her glass, peers into its empty depths, and then glances meaningfully at Vic.

"Let me get you another. Same?" He catches Rosa's eye and holds up three fingers.

"Were we getting some food, too?" Spiro twirls a lock of hair around her finger, her voice as husky as if she's asking about renting a room instead of ordering bar food.

"It's coming." Vic gives her a slow, easy smile, letting his eyes close just a little so he looks sleepy and stupid. Or maybe it's meant to be sexy.

I roll my eyes.

"Here's the thing," Spiro says. "I feel bad, like I'm gossiping, but since you were in that car, and since you're involved in this party and expecting to be paid and all..." She lets the unfinished sentence hang in the air suggestively.

"Leno was broke?" I think about the check I dropped in the bank and wonder if it's cleared yet.

"Oh, no. Leno had millions. But the family? That mansion of theirs up on the hill? Mortgaged to the hilt. Debts rolling in that nobody can pay. The old queen of the castle is about to go bankrupt and move into a tiny home."

Rosa comes over with a tray of drinks plus an order of everything fries and a platter of nachos. Spiro digs in as if she's famished and keeps talking with her mouth full.

"Old man Masterson died a few years ago and left everything in a mess. Bad investments, gambling debts, owes money to some not-nice people. Poor old Owen got pressured into taking over the company business when his dad died, and it's been circling the drain ever since, things getting worse and worse. Might be some enforcers are tired of waiting and sending a message."

"Someone like that might have hurried Leno along," Vic muses. "I assume the family is in the will. Sooner Leno dies, sooner they inherit the money and can pay the debt."

"Pre-cisely." Spiro scoops up a cheesy nacho directly from the platter with her fingers, trailing a string of cheese all the way to her mouth. "Or someone in the family doesn't want to move into a tiny home. Or couldn't wait to be clear of running a floundering business."

I think about Owen's gentle hand on my hair. The look in his eyes as he asked if I was all right.

"Did anybody visit Leno the night he died?" Vic asks.

Spiro shrugs. "I was out. Asked the security guard if any visitors came through the gate, but she wouldn't tell me." She guzzles half of her new drink. "In any case, I wouldn't worry. If they'd really wanted to kill you, you'd be dead."

This is not as comforting as she apparently thinks it should be. My mouth goes dry. My whole body feels cold.

"Maybe the party isn't such a good idea," Vic says.

A little shiver runs up and down my spine. What if these people think I know too much and it really was me they were trying to kill? Did they really kill Leno? I could back off, walk away, let this whole thing go.

I find myself twisting the ring on my finger and realize that I can't. I'm in too deep. I've found out too many things already.

I push the paper toward Spiro. "I think we should get this contract signed."

"Cool. We're in. Let me just read it." She picks up the pen.

Ethically, we should have gotten her to sign before she slammed two double-sized drinks, but I'm not about to say anything.

"Note that you'll be playing for free," Vic says. "Food and drinks provided, of course, and we're highlighting the band on socials and media posts."

"Worth it," Spiro says. "All of us are looking for new gigs—either with the band as it is, with a new front person, or with other acts. You promise this is going to be a big deal?"

"The biggest," I say, even though I'm currently having doubts about pulling any of it off.

Spiro signs the contract with a flourish. "We're in."

Vic slides the paper over to me, and I sign as the representative of *Next-Level Parties by Addy*. Vic signs as a witness, and the deed is done. He picks up his phone and initiates a call.

"Britt, hey. I'm with Spiro and Addy. Contract is signed. Ready to launch."

I hold out my hand for the phone. "Let me talk to her."

Vic always knows when something is up with me. He hesitates before passing me his phone.

"We need to talk. Meet me at *Grounded*?"

A breath. A pause. "Will do," she says. "Right after I send out the press release."

"What's that all about?" Vic asks.

"Party stuff."

He doesn't believe me, but he doesn't push me in front of Spiro. "Before you go, let me make some copies," he says, sliding down off his stool.

Spiro watches him walk down the back hallway that leads to his office. "He's not really your company attorney, is he?"

Maybe she's not as drunk as I thought she was. "What was your first clue?"

"He's obviously your brother."

"Most people don't see a resemblance. Including me, to be honest."

"Well, obviously, your features are different. Body type, all that. It's the facial expressions. The way you both move."

"Huh," is my brilliant response.

Then we sit in silence, Spiro eating, me thinking, until Vic returns with copies for himself and Spiro and the original for me.

"All right. I'll be in touch," I say. It's a lot farther down from the stool for me than it is for Vic, and I'm much less graceful. I have no idea what similarity Spiro thinks she sees in the way we move.

Vic gives me a look, a reminder to pay attention and watch myself. I give him a quick thumbs up to let him know I'm good, even though I'm not and he knows I'm not. If he knew what I know, he'd be more upset than I am, which is another reason not to tell him anything until after I've confirmed my facts.

CHAPTER 18

I'M ALREADY SETTLED at a table with my macchiato and Britt's tea when she walks in. I've picked the back corner again, wobbly table and all, and lift both of our drinks to safety as she slides into a chair.

"One of these days, I'm going to fix that myself," she says, reaching for her tea. "What's up? You look like the world is coming to an end."

In answer, I strip the ring from my finger and set it on the table between us. "Found this under the passenger seat in the Maserati."

She looks at it and says nothing. Doesn't move. Barely breathes.

"Were you going to tell me?" I ask. "Maybe in another ten years or so?"

"It's not mine."

Those three words drive a spike through my heart. I don't know what I'd been hoping for, what kind of explanation would make everything all right again, but the fact that she can sit there and lie to me is devastating.

"You might as well tell me the truth."

"Oh, for God's sake, Addy. Yes, I dated Leno and didn't tell you. Yes, I should have. I was seventeen. Whatever it was between us was over by the end of my first year in college. I certainly haven't been carrying on a clandestine relationship with him recently." She has the nerve to sound pissed, as if I'm the one who is in the wrong.

"What happened when you were seventeen is one thing. Finding your ring in his car is another thing entirely."

"I'm not the only girl who has a class ring."

"You're the only girl whose doctor daddy bought her a class ring with a genuine sapphire," I retort.

Britt holds the ring up to the light, squinting at the inside of the band. Then she tosses it back onto the table.

"You might have looked at the engraving, Addison, if you weren't busy jumping to conclusions." Her voice is cold, and the use of my full name is even colder. "Mine has Valedictorian engraved on it. This one has two sets of initials and a little heart. Also, I haven't been in that Maserati even once. Maybe I kept Leno a secret from you back then, but I can't believe you think I'd lie to you about this now. I suppose you also think I killed him while I was at it."

She gets up from her chair. Neither one of us thinks to secure the table, and both of our drinks tip over and start running everywhere. Neither one of us makes a move to pick them up.

Britt has tears in her eyes, and her voice is choked as she says, "I can't believe you'd think... Shit. I can't do this."

I watch her walk away, head bent, steps rapid, and I want

to run after her, but I can't seem to make myself move. Of course, she's right. If I hadn't let my own hurt and jealousy blind me, I would have seen that the ring wasn't hers right away.

"Everything okay back here?" Kathy appears with a rag in one hand. She rights the spilled cups and starts mopping up the mess.

"No," I say. "It's not okay. I'm an idiot, and I think I just blew up our friendship."

"You and Britt? No way. The two of you are solid. You'll work it out, whatever it is." She flashes me a reassuring smile.

I try to smile back, but my lips are trembling and I can't pull it off.

"Hey," Kathy says, touching my hand. "Things will work out. You want another coffee?"

I pick up the ring and slide it back onto my finger for safe-keeping. "Thanks, but no. Places to go, people to see, parties to plan."

She drops into the seat across from me. "Addy, be careful, would you? I'm not sure what all you're mixed up in, but I'd hate to see you get hurt."

I look up into her eyes and try to think of what to say. "Kathy, you're the best, you know that?"

"Only..." she adds, with a half-smile. "Only you don't swing this way. I know that, honey. Maybe we can be friends, though, do you think? Benefits entirely optional."

I feel my face heating, and I'm trying to think of what to say when she laughs and gets to her feet.

"Just kidding. We're good, Addy. Really. But I mean it about being careful."

HOURS LATER, I have just turned off the lights and laid my aching head down on the pillow when my phone rings. No need to look to know it's Mom; it's her ringtone—"Danger Up Ahead." I close my eyes, telling myself I'll call her back in the morning. But then I remember, her mother died and I haven't been over to check on her all day. Not only am I a bad friend, but I really am a bad daughter who should be supporting my mother more.

So I call her back.

"You need to come over here now," she says. "We have a situation."

"Now? I'm just crawling into bed. What kind of situation?"

But she's already hung up. This is not like Mom. When I hit redial, she doesn't answer. God. What if some unknown bad people really were targeting me, and now they've gone after my mother? I try to call Vic, but he doesn't answer, either. So I text him.

> Addy: Some kind of urgent thing with Mom. Call me!

I put my jeans back on, snuggle into a sweatshirt, and drive Hannibal over to Mom's house. There's an unfamiliar car in the driveway, a rental, and my heart skips a beat and kicks its rhythm into overdrive. I can't call the cops based on nothing more than a bad feeling, but something is up and I'm not going in there unarmed.

I carry bear spray in my bag, not that it would ever do me any good because even a slow-moving and hesitant mugger could knock me out three times before I could even find the damn thing. Finally, my fingers locate the canister. I figure out which way to point it and sneak up to the door, holding it at the ready. I stop to listen but can't hear anything, so I ease the door open and tiptoe down the hall until I hear Mom's voice coming from the kitchen. She sounds annoyed, not frightened, but that's exactly how she'd talk to a kidnapper. I continue with caution, imagining her tied to a kitchen chair, lecturing a man with a gun who stands over her.

My wildest imaginings could never have prepared me for the sight that meets my eyes.

Dad is the one in the kitchen chair, and Mom is hovering over him. He's wearing a pair of worn Levis with an unstylish rip in one knee and a once-white T-shirt, now bloodstained, with a slogan that reads, *Boobs and Beer That's Why I'm Here.* His hair sticks up every which way, and there's blood matted in it, too. His right hand holds a bag of frozen peas to his jaw. His left grips a can of Raven Brew. His lip is puffy and bloody, and one eye is swollen shut and turning a livid reddish purple.

There's a basin full of bloody water on the table, and Mom is dabbing at his face with a washcloth.

I stand there, blinking, bear spray still held out at arm's length, ready for action, wondering what alternate reality I've stepped into.

"Your father was hurt," Mom says, in the tone that makes it clear it's my fault somehow. "He came here because he had nowhere else to go for help."

"You didn't think maybe the emergency room would have been an option?"

"He's fine," she says. "Just needs to be cleaned up a little."

My brain catches up to the action enough to suggest that I

stow my weapon and maybe ask a meaningful question. "Geez, Dad. What happened?"

"Went to talk to that Perch fellow, like I promised." His words are slurred and a little garbled due to the combination of a swollen lip, bruised jaw, and possibly a blood alcohol well above the legal limit.

"Perch hit you?"

"Ow! Easy there, woman!" Dad squawks, trying to pull away from Mom's not-so-gentle ministrations.

Mom *hmmphs* and dabs a little harder. "Well deserved and a long time coming," she mutters under her breath.

"Not Perch," Dad slurs. "Nice young man, Perch. Alvin started it. Old score to settle, he said; guess some folks never forget."

"Alvin did this?"

I know Alvin. He's Dad's age, and he's an accountant. Unless he's got secret ninja moves or carries brass knuckles, he can't have done this level of damage.

"He started it. Then some other guys jumped in. Best fight scene ever! Hope somebody caught it on their phone." Dad laughs—actually laughs—followed by an exclamation of pain and a string of profanities.

"Richard!" Mom reprimands, dabbing even harder.

"First time in my life I've been in a real bar brawl. Can you believe it? Total free-for-all broke out. Fists flying. Couple of chairs."

"Do you have a concussion?" I ask. "Do you need to see a doctor? Or are you just drunk?"

He lifts the beer to his mouth, winces, but drains it. Belches. Tries to crumple the can in his fist and lets out a whimper, which is when I notice that his knuckles are also bloody and swollen.

Mom eases the can out of Dad's hand. Then she goes to the fridge to get another, pops the top, and hands it to him.

"Do you think that's wise?" I ask. "Seems like he's had enough."

"He's in pain, dear. Alcohol is an anesthetic."

"Clearly, you don't understand hangovers," I begin, thinking about how much Dad's head is going to hurt tomorrow, how much extra harm alcohol poisoning will do if he already has brain damage.

Mom shifts her feet a little and glances off to the side, which is when I realize the truth.

"Mom!" I exclaim. "You are evil."

"Just trying to help," she says, setting the empty on the kitchen floor and crushing it beneath her heel.

I cross the room to Dad and tug the new can out of his hand. "You have to stop."

He's sloshed enough, or concussed enough, that he doesn't offer much resistance.

"I don't suppose you learned anything from Perch, other than how to throw a punch?" I ask him.

"Nice young man," Dad slurs, head lolling against the back of the chair, the hand with the ice bag sliding into his lap. "Good Christian boy."

I kneel on the floor in front of the chair and cup his face in my hands, gently, but still his eyes fly open and he tries to glare at me, only he can't decide which one of the Addys in front of him to focus on.

"Did he tell you anything about the crime scene?"

"Addison Winters," Mom reprimands. "What have you been up to?"

"I hardly think you've got room to talk right now," I say, not looking away from Dad. I press my palms a tiny bit harder against his cheeks. That rouses him.

"Jesus, mother of Christ! That hurts!"

"I will not suffer profanity in this house," Mom says.

I ignore her. "Dad, stay with me. What did he say about Leno?"

"Left a suicide note on the nightstand. Empty pill bottle. Morphine. Phone. Don't feel good, Addy baby. Think I'm gonna..."

He does. I dive out of the way just in time to avoid being spattered. As soon as the spasm eases, his eyelids close and his head lolls sideways.

"Dad! Who called in the body? Did he say?"

But he's out cold. His eyelids don't even twitch when Mom scrubs at his face again. The ice bag has fallen to the floor.

"Just like him," my mother says, nose wrinkled. "Get drunk, make a mess, and then expect me to clean it up."

"You gave him the beer," I remind her, checking to make sure Dad is still breathing. "How many has he had since he got here?

"You always did side with him," Mom retorts, an accusation that is so manifestly untrue I don't even bother to defend myself.

"We need to take him to the ER to check for alcohol poisoning and concussion."

"Like this? We'll have to clean him up first. You know how this town is. Talk, talk, talk."

"Do we care, really, if they gossip about him?" I ask.

"It all reflects back on us," she says. "On me. Get me another basin and some warm water and soap. And towels."

There's no point arguing with her. Even if I call an ambulance, she won't let them in until Dad is "presentable," which means I have to help her lower him to the kitchen floor and strip him out of his T-shirt and jeans. And then watch while she gives him a sponge bath. Thank God she doesn't insist on taking off his tighty-whities because I'm pretty sure I'm already scarred for life by what I've seen.

I'm torn between trying not to look at his aging body, checking to make sure he's still breathing, and wondering if he'll die right here in Mom's kitchen and we'll be responsible. But Mom is insistent that since she has failed to bring him to godliness, at least she can restore him to cleanliness. Finally, the task is done, and we dress him in an old pair of sweatpants and a T-shirt that Vic left here. I commandeer his wallet and phone and cram them into my already overfilled bag.

"Let's call Vic to help get him in the car," I suggest.

"We can handle it. The poor boy needs his rest."

"You know, I could use some sleep myself," I mutter, but I help her drag Dad onto his feet.

Mom steps on his foot, which is possibly an accident, and he rouses enough to support some of his own weight and we're able to lurch outside.

"I'll hold him. Get your car door open," Mom says.

"Wait, my car? This car? The *Maserati*?"

"Unless you've got that other monstrosity around here somewhere."

"What about Dad's rental?"

"Addison, open the door. Hurry up before I drop him."

I have to admit that the idea of trying to drag Dad's dead

weight up off the ground, or worse, calling the ambulance after all and then explaining why he's lying in the middle of the driveway is much worse than the idea of Dad in the Maserati. So, I unlock the doors with my fancy-ass fob thing. We drag Dad over to the passenger side, open the door, and stuff him in. He remains more or less upright, and I manage to get a seatbelt around him.

Mom doesn't even ask about the car, so I assume gossip about it has reached her. Or maybe Vic told her.

"What if he throws up again?" I ask, silently apologizing to Hannibal for sullying his pristine interior. The luxurious smell of leather has already been overtaken by beer fumes.

"You brought this all on yourself," Mom says, "so don't be whining to me."

There's some truth to that. I did willingly dispatch Dad to talk to Perch. But I'm certainly not the one who then plied him with extra alcohol or refused to call 9-1-1.

"Could I at least have a bag or a bucket or something to take with me?" I plead, and she stalks, stiff-backed, into the house and returns with a Tupperware bowl big enough to hold a sandwich.

"Really, Mom?"

"Better get going, before he dies of a brain injury," she says, heartlessly.

As soon as we're underway, I employ the car phone system to call Vic. He still doesn't answer, but this time I leave a message.

Dad stirs, rousing himself enough to slur, "Don't feel good. I'm gonna..."

As predicted, the tiny Tupperware is not equal to the task. Apparently, he didn't even begin to get his stomach empty properly the last time, and apparently, he also ate things at the bar. I open both windows and breathe through my mouth, but I'm feeling decidedly less than awesome when I pull into the unloading zone in front of Fox Valley Hospital's small emergency room.

Vic is waiting. "That's not revolting or anything," he says, nasally, keeping his distance from the window.

"You didn't have to help Mom sponge bathe him," I gasp, turning away from the car to breathe some fresh air.

"I don't want to know," Vic says. "Hang on, let me get a wheelchair. I'm not carrying him."

"Respect," Dad mutters.

The two of us get him out of the car and into the wheelchair and roll him into the ER, where it rapidly becomes clear why our mother opted not to be here—apart from the fact that she wants Dad to suffer, I mean.

Zelda Anniston is behind the desk. "Fill this out, please," she says, shoving a form across the high counter at me without taking her greedy eyes off Vic.

"Hey, Zel," he says. "How you been?"

I write head trauma on the slip of paper, along with Dad's name and birthdate. "Look, he's not doing so hot. Could we expedite this?"

Zelda peers over the top of her fortress and her jaw drops. "Dear Lord, have mercy, is he dead? Is that some...homeless guy?"

"It's Dad," I say, shoving the form back at her.

"Are you sure? I mean..."

"I'm sure," I say. "Please. A nurse? A room? He might have a brain injury."

Vic flashes a smile that manages to convey appreciation,

apology, concern, and a tiny bit of flirtation, but even this fails to mollify Zelda.

"You should have called an ambulance," she says, all judgy, like she has any idea about the circumstances behind us being here. But she picks up the receiver, dials, then says, "Got an unconscious guy out here...pretty beat up. Can you... Thanks!"

The double doors on the far side of the waiting area, the ones with the sign that reads AUTHORIZED PERSONNEL ONLY, swing open, and a woman in green scrubs strides over to us.

"What's his name?" She leans over and checks for a pulse, watches his breathing. "What happened?"

"He was in a bar fight," I say. "We're not sure if he's passed out from booze or—"

"Oh, God," the woman says, her professional demeanor slipping away. "It's Rich. Rich, can you hear me?"

Dad's eye, the one that isn't swollen shut, tries to open and focus. His lips move. "Glenda?"

At least that's what I think he says.

She says, "Oh, thank God, you're still conscious. Stay with me, Rich. Let's get you in a room, stat." She shoves Vic out of the way, grabs the handles of the chair, and pushes Dad toward the AUTHORIZED PERSONNEL ONLY doors at a fast walk.

Vic and I start to follow, but she calls back over her shoulder.

"Wait in the waiting room, please."

Since neither one of us really has any burning desire to sit beside Dad's bed and hold his hand, we don't make a fuss about following.

"What happened? And did your message really say he was at Mom's?" Vic asks, when we're sitting on uncomfortable vinyl seats, looking at each other's pale faces in the harsh glare of the fluorescent lights.

"Bar fight. He was doing his undercover routine and got way too into the role. Then he went to Mom's because he's Dad. He figured she'd help him. Only, she was...maybe trying to kill him while pretending to help." I shudder. "You know what, Vic? I don't ever want to talk about what I saw tonight. Also, he puked in my car."

"I noticed. You've got to sell that before you manage to turn it into another Jezebel."

I'm too tired to argue. Plus, I think maybe he's right. "So, do you think he's okay?" I ask, instead.

"Who, Richard? Absolutely. The man is unkillable. How does he do that with women, anyway? They're all over him. Can't take their eyes off him even when he's barely conscious and bashed up enough to be mistaken for a street drunk. What's the matter, Addy? He'll be all right."

"This is my fault, Vic."

"Don't go blaming yourself. Richard was excited about the idea. All he had to do was go talk to Perch. Nobody said he had to drink himself under the table and get into a brawl."

"Some of the alcohol was thanks to Mom. Don't ask. Anyway, it wasn't even Perch who beat him up. He had some old beef with Alvin, who started the fight, sounds like. Can't imagine..."

My voice trails off because Vic, whose facial expressions are like a billboard for me, has definitely reacted to this bit of information. His cheeks flush. He looks away.

"What?" I ask.

"Nothing."

"Tell me."

"Trust me. You don't want to know about this."

"I'm already scarred by watching Mom pour alcohol down Dad's throat and then give him a sponge bath. How much worse could it get?"

His gaze comes back to me and there's rage smoldering in his eyes. "Fine. You really want to know? I'll tell you. One day, when we were twelve, I came home from a half day at school—teacher training in the afternoon or something, I don't remember. You went home with Britt. Mom was gone somewhere—work trip, I think. The details are fuzzy.

"What isn't fuzzy is walking into the house and seeing our beloved father naked, in the act of ravaging some woman on the kitchen table."

I'm speechless, staring at him with my mouth gaping, my brain absolutely incapable of processing not only this image but also the fact that Vic has kept this secret. From me.

"I tried to sneak back out, but I think I made a noise, or they saw me, or whatever, so they broke apart, which was worse. Then I could see...all of her...butt-naked. And her face. It was Alvin's wife, Minna."

"I can't believe you didn't tell me." This is somehow the most salient point.

I've known Dad was having sex with a wide variety of women for most of my life. I know he cheated on Mom. But the fact that Vic would keep this from me, when I thought we told each other everything, makes the world feel like it's spinning out of control. First Britt and her secrets. Now Vic.

"Did you really need to know this, Addy? Would it have made your life better in some meaningful way?"

"Well, no, but—"

"And you have no secrets from me? Nothing that happened

when you were a kid, or recently, that you just decided didn't need to be shared?"

A whole kaleidoscope of things I've never told anybody lights up my brain, and I feel a little better. Vic has a point.

"So, did he find out anything?" Vic has apparently already moved on, and I scramble to catch up.

"What a bar brawl is like. He said that was a first."

"I mean about Leno."

"He said there was a suicide note. Also, an empty morphine bottle. Oh, and something about a phone. And then he puked and Mom gave him a sponge bath. That's all I know."

"So, maybe Leno really did take himself out after all," Vic says.

"He didn't."

"Addy," he says, "you have to look at the logic and not get sucked into the drama. Don't take this the wrong way, but you're just a bit like Richard—"

"Oh, perfect. Thank you so very much."

"I knew you'd take it like that."

"How else am I supposed to take it? Like I don't know your opinion of him? And especially after what you just told me."

Vic closes his eyes. His chest rises, his nostrils flare, as he sucks in the biggest breath in history and then—just holds it. Like he's forgotten to breathe out. This is what he does when he's uber frustrated because he thinks I'm being obtuse. His word, not mine.

As for me, I've had a hell of a day, and I say, "You know what, you're like him, too."

The breath comes out all in a whoosh, and Vic's eyes fly open. "Do tell."

"You know the way the women can't keep their eyes off

Dad? The way he charms them and gives them that look? Then they go all melty and gooey and pretty much fall at his feet?"

"Your point?"

"God. You don't even know, do you? It's like it's genetically baked in."

"You know what?" Vic gets to his feet. "I'm going home. I don't even know why I'm here."

"To help me with Dad? To figure out who killed Leno?" But I've pushed that one big, red button with the WARNING, OFF-LIMITS signs plastered all around it, and now there will be nuclear fallout.

"Have fun," Vic says.

"Wait, don't go! What if it's serious? Like he has brain damage or whatever?"

"My sitting here isn't going to help him. If you had any sense, you'd go home, too. Night, Addison." And he walks away and leaves me there.

Exhausted as I am, the adrenaline is really flowing through me now and I can't sit still. I get a cup of horrible coffee from a carafe with a FREE sign hung over it. It tastes awful, bitter and burned, even after I add six of those little plastic cream things and three packages of sugar, but at least it's hot and caffeinated.

What if Dad is actually dying? I poke at my lack of emotional reaction to that thought and uncover a pale, shadowy sadness that is more about what never was than any sense of impending loss.

Guilt? Yep. Present and accounted for.

Grief, not so much. You can't miss somebody who has never been there.

I want to talk to Geneva about all of this. About Leno and

how he died so young. That maybe he was murdered, but nobody wants to believe it. Also, about Owen and Britt and Vic and the way that maybe you can't ever really know even the people you're closest to.

Zelda is still ensconced behind her desk. She looks all around for Vic and pretends not to see me until I speak.

"Zelda. How can I find out how my dad's doing? Can I go in?"

"I'll check. Just you? Or is Vic coming back?"

I try not to roll my eyes. "Vic's gone home. Could you…" I gesture toward her phone.

She picks up the receiver. "Hey, Mr. Winter's daughter would like to come back." She listens. Hangs up. Says, "They'll be out in a minute. So, about Vic…"

I just look at her, and she has the grace to flush a little.

The double doors open and a man in scrubs waves me over. "I'm Dr. Kennedy," he says. He looks tired, but his eyes are kind, intelligent, and possibly even understanding. "You're next of kin?"

"I'm the only kin available." And then I realize that I truly am next of kin, given that Dad and Mom are divorced. I'm the oldest, even if it is only by five minutes.

"Your father has a mild concussion," he says. "Complicated by a blood alcohol of .30. We've got an IV going, which will help. We'll admit him overnight, just for observation, but I'm sure he'll be fine."

"Fantastic. Thank you." I repress the impulse to hug him.

Vic had a concussion once in high school, and Mom and I took turns waking him up every hour or so to make sure he was still conscious. This is not the kind of closeness I need with my father. What I do need is sleep.

"Having an alcoholic in the family can be challenging," Dr. Kennedy says. "I've asked the nurse to include referrals to Al Anon for the family, and AA for your father."

I don't bother to explain that Dad's not an alcoholic, that the only reason he's totally plastered is because we sent him on a reconnaissance mission to a bar and then Mom practically poured beer down his throat.

"Can I talk to him?"

"You can go in. He's sleeping right now." Dr. Kennedy leads the way to one of the rooms. "He's in here. Not very coherent and only semi-conscious, but again, that's mostly the alcohol. Nothing broken. No permanent damage." He smiles in what I'm sure is meant to be a comforting way and heads off down the hallway.

Dad lies on his back, not looking at all like his usual carefully presented self. His left eye is swollen shut, and the bruising is spreading to the skin below his right. His lip is huge and distorted and his jaw is swollen. His right hand is wrapped in gauze. An IV is taped to his left arm. EKG wires snake out of the top of a blue hospital gown and a monitor beeps out the regular rhythm of his heart.

I take his left hand in mine, not so much because I want to touch him, as because it's what people do. "Dad?"

His good eye flutters open and he squeezes my hand. "Addy, did I do good?"

"Rest now. We'll talk in the morning."

A guy rolls a cart into the room with a laptop to take a history and get Dad properly registered. I'm able to supply his address and insurance info, thanks to cards in his wallet, but there's not much I can contribute by way of medical history. I think I'd probably know if he'd had a stroke or a heart attack or cancer, but the smaller things—diabetes or high blood pressure or medications? Haven't a clue.

Not my choice, I remind myself. He left us. After getting it on with the wife of one of his friends in my mother's kitchen, an act witnessed by my brother. Which explains so many things.

I give my number as the contact number and decide that Vic was right about losing more sleep. The hospital can take care of him tonight. "Good night, Dad. I'll come see you tomorrow."

His eye opens and his lips move, but nothing comes out.

"Sorry, didn't catch that." I pat his arm. "You can tell me in the morning."

His hand grabs mine. "Phone. Recorded."

"You recorded your conversation?"

He nods, grimaces with pain, then whispers, "052165."

"That's your birthdate."

His eyes have closed and he doesn't answer, but finally my brain catches up.

I scrounge in my bag for his phone and punch in his birth date when it asks for the password. When the lock screen clears, I swipe through his apps for a voice memo. Sure enough, there's a recording made tonight.

"Go, Dad," I murmur.

Curiosity is strong, but I don't want to listen to it here. I drop a kiss on his cheek and leave the room. I ask a woman sitting at the desk to please call me if there are any changes, and then head out of the hospital and into the blessedly cool, fresh air. Okay, it isn't that fresh. It smells a bit like exhaust and tarmac, but at least it doesn't stink of antiseptic and bleach and second-hand alcohol.

Hannibal gives off a definite vibe of hostility and resentment, which is no big surprise. He's gone from being garaged and cosseted to outdoor parking lots and being drunk-puked on. I miss the familiarity of Jezebel, even her temperamental way of not starting when I want her to, backfiring at inconvenient moments, or even just deciding to stop running in the middle of the road.

But I have to admit that his speaker system is absolutely stellar, so even though there's a ton of background noise on Dad's recording—people laughing and talking, music blaring —I still hear Perch's description of Leno's death scene loud and clear. Peaceful. Looked like he was asleep. Empty morphine bottle. A suicide note. Dad, bless him, actually made an effort to find out what it said.

"Goodbye cruel world? That sort of thing?" his recorded voice asks.

"Funny you should say that, because that's how it started. Long, wordy document. Computer printout, not handwritten. He went on about some party. I only scanned the highlights, you know? It was stapled to Death With Dignity paperwork, signed by all the doctors, with a sticky note on top that said Do Not Resuscitate. It would have been too late, anyway. He was already cooling."

"Who called it in?" Dad asks.

"Some woman. Anonymous caller." Loud rowdy laughter and comments about dispatch being mushrooms in the dark follow.

After that, the conversation derails. There's a rambling story about some girl another guy at the table knew who killed herself. Perch proposes a round of shots.

And then Perch says, "Phone was in his hand. Kinda sad

that, isn't it? Guy dies alone, but maybe trying to connect? I need another drink."

And then another voice, Alvin's I'm guessing, shouting, "You've got your nerve coming back to this town, Richard. I'm gonna kick your ass!"

The recording ends abruptly which is fine. I can imagine the bar fight perfectly well on my own.

All the rest of the way home, and while I shower—again—and climb into bed—again—I turn the bits of new information over and over in my mind. Who found the body and called 9-1-1? Why didn't they wait with him until the responders arrived? Why call anonymously? Did Leno really write the suicide note, or was somebody trying to make it look like he killed himself when he didn't?

My last thoughts as I finally slide into sleep are about the phone. Who was Leno calling? Or who called him? And where is his phone now?

TUESDAY

CHAPTER 19

A REPETITIVE BUZZING drags me up out of oblivion. For a hazy moment, I think there's a fly in my room, but then I get my eyes open and see light pouring in the window. The buzzing is not a fly but my silenced phone, vibrating on the bedside table. I squint against the light and moan out loud as the events of the last few days come flooding back into consciousness.

I'm on the outs with both Britt and Vic. Dad's in the hospital, there's a damaged Maserati in my parking lot that has also been vomited in. I have a murder to solve and a giant party to plan that might—just might—be out of my league. Oh, and there's that little scene I witnessed between Mom and Dad last night.

I ignore the phone and pull the quilt up over my head.

"I'm in a bit of a mess, Geneva," I whisper.

Her absence is like a physical ache in my belly. She was my advice person, and if I ever needed somebody to give me some direction, it's now. I think back to all the other messes I have gotten into that she guided me out of and what she had to say then, but nothing in my life so far has come even close to this situation.

And then I feel a butterfly kiss on my cheek, and her voice whispers in my head:

You've got this.

You're stronger than you think you are.

Making mistakes is good, as long as you learn from them.

Bruno jumps onto the bed and lies on my chest, purring.

"I don't feel very strong," I tell him. "I do not have this situation under control. I'm actually much more fragile and breakable—and killable—than I thought I was, and the mistakes I've made have consequences. Real ones."

Trust your inner guidance, Geneva's voice whispers. *And for goodness's sake, answer your phone.*

I sigh, and reach for the annoying object, trying to focus my still bleary eyes to read the display. What I see brings me instantly awake, and I dislodge the cat and sit up to see better. The entire screen is filled with missed calls and there are five voicemails. The first one, the only one from a known number, is from Owen.

"Addy. Listen, I've been thinking about what happened and I think we should talk. Would you meet me, maybe? At that *Grounded* place? Call me. Or text. Whichever you prefer."

The other four messages are from media people, all wanting to talk to me about the party, which means Britt has launched the press release. Which means I need to get my ass out of bed and move into super party planner mode. I'm already behind the eight ball on getting everything put together.

My phone buzzes again, and this time I answer.

"Good morning! Is this Addison Winters?" The voice is female, bright and bubbly. Boston accent. Not from here.

"Yes, this is her. She. Me." I wince at the stupid response. Never, ever, should I talk to strangers before coffee.

"Oh, my goodness. It's really you. I can't believe you answered. You are absolutely going to have to spill all the tea about Leno Masterson and this party you're planning. How did you know him? Did you grow up together? I bet you know things nobody else does."

She pauses to take a breath and I seize the opportunity to say, "I'm sorry, but I think I missed your name?"

"Oh, pesky details, right?" She laughs, effervescent and breathless. "Sorry about that! I was just so surprised you answered. I've called five times this morning, and they all went to voicemail. This is Lindy Lind, aka @FlatzandSharpz?"

"I'm sorry, I—"

"Oh Em Gee! You don't know who I am. I can't believe it. You can check, though, I've got like a million followers on TikTok and a jillion subscribers on YouTube. I promised them I'd get the scoop on Leno. You will meet with me, please, please?"

"When were you thinking?" I ask, cautiously.

"Today? I'm in Fox Valley, just to meet you. And cover the party, of course! Don't worry, I'm not going to try to make you look bad or anything. Of course, if you don't meet with me, then I might have to tell everybody you were too stuck up."

I hold the phone away from my ear as another effervescent chime of laughter blasts my eardrums.

"I'm kidding, I'm kidding, only not really. I mean, I'll have to tell them *something*, but I can't help what spin they put on it, can I?"

"Lindy, hey. Let me see if I can find a time to meet. It's a very busy morning, and I've had a lot of media calling."

"You do not want to blow me off." Her tone is no longer bubbly. "My fans are very loyal."

I'm awake enough now to realize that this bitch is actually threatening to unleash trolls on me. I have an Instagram for my business. It's not huge, but I'm proud of it. A troll attack could totally ruin it, cut back on my bookings even though they're all local. I need a strategy, and it needs to be a good one.

"Believe me, I am not blowing you off." I make my tone match hers. "I would absolutely love to meet with you, and I am going to move heaven and earth to make that happen. Give me a minute to have my assistant check my schedule, and then I'll call you right back. Promise."

"I'll hold you to that," she says.

I disconnect and sit there, fending off an onslaught of panic. God. Owen was right about the media. I didn't ever think they'd come after me. I'm the behind-the-scenes person, used to fading into the woodwork while my brides and other VIPs are in the limelight. I don't know how to deal with this.

Britt would. But I can't ask her for help, not with the way things are between us.

Looking up Lindy Lind and her @FlatzandSharpz accounts heightens my panic. She wasn't lying about her following or the engagement she gets from her people. She's already posted a live video she recorded at the "WELCOME TO FOX VALLEY" sign on the edge of town, and another post shows the gate (closed) that leads up to the Masterson house, with a caption: **Gates locked and barred but you know me! I'll find my way in.**

I need to talk to somebody about all of this, and since it can't be Vic or Britt, I text Owen.

Addy: Media besieging your gates. This is not a drill.

Addy: You were right. OMG they've come for me. 🙈

He doesn't respond and I try to come up with a plan.

Think, Addy. What next?

If—make that when—I meet with this Lindy person, she's going to insist on a photo. Maybe even a live interview. I need to look put together for that. Hair. Makeup. Wardrobe. I'm honestly not great at any of it. Obviously, I need professional help.

Foxy Lady is generally booked weeks in advance, but maybe, if I'm lucky, Lisa will fit me in. When I call the salon, I draw a breath of relief when her voice answers.

"Hey, Lisa, it's Addy. I'm hoping you can do me a favor? I know you're busy and this is short notice, but there's this big influencer in town and she wants to meet about Leno's party. Is there any possible chance you could get me in this morning before I connect with her? I'll pay double."

"You know what?" Lisa says. "I owe you big time. If you can be here in fifteen minutes, I can fit you in."

"You are the best. I'll be there."

Fifteen minutes means precisely five minutes to get some clothes on and make it to the car. Ten to drive to the salon. No time to put myself together at all. Not even time for coffee. If I had coffee, which I don't, since I haven't had time to go buy it. My hair is exceptionally wild this morning, corkscrews poking out everywhere, thanks to going to bed with it wet. An attempt to tame it with a hairbrush just turns it into frizz, so I wet it down and wrestle it into a messy bun. Then I pull on the first clean T-shirt I find in the drawer without even looking at it, grab my keys, and run for the door, only to find Mom standing there with her fist raised, poised to knock.

She looks me over critically and says, "You know, if you want to make something of yourself, Addison, you might try getting up earlier so you can put more effort into your appearance. Did you know it's already noon on the East Coast?"

"And it's already tomorrow in Japan," I retort, "and sure to be night time somewhere, so maybe I should just go back to bed."

She brushes by me. "Coffee?" she inquires, which is just another dig because, obviously, there is no coffee in my kitchen this morning.

"Mom. I have to go. I'm late for an appointment."

"Like I said, you should get up earlier." She reaches her hand up as if she's going to smooth my hair and then rubs at an imaginary smudge on my cheekbone with her thumb instead. "What kind of appointment?"

"Getting my hair done. It's an emergency."

"I can see that."

"Thanks, Mom, for the moral support. Can I take your car?" Mom's car is just a car. No jealousy, no hate, no drama. The last thing I need right now is to attract attention.

Mom looks as shocked as if I've proposed leaving her stranded on a desert island infested with rats. "And leave me here?"

"Well, Dad puked in mine. So?" I hold out my hand for the keys.

"How is your father?" she asks, ignoring my hand. "I called, but you didn't answer, so I came over to ask."

"Concussion and too much to drink. They kept him

overnight. What were you thinking, Mom? You could have killed him."

"He deserves to be killed," she says. And then, accusingly, "You haven't checked on him this morning?"

"I have done nothing this morning but get dressed and—"

"You haven't really done that, either," she says.

I hold my breath and start counting to ten. Yes, I know you're supposed to keep breathing while you count, but if I let any air out, a lot of swearing is going to come with it.

"Why don't you go check on him if you're so worried?" I say after I reach ten. "I really need to go."

"Probably that would be the Christian thing to do, wouldn't it?" She turns around and walks off, still with her car keys, which means I'm going to have to drive Hannibal in his current condition.

Which is worse than it was when I left him last night because somebody has written "Just Slumming" on the rear window in lipstick, which I'm sure is exactly how Hannibal feels.

"Don't worry," I tell him as I start the engine. "Your slumming days are numbered. Just hang on for a little longer."

I drive with my eyes glued to the rearview, my muscles tightening every time a vehicle comes up behind me. I've got a thudding headache by the time I park outside the salon. I'm already three minutes late, but I take time to dig out some Tylenol and dry swallow them before going in.

Lisa glances up from the cut she's just finishing. "Addy. I'm so glad you came in. Have a seat. I'll be with you in a minute." The words are perfectly ordinary, but she utters them in a robotic sort of way, her tone saccharine sweet, and something is wrong with her smile. A little warning shiver travels up my spine.

The woman Lisa is styling is a stranger. She's model thin, with high cheekbones, purple eyeshadow, and plum lipstick, her short hair a harsh, dramatic black. A black rose is tattooed on her neck, vines with emphatic thorns winding over her right shoulder and all the way down her arm. Her eyes are sharp with curiosity.

"You're that party planner," she says. "Leno Masterson's friend."

"No shit?" This from a guy in the chair at Margie's station, a kid who could be anywhere between sixteen and twenty-five.

I don't know either of them. They could be Fox Valley residents. They could be influencers or reporters. Lisa is still smiling in an unsettling sort of way, and I suddenly feel like a rabbit that has blundered into a room full of coyotes.

"I heard about the accident," Lisa says. "That corner is a nightmare—wish they'd do something more about it than that guardrail."

"So, what happened, anyway?" Margie asks, snipping away at the young man's hair. "Heard somebody bashed right into the back of that fancy car and rolled you over, but the guardrail actually did its job this time."

"Did it explode?" her client asks, with way too much enthusiasm. "Did they have to cut you out of the vehicle?"

"Sorry to disappoint, but nothing so dramatic. Hit and run. Probably some drunk kids in a pickup truck. They tried to pass on a corner and caught the back end. We ended up in the ditch. Nobody was hurt, and the car is still drivable." This is the spin I've decided to put on the attack in public. Word gets around, and I'd prefer that the person responsible doesn't know I think they tried to kill me.

"No shit?" the kid breathes.

"No shit."

"Heard you were on the way out to talk to Spiro when it happened," says the woman in the chair.

"You know Spiro?" I ask.

The woman shrugs. "I know who she is."

"Roxy owns that new tattoo parlor on Elm," Lisa says, as if the fact that Spiro has tattoos and Roxy creates them means they must be friends. "Don't suppose they have any idea who did it?"

The tiny hairs on the back of my neck are twingling with the warning sensation I get when one of my clients is about to have a major meltdown. *Maybe today is a bad day for a haircut*, it whispers. A glance at myself in the mirror persuades me to ignore it. I'm just imagining trouble, and I really need my hair fixed before I face the Lindy Linds of the world.

"Not a clue," I say. "Too dark to make out a license plate number."

Lisa shakes her head, indicating the craziness of this world. She squirts gel into her palm and works it into Roxy's hair, creating spikes that amplify an already edgy appearance.

"There you go, Roxy. What do you think?"

"It'll do," Roxy says, but she's not looking at her own image in the mirror; she's watching me.

"Go ahead and have a seat," Lisa tells me. "I'll be right with you."

This is my moment to make an excuse, to take myself elsewhere, but I don't. I sit myself down in the empty chair, tight with dread. Roxy pays and exits. Five minutes later, I begin to relax. I've been shampooed and conditioned and am looking at my pale, sleep-deprived, face in the mirror. The kid at Margie's station has also moved on, and she's taking a well-earned break, sitting in her client chair and watching Lisa and, therefore, me.

"Her hair is so fine," Margie says. "Something short and layered, maybe, for more body."

"Short doesn't work on me," I protest. "The curls go crazy. I end up with a carrot-colored afro sort of thing."

"Good to know," Lisa says, with a dangerous edge to her voice. The comb catches viciously on a tangle. When I gasp, she smiles at me in the mirror and says, too brightly, "I forgot the detangler, didn't I?"

But she doesn't reach for the detangler; she just continues raking that comb ruthlessly through my hair. She looks more bridezilla now than she did the last time I saw her. Lisa, in this mood, will not pair well with scissors.

Time to go.

"Oh my God," I exclaim. "I just remembered. I don't know how I could be so stupid, but I have this urgent thing. I'm going to have to go right now, or I'll be late."

"Nonsense. You've got all of those media people in town. You need to make a real impression." Lisa's fist tightens around a hank of hair, and our gazes lock in the mirror. The smile is gone, replaced by an expression of outright malice.

She drops the comb with a clatter and picks up the scissors, one hand twisting my hair so tightly that tears spring to my eyes. I glance at Margie for help, but her face, too, has gone hard. There are no other customers in the shop. Lisa opens and closes the scissors, *snick snack, snick snack,* still staring at me in the mirror.

"I heard Leno left his fancy car to you for some reason," Margie says.

Lisa tugs harder. The scissors snick. A long lock of still tangled hair falls, in slow motion, onto my plastic-cape covered lap.

Snick. Another lock, leaving a patch of hair just behind my temple that is only a couple of inches long.

"What are you doing?" I screech, trying to pull away, but Lisa's hand twists even tighter in my hair.

"We agreed on a shorter, more stylish cut," she says. *Snick.*

"I didn't agree to anything. Let me go, Lisa. You're hurting me."

"You can't leave now. You can't walk around like this, not with all the people staring at you because you're driving Leno's Maserati. Not to mention all of those *reporters.* And *influencers.*"

Every emphasized word comes with another *snick.* Another fallen lock of hair.

The bell over the door jingles, signaling a new customer, and I suck in a breath, thinking this will mean a reprieve. And then Aunt Rachel appears in the mirror behind me.

"Addison," she says. "I might have expected I'd find you here." From her tone, you'd think she'd found me in a crack house or a brothel.

"Where should I be?" I ask, and even Lisa, scissors positioned to make another devastating cut, pauses for the answer.

"Comforting your poor, dear mother. Honestly, first, you skipped the funeral—"

"The burial. I skipped the *burial.* I was at the funeral, as I think you'll remember."

"And now here you are, indulging your own vanity—"

A hysterical laugh bursts out of me. "Does this look like vanity to you?"

She cocks her head. "I never did understand modern hair styles. Is this one of those shaved on one side and long on the other dos?"

Lisa, taking advantage of my distraction, snips again, shorter this time. She's not even pretending to do any sort of style now. This is a scalping.

"Come sit down, Rachel," Margie says, as if what Lisa is doing to my hair is perfectly normal. "A trim up and fix those roots, yes?"

"Please. I've let myself go horribly while Geneva was ill," she says, sinking into the chair like a Victorian lady onto a fainting couch.

She looks the same as she always has to me: thin, pinched, her hair dyed an uncompromising walnut even though her brows and lashes are as pale as mine. Grandma Geneva lived with us while she was dying, not with Rachel, and my aunt's version of caring for her to come over and spend hours telling Mom what she should be doing.

"About that car," Lisa says. "And Leno's big party that you're throwing on what was going to be my wedding day—"

"Which you called off."

"Because you said my ring was fake." *Snip*

"I didn't—"

"You know what?" *Snip*. "I took it to the jeweler, and it's not fake. It's a real diamond." *Snip*.

"Lisa. I never said the ring was fake. I said I didn't know how Brad could afford a ring like that—"

"And all the while, you just wanted that venue for Leno. Who gave you his Maserati."

Snip.

"I bet you were sleeping with him. Talked him into changing his will so you'd get all his money."

Snip.

"Sounds about right," Aunt Rachel sniffs. "You always were just like your father." She's been watching this whole disaster and hasn't said one word to stop it.

"What?" I protest. "No! Leno was too sick to be sleeping with anybody. Aunt Rachel, I am not like Dad. For God's sake, Lisa, put the scissors down!"

She throws them onto her workspace with enough force that a bounce might put an eye out. Picking up her phone, she taps a couple of times and shoves it in my face so close it makes me cross-eyed. Wrapping one hand around her wrist, I tug both phone and hand far enough away that I can see what looks like some tabloid article with a grainy picture of Leno and me. It's the same altered photo I saw earlier. I appear to be gazing at him in rapt adoration. He's laughing. We're holding hands.

My reality quavers, and for a fraction of a second, I find myself believing my own eyes even though I was there when this picture was taken and it was certainly not Leno holding my hand.

"This is photoshopped, Lisa. They put Leno's head on Alex's body."

"Try making up a better story next time," she says.

"Lisa, listen to me. Does that look like the arm and hand of a dying man? Leno was practically skeletal. And he'd never have been caught dead in those clothes."

Taking advantage of her distraction, I pop up out of the chair before she can grab me again.

"Let me see," Aunt Rachel says.

Lisa walks over to show her, and Margie joins them. While the three of them examine the photo, debating whether or not it has been altered, I shed my plastic cape and make a run for the door. But my escape attempt is thwarted by a woman standing outside on the sidewalk, taking a selfie with the salon behind her.

Lindy Lind, @FlatzandSharpz in the flesh.

"It really does look a little strange," Margie says.

I edge away from the door and work my way toward the back of the shop, my eyes flicking back and forth from the three women inside the shop to the influencer outside.

"He still gave her the Maserati." Lisa glares at me. She reaches for Margie's scissors.

I glance back toward the door, thinking maybe @FlatzandSharps is the safer bet, but my own reflection in all of the mirrors stops me. My hair looks like I've been in a fight with a lawnmower. The T-shirt I'm wearing is one Britt bought me a couple of years ago as a joke. The slogan reads: YOU DON'T WANT TO MESS WITH ME TODAY. It has an image of a hand holding a bloody knife and a body outline surrounded by yellow crime scene tape.

Well, all right then. Since I look like a crazy bitch, I might as well act like one. Instead of running, I take a step toward Lisa, hands up in the air like claws, teeth bared in a feral grin. "Why would you care if I *was* getting it on with Leno? What could it possibly matter to you? Unless the two of you were having a fling. You told Lindy Lind I was going to be here, didn't you? How about if I bounce out that door screaming and tell her viewers, all gazillion of them, that this is what they can expect at *Foxy Lady*? And that you were having an affair with Leno and called off your wedding because you were going after all that money yourself?"

I take a step closer.

"Maybe I'll tell Brad you just wanted out because you were in love with Leno. Or wanted his money."

"Mom?"

A kid, apparently Lisa's, has just come in through the back door. This is so not good.

"Jackson," Lisa says, her face first going pale and then flushing crimson. "What are you doing here?"

"No school today, remember? I got bored at the house."

This is it. I'm out of here.

"Well, this has been fun," I say, "but I'm gonna leave now."

"Don't go," Margie calls after me. "We messed up. Come sit down. I'll fix you."

"Are you kidding? Nobody in this place is touching my hair again. Ever."

"You can't tell anybody what happened, though," Margie says. "It will ruin business."

"If you really think I'm going to walk around letting people think I had a Brittney Spears moment and did this to myself, then you're as crazy as Lisa. Sorry, Jackson."

"Well, you're the one that *looks* crazy, anyway," Lisa screeches. And then her face crumples. Her mouth goes square, her eyes squinch shut, and tears start to flow down her cheeks. She runs into the restroom, slamming the door behind her. We can still hear her sobbing.

"What's the matter with Mom?" Jackson asks.

"She's just having a bad day, Jackie," Margie says.

Jackson assesses me and shakes his head. "That looks like more than just a bad day. Did Mom really do that?"

"Your mom is, as Margie says, having a very bad day," I say. "What's really interesting is the complicity of everybody else in this room."

Margie flushes and bites her lower lip.

Aunt Rachel sniffs. "Vanity," she begins, but then she pinches her lips together and doesn't continue what I'm sure was going to be a pep talk on how I needed to be taken down a peg and got what I deserved.

"At least let me even it out," Margie pleads. Now it looks like she's going to cry, and I feel weirdly guilty, like I'm the mean girl who came in here and bullied everybody.

"You want to make it better? You can stop the gossip about Leno and me. He asked me to plan the party. I said no. Then he died and I changed my mind. There was no relationship. I don't know why he gave me the car."

"Holy shit," Jackson says, still staring at me, his eyes wide. "I can't believe Mom did that to you."

"Don't swear, Jackie. All right, Addison. I'll do my best."

"And if that influencer person comes in here looking for me, I never showed up. Okay?"

Margie nods.

"Aunt Rachel?"

"Lying is a sin."

"So don't lie. Just keep your mouth shut."

I don't wait for more. Keeping my head down, hoping nobody will recognize me, I head for the back door.

It opens into a small parking lot—employees and

customers only—but I still feel exposed. I can't get to my car, not with Lindy Lind out front of the salon. I need a ride, and I need it now. Vic will rescue me, even if he's still mad, but my call goes to voicemail. I can't call Britt. Desperate, I try one last person.

"Owen? I wonder if you might be willing to do me a favor?"

CHAPTER 20

OWEN ROLLS up in a silver BMW, all understated luxury, unlike the Maserati. All that matters to me is that the windows are tinted. I'm pretty sure nobody sees me dash across the parking lot and slip into the passenger seat, but I still lock my door and duck down low, feeling like I've just escaped from a war zone.

"I'm listening," Owen says. That's all. No shock and dismay at my appearance, no sympathy, no judgment or offers to protect me or exclamations of horror.

"If we could just get out of here?" I request. "There's a super influencer out front waiting for me."

"Right," he says, shifting into gear without further question and heading for the alley. "Back roads, then. Did you want to flee town, or do you have another safe haven in mind?"

"God, I don't know. Home?"

"They might be watching your place," Owen says.

"Right. Of course they are." My brain scurries around,

latching onto possibilities and discarding them. There's only one very bad option available.

I'm hoping Mom is still at the hospital, or at least out, but no. Her car is in the driveway, right beside Dad's rental car.

"Maybe the influencer would be preferable," I mutter when Owen parks on the curb.

"Family trouble?" he asks.

"My mother is ...well. Mothers, right?"

"I hear that. There's nowhere else you can hide out for a bit?"

"Last night, I accused my brother of being like my father, which is the ultimate sibling insult. My best friend isn't talking to me because I found a ring in Leno's car, and I honestly thought it was hers because they apparently used to date and she never told me. So I thought maybe she'd been seeing him again but didn't tell me..." I try to laugh, but it comes out like a sob and I bury my face in my hands.

"And now you are being stalked by media people, and somebody at the hair salon obviously hates you."

"You think?" I manage a strangled laugh.

"Don't take this wrong," he says, "because I know you're a smart woman. But why would you let someone with a grudge get anywhere near you with sharp objects?"

"It was an ambush. We went to school together. She was my client and I had no reason to expect an attack."

"Except?" Owen encourages, accurately reading my expression.

I sigh. "Except —I did sort of plant some suspicions about the quality of her engagement ring, and she *did* call off the wedding based on that and I *am* using her date at the venue for Leno's party. Oh, and she had the ring appraised, and it turns out it really is a good diamond and now she regrets breaking things off with Brad."

"This would be the woman who was going to marry the tow truck driver?"

"That's the one. This is me, making friends and influencing people. Speaking of influencers, there was one out front of the salon, which is why I called you for a rescue. Actually, she's the reason I went to the salon in the first place. She'd threatened to send her trolls after me if I didn't meet with her, and I wanted to look my best so I thought I'd go to the salon first and then..."

A sob rises up and chokes me before I can stop it. I bury my face in my hands to hide the tears, but there's not much point because my ragged weeping is a dead giveaway.

"Hey," Owen says, "Hey. It's going to be okay." His hand settles on my head, so very gently, and begins to stroke my ruined hair. "It's a shame, for sure. Your hair was so pretty, but it will grow. And this can be...well, better, anyway."

"There's nobody to fix it," I wail, even as part of me is registering the fact that he actually called my hair pretty. Also, that I didn't cry like this when Geneva died and that maybe I'm my father's daughter after all, weeping over wounded vanity but not people who have died.

"I'll fix it," Owen says. "I have secret skills. Come on. Let's go in the house."

"You don't understand. You don't want to go in there."

He laughs. "Are you kidding? You've met my mother. And she's gentle and sweet compared to my dearly departed Dad. Come on, Addy. How bad could your parents be?"

Little does he know. I keep my face in my hands and stay where I am. I hear his door open and shut. And then my door opens and he's standing there, holding out his hand. I scrub my tear-wet palms on my jeans and hold my hand out to him. His fingers wrap around it, warm and strong, and he pulls me out of the car and then into a gentle hug.

I let my forehead rest against his chest. His body feels good, strong but still soft enough to be comfortable, and he smells of shampoo and shaving cream and clean clothes and something that is just Owen. I want to stay here like this, maybe forever, but my brain wakes up enough to remind me that I don't even know this man, no matter what my heart is trying to tell me. Also, nothing but trouble will come from us being seen in an embrace.

I pull away. On autopilot, I reach up to run my fingers through my hair, but Owen stops me, his hand circling my wrist, a reminder that I don't want to do that. And then he laces his fingers with mine and leads the way up the driveway to the front door.

Maybe, I think, this won't be so bad after all. Owen is polite and successful, so Mom will like him. Maybe she'll even refrain from pointing out my shortcomings if we have company. All of which just goes to show that I'm sleep-deprived and rattled because once things start going downhill, there's a universal law of momentum that means they're just going to keep getting worse until I land on sharp, pointy rocks or hungry alligators or, in this case, Dad.

He's reclining on the living room couch, still wearing Vic's clothes, his head propped up on a couple of pillows, looking for all the world like he belongs there. Mom is knitting something, the click of the needles sharp and angry in the silence. The TV is on but muted. Both of them probably watched Owen and me hugging through the window.

Sometimes, the best thing to do in an impossible situation

is just barrel through it as if everything is normal. So, I smile brightly and chirp, "Dad! You're looking so much better than the last time I saw you."

"Can't say the same for you," he says. "Looks like you put your head in a woodchipper." That's Dad for you. Ever and always encouraging and supportive.

"It's not exactly the improvement you were going for," Mom says, possibly the understatement of the year. "Who's this? One of the media people?"

Dad's face is too swollen to be capable of a range of expression, but his eyes convey horror. Dad being Dad, I'm pretty sure the problem is that a media person might see him not at his best. He flounders around, trying to move into an upright, wounded-hero position, and I can't help tormenting him a little.

"This is Kristoff," I say, gesturing toward Owen. "He has a TikTok feed to die for. I told him all about you getting beat up last night in the course of gathering intel on Leno's death, and he just begged to meet you."

I don't actually have a plan beyond giving Dad a moment of panic. I mean, there's no way I could have guessed that Mom would bring him here.

But Owen runs with it. He positions himself where he can hold out his phone and snap a selfie with Dad in the background, then pushes the video record. "People, you will not believe where I am! This is the home of the selfless hero who sacrificed his face last night for the cause of justice. I knew you would want to meet him, and I am standing in his house right now!"

"It's not my house, actually," Dad protests, his eyes

tracking the shabby décor which dates back at least to the eighties. "I'm just visiting."

"Better and better," Owen crows. "And whose house are we in, viewers? Can you guess? This is the home of our hero's ex-wife. The scoop is that the two have been on the outs for years, so are you as curious as I am as to what he is doing here?"

He turns the phone and points it toward Mom. "Can you tell us—"

"Don't you point that thing at me, young man," she says, waving her knitting threateningly.

Owen turns back to Dad. "Mr. Winters, can you tell us what is going on?"

You've got to give it to Dad. He knows how to work a camera. "It's Rich, please," he says. "Bethany took me in out of Christian charity and the goodness of her very big heart after I got beat up in the course of my investigation. Don't you worry, now. This looks worse than it is. Just a little concussion, and what I discovered was worth it."

"Oh, do tell us!" Owen says.

"I'm afraid I...can't." Dad continues to try to smile for the camera, but his shoulders sink, and his chest collapses as his body deflates. He suddenly looks like what he is—a sixty-year-old man who has been badly beaten.

"Of course," Owen says. "Keeping secrets until all the truth comes out."

"Enough." I touch his arm, and he lowers his camera.

"Off the record?" Dad asks.

"Maybe?" Owen says.

I touch his arm again. "Please."

"All right, Rich. Off the record."

"I failed, Addy," Dad says in a hollow voice. "I'm afraid it was all for nothing. I don't remember a thing."

This is when I should reassure him that he did great, that he recorded everything on his phone, that he got some good information. I should tell him that Owen is Owen and not an influencer at all. But here's the thing.

Dad has just proven that if a reporter or influencer points a camera or a microphone at him, he will tell everything he knows. And I've tasked him with dealing with the media. His memory blackout is the only good thing that has happened so far in this day because I don't want him repeating what he knows to anybody.

"It's okay, Dad," I say. "At least you tried. Just glad you're all right."

He frowns, I think. It's hard to tell the way his face is swollen. "I can't find my wallet and my phone. Do you know where they are?"

I catch myself glancing down at my bag, where both the phone and the wallet are currently located, and force myself to look directly into his eyes while I lie outright. "Oh, duh. I'm sorry. I left the house in a hurry and didn't bring them for you. Maybe Carmen will fetch them. Right now, there are too many media people around for me to go back there."

Dad sighs, pathetically. "I need to make some phone calls, but maybe I can use the house phone. You'll let me crash here for a bit, won't you, Bethy?"

"My Christian duty is to let you stay until you're out of danger from the head trauma," Mom says, folding her hands. "The doctor said you shouldn't be alone for forty-eight hours, at least."

I narrow my eyes at her and say, with meaning, "I'm

certain he'll be perfectly safe with you." And then I gasp as I look up to see Spiro on the TV screen, talking to a reporter.

"Dad. Volume. Quick."

Any mental impairment he may be suffering does not affect his reaction time with the remote, and sound comes up just in time to hear Spiro say, "Yes, Leno and the Lonely will absolutely be playing a tribute concert at Leno Masterson's send-off party. We're bringing back all the old hits, plus we have a couple of new surprises for you."

"We're excited about the concert," the reporter says, "but I do have to ask the question I know all of Leno's fans have right now—how can there be a Leno and the Lonely concert without Leno?"

Spiro smiles big for the camera. "I guess the fans will just have to wait to find out. You might be surprised what the rest of the band is capable of. Also, we're raffling off a few exclusive tickets for the party over at L&Ltribute.com, so make sure you pop on over and buy yours."

The camera focuses back on the reporter. "This party promises to be bigger than any event we've ever seen here in Fox Valley, but if you're planning on sneaking in, think again! It's invitation only, I understand, plus those exclusive raffle tickets! Our own hometown party planner, Addison Winters, is organizing the event, so if you're trying to schmooze an invite —you know who to talk to. And now, over to Brett, who is going to tell you all about the storms we're expecting this weekend. Brett?"

Dad kills the volume as a guy who looks to me like he should still be in high school starts talking about the weather.

My phone buzzes with a text.

> Unknown number: Addy, hey. This is Jer. Been a while, but, hey—I'd love to go to that party. Can you hook me up?

And then another, this time from Brad, of all people:

> Brad: Got your car almost running. Any chance I could score one of those tickets to the party?

"This is stellar," Dad says. "We need to leverage the media."

"I'm meeting with an influencer this afternoon."

"You can't go looking like that," Dad says.

"Yes, well, since I'm never going back to the only salon in Fox Valley, I'm not exactly sure what I'm going to do. No time to drive to Spokane. I suppose I could wear a hat."

"Wrong look for this party," Dad says. "You need to look glam if you want to bring in stars."

"They walk around in ball caps and sunglasses all the time!"

"Only because they don't want to be recognized."

"Well, maybe I don't want to be recognized, either."

"You're not famous, honey," Dad says.

"I have an electric shaver from when I used to do Vic's hair," Mom says. "It probably still works."

"I am not having a buzz cut."

"It would be better than what you've got going on now. You could be like that one singer—what was her name? Something Scottish or Irish, maybe."

I stare at her in absolute horror. Spiro could easily pull off a Sinead O'Connor vibe. Me? No possible way. But then I catch a glimpse of myself in the living room mirror and realize, with despair, that bald would probably be better.

"We're going to fix your hair," Owen says. "And we're not shaving your head. What time is your meeting with Lindy?"

"Noon."

"Okay. We've got time. Mrs. Winters, do you have a pair of scissors, a comb, and maybe a bed sheet we can use? Oh, and the shaver while you're at it."

To my surprise, rather than asking questions or offering advice or censure, Mom says, "Yes, of course. I'll go get them."

And then Dad says, "Don't worry about the media, Addy. We've got this. You're going to need a ton of security at the door of the venue. I know a guy. You have a budget, right?"

"Yes, we can pay him, but—"

"And if you'll give me Britt's number, I'll get with her to put together some talking points for all of us. Okay?"

"I don't think Britt's talking to me."

"Doesn't mean she's not talking to me, though, does it?"

I grab a sticky note and pen from my bag and jot down Britt's number, then lead Owen into the kitchen.

Mom bustles in with the requested items. "You should wet your hair," she says. "Come over to the sink."

I do as she says, but warily. Mom is acting all nurturing and motherly, which means she has an ulterior motive. She waits for the water to warm before she activates the sprayer and uses one hand to gently rub the water through my hair. It feels soothing, and I'm just beginning to relax when she asks, "So, what did you do to Lisa?"

And there it is.

"You're trying to make this my fault now? What the hell, Mom? Maybe you could be on my side for once."

"Language," Mom says. "Rachel called."

"Of course she did," I say bitterly. My aunt did nothing to help me but was certainly quick to get on the phone and tattle to my mother.

"Rachel said Lisa was upset about Leno giving you his car. And a social media pic of the two of you together—"

"The pic was photoshopped! And I didn't ask for the car. I have no idea why any of that should matter to Lisa, anyway. It's not like she was dating Leno."

"Well, really, it's not so surprising that she might be a little upset, don't you think? I mean, they do have a child together."

I jerk upright, flinging water everywhere, as the truth dawns.

Jackson. Those blue eyes. That red-gold hair. I knew there was something familiar about that kid. If I hadn't been in the middle of an ambush, I would have seen it myself.

"Addy, you're making a mess. Over the sink," Mom reprimands. She turns off the faucet and wraps a towel around my head.

"Mom, what do you know about Jackson?"

"Why is an influencer here at the house and about to do your hair?" she counters.

I sigh. "Mom, this is Owen, Leno's brother. He's not really an influencer. We were just messing with Dad."

"Sorry about that," Owen says, but he doesn't sound sorry.

"Does *he* know about Jackson?" Mom whispers, as if Owen is hard of hearing and not standing right there.

One glance at Owen's face tells me that he does not, in fact, know about Jackson.

"If my brother has a child, this is the first I've heard of it,"

Owen says. "Though I can't say I'm surprised. I'm still not clear what that has to do with what happened to Addy."

"It's quite obvious, isn't it?" Mom says, in the superior but disappointed tone of a teacher charged with a class of inattentive students. "Lisa thinks Leno owed her something special, her being his baby mama and all. And then he goes and gives that fancy car to Addy. I can see how that might set her off."

"How do you know Jackson is Leno's?" I ask.

"I have eyes," Mom says smugly.

"Also, you're tapped into the Fox Valley gossip network."

"Well, there is that. Lisa was always tight-lipped about her baby, wouldn't say a thing about who the father might be. And she didn't act traumatized like she'd been raped or something, so we thought, at first, it must have been some casual hookup. She'd taken a spring break trip to Florida, and we all know how those trips go. Girls gone wild, that sort of nonsense. But when Jackson got older, it became pretty obvious who his daddy had to be, whether Lisa would admit it or not."

"I never saw him before today," I say. "Not since he was a baby. It's not like Lisa and I hang out."

"You sure you didn't know about this?" I ask Owen, who is taking the news much more calmly than I'd expected.

He shrugs. "He never told me. But women have been lining up to sleep with him since junior high. I could have nephews and nieces all over the country, for all I know. Let's get your hair fixed, shall we?"

He pulls a kitchen chair out for me. "Sit."

I plunk down into the chair, and he wraps the sheet around my shoulders and begins, very gently, to ease the comb through a section of hair that is still long enough to tangle. "Sorry if I pull," he says. "I'll do my best to be gentle."

"You're good," I say, squeezing my eyes tight and bracing for pain as the comb snags on a tangle and it pulls against my tender scalp. But Owen immediately stops tugging and begins to tease the strands free. I relax into his hands, into the warmth of him behind me, the easy rhythm of his breath.

"I guess you can't make it any worse," Mom says.

This is so typically Mom it draws a giggle out of me. As laughs go, it's a poor specimen, but I feel marginally lighter. It fades immediately, though, when Mom gets down to business.

"Did Leno leave her anything? Lisa?" she asks. "I know what it's like trying to raise kids without support."

"Haven't seen the will yet," Owen says. "I'm meeting with the attorney tomorrow to go over things."

Realizing she's not going to get any gossip-worthy info out of Owen, Mom switches gears. "Why are you lying to your father, Addison?"

I jerk my head around to look at her, and that makes Owen pull my hair. "Ow!" I squeal.

"Sorry," he says.

"Not your fault," I breathe. "I'm not lying to him."

"You let him believe he failed to get any information for you last night."

"What makes you think he told me anything?"

"You have his phone in your bag, but you told him it was at the apartment. Did he videotape something?"

"How can you possibly know I have his phone?"

"You looked at your bag when he asked for it. And I'm your mother. I know when you're lying."

"I'd like to know what he found out," Owen says.

I'd had no intention of telling either my mother or Owen any of this. I'm still not one hundred percent sure he didn't kill

Leno. He's probably got more motive than anybody. But I'm trusting his hands right now. That he won't hurt me. That he will honestly do the best he can to make me look, if not classy, at least relatively normal.

"I'll tell you right after Owen tells me how he learned to cut hair," I say.

He laughs. "It was all for love. Well, partly love and partly as a dig at my mother."

"I think you might need to unpack that a little."

"Right. Well, you've met Mother. I went through a little rebellious phase while I was in college. She wanted me to be a doctor or a lawyer—not just the garden variety of either, mind you. World-class surgeon. Lawyer turned politician, preferably president. I thought maybe I'd be a mechanic or a plumber instead. And then I fell for this girl who was taking cosmetology, and I thought if I signed up for the classes, too, maybe she'd notice me. She didn't. But, I had a knack for hair, as it turned out. I was enjoying myself and making decent money, but then Dad died and somebody had to take over the family business. Leno was a rock star, so obviously that fell to me."

He takes a breath. "Now you. What did your father find out about how my brother died?"

"Do you have Leno's phone by any chance?" I ask.

"I couldn't find it."

"Hmmmm."

Owen's hands go still. "Addy, please tell me."

I glance at my mother who has made herself small and quiet, and I know she's hoping I've forgotten she's there. She shrugs and smiles. "Obviously I'm not going anywhere until you spill," she says.

I sigh. "Okay. Mom was half right; Dad got an audio

recording at the bar. Perch—he's an EMT—told him that when they responded to the condo, they found an empty bottle of morphine and a suicide note—and that Leno died with a phone in his hand. So, I was wondering who he was calling. Or who might have been calling him."

Owen's hands start moving again, combing through what's left of my hair. He picks up the scissors. *Snick.* A long lock of hair falls to the floor.

"Spiro," he says. "If anybody has his phone, it will be her."

"Is that the woman we just saw on the news?" Mom asks. "Maybe she killed him. You can't trust a woman like that."

"Mom. Just because she's got tattoos and facial jewelry—"

"And a belly button ring," Mom interrupts. "Don't forget that. Probably got a nipple piercing, too."

"Mom!"

"What? You think I don't know about piercings? But that's not why you can't trust her. It's the way she looks out through the camera, like she wants to eat you for dinner. Just like your father. And speaking of Richard, I'm going to go keep an eye on him. You never know what he might be up to."

A little shudder runs through me, thinking about what Vic once caught Dad getting up to. I wonder whether Mom, who is better at secrets than I suspected, knew all about that—both what Dad did and what Vic saw. Maybe she's also better at reading people than I've given her credit for.

But I also know that lies, whether tiny and white or blatant and deadly, are right up there with Mom's version of the seven deadly sins: smoking, adultery, tattoos, rap music, rock'n'roll, and vanity. I would have said murder, but after what happened last night, I'm not sure where she stands on justified homicide.

"Mom, you can't tell Dad about this."

"About which parts, dear? That he actually shared information with us last night but blacked it out, that Jackson is Leno's love child, or that Owen is Owen and not an influencer?"

"Any and all of it."

"Well, I can't make any promises," she says. "If he asks me outright, I'll tell the truth. Otherwise, I suppose I'll keep your little secrets."

"You have an interesting family," Owen says after she leaves the room.

"Tell me about it."

"Leno wasn't texting anybody," Owen says. "With the phone. All of his texts showed up on his laptop. I wonder who would have warranted a phone call?"

"It wasn't me. If it wasn't you, who is left?'

"Mother," Owen says. "Draco. Maybe this Lisa person."

"Or 9-1-1. Maybe he was calling for help."

"God, that's a sobering thought," Owen says. "We need to find that phone."

"Can you get us into the condo?"

"Shouldn't be a problem getting in, but Spiro is another story. I want to do some snooping without her watching. Hey, where are you meeting that influencer?"

"I was just going to meet her at *Grounded*."

I can practically hear him thinking as he continues snipping at my hair.

"Not a good idea?"

"It has the benefit of you being on home territory. But what if we have her meet us at the condo? Tell her we also got her an exclusive with Spiro. While Spiro's eating up the attention from this Lindy Lind person, we'll have an opportunity to poke around Leno's bedroom and the rest of the place. Find the phone. Look for clues. What do you think?"

What I think is that somebody in my life is offering a suggestion rather than telling me what to do. It's a refreshing novelty.

"It also has the advantage of getting Lindy's focus off of the train wreck that is me," I say.

"You're not a train wreck," Owen says. "Although this style would be better with some gel or some mousse or something. Your mom have any styling products?"

I snort. "Unless you want to empty a bottle of Aqua Net on my head, no."

He picks up the trimmer and plugs it into an outlet.

"You can't shave me!" I cry. "I can never pull that look off! I thought you were just evening things up or whatever!"

"Easy," Owen soothes. "I was thinking about just shaving up the sides and leaving your curls a little longer on top. But we don't have to do that. Breathe, you're turning blue."

He sets down the trimmer, and I breathe again. He makes another couple of snips and lays down the scissors. "Best I can do with what we've got."

I lift a had to tentatively touch my head. "How bad is it?"

There's no mirror in the kitchen, and I'm grateful since I'm not quite ready to look. I've worn my hair long since I was a child, and now my head feels foreign and strange, not like me at all.

"I kind of like it," Owen says with a half-smile. "And it will grow."

"Well—thank you."

"Aren't you going to go look?"

263

"Not quite yet."

I dig Dad's phone out of my bag, pull up the voice memo, and AirDrop it to my own phone. Then I double-check to be sure I've received and saved it, delete Dad's recording, and shove his phone back into my bag, making sure it's buried at the bottom, just in case.

"What?" I ask, feeling Owen's eyes on me.

"You're alarmingly devious," he says, in a way that might be a compliment rather than a criticism. And then, out of the blue, he asks, "What's your favorite color?"

"Why? Are we going shopping?"

"I've just realized that I don't know the most basic things about you."

He's right, of course. He's held me while I cried. Trimmed up my ravaged hair. Helped me formulate a plan. Hell, we almost died together. But our external knowledge of each other hasn't caught up to all of the intimacy.

"Blue," I say. "Any shade. Yours?"

"Purple. Tea or coffee?"

"Macchiato, frozen, extra whipped. You?"

"Just coffee. Black. No sugar. I'd ask dogs or cats, but I know the answer. I think. Who names their cat Bruno?"

"He named himself. He's not your average cat."

"Addy," Owen says, his voice gone husky, a new intensity in his eyes that turns my heart upside down and inside out.

My whole body lights up in response. If I take one step toward him now, I'm going to back him up against the counter and kiss him. The way he's looking at me, I'm pretty sure he'll have no objection. But an image pops into my head of my father naked with Alvin's wife right here, in this kitchen, and that saves me from myself.

"Gonna go look at my hair," I croak. I turn my back on him and the energy crackling between us and run for the bathroom, locking myself in. Breathing hard, I brace my palms flat on the countertop and confront myself in the mirror.

"Get a grip, Addy. He could be a killer."

A killer who has fixed my hair for me, because Owen has worked a miracle. Whatever he's done to my hair looks like it was done on purpose. Still, I don't look like me. My eyes seem bigger, my cheekbones more defined, my neck longer. Short, my hair is a shade darker than I'm used to, more copper than carrot. It nestles against my scalp in glossy curls and spirals. A little wild, a little frizzy, but this is a look I can live with, at least while my hair grows out.

The eyes looking out of the mirror at me are questioning, unsure, the sort of expression that will get me eaten alive by women like Spiro and Lindy Lind, and apparently, also Lisa. Maybe an expression that would also get me ravaged by Owen. So what if he is a murderer? Is that really a reason not to have steamy, hot sex?

Addy. Focus.

I stare myself down in the mirror, trying all sorts of ridiculous mantras like, "I am a tiger. I am Wonder Woman. I am strong. I am invincible." My gaze drops to the slogan on my T-shirt.

"You do not want to mess with me today," I say to the mirror. And then again. "You do *not* want to mess with me today." I repeat it once more, the words beginning to feel like a magic spell. I feel my spine straightening. Resolve ignites my muscles, firing something at my core.

I'm going to get justice for Leno. And I'm going to throw him an amazing party. Any influencer or reporter or murderer

—or hairdresser—who wants to get in the way of that can kiss my ass.

Whatever this is between Owen and me, it is going to have to wait.

CHAPTER 21

"I'm sorry," Jen says when Owen pulls his BMW up to the gatehouse. "I can't let you in. Spiro said absolutely nobody gets through."

"Come on, Jen. You know she didn't mean us," I say.

"Everybody means everybody. Random people have been showing up here all morning. Leno and the Lonely fans, reporters, influencers, you name it, they've been here. Spiro was very explicit."

"I imagine she was," Owen says. "But as Spiro is actually a guest, and since I'm now responsible for my brother's property and his affairs, perhaps you might make an exception."

Jen flushes. "Oh, sorry, Mr. Masterson. I didn't know you were you. Yes. Of course. I'll just tell her you're coming."

"Do me a favor and don't. We'd prefer to surprise her." Owen smiles, but the tone of authority is clear, and I'm reminded that while Owen might be able to cut hair, he's also the head of a multi-million-dollar company.

"Yes, sir. Of course, sir," Jen says. I almost feel sorry for her, caught between Spiro and Owen's power persona.

"Also, we're being joined by a woman named Lindy Lind," he says. "Please let her through when she arrives."

"Yes, sir. Want me to call up when she gets here?" Jen is practically groveling now.

"I think we'll just let it be a surprise." Owen hands her a couple of folded bills and smiles. "Sorry for the extra trouble, and thank you for accommodating us."

He starts to roll forward through the now open gate, but I stop him.

"Hang on a sec. I need to ask her something."

Owen backs up, and I lean over the console to look up at Jen. "Do you keep a record of who all comes in and out?"

"I keep track of visitors. Who they were coming to see and when they came and left. Residents usually just use their key card and go in the back gate."

"Could you tell us who visited Leno the day he died?"

"I'm not supposed to do that."

"Surely it's okay for you to tell Owen, right? I mean, since he's responsible for the condo."

"I'd really appreciate you doing that," he says. "If you could stretch that to include all guests, not just people who said they were here to see Leno, that would be even better."

Jen touches her hair. Flashes her dimples. "I guess I could. I'll start working on it right away."

"Thank you," Owen says. "You've been most helpful."

He drives through the gate and into the lot, while I drag my brain back up out of all the rabbit holes it's trying to scamper down, one of which involves making out with Owen in the car. After he parks, we both sit quietly for a minute, listening to the ticking sounds of the engine cooling, and the distant sound of well-known music.

"That's not the album, that's live. Spiro's not alone in there," Owen says.

"Do you think this will make our mission easier or harder?" I ask. "You know all the band people, right?"

"Not so well as you'd think." He opens his door. "We need to get up there before Lindy shows up."

Owen has a key card that gets us into the lobby, so there's no need to be buzzed in. A good thing because up close, the music is blaring, and it's pretty obvious Spiro wouldn't hear a door buzzer. I'm surprised the neighbors haven't been complaining, but maybe they are all excited by this brush with fame. There's a young couple down in the lobby, slow dancing to "Midnight Dreary."

Owen's jaw is tight and set, like he's in the middle of an arduous and unpleasant but necessary task. His expression looks like mine feels when I have to clean up cat vomit. Or person vomit, for that matter.

"You don't like your brother's music much, do you?" I shout as we climb the stairs.

"It's complicated," he says.

Or at least I think that's what he says. My lip-reading skills are not well developed. He could be saying "something is amputated" for all I can tell. Also, to be fair, this isn't entirely Leno's music. Spiro's clear, sharp vocals are winter ice where Leno's made me feel like a warm summer night.

The door is unlocked, and we walk right in.

It's been years since I've seen the guys, and they both look a little worse for wear. Sig's face is puffy, with bags and black circles under his eyes. Jax has put on a good fifty pounds, and I wonder whether the fact that he's shaved his trademark dreads is a fashion statement or whether he's compensating for hair loss.

Also, there are only three of them, and it's painfully obvious that something is missing. That something is large as life in the mural on the wall behind them.

"Dude!" Sig calls out when he sees Owen. "Long time no see! Grab an axe and join in!"

"I think we can all do without that," Owen says. "How long has it been, man?"

"Eons." Sig sets his guitar on a stand and comes over to give Owen an exuberant hug.

Jax, after carefully leaning his bass up against the amp, comes to join them. A flurry of back-slapping and enthusiastic greetings follows.

"Thanks for doing this," Owen says.

"Least we could do," Sig says. "Can't believe he's really gone."

"We sound like shit without him," Jax says.

"Maybe if we could focus and, you know, practice, we'd get better," Spiro barks. She hasn't moved from her place behind the drums. "I told that useless chick at the booth not to let anybody in."

"Since the apartment doesn't actually belong to you, your mandate didn't apply to me," Owen says.

I can feel the hostility arcing between them.

"We came to get some of Leno's things. Don't let us bother you. Carry on with your...practice." The tiny space he inserts before that last word is heavy with sarcasm.

Spiro glares at him.

"Addy, right?" Jax asks, turning to me. "You're the one

putting this party together, right? Thanks for hooking us up with this gig."

Sig is a hugger. He wraps his long arms around me and pulls me in close. He smells of pot and patchouli. "Yeah, thanks. Feels good to have a chance to do something for Leno. Always thought he'd go out in some fireball crash or something, you know?"

"Nobody is going to be playing anywhere until we clean up these tunes," Spiro says. "Again, from the top."

"Permission to speak up," Sig says, "but I'm not so sure you're the one who should carry vocals on this one."

"I suppose you want them?" Spiro's tone is cutting. "You're barely capable of carrying the harmonies."

"I was thinking Jax," Sig says mildly. "His vocals are the closest to Leno's, and this song needs that warmth."

"Last I checked, I'm leading this band," Spiro retorts. "Do we want to sit here and bicker all day? Maybe take a vote and pick a new leader? Or are we going to nail this song down?"

"If you'll excuse us," Owen says, moving through the room toward the hallway. "We'll just leave you to it."

"From the top." Spiro taps her sticks, setting the tempo, and then bass and guitar join in, and she starts to sing. Sig is right. Spiro's voice is too cold, too edgy, too not Leno.

I follow Owen down the short hallway and into the room on the right. He closes the door, which gives us a modicum of privacy but does nothing to take the edge off the volume. He sinks down onto the bare mattress of the queen-sized bed and drops his face into his hands. His shoulders are hunched. A spasm runs through him, and then another, and I hear the dry tearing sound of a grieving man unused to weeping.

For an instant, I stay where I am, frozen by uncertainty and not knowing what to do, but only for the space of a breath. I sit down beside him and rest my cheek on his shoulder, just being quiet and present while the wrongness of the music buffets us both.

"Sorry," he says into a space of relative silence, scrubbing at his face with both hands. "The absence of him from the music just slapped me upside the head there for a minute, you know?"

"I do," I say. "The room is also kinda sad."

"It's not like he lived here," Owen says. "Just for the last few weeks. But yeah. That, too."

Apart from the bed, which has been stripped down to the bare mattress, nobody—namely Spiro, I suppose—has bothered to tidy up the rest of the space. There's a laundry hamper, half full of jeans, T-shirts, and underwear. A glass carafe and water glass sit on the bedside table, both still half full. An array of pill bottles is neatly lined up on a dresser. The closet door is open. In addition to a jacket and a couple of sports coats on hangers, there's a black carry-on, a spare amp, and a huge, wheeled plastic crate overflowing with cords and other electronic equipment that I presume is for the guitars.

Muddy footprints on the carpet are a harsh reminder that it was raining on the night Leno died. Overall, the effect is dismal and lonely. I can't help thinking about him dying here alone, the phone in his hand. Who was he reaching out to?

"I guess we'd better get moving. That Lindy person will be here any minute," Owen says.

I'm already moving around the room, looking for clues. "If the phone is here, then it's somewhere it got tossed or fell or whatever while the paramedics were doing their thing."

"Wonder if he shut down his apartment in New York before

he came back here?" Owen muses. "Draco will know, I guess. That's a job I'm not looking forward to."

"Let's focus on this one first." I get down on my hands and knees and then flat on my belly to peer under the bed. "Don't suppose you've got a flashlight?"

"Doesn't everybody?"

"Obviously, *everybody* is not as put together as you are," I growl, but I don't mean it.

His comment doesn't feel like a putdown. He hands me a pocket-sized flashlight, and I press the on switch and scan beneath the bed. A lonely sock. A pair of underwear. A guitar pick. A whole lot of dust bunnies. "Nothing here."

Not bothering to get up, I crawl across the room to look under the dresser. I shine the light into the dark spaces, illuminating more dust bunnies and a spider. "Nothing here, either."

Owen doesn't answer. He's standing beside me, staring down at something on the top of the dresser, his entire body gone rigid and still. Scrambling to my feet, I stand beside him to see what's caught his attention.

It's a computer printout, half a page, with a signature in blue ink at the bottom.

Dearly beloved, we are gathered together.
   Goodbye cruel world.
   Ashes to ashes, dust to dust. Don't want to leave, but I reckon I must.

   Please forgive that bit of inane throat-clearing. I find it extremely difficult to say what I want to say, so I opted for the "just start somewhere" philosophy. Listen. Please don't be sad, not today. The world isn't cruel, not really, but the cancer was. Wherever I am now, I'm sure it's a better place and I'm happy to be free.

So, let's not mourn my dying. Face it—you are all secretly very grateful that it wasn't you. That you're still breathing the air and hearing the music and loving the fact that you still have time to eat and drink and be merry. Sorry, the old clichés are everywhere today, but maybe they stay with us for a reason.

Let go of the guilt and just embrace that truth—you're here, you're alive, and yes. You are having fun. Make sure to thank Addy Winters for throwing this fabulous bash.

Now—have another drink. Dance! Eat some good food.

With love, Leno

"I thought you hadn't agreed to throw the party when he died," Owen says.

"I hadn't. What if..." I hesitate, not sure whether what I'm thinking is something I should bring up with Owen. But I've underestimated him.

"What if somebody else wrote it?" he asks.

A cold thread of unease winds itself up my spine. Because if Leno's death was murder, there is somebody who had motive and means and all the time in the world to cover up the evidence—and that person is beating on the drums in the other room right this minute.

"Is that his signature?" I ask.

"It looks like his, but it's such a flamboyant scrawl it would be easy enough to forge, wouldn't it? By somebody who maybe signed for him sometimes, anyway. Like his business partner."

We've been half shouting in order to hear each other, and his voice echoes in a sudden pocket of quiet. I spin around as the door opens, and Spiro steps in.

"Something you wanted to say to me, Owen?" Spiro's eyes narrow into slits. Her right hand is fisted around both drumsticks, turning them into a club, and I'm aware of how powerfully she's built, how much rage lies contained beneath her edgy persona.

"Not particularly," he says coolly. "I do think Sig was right about the vocals on that song."

"Everybody's a critic," she says. "I thought I heard something about forging signatures."

"We just wondered if you might have helped Leno...die." Owen is carefully rolling up the sheet of paper, printed side in.

Spiro taps a rapid rhythm against her thigh with the sticks. "I didn't help him. I didn't kill him. I already told your little girlfriend that."

I press my shoulder into Owen, trying to convey that he needs to shut up, to go along, to placate her, and let us get out of here before she decides to use the drumsticks as a weapon. Vic would have understood, but if Owen gets the memo, he ignores it.

"Maybe Leno was getting in your way," he says. "Taking too long to die..."

Spiro paces two steps forward, the hand with the drumsticks half-raised.

Before I can scream for the guys in the other room to get their asses in here, pronto, Sig pokes his head in. "There's some influencer chick at the door. She says Owen and Addy wanted to meet her here."

"Tell her to go away," Spiro growls.

"Maybe not the best idea," I suggest. "It's Lindy Lind. You know, @FlatzandSharpz? She already threatened to unleash her trolls on me, and I can only imagine what they could do to you if she thinks you've dismissed her."

Spiro shifts the ferocious intensity of her gaze away from Owen and over to me. "You invited her here?"

"Figured you'd want to talk to her. She can really drum up some excitement for you and the band playing at the party. Or she could really do some damage. Your call."

"You're a manipulative little creature, aren't you?" Spiro says, but it sounds oddly more like respect than an insult. She lifts one bare, tattooed shoulder in a half-shrug. "Let her in, Sig. Let's give her an exclusive."

"Don't suppose you've seen Leno's phone anywhere, have you?" Owen asks before she can leave the room. "Seems he had it with him when he died. The first responders haven't seen it since."

She turns around and stalks back over to him, standing so close there's not room for a single sheet of paper to slide between them. Her head is tilted back so she can glare directly into his eyes. "If you insinuate one more time that I'm implicated in Leno's death, you will wish you hadn't. I swear that on my daddy's grave." For one long drawn moment, they stand there, gazes locked, breathing harshly.

"Hey, people," I say, pleased that my voice comes out casually without any evidence of my internal trembling. "This little thing between the two of you would make a great photo for Flatz and Sharpz. Should I tell her to come on in, or do you maybe want to wait until later to hash this out?"

It works. They suck in simultaneous deep breaths. Spiro takes a step back. "This isn't over, Owen. You don't get to throw around accusations like that and walk away clean." Then she turns and stomps out of the room.

A loud squeal marks her return to the living room. "OMG. It's Spiro in the living flesh. I am such a fan! You have no idea how long I've wanted to meet you. But I'm ahead of myself. You probably don't even know who I—"

"You are Lindy Lind," Spiro says. "Anybody who is anybody in music knows about Flatz and Sharpz. We're all super pumped you're here. Did you want a group photo? Maybe over here?"

"I was thinking right in front of that huge mural of Leno. Makes it like he's still part of everything, don't you think? I mean, without Leno, the band is just—"

"The Lonely. We know," Spiro says. "Look, we're all set up over here already, and it's a hassle to move the kit, so maybe—"

"Oh, but we don't really need the drums, do we? Just the three of you standing right over here. I mean, Spiro, you are already a legend. Hold the sticks, and everybody will know you're the drummer."

Owen laughs, low, gleeful, and malicious. "Sounds like Spiro has met her match. Let's go watch."

"Or we could just hide here. Lindy has forgotten about me. I'm off the hook."

"We don't want her to forget about you. This is about the party, too, remember? Not just Spiro."

I follow him back into the living room. Sig and Jax have already been herded over in front of the painting, instruments in hand. Spiro is stubbornly sitting behind the drums.

Lindy's got her blonde hair up in a high topknot. Her three-quarter sleeve, shapeless black sweater exposes one bare shoulder and an expanse of lacy black bra. Across the room, a pony-tailed guy with a camera hanging on a strap around his neck finishes setting up a couple of lights on stands.

"Ready whenever you are," he says, straightening up and looking to Lindy for direction.

"Maybe we could take pictures in both places?" I suggest. "One in front of the drums, one in front of the mural. In fact— maybe you could shoot a short video of the band playing for your TikTok?"

Lindy swivels around, hands on hips, eyebrows raised. "I'm not sure why you think you have an opinion?"

Spiro snorts, most likely in agreement.

I paste on a smile. "I'm Addison Winters. I'm arranging the—"

"I know who you are," Lindy says dismissively. "And I know you're obviously dying for some media exposure, but I hate to break it to ya; the band is bigger news than you. Genius move to get them to play the party, though, I'll give you that. Here. Tell you what." She comes to stand beside me. "Let's do a selfie for this one." She whips out a phone and snaps a shot of the two of us, not bothering to wait for me to smile. I'm pretty certain my eyes were closed, and my mouth was open.

And then she sees Owen. "You!" she squeals. "Here, really? You're Owen, right?" Her voice goes all soft and croony as if he's an adorable puppy and her heart isn't made of granite. "Oh my God. I'd be so honored if we could take a photo together."

She flits over to stand beside him, clinging to his arm, head nestled against his shoulder. "Run video," she directs the photographer. "Use your phone. Make it look spontaneous."

Owen stands like one of those guards at Buckingham Palace, expressionless and stiff.

"You'll never guess where I am and who I'm with!" Lindy turns herself so she's mostly facing the camera, but without letting go of her victim. "This is Owen Masterson! Leno's big brother. And I'm here to tell you that this man has secrets! Tell me in the comments if you already knew that—".

"Enough!" Owen jerks away from her with enough force that she loses her balance and very nearly falls.

On reflex, I stick out a foot to trip her, but I'm too far away and she recovers her balance and pouts, prettily.

"Don't be like that, Owen."

Owen wipes lipstick off his cheek. "For the record, I do not give my permission for any of this footage to go on your feeds."

"But it will be so awesome for you," she purrs. "When I share that you—"

"Don't do it. I'm warning you."

"And what are you going to do about it?" Laughter bubbles up out of her. "You invited us here, or at least your little girl-friend did, to get material for the party. And now here we are, and anything is fair game, isn't it?"

"No, anything is not fair game. You're here for the band. And to buzz up the party. Talk about Leno all you want. But do not talk about me. Delete that, would you?" he asks the camera guy.

"Sorry, man, I don't call the shots," the guy says.

Owen looks equal parts furious and sick to his stomach. For a minute, my curiosity and my better self fight a pitched battle. Whatever it is that Lindy knows, I want to know it, too. But the good angel wins out. I wouldn't want my own life splattered all over Lindy's feed, and I've kind of dragged Owen into this mess.

"Hey, Lindy!" I snap my fingers. "Over here." She turns her head in my direction.

The camera guy points the phone at me.

"The band is setting up a donation fund for kids with cancer, right, Jax? Do you want to tell her about that?"

Jax blinks at me, and I'm afraid my attempt at deflection is going to fall flat. But then he grins and turns mega-watt charm on Lindy. "That's right, we are. It was Spiro's idea, of course, she's cool like that. Since we're doing a tribute concert for Leno, we'll be making some commemorative Leno and the Lonely T-shirts special for the occasion. Follow us on TikTok and Insta to get the deets, or you know, do the boring thing and hit the website. When you buy a shirt, all proceeds go to St. Jude's."

"Only on the day of the concert," I chime in because, obviously, no such shirt exists yet, and we need time to put this together. "Check out lenoandthelonely.com on Sunday morning."

"That's amazing!" Lindy actually hops up and down.

I bet she was a cheerleader in high school. Also a mean girl. But whatever.

"Can I have a T-shirt? Will you all sign it for me? I mean, it would have been even better if Leno could have signed it, but still!"

"I'm sure Addy will hook you up," Spiro says. If looks could kill, I would be deader than Leno about now.

I ignore her, beaming at Lindy. "Of course! When you talk about it, make sure to let your followers know it's day-of-the-party only and only available through the website. So, let them know it's coming; let them know we'll be dropping the buy link on Sunday. A one-day special commemorative T-shirt of the Leno and the Lonely tribute."

Right then, I remember that Britt and I are not in a good place and that I can't possibly pull this off without her. I was already in over my head, and now look what I've gone and done. But I'll have to worry about that later because right now, I need to get Owen and his secrets safely out of here.

I grab his hand and tow him toward the door. "You all have fun with the photos! Owen and I have got so much to do getting ready for this party, so we are out of here!"

Lindy makes a move to follow us, but right then, Spiro, who has probably had enough of the attention being directed at people other than her, starts a rhythm on the snare, adds in the kickdrum, and conversation is no longer possible. Lindy turns back toward the band, and we are out the door, running down the stairs and out to the car.

"Thank you," Owen wheezes once we're safely ensconced in the car with the doors locked and the engine running. Both of us are out of breath, due to running like the hounds of hell were after us. "Anybody ever tell you that you're a brilliant manager of people?"

I grin. "A manipulative little bitch, you mean? That I may have heard before. Brilliant? Not so much. I have no idea how we are going to pull off this T-shirt thing."

He starts laughing, and I join him, the two of us feeding off of each other's gasps and snorts until we're out of breath. And then the mood between us shifts. My heart, which had just begun to settle down to normal, speeds up again as the laughter in his eyes is replaced by a slow-burning smolder.

If I make a move right now, even a small one—turn to him, glance at his lips, lean toward him, return that gaze—I'm pretty sure he'll kiss me.

But.

It takes a good manipulator to recognize another one.

What is he hiding? What secret does Lindy know? I fell for Alex and look where that got me.

"Spiro and Lindy deserve each other. Where to next?" I turn my head away to look straight out the windshield.

Owen starts the engine. "First, we get the visitor list from your friend at the gate—"

"She's not my friend."

"Figure of speech. I'm not the most observant man on the face of the planet, but I had actually picked up on that. Then, if you wouldn't mind, I'd like you to come up to the house and look at some files on Leno's laptop."

"We could take the laptop somewhere else," I suggest. "You could meet me at *Grounded,* maybe."

"Don't tell me you're scared of my mother?"

"I'm scared of your mother. Also, I've had a police warning to stay away."

"From your boyfriend detective?"

"He's not my boyfriend."

"Are you sure? Because he has a way of looking at you."

"I'm sure. Trust me. I'm the one who ended it."

"Good," he says, in a tone that makes me rethink my earlier decision about that kiss, but the moment has passed.

When we drive up to the gate, Jen holds out a folded piece of paper. "Your list."

"You are fabulous," Owen says.

Jen gives him a dazed sort of smile and the gate opens. Owen drives through while I unfold the paper and read the notes.

"You going to share that with me?"

"Draco stopped by. And...so did your mother. That's it."

Owen grimaces.

"Forgive me even asking this, but any chance your mother might have...helped him?"

"Are you kidding? She objected to him even going into hospice. Wanted him to get more second opinions, try another medication, another round of chemo. She thought he hung the moon and stars. Absolutely no way."

He's quiet for a breath or two and then says, "There's something I need to do. I know it's a big ask, but will you come with me? I don't want to do this alone."

CHAPTER 22

"You don't have to do this," Owen says. "You can just wait here, if you'd rather."

We sit in silence, staring at the low brick building and the sign that reads Ever After Funeral Parlor and Crematorium. The building wants to look like a church, but the smokestack does away with any comforting lies the rest of the building might try to tell. A few manicured shrubs and carefully regimented flower beds, nothing too bright or too cheerful, are set into a green lawn where a dandelion would never dare to show its perky yellow head.

"They should have a sunflower patch," I say, shivering. "Something a little more cheerful, don't you think? It's all so, I don't know, sterile and conservative and foreboding all at the same time."

"I can see why Leno chose you to throw this party."

"We were friends, you know. Once. A long time ago. So, he maybe thought he knew me still."

Owen's gray eyes search my face, and I turn back to the window to hide what I'm feeling. "Let me guess," he says, with a trace of bitterness. "You were friends and then he got famous and dropped you?"

"Something like that."

"Well, he was an idiot."

Speaking of being an idiot, how could my younger and stupider self have ever thought Owen was less interesting than Leno?

Owen opens his door. "I'm going in. You do not have to come in if you'd rather stay here."

I'm not crazy about the idea of viewing Leno's body, but at this point, I'm prepared to go anywhere with Owen, and I follow. He reaches for my hand, and we walk up to the building in silence, fingers intertwined.

I've never set foot in this place. I didn't come to "view" Geneva's body, and I've certainly never viewed anybody else's. All of the funerals I've attended have been held in a church. I'm not sure what I was expecting, but it's not this overly pleasant waiting room, tastefully decorated with green plants and a basket of cut flowers. Two small sofas and a couple of armchairs are placed at the perfect distance from each other to allow either privacy or intimacy, depending on the occupants. There's a fountain in the corner. The peaceful sound of falling water overlays the background Muzak coming from invisible speakers.

A picture on the wall behind one of the sofas is of a white-robed angel with his arm around the shoulders of a woman standing by a grave, her head bowed in grief. And the magazines on a wooden coffee table have images of coffins, urns, and tombstones on the covers. The fountain makes me need to pee, the supposedly soothing music makes me want to scream, and I am not going to sit in one of those chairs and consider all of the different containers Leno's remains could be concealed in.

"Rather ghoulish, isn't it?" Owen murmurs, bending to pick up a brochure advertising coffins.

Speaking of ghoulish, a door down the hallway opens, and Ricky Hamilton appears.

"Addy!" His face lights up like I'm absolutely the best surprise of the century.

"Hey, Ricky." I smile and summon all of the warmth I can manage, which is admittedly not a lot.

Ricky has always been totally inoffensive, and there's no logical reason whatsoever why, every time I'm in his vicinity, I want to be elsewhere. He's of average height and average weight and has an average, trustworthy sort of face, with regular features, wide blue eyes, and a scattering of freckles.

But interactions with him always leave me feeling like something is missing, some understanding of boundaries and human interaction, something off about his emotional responses. Even now, it feels like he's standing too close, even though my eyes tell me he's at an appropriate distance.

"If you're here for Geneva's belongings, your mother already has them."

"Right, of course." I glance at Owen, who looks a little woozy, and add, "We're actually here to...um...say goodbye to Leno Masterson."

"You too? We should have had a guestbook for this guy!" Ricky looks pleased and proud, as if *Forever After* has scored major death points by attracting so many visitors to view a body.

His smile dims, and he says, "He's not dressed for visitors. Cremation is scheduled for later this evening, and we've prepared him for that already."

"We weren't planning on chatting over a cup of coffee," I say before my mouth gets the memo to keep itself shut. "Also, this is Owen Masterson. Leno's brother."

"I'm so sorry for your loss," Ricky says, schooling his face into an expression of professionally restrained grief. "If you'd like to wait a few minutes, I can make him more presentable."

"That's not necessary," Owen says. "We can just see him as he is. But I'm confused. My mother has chosen a coffin, I believe. We weren't planning on cremation."

"Oh, dear," Ricky says. "My goodness. Mrs. Masterson and Mr. Dawlish were in earlier and explicitly requested a change to cremation. Apparently, your brother was very clear about his wishes in his will?"

"You said a lot of people have been here. Can you tell me who, besides my mother and Leno's lawyer?" Owen's voice is calm, but his hand tightens around mine.

"Sure thing," Ricky says. "No confidentiality laws to visiting the deceased. Let me think. Bunch of our old classmates, Addy. Millie and Jen came by. Glen was here...and Kevin. And some woman I don't know... Didn't give her name."

"What did she look like?"

"Tall. Long black hair and tattoos. Not very friendly."

A thought occurs to me and I ask, "Lisa didn't come by?"

"No, haven't seen her. Given their kid and all, you'd think she might have, but no."

"You know about Jackson?"

Ricky looks confused. "I thought everybody did. Been a

long time though; I suppose they haven't kept in touch much except maybe to arrange child support or whatever."

"Clearly, I need to get out more," I mutter, but Rick is already moving.

"This way," he says. "Sad, Leno dying so young, but at least he took his own way out, right? Which reminds me. Almost forgot that Alex was here in his detective capacity, which was weird because it was medically assisted suicide, right? I don't understand why everybody doesn't take the quick and easy way out."

"Some of us kind of like living, Rickster."

"Oh, naturally. I meant people who are going to die anyway. If you're really old, or you've got cancer, say, or some other thing that you know is going to kill you slowly and painfully. People are scared of death, that's why. If they weren't, people would be helping themselves out all over the place."

A chill creeps up and down my spine, even though the building is warm. It's not the words so much but the way he delivers them, with that big sunshine smile of his and way too much enthusiasm for the subject, as if he's talking about cute kittens and puppies or arguing for the existence of unicorns.

As he talks, we follow him down an ordinary, white-painted hallway with industrial beige carpet. He opens a door to a small, windowless room, empty except for a couple of chairs along one wall. "Wait here. I'll go get him for you."

We wait in a heavy silence, me sitting in one of the chairs, tapping my foot, Owen pacing. We hear the sound of wheels in the hallway. Then the door opens, and Ricky rolls in a stretcher with a clean white sheet draped over an unmistakable shape.

I feel like I'm floating as I get up and cross the room, my feet not touching the floor.

Rick folds back the sheet, revealing Leno's face. His skin is a grayish-blue color. His bones are sharp and far too well-defined beneath it.

"If we could maybe be alone?" Owen says.

Leno looks cold. He should be wearing a sweater. Maybe a down jacket and gloves and warm winter boots. I shiver in sympathy. But what strikes me most is how overwhelmingly alone his body is without a soul in it. Cast off. Abandoned. Which seems unfair, after all it has done, all it has suffered.

"Take as long as you need," Rick says, stepping out into the hallway and closing the door behind him.

"If you want to be alone with him, I can wait outside," I offer.

"Stay." Owen glances up at me, then back down at his brother. "Please."

And so, I do. Time stretches out like a vast, empty desert, although in reality, it's probably only a couple of minutes before Owen clears his throat, leans over Leno, and says, in a low voice, "I forgive you."

He straightens, wipes his hand across his mouth once and again, then lets out a sigh so long and deep I figure he must have been holding his breath. "Ready?" he asks.

I was ready to leave before I ever walked in, and I beat him out into the hallway. Rick is nowhere to be seen, and I don't bother looking for him. Owen walks as fast as I do, both of us racing toward the great outdoors, where there is sunlight and fresh air and no dead body.

"You were right about the sunflowers," Owen says. He

looks drained and pale, and I want to put my arms around him and comfort him. I want to ask what it was Leno did that required forgiveness.

Instead, I say, "He's not in there, you know. With his body. He's moved on to the next dimension, or he's hanging around right now watching us."

"In that case." Owen holds up both hands, curls them into fists, and then releases the middle fingers. "Fuck you, little brother!" he shouts.

"Didn't you just say you forgave him?" I ask.

He laughs, ragged and sharp. "Forgiveness is a process, right?"

He's got a point. I think about Dad, wondering if I'll ever entirely forgive him for his many transgressions.

My phone rings. It's Vic.

"Addy. About this party."

My heart knifes sideways. "You can't bail on me, Vic. I know I pissed you off, but—"

"Who said anything about bailing? I just think it's time to up our game. Can we meet?"

I glance at Owen, remembering we need to swing by his place for Leno's laptop. "Half an hour? *Grounded*?"

"There are two reporters and a bunch of fans at *The Raven*. How many do you think are at *Grounded*? I vote for your place."

I consider this. The cramped space. The mess I left it in when I ran out the door this morning. The distinct lack of coffee and food. My stomach feels hollow, and I realize that it's late afternoon and I haven't eaten anything yet.

"I would kill for a macchiato right about now. And food. Besides, it's good to feed the media machine, right? We'll just give them an update, buy them a coffee, and they'll go away happy."

"Oh, fine. I'll be there. And I'm bringing Britt."

"Vic, do you really think..."

But he's already hung up, and I'm talking to myself.

CHAPTER 23

"You look great," Kathy says, assessing me as she rings up my macchiato and Owen's coffee, along with an Americano for Vic and tea for Britt. "I heard Lisa totally massacred your hair, and I was worried for you. That's what I get for listening to gossip. Short is cute on you."

"Between you and me, the gossip was accurate. Owen fixed me up after."

"You?" Kathy eyes him with new interest. "You don't look the hairdresser type."

"What exactly does a hairdresser type look like?" he asks. "I'm a man of many talents."

"Don't doubt that for a minute," she says. "Let me get your drinks, and I'll bring the food over when it's ready. Been busy in here."

"That would be great, Kath. Much appreciated."

I survey the patrons while we wait. Mostly locals, all checking out my hair and Owen with equal parts curiosity. But there are people here who don't belong. A guy in a suit, a keen-eyed woman watching us over the top of a newspaper, and a group of seven thirty-somethings in Leno and the Lonely T-shirts, all crammed around a four-top.

Our table in the back is the only one empty, which is fine by me. "Watch out, it rocks," I tell Owen, holding my macchiato and Vic's coffee aloft as I settle into a chair.

Owen follows my lead, doing the same with his coffee and Britt's tea. "You should ask them to fix this."

"Are you kidding? This is our confab table. Nobody else wants it, thanks to that wobble. Back of the room, under the speakers and the fan. Best place to talk when you don't want everybody listening in."

"A valid point. Remind me to never underestimate you." He leans down to unzip the worn leather briefcase he stopped to retrieve from his mother's house before we came here and withdraws a MacBook, setting it on the table while I steady all of the drinks.

"I had a quick look through the computer earlier, and I think you'll find this of interest."

He enters a password, then clicks open a file folder labeled "Goodbye Party," and a list comes up in a Word doc, each item complete with a clickable hyperlink:

Proposed Schedule

Ideas for Activities

People to Invite

My Last Goodbye

Notes for Addy

"Might as well start with the notes he left for you," Owen says, sliding the laptop over to me.

I connect the computer to *Grounded's* Wi-Fi, then click on

the item labeled "Notes for Addy." A Google Docs page opens up. The first page is a clear message in bolded, over-sized all caps: OWEN DON'T READ THIS. FOR ADDY'S EYES ONLY. YOU'LL SPOIL THE SURPRISE.

"That sounds ominous." Owen reaches over and starts scrolling, but I grab his hand and yank it off the trackpad.

"You're not supposed to read this." I drag the laptop over to my side of the table, well away from him, and start scrolling.

"Let me guess," Owen says. "You're supposed to talk me into singing with the band. Or ambush me with an invitation to come on up to the microphone at the party."

"You're psychic," I say, even though he's actually way off track.

"I knew my brother," Owen mutters tightly. "But he obviously never knew me at all. I am not going to sing at this party."

Owen didn't know Leno as well as he thinks he did but I decide to keep that bit of intel to myself for now. I close the "Notes for Addy" file, and click open "Last Goodbye."

I read the document once. Then I read it again.

"What is it?" Owen asks. "You look like you've seen a ghost."

"Do you still have that suicide note?"

He lowers his cup to the table. "This is going to be bad, isn't it?"

"This is going to be evidence, I think."

He bends down and withdraws a piece of paper from the briefcase, still carefully rolled into a tube.

"Try not to touch it. I meant it about evidence. Actually, hang on. Kathy can give us some gloves." I get up, carrying my drink with me and sucking up a fortifying mouthful as I walk.

Kathy's eyebrows go up at my request, but she reaches down under the counter and hands me a pair of disposable blue gloves.

"Whatever this is, you are going to tell me all about it," she says.

"Of course! Very soon."

I carry the gloves back to Owen. He puts them on and then unrolls the paper like it's an ancient scroll that might disintegrate if handled roughly. I set our cups on the floor so there's no chance of upset and then the two of us start comparing the words on the page to the words on the laptop screen.

"What are you two so focused on?" Vic's voice asks, startling me out of my concentration. He lowers himself into a chair across from us, setting a tray of pastries carefully on the table and grinning at me. "Sorry about last night, Addles. You were right. A little. Maybe."

Britt, who has come in with him, stays on her feet, as if uncertain of her welcome. I feel the fracture between us like a physical pain.

"You might have been right, too, maybe just a little," I tell Vic.

"Genetics," he says. "What are you going to do? Sit down, Britt, you're making me nervous."

Britt still doesn't sit. "I heard about Lisa," she says. "You look good, though. Really. Not butchered at all."

"Thanks to Owen. Britt, I'm so sorry—"

"Me too. I should have told you, and I can totally see why you'd think I knew something. I don't, though. And it wasn't my ring."

"I know."

I hate the way we're both acting like we're strangers, as if the secret she kept and the accusation I made have undone all of the years of closeness between us. I want to throw my arms around her, maybe fling myself at her feet and grovel, but that wouldn't fix the fact that she hurt me, too.

Then, because I know Britt and I know myself and because Vic is back, I take a different tack entirely. I give us all a gift and pretend that everything is normal.

"We have discovered something of interest. Sit down, and I'll tell you. I got you tea."

She settles into a chair, accepting the cup I pick up from the floor and sipping as she takes in the gloves, the paper on the table, and the open laptop. "What is all this?"

"This is the supposed suicide note Leno left. And here on his laptop is an identical version in a Google doc, along with his instructions to read it aloud at his party."

Owen turns the printout around so they can read, and I turn the laptop so they can see the screen. "We've probably already ruined any fingerprint evidence, but don't touch it anyway," I say.

"Thus the gloves," Vic says.

They lean their heads together, both sets of eyes going from the paper to the screen and back again.

"Could somebody have forged that signature?" Vic asks, after a moment of silence.

Owen draws the document back toward himself and gives it another long look. "Pretty sure it wouldn't be the first time Spiro signed something on his behalf. Of course, it's possible he printed it off and signed it himself, but Leno would never have wasted something he intended for his public on close family and friends."

Vic considers for a minute. "Never thought I'd say this, but I think we need to call Alex."

"Are they doing an autopsy?" Britt asks.

"Nope. And he's set for cremation tonight."

"Can you stop that, Owen?" Vic asks.

"That's all up to Mother," Owen says. "And therefore, unlikely."

I think about Sylvie warning me to leave the funeral up to her. *Details of the funeral have already been arranged. Everything is already in order.* That didn't sound at all like a woman about to honor her son's last wishes. And Sylvie is not the sort of woman to lightly change her mind.

"You think she'd object to an autopsy?" I ask Owen. "I mean, if you told her our concerns would she agree?"

"You've met her. What do you think?" he retorts.

Vic swirls his cup and sips meditatively as if it contains a finely aged brew. "Look, like it or not, the detective on the case is Alex, who we all know is not the sharpest knife in the drawer—"

"And who has a chip on his shoulder because of Addy," Britt says.

"Still. If Owen doesn't have the authority to make an autopsy happen, then we need law enforcement to get a warrant."

"Let's go over everything we know before we talk to Alex," I suggest. "Get our ducks in a row so we can make a convincing enough case for him to at least ask for a hold on the cremation. If we don't stop that, any physical evidence on Leno's body is going to go up in flames. Oh, God, I'm sorry Owen."

Owen's face has gone dead white. He sets down his cup

and presses the back of his hand against his mouth while he takes a long, quavery breath. "It's just...I know Leno chose cremation, but the thought of the burning is so..."

"Ghastly," Britt offers. "Cremation makes total sense but it still gives me the shivers. Listen, I have an idea. How about we call Julie? She's smarter than Alex. And she needs less evidence. All the coroner needs to do is change the ruling on his death to suspicious. Then she can call for an inquest and order a hold on the cremation and ask for an autopsy."

Vic taps the screen on his phone exactly twice, and it starts to ring. Julie's voice answers almost immediately. Interesting that he has her programmed into his contacts. Yet another thing I didn't know about my brother.

"Vic! It's been a while," Julie's voice says, tinny through the phone. "We should grab a drink one of these days."

"We should! You haven't been by *The Raven* in weeks."

Britt's brows draw together in a frown, and Vic turns away from us slightly, pressing the phone closer to his ear, as if that will keep us from hearing the other side of the conversation. "Hang on. I'm stepping outside." He shoves back his chair and heads for the exit.

We wait for him in an uneasy silence. Owen's brow is furrowed, his jaw tight. He keeps drumming his fingers on the tabletop, catching himself, and then starting up again. Britt gazes off into the distance, her right leg jiggling up and down and rocking the table, and I know her brain is zipping along at a gazillion thoughts a minute.

When Vic comes back, his face is flushed and he avoids my eyes.

"Well?" I ask.

"On the theme of ways I'm like Dad," he says. "Apparently, Julie doesn't appreciate being manipulated. However, she did say she would change her ruling and open an investigation."

I reach across the table and pat his arm. "Nobody has beat you up lately for sleeping with their wife, at least. Could be worse."

Before he can snipe back, I rummage in my bag for the college-ruled notebook and pen I always carry with me. You never know when you're going to have to take notes, and I want them where I can cross things out and add little details and corrections, which means pen and paper and not the computer or my phone.

"Okay, who are our suspects, and what are their motives?"

I write Spiro's name right at the top and put a big star next to it. "My money's on Spiro. Financial reasons. Jealousy."

"The Ice Queen," Britt says, and then remembers Owen. "Sylvie Masterson, I mean. Sorry, Owen."

"We can't add somebody to the list just because you don't like her," Vic objects.

"You don't think a mother might want to ease her son if he's in pain?" Britt persists. "I'm not saying she murdered him out of some sort of malice. Maybe she just couldn't stand to see him suffer. I mean, she didn't know he was planning to invoke the Death with Dignity Act, right?"

"She *said* she didn't know," I add, with an apologetic glance at Owen. "We don't know that she didn't know. And it is weird that she's suddenly decided that she wants him cremated."

"Alternately," Vic says, not looking at anybody, "there might be some family financial issues and she needed the money now, not later. To pay off some debts, maybe."

"I'd ask how you know about that," Owen says, "but I'm guessing Spiro. Like I told Addy, Leno was Mother's golden boy. She would never have helped him die. Still, if you're considering her, you should add Draco to your list. Any motive Mother has, he shares, possibly even the bit about ending Leno's suffering. I suppose it's possible that Mother might try to cover for Draco. He wouldn't be much use to her in prison."

He rolls up the letter as he speaks, tucking it back into the briefcase before stripping off the gloves.

I add both Sylvie and Draco to my suspect list.

"Maybe you also have some financial concerns, Owen," Vic says.

"Maybe I do," Owen replies quietly, directly meeting Vic's challenging gaze. "Did you want to add me to the list, too?"

"My money is still on Spiro," I say. I don't add Owen to the list—not because I'm sure he didn't do it, but because it feels insensitive with him sitting right there, watching me. "We should also consider Lisa."

"Not adding people because we don't like them," Vic says.

There's something bothering him that goes beyond whatever Julie said to him. He keeps shifting restlessly in his chair, darting glances at the door.

"Lisa had a secret love child with Leno," I say. "And she was pretty pissed about the media linking him and me together. So, this isn't just about payback."

"She's also a mean girl in general and was probably having sex with Leno at the same time I was." Britt gives me a sad smile and a half-shrug.

"Motive isn't enough," Vic says. "Did she have opportunity? Besides Spiro, who had access? We should find out who all visited Leno the day he died."

"Draco and Sylvie," I say. "We got Jen to tell us who had been in."

"So, Lisa didn't have opportunity," Vic says. "As for means, we're pretty short on any kind of actual evidence."

I strip the class ring off my finger and drop it in the middle of the table. "There's also this. Whoever it belonged to has been in his car recently. I would guess another old girlfriend, given the engraving."

"Let me see that." Vic picks up the ring and holds it up to the light. I know what he's seeing. Two hearts. The initials LM + AR.

"Who was in our grade whose name starts with A?" I ask. "I can't think of anybody, but we can pull out the yearbook. Okay, let's organize this a little. I'm making columns. All of our suspects, plus motive, means, and opportunity."

"We can't do means when we don't know how he died," Vic objects.

"Wasn't it a morphine overdose?" Britt asks.

"We don't know that," Vic says. "Not without an autopsy. It's assumed that's how he died because of the empty bottle. But we don't know for sure. And—this is important. If it was a morphine overdose, then he did it himself. It's not possible to force somebody to swallow that many pills."

"Point," I say. "We'll go with motive and opportunity for now. Anybody who had access to the condo, especially if they were there the day he died, has opportunity. Here we go. Names first."

I jot them down in column one, labeled **Suspects**:

Spiro
Sylvie Masterson (unlikely)

301

Draco
Lisa (sadly unlikely)
AR (?? Who the heck is this?)

"Anybody else?" I glance up at all of the faces around the table.

Britt is reading upside down from across the table. Owen is gazing off into the distance. And Vic isn't paying attention at all. He's turned sideways in his chair and is now openly watching the door the way Bruno watches me when I get out the bag of treats.

Then the door opens and Alex walks in, and Vic's behavior makes perfect sense.

"Victor Aloysius Winters," I snap. "What did you do?"

He lifts his chin defiantly and stares me down. "I wanted you to stay out of this, Addy. But no. You do what you want without caring about your own safety or any of the rest of us—"

"That's not fair! I can't believe you'd set me up like this!"

Alex saunters over to stand beside me, smirking insufferably.

"Go away," I say.

He drags a chair over and sits, resting his elbows on the tabletop, which rocks wildly. We all grab our drinks. "No can do. I've been informed there is actual evidence indicating that Leno Masterson may have been murdered. The coroner has changed her ruling and called for an inquest. We can talk here, or you can come down to the station and tell me all about it there."

I ignore him, completely focused on my twin and his latest betrayal. "I said we'd call him later."

"I decided to call him now."

"He was worried you were in danger," Owen says. "Am I right, Victor?"

"Of course I'm worried! Spiro told us about your father's business practices and his...associates. Then your brother maybe gets whacked, and somebody tries to run you and Addy off the road. The guy with the money was already dead. The one who stands to inherit needs to go next, and then—"

"And then there's nobody left to pay them what's owed," Owen says evenly. "I would never put Addy in danger."

"You don't need to. She's plenty good at doing that herself."

"Vic, stop it!"

"If I might?" Alex sets his own notebook on the table and opens it to a fresh page. "Somebody should fix that," he says, as we all protect our drinks and reach to steady the table. "Perhaps we could backtrack to this alleged murder and you could all tell me what you think you know?"

"If we must," I grumble. "We've made a list of suspects and any motives and evidence for each of them." I pick up the pen and add "Owen's nefarious business associates" to the bottom of column one, then hand it over to Alex.

"I don't suppose you have anything other than conjecture?"

"For starters, the suicide letter isn't a suicide letter."

"Oh, come on, Addy," Alex says. "I saw it. It was signed and everything. Right by the bedside of a man who had completed Death with Dignity paperwork."

Owen slides the laptop over to Alex. "What you saw in Leno's room is a printout of this. If you read the notes in my brother's party plans, you'll see that he wanted it read at his send-off party."

"So, you think somebody faked his signature?" Alex asks.

"Not that hard to do," I say.

"Where's the suicide note now?" Alex demands. "Why do I think it's no longer in his bedroom?"

Owen hands it over.

"Too bad your fingerprints are smeared all over all of this evidence."

"Too bad nobody decided to call it evidence until right this minute," I retort. "Too bad the morphine bottle found by the body didn't get fingerprinted before it was discarded or tested to see if it had anything other than morphine in it. I did try to tell you, Alex."

"If you would pass me that briefcase?" he says to Owen, ignoring me. "I'll take that and the laptop. We'll have the forensics people go through all of this. I'll also take his phone."

"We don't have the phone." I glare at Vic, the traitor, as Leno's computer slips beyond my reach. "Another piece of evidence that should have been collected at what is now, belatedly, a crime scene."

"Could have gone with him in the ambulance and gotten lost along the way. Given that nobody considered the possibility of foul play," Vic offers.

"Or Spiro knew it was evidence and got rid of it," I counter. "Speaking of Spiro—"

"I'd like to hear about your role in the Masterson family business," Alex interrupts, focusing in on Owen. "I'll want the company records going back to before your father died."

"It's good to want things," Owen says.

"It's also good to cooperate with the law."

"The law I will cooperate with. You, on the other hand, can kiss my ass," Owen says.

"I can get a subpoena."

"You do that."

I drop my face in my hands. This is, predictably, not going well. How could it? I am going to kill Victor with my bare hands.

"Who made the 9-1-1 call?" Britt asks, out of the blue. "It wasn't Leno, obviously, or you would have investigated sooner."

Alex squares his shoulders and tries to look threatening. "Let me tell you how this works. I'm investigating. I ask questions. You tell me what you know. I will not be sharing any evidence with you."

"We already know it was an anonymous woman," I volunteer.

"That doesn't get Draco or Owen off the hook," Britt says. "Sorry, Owen. Could have been a female accomplice. Or just a woman who found the body but didn't want to be involved. Our mysterious AR, even."

Alex clears his throat. "Who is AR?"

"You need a drink?" Britt asks. "I recommend tea and honey for that."

"What I want—"

"Is evidence. Right. Of course." I smile at him. "Just to make sure we don't forget anything, I'm going to go through it all in an organized way for you, okay? Let's start with Spiro."

"Fine." He practically spits out the word, but he does write down Spiro in his notebook. "Last name? And who is she?"

"God, really?" I exclaim. "You don't know who Spiro is?"

"Hottest female drummer ever," Britt enthuses. "And it's just Spiro. Like—Beyoncé or Lizzo. She doesn't need a surname."

"All of those are stage names. What's her name, really?"

"Legally, I think you'll find that it's really Spiro," Owen supplies. "But I believe she was born Elizabeth Jane Smith. Her parents are still in Seattle, but I have no idea how to contact them."

"And you think Spiro might have killed Leno? Why?" Alex asks. "I don't see what she would stand to gain from his death."

"Tell him," I say to Owen, who stares back at me blankly.

"Which thing?"

"The grab at fame thing."

"I wondered about that," Vic says. "I saw that interview."

Alex clears his throat and taps his pen on the table.

"Spiro has always been fame-hungry," Owen explains. "Now that Leno is no longer the front man, she wants to move more into the spotlight. She was already his business partner. And if Leno didn't sign that suicide note himself, my money is on her as somebody who knows how to forge his signature."

"We got the list of who all went in and out through the gate that day, and Spiro could have been there, depending, of course, on how he was killed and what time he actually died." I pull the list Jen gave us from my bag and spread it out on the table. "Spiro left at 4 pm. Draco Dawlish, Leno's lawyer, came in at 5 pm and left at 6 pm. Sylvie Masterson came in at 6:25 and left around 7:30. Spiro came back in at 8:05 pm, went out again around 9 pm, and then didn't come back until after somebody called and the body was taken away."

"She was the last one to see him alive then," Owen says.

"Because I'm going to assume that if my mother had found him dead, she would have called and it wouldn't have been anonymous."

"Another thing," Vic says, in his thinking voice. "Spiro knew Addy and Owen were coming up to the condo the night that someone tried to run them off at Suicide Corner. She could have made a call, gotten somebody to try to kill them."

Alex lays down his pen and glances around at all of us condescendingly. "You do realize that every bit of this is conjecture and there is no evidence whatsoever? Even the motive is thin, given that Leno was dying anyway."

There is more to Spiro's motive, but I'm not ready to talk about it yet. Owen deserves to hear it first. "So, you're not even going to look into her?" I ask.

"I will talk to her," Alex says. "And I will subpoena those Masterson business records. Anybody else on your little list of people who came and went from the condo that day besides Draco Dawlish and Sylvie Masterson? People who could be actual suspects?"

"Both of them have motive," I say.

"Mr. Dawlish is a respected attorney who has practiced law here in Fox Valley for twenty years," Alex says. "I hardly think—"

"We're looking at motive and evidence. Anybody can be a murderer given the right motivation and set of circumstances," Vic cuts him off. "Although, if he'd killed Leno, I suppose Owen is right. Sylvie Masterson would have found him and called it in."

"Unless she was in on it," Britt mutters. "Or covering for him."

Vic rolls his eyes. "Pretty sure Leno's mother didn't kill her

KERRY SCHAFER & KERRY ANNE KING

already-dying son for his money. Whatever financial motivations the Masterson family has could also apply to Draco, who
was involved in the business before Owen took over, I'd guess."

Alex is actually jotting down some notes. I guess it's not a
big surprise that he would like to solve this case. But I want to
be sure he actually does due diligence and gets the right
person.

"Let's not forget Lisa," Britt says.

"Lisa, who?" Alex asks.

"Lisa, the owner of *Foxy Lady*, who had a secret love child
with Leno," Britt says. "Also, she tried to scalp Addy this morning, apparently because of jealousy."

"So that's what happened to your hair," Alex says. "Is that
everything?" He glares at me, as if I'm responsible for all of
this.

"Well, there are also the bad business associates of Owen's
father who could have been sending a message or trying to get
paid." I grin at him cheekily. "And AR."

Vic hands Alex the ring. "Addy found this in Owen's car.
Check the engraving."

"More compromised evidence," Alex says, frowning, as he
inspects the ring. "With any possible fingerprints obliterated
by all of you." He slams his notebook shut and gets to his feet.

"Don't forget the faked suicide note," I remind him. "And
we need the laptop back ASAP. Leno left notes in there for his
send-off party."

"It will be returned to his next of kin, which I'm guessing is his
mother, as soon as forensics is done with it. Which, I'm warning
you, will not be soon. It will have to go to Spokane to be processed."

Dammit. I shoot a murderous look at Vic. If he hadn't

308

called Alex, we could be going through all of Leno's files right now. I would have access to his invite list and his party suggestions. Britt could dig deep into the computer memory for clues. Now we've got nothing.

"Don't leave town," Alex says to Owen as a parting shot.

I wait until he's out the door before I turn my frustration on my twin. "Nice work, Vic. We've now lost all access to any evidence we actually had. Like you think involving Alex is going to actually protect me from the bad people?"

"Alex isn't a bad cop when he can pull his head out of his ass," Vic retorts. "I'm sure his investigative abilities are better than ours, anyway."

"Unless Leno had something super secret encrypted on that laptop somewhere, I've backed up all relevant files to my own computer," Owen says. "He used Gmail, and I have his passwords, so we can still look at email and get into his Google docs. And hey, maybe your boyfriend will actually find something helpful."

"He's not my boyfriend."

Owen grins, teasing, and I grin back.

"You're a genius. I thought you said you didn't look at those files."

He shrugs. "I didn't actually open them. But I figured we'd have to get the cops involved at some point, so I'll admit I saw this coming."

"What now?" Britt asks.

"Now, we need to see the autopsy report as soon as there is one."

"Don't look at me!" Britt says. "Just because I hacked Julie one time doesn't mean I'm going to risk doing it again."

"She's sure as hell not going to tell me anything," Vic says. "Not about this. Not now."

"Come on, Britt. You know you want to," Vic says. "It's a challenge for you."

"We'll see," she says. "You do realize that no matter how he died, Leno's murderer has to be the last person to come in that evening."

We all go quiet, staring down at my paper and the starred name at the top. Things are not looking good for Spiro.

CHAPTER 24

It's time for me to come clean. I clear my throat. "There's something else I haven't told you."

Three faces turn in my direction, wearing three very different expressions. Vic, grudging admiration, that for once I might have figured out something first. Britt, pure curiosity. Owen, trepidation.

"I read Leno's list of things he wanted me to do at the party before we lost the laptop. And I think I know who did it and what the real motive was."

"You didn't think you should maybe share that with Alex?" Vic asks.

"He'll be happier if he does the work himself," I say. "He's got the computer. He can figure it out. Do you want to know or not?"

"Does it have something to do with this?" Britt, who has been scrolling on her phone, sets it in the middle of the table.

It's open to a YouTube video featuring Lindy Lind in Leno's condo.

Lindy beams at us through the camera. "Three guesses where I am right now! Wait, you only get one because if that mural right there on the wall doesn't tell you, then you don't deserve to know. That's right, Leno and the Lonely fans, I am right here in Leno Masterson's condo—the place where he lived his last few days—and took his very last breath! No, OMG, I am not going to show you the deathbed. What is wrong with you? How could you think such a thing?"

A banner scrolls across the screen that reads: *Shhh, maybe later, if I get a chance... Don't go anywhere or you'll miss it...*

"My God, she's awful," Vic says.

Lindy hasn't even begun to be awful yet, but she's warming up to it.

"You know who else is here? The rest of the band!" A clip from "Not Lonely Now" begins to play, accompanied by a photo montage so rapid-fire it makes my head spin. Spiro at the drum kit, the guys with their instruments, all three of them standing in front of the mural of Leno. All three of them playing.

The music fades, and video of Lindy comes up again. "I know you're excited about the band and will want to hear all about the farewell tribute concert they are planning for Leno's send-off extravaganza on Sunday, including your chance to get a limited commemorative T-shirt and help kids with cancer, but wait! I'm about to spill a secret about the band that nobody knows! Well, except for me. And you, in just a minute. Remember, when the news breaks elsewhere, that you heard it here first.

"Isn't the T-shirt a licensing violation?" Vic asks.

"It was my idea," I say. "Spiro's on board. We need to come up with a design and figure out how to sell them on the L&L website."

"We're going to sell T-shirts? When? How? Don't you think we should—"

"*Shhh*. Later."

"Are you ready to hear my super-special secret?" Lindy gushes. "It's not even really a secret, which is what makes this so mind-blowing! Check this out."

A transition screen pops up with the words "Are You Guessing? Comment below!"

Then, a clip of Lindy clinging to Owen's arm. "This is Owen Masterson! Leno's big brother. And I'm here to tell you that this man has secrets! Tell me in the comments if you already knew that—"

The Owen in the video looks cornered. The Owen beside me at the table groans, as if he's in mortal pain.

"Can you guess?" Lindy asks. "I want to see those guesses in the comments! Exactly fifty of you are going to win one of those commemorative T-shirts, so type in your answers now while my staff is watching! Ready? Okay, I'll tell you.

"Leno's big brother, Flatz and Sharpers, is the best kept Leno and the Lonely secret of all time. First thing—big brother Owen, had a band of his own in college and they were knock-your-socks-off fantastic. I dug up a clip for you. Listen up. You'll find the clue to the second secret hidden in the first one!"

Jerky footage of a band comes on, obviously recorded by somebody's cell phone. This is a five-piece—lead guitar, rhythm guitar, drums, bass, and the singer. The guy with the microphone, wearing a leather vest and ripped jeans, brown hair darkened with sweat, his soul in his voice and his face, is

Owen. Younger. Unfettered and unguarded and oozing charisma, but definitely Owen. His voice is like Leno's on overdrive. Similar in tone but with a quality that bypasses my brain and travels straight to every cell in my body.

Most importantly, the song is "Light Me Home," which all of us first heard on L&L's *Midnight Dreary* album, with the writer credit going to Spiro.

The music fades out, and Lindy comes back on. "Did you see it? Did you guess it? I'm not going to tell you if you didn't!"

"Enough." Owen grabs Britt's phone and taps the video off, but it's too late. We've all heard what we've heard.

"How did she do that?" I ask. "She just recorded that bit with Owen this morning."

"I bet she knew all about Owen's band already," Vic says. "Had that old clip all ready to go."

"Can't imagine how," Owen says. "Nobody remembers us. That was from a college talent show, not a concert venue."

"'Light Me Home' was your song?" Britt asks, coming around to the salient point.

Owen doesn't answer, so I do.

"Turns out that Owen is a brilliant songwriter. Most of L&L's hits on the *Midnight Dreary* album were his. They had a deadline on a new album but they were out of material and needed new stuff fast. Spiro presented a bunch of songs as hers and they just...recorded them, took the credit, and the album was out before Leno realized they were Owen's."

Owen slumps back in his chair and scrubs both hands over his face before he says, "One of the guys in my band used to jam with Spiro; I can only guess that's where she picked up my tunes. Anyway, the album took off immediately. First I knew what they'd done, I heard my songs playing on the radio. Leno kept telling me he was sorry, that he'd give me credit in just a bit when things settled down, when they got their next deal, that they'd at least cut me a share of the royalties... I think he meant it, but Spiro fought him on everything."

"Leno wanted to make it right," I say. "He wanted me to announce it at the party that the songs were yours. He talked to Spiro about switching the copyright over to you and making sure you were back paid for royalties. He said it didn't go over well, which was why he wanted me to announce it, in public, at a huge star-studded party. You've still got the files—you should read what he said."

Vic's face darkens. "Sorry to say this, Owen, but your motivation factor has just skyrocketed."

"I went to the condo that night," Owen says wearily. "Might as well tell you now, as I'm sure the detective will unearth it."

"But you're not on Jen's list," I protest.

"I used Leno's keycard," Owen says. "Went in the back gate. Jen wouldn't have seen me."

"Was he still alive?" Britt asks.

"I...don't know. I didn't go in. Draco's car was parked out front. Leno had called me and asked me to come over to talk. I'd been hoping to catch him alone, to hash some of this out and make peace before he died. But I wasn't up for a legal discussion about the will and the estate, and I just turned around and drove right back out."

"So you say," Vic challenges.

"So I say. Your buddy, Alex, will be able to pull the card entries from the automatic gate, I suppose."

He glances at me, eyes dark with misery and then away.

My body goes cold as my brain forces me to confront the

facts. Owen as the killer makes perfect sense. Vic is right about motive. Leno got all of the success and the fame, and he did it with Owen's music. I remember him saying, in that tone of bitter resignation, "Everyone wants to dance with my brother." And now it turns out he also had opportunity.

Vic's voice sounds strangely far away as he keeps on working through the rest of what we know.

"Supposing we believe your story, that confirms that Draco was there at that time. According to Jen's notes, he left and your mother came over."

"She went over every evening to make sure Leno got to bed okay and to say goodnight," Owen says.

"The Ice Queen might have been the last person to see him alive," Britt says. "It would be good to know how he was when she left him. It would rule out Draco, unless she's covering for him."

"I'm sure Alex will talk to both of them," Vic says.

"Like she's going to tell the cops anything." Britt takes a bite of her turnover and makes an approving noise as she chews. For possibly the first time in my life the thought of food makes me feel ill.

"I'll go talk to her," Owen says.

"No offense, but it's not like we can trust you, is it?" Vic says. "You could just be going to get your stories straight."

"I'll go with him," I say.

"You think I'm letting you go anywhere with him alone? He could be the murderer. Think, for once, Addy."

"We'll all go," Britt shoves her empty plate toward the center of the table.

"No," I say. "We won't. Owen and I will go. I promise to keep my cell on and to check in. Okay?"

Vic doesn't look happy, but he also knows he can't stop me. I get up and follow Owen.

"Excuse me." A woman reaches for my arm as I pass by. "You're Addy Winters, aren't you? The one who is planning the party? Could we talk for a minute?"

I smile and point over at Britt and Vic. "Those are the people you want to talk to," I say. "Trust me on that."

Owen has kept walking, and I speed up my steps into a near-trot to catch up to him.

"Should we let her know we're coming?" I ask as we get into the car. "And by we, I mean me, so she doesn't call the cops or something."

"Better to surprise her," he says. Then, "You think I did it, don't you? Killed my brother."

For once in my life I'm incapable of telling a lie. "I don't know what to think."

"Thank you," he says.

"You're thanking me? For what?"

"Your honesty."

After that there's nothing to say. We drive in silence; Owen deep in his own thoughts, me beset by misery.

Owen slows as we round the final curve of the driveway leading up to the Masterson mansion. "Well, that's interesting," he says. "Too bad you weren't still driving that behemoth of a Crown Vic. We could box him in."

"Her name is Jezebel, and box who in?" I assume the Lexus in the parking lot doesn't belong to any uninvited guests because the gate was closed and locked. Owen had to enter a code to get us through.

"That's Draco's car. Wonder what he's doing here?"

"Something about the will, maybe?"

"Last I heard, I'm the executor. If they're having a confab about the will, I should be part of it. Well, only one way to find out."

"Awesome. Let's do this," I say, feeling suddenly better.

"That didn't even sound like sarcasm," he says. "Tell me you're not enjoying yourself right now."

"It's possible that I enjoy antagonizing certain types of people."

"Mom and Draco both being those types," he says. "Excellent. Let's get on with it then."

Owen doesn't announce our arrival. In fact, he enters the house the way I used to when I was a teenager and had been out past Mom's curfew—opening the door slowly, placing his feet carefully, all of it as close to soundless as he can get. He glances back over his shoulder at me, and I nod to let him know I got the message.

We leave our shoes by the door, and I tiptoe barefoot behind Owen down the hallway that leads to the parlor. But halfway along, Owen takes a right, and a moment later, I hear the voices.

"Since you're such a brilliant mastermind, then you tell me what we do next." Sylvie Masterson's icy tones are unmistakable.

"I do have a plan," Draco replies, an edge to his voice. "If you'd just listen for once."

"I've done nothing but listen, and now look where we are."

"You're not listening now."

"Okay. Fine. I'm listening. Are you happy? Speak wisdom to me."

"Dear God. One of these days, Sylvie, I'm going to—"

We never do find out what Draco is going to do because,

distracted by the conversation, I bump my hip against a credenza. The legs make a screeching sound as they jump along the floor. A display of particularly ugly collector plates on stands teeters precariously and one falls over with a crash.

"Someone's here," Draco's voice says.

Owen strides forward and flings open the door, as if we'd meant to announce ourselves all along.

"Good to see you, Draco. Good evening, Mother." He bends down to drop a kiss on her cheek, careful not to muss her hair.

She shoves him away and wipes the spot with the back of her hand. "What is that girl doing here?"

"That girl's name is Addy. She's with me."

"I thought we'd agreed she needed to stay away from here."

"There was no agreeing," Owen says.

"My house. My rules. Go back to Chicago. I don't know why you're still hanging around."

There's a cut glass tumbler on the table beside her, with only a puddle of amber liquid at the bottom. Her words are slightly slurred, and her hair has started to come undone, strands of it falling around her face.

"Wow, you're a mean drunk," I say. "Who would have guessed?"

From the silence that follows, you'd think I'd axe-murdered somebody in the middle of the room rather than just telling the truth. Then Owen barks out a laugh. Draco, who was standing, drops into a chair as if his knees have gone weak.

Sylvie holds out her glass. "Somebody get me another."

"I think you've had enough," Owen says.

She waves the glass at Draco. "I'll fire you." And then at Owen. "And disown you."

"I'll take my chances," Owen says.

"You, then." Sylvie aims the glass at me. "You might as well make yourself useful. The drinks cart is in the corner. Scotch. Neat. Get yourself one, if you like. And then tell me what in hell you're doing here."

Owen and I exchange a look. He nods, ever so slightly, a gesture that I guess means, 'Let me.'" He turns toward his mother and says, "Would you like to tell me why you suddenly decided to have Leno cremated?"

"Get me a drink or get out." Sylvie staggers up to her feet and stands there, swaying. She's barefoot, her shoes kicked off beside her chair.

I half expect her heels to stay in the air, like Barbie in the movie, but she turns out to be as flat-footed as the rest of us.

"My God, how much has she had?" Owen reaches out to steady her.

"Don't touch me." The act of pulling away from his hand very nearly drops her, but she catches her balance and lurches unevenly toward the bar, where she fills her glass to the brim.

"Please. Mother. Whatever's going on, this isn't helping."

She swings around, amber liquid arcing up over the top of the glass and spilling down over her fingers, dripping onto the floor. "Oh, I've had enough, all right. Enough of you. This is your fault, Owen Masterson."

"I suppose I was supposed to find a cure for cancer?" Owen asks. "Or do you mean interfering in the rushed cremation? Are you worried about what they'll find in the autopsy?"

She takes a swig out of her glass and points at him with her free hand. "Leno knew how to make money. Leno should have inherited the business. You should have..." She breaks off on a sob, her breast heaving with emotion.

"I should have what? Been the one to die?" Owen asks.

She lurches sideways, steadies herself with a hand on the top of the bar, and slugs back half of the contents of her dripping glass. "If he'd been you and you'd been him, maybe he'd have fixed everything by now. Maybe I wouldn't have had to—"

"Sylvie. Don't." Draco has crossed to her side while she's been talking, and now he lays a hand on her shoulder. His tone, his touch, are familiar, intimate, and for an instant, she sags against him.

Then, without warning, she flings the contents of her glass into his face. "You weren't there!" she shrieks. "I held him while he took his last breath, my beautiful, beautiful boy, and now they are going to cut him open. For what reason? How can it possibly matter how he died? It only matters that he's dead." Her voice breaks on the last word and is followed by a deep, guttural sob.

"Wait," Owen says. His face is so pale I'm afraid he might pass out, but there's also a hardness to him that makes me think strength of will is all that's keeping him upright. "He was dying when you got there?"

Draco, I think, relief washing over me. It wasn't Owen, it was Draco.

Sylvie nods, her face contorted with weeping. She sucks in a deep breath and gasps, "He was in his bed, unconscious. I thought he was just asleep, but then I saw he was barely breathing."

"And you didn't call anybody?"

"Who would I call? What would they have done? There were Death with Dignity documents right there on his bedside table. A sticky note on top that said DO NOT RESUSCITATE. So,

I sat with him. I held his hand. And then he breathed his last, and I..." her voice chokes off.

"Sylvie." Draco reaches both arms out toward her, then lets them fall to his sides. He looks smaller, older, less sure of himself.

"You were there right before she was," Owen says. "What did you do, Draco?"

Draco waves the words away, impatiently. "I didn't do anything. Leno summoned me to go over his last wishes yet again. He asked me to help him die, and I advised him that he should let the cancer take its course."

"You're lying," Sylvie shrieks.

"Sylvie, I swear to you."

"You helped him, or you tricked him."

"Why would I—"

She drops the glass, and it shatters at her feet. "I might have had him another day, another month. You took him from me. I wasn't ready." Pressing both palms against his chest, she shoves, the effort making her stagger backward.

Draco catches her and holds her tight while she beats against his chest with futile fists.

"You killed him!" She hurls the words like a missile, her face twisted with grief and fury. "You're the only one who could have done it. There was no note when I was there. The pill bottle was almost full. You went back and made it look like he did it himself."

"I didn't," Draco says. "Sylvie, I didn't kill him. He was fine. Laughing, talking about his plans for this insane party. Lighting up a joint, in fact. You were distraught. Maybe you—"

"There was no fucking note! I looked for one, all right?

There was nothing! Just the right-to-die paperwork. The sticky note. The empty bottle. I know what I saw."

"What about his phone?" I ask. "The EMT guys said he had a phone."

"It was in his hand," Sylvie wails. "I don't know why. Maybe it gave him comfort or something. I left him holding it."

Either Sylvie Masterson is worthy of an Academy Award, or she's telling the truth. And if she's telling the truth, and there was no note, then somebody put it there later. If the pill bottle was still full, then somebody emptied it. Probably the same somebody who disposed of the phone. Draco is a likely suspect, but not the only one.

Owen, who has looked shell-shocked throughout this entire exchange, suddenly shifts into anger. "You were with him when he died, and then you just drove off and left him there? You didn't think maybe I'd want to know my brother was dead? You didn't think maybe you should have called somebody to come and get him?"

"There was nothing to be done about it," Sylvie says. "What were you going to do? Gloat? You were always jealous of him. You couldn't wait for him to die so you could be the star. Oh, yes. I've seen the social media posts today, all about poor Owen, shoved out of his rightful place by his upstart brother. I didn't call you. I came home. I went to bed and slept deeply, knowing my beautiful boy was at peace."

"And that your financial worries were at an end, I suppose," Owen says. "Seeing as I've failed so miserably at fixing the disaster Dad created."

"What does it matter?" Sylvie moans. "He's dead. I just want to die, too." She collapses against Draco's chest, sobbing dismally.

He lifts her into his arms. "Clean up the glass," he says as he carries her across the room. "I'll put her to bed to sleep it off. Don't be here when she wakes up."

Owen and I stare at each other in the echoing silence.

"Will you tell Alex?" he asks after a long moment.

I nod. "I'm sorry, but I have to. Are you...all right? That was intense."

"Ugly, wasn't it?" He stands there, the whole room between us, and looks at me. His eyes are wary, his shoulders slumped as if reality is too heavy. "Addy..."

"What?" I ask, when he doesn't finish.

"Nothing." He squares his shoulders and offers up a smile that is anything but genuine. "As soon as I sweep up this mess, I'll drive you wherever you want to go."

"And what are you going to do?"

"I am off to have some words with Spiro."

"Take me with you, Owen."

"Addy, I don't think—"

"Please," I say.

This time, his smile lights up the stars. My stars, anyway. He's not going to shut me out.

CHAPTER 25

I KEEP GLANCING back over my shoulder, memory and imagination working together to conjure a giant pickup truck with a spiked grill, gunmen hang out the windows, ready to shoot. There's no such vehicle, of course. We have the road to ourselves for the most part, and I take a break from my vigilance to text Vic, who will have a meltdown if I don't let him know where I'm going. I also call Alex's cell. When it goes to voicemail, I nearly hang up. But I hear Vic's voice in my head, telling me not to be stupid, so I leave a detailed message. It does occur to me to call the actual station and demand to speak with an officer, but I figure Owen has the right to confront his brother's murderer.

Even if Spiro's the killer, the rest of the band will still be there. What's she going to do, shoot all of us? She probably doesn't even have a gun. Leno wasn't shot or stabbed or bludgeoned with drumsticks. Poisoned, maybe, but how?

Jen lets us through without any questions, but Owen has one for her.

"How long have the cops been here?"

"Fifteen minutes? They asked me what you did, about who all had been here. And then they started going through the dumpster."

Owen parks the car where it won't be immediately visible to Operation Dumpster.

"Hurry," he says, opening his door. "Act natural."

These two things don't pair well, and we do an odd run-walk-shuffle sort of approach to the condo. Fortunately, the cops are focused on their task and don't notice us.

When we enter the condo, Jax and Sig are gone. Spiro stands alone at the window that looks out onto the parking lot and the dumpster, watching the cops.

"You killed him," Owen says. No preamble. No pleasantries.

She doesn't turn around. "I didn't."

"They're going to find his phone out there," Owen says. "With your fingerprints all over it. Probably see you on the security footage tossing a bag of trash."

"Me and everybody else who lives here," she says. "Tossing bags of trash in the dumpster. It's a thing we lowly mortals do. Take out the trash."

"What was on the phone?" I ask. "Somebody he called? Something he recorded?"

"The jig is up, Spiro," Owen says impatiently. "It has to be you. Bet you didn't know that Mother came in while he was dying."

Spiro's shoulders twitch, but she still doesn't turn around.

"She didn't see a note. The morphine bottle was still full. She checked because she'd been worried he might take himself out. After he died and after she left, somebody else set out the note and emptied the bottle. Nobody else came in or out. The only possible somebody is you."

Spiro swings around, her back pressed against the window. She looks weary and frightened, her eyes puffy as if she might have been crying. "I don't know what to tell you. Maybe your mother killed him; maybe she's lying. Maybe his lawyer did it. Maybe it was you, and you're wanting to pin it on me. All I know is, I didn't do it."

"Come on, Spiro. Give it up. The detective is on his way."

"To arrest me? You'd like that, you and your frumpy little party planner girlfriend."

"Hey," I protest, but only half-heartedly because an interesting text has just rolled in from Britt.

"How am I supposed to have done this thing?" Spiro asks. "And even if I had helped him along, how is that a crime? He had a license to die."

"Fentanyl," I say, dropping the word Britt texted me into the conversation like a penny into a fountain.

"What?" Owen and Spiro chorus.

"Tox screen results are in. Leno had fentanyl in his system."

"But he was taking morphine," Spiro says blankly. "Not fentanyl."

"Exactly my point. No reason for fentanyl to be in his system. Not like I'm an expert, but I know it doesn't take much, does it? I bet your pal, Roxy, local purveyor of tattoos and illegal drugs, hooked you up."

"No," Spiro says. "I don't even know a Roxy. And if I'd done what—injected him? He'd have been dead long before Sylvie showed up."

"Unless you cut it into some pot," Owen says. "That would

almost be a kindness, wouldn't it? Give him some nice, friendly weed. Make him feel better. Ease the pain. Help him sleep. Meanwhile, you have an alibi because you weren't here when the dose was delivered."

"But he hardly ever smoked anymore. He got gummies from that dispensary in town. Said they were better for the pain. What would I possibly have to gain by killing him? Maybe I'm not the greatest at impulse control, but he was planning to kill himself. Even I could wait that long."

"Not if he was going to tell the whole world about you stealing Owen's songs. He was going to make sure Owen got recognition and money. And that the whole world knew what you had done. All pretty good reasons for you to end him before that could happen."

In slow motion, she brings a hand up to her head and puts the flat of it against her temple, then just stays like that, horror moving across her face. "Oh God. Oh shit. You have to believe me. Yes, we had a fight about the music and him wanting to tell everybody what we did, and he fucking recorded a video of the whole conversation. I knew if anybody saw that, I was done for. But he was alive when I slammed out of here, I swear it. So, when I found him dead, I figured he probably had just decided to end things early. But I also knew if it got out what I'd done, everybody would think I killed him. He'd given me a copy of the letter, so I put it out by his bed, signed it for him, and I flushed the pills to make sure the cops would call it suicide. And then, yes. I threw away his phone, and I left and called 9-1-1 from a bar...but I swear I didn't kill him."

"Tell it to the cops," Owen says.

Right on cue, I hear heavy booted feet in the hallway.

Spiro looks around wildly. My imagination summons up

rapid-fire scenarios—Spiro flinging her body against the window, leaping through, crashing down to the pavement below. Spiro grabbing her drumsticks and beating on me and Owen in an adrenaline-fueled rage.

None of these things happen.

There's the sound of a fist on the door, followed by Alex's voice. "Fox Valley Police. Open up."

Spiro looks pleadingly at Owen, then me, then back again.

Owen opens the door. Alex enters, accompanied by another officer. He looks at us and shakes his head. "Of course you're here. Contaminating evidence, most likely. Wrecking my case."

Which is outrageous, given that he wouldn't have a case at all if we hadn't made it for him, but I don't bother to argue. He's on a mission and doesn't waste any more time on us.

"Spiro, aka Elizabeth Smith, you are under arrest for the murder of Leno Masterson. You have the right to remain silent. Anything you say may be used against you in a court of law. You have the right to an attorney—"

"I don't have an attorney," she says as they pull her hands behind her back and snap handcuffs on her. "Would yours help me, Owen, do you think? Draco?"

"You're insane," Owen says. "Either get your own or go with court-appointed."

"I didn't do it, though," she pleads, looking back over her shoulder as they march her out the door. "You have to believe me."

Owen and I stay where we are until the door closes behind them, until we hear their footsteps at the end of the hallway, the ding of the elevator. Then we move to the window and watch as Spiro is loaded into the back of a cop car and driven away.

"Think it will stick?" Owen asks.

"They've got motive and circumstantial evidence. And covering up a crime." I'd wanted Spiro to be guilty. Had fully expected to feel validated and exuberant when justice caught up to her. Instead, I feel like I've got indigestion after a delicious dinner. Not just because Spiro being arrested throws a huge wrench in my party plans, either, although that's part of it.

"What will you do now?" I ask Owen.

"I only know for sure what I'm not doing, which is going back to my mother's tonight," he says.

"You can come to my place," I offer. And then, just in case he thinks I'm suggesting what it sounds like I'm suggesting, I add, "The couch isn't bad, if you can tolerate a cat sleeping on your belly."

He smiles, but it doesn't reach his eyes. "You know what? I think...I'll just stay here. There seems to be an available bed. The guys will be back at some point. Probably, we should all talk."

"I get that," I say. "One small problem, though."

"What's that?"

"Um, you drove? How am I getting home?"

He laughs. "Take the car. Since we've proven that they do actually exist in Fox Valley, I'll get an Uber."

He crosses the room and gives me the keys. Then, instead of turning away, he cups my chin in his hand and tilts my face up toward his. "Thank you. For everything."

For a long moment we stand there, gazing into each other's eyes, and then he bends his head and presses his lips to mine, soft, lingering. Just when I lean into him, thinking he's going to deepen the kiss, he pulls away.

"Goodnight, Addy."

"Goodnight, Owen."

As I walk out and close the door of the condo behind me, I find myself wondering whether he's just kissed me goodnight or goodbye.

WEDNESDAY

CHAPTER 26

A PERSISTENT KNOCKING drags me out of a deep and oblivious sleep. For a minute, I lie there, collecting my memories and my wits and what feels like little pieces of me that have been scattered from hell to breakfast.

The knocking continues, and I groan out loud and pull the covers up over my face. Instantly, I realize my mistake. I need a shower. I need to brush my teeth. When I fling the covers back so I can breathe again, Bruno expresses his own annoyance by digging his claws into my chest.

"Can nobody allow me to just sleep in ever?" I shout at the door.

"Stop being dramatic. I'm coming in!" Vic shouts back. "Just wanted to make sure you were decent."

Decent, I am not, but at least I'm not naked. I fell into bed wearing yesterday's T-shirt and a pair of yoga pants. It's only Vic, anyway, who has seen me at my worst, so I sit up and shove the covers back into a heap at the foot of the bed.

As the door swings open, though, Carmen and Britt troop in behind him. The invasion comes with compensation. Vic carries two promisingly fat, greasy paper bags marked with unmistakable golden arches and the smell of fried food wafts into the room around him. Britt carries the drinks tray, which is not from the golden arches and includes a large, clear plastic cup that looks very much like a *Grounded* macchiato.

Carmen follows with a plate of homemade cinnamon rolls, and behind her, I'm shocked to see dear old Dad, who is, of course, empty-handed.

"What are you all doing here?" I ask plaintively. "Does nobody sleep anymore? Or go to work?"

"Fortunately, we all have flexible schedules," Vic says, unpacking the bags.

My mouth waters at the sight of breakfast sandwiches and hashbrowns. I can also smell cinnamon now from Carmen's contribution.

"Some of us don't have schedules at all," Vic continues. "You do realize that it's Wednesday and we have exactly four days to pull off the party of the century—and the leader of your band is now in jail?"

"Trust me, I'm well aware. I was up until nearly three working on it." I grab my macchiato off the counter and sink cross-legged onto the floor, too demoralized to take more than a half-hearted sip until Bruno climbs into my lap and makes a play for the whipped cream.

Nothing like almost losing something amazing to make you value it. "You can't have that," I tell him firmly. "It's mine." A creamy-sweet lick of whipped cream and a proper gulp of coffee later, I feel more like my usual self.

"Too late to call it off," Dad says, unwrapping a bacon, egg, and cheese biscuit. "Media is all over this shit. We need a spin."

"And to finalize the guest list," Britt says, sipping meditatively at her tea and wrinkling her nose at the food choices on the counter. "You have yogurt and fruit in your fridge, by any chance?"

Vic laughs. "You're forgetting who you're talking to here."

"We don't have to call it off," I say. "Everything is mostly under control already. Honestly, I think Leno would love the whole murder spin—he didn't want to go out with a whimper and have people pitying him."

"But they will, won't they?" Carmen asks. "I mean—dying guy gets basically poisoned by his bandmate and business partner. Have you seen Lindy's latest?"

"There was a vigil in the park last night," Vic says. "Candles, second-rate band covering all the Leno and the Lonely songs. The motels are overflowing, and people are sleeping on picnic tables."

"How about this for the spin? 'Even though he was afflicted with cancer, Leno Masterson was heroically determined to make things right in the face of overwhelming odds...'" Dad waves his half-eaten biscuit and crumbs fly everywhere, much to Bruno's satisfaction. "Of course, it needs one of the band tracks running behind it, something with a powerful vibe. And you're doing that T-shirt thing, right? Hey, wasn't there a reporter out there in the parking lot when we came in? We should invite him..." Dad's voice trails off as his gaze rests on me. "Or not. Addison, you look like a street person. Stay away from the windows."

"If people would maybe call and let me know they are coming over, I could shower and get dressed before they arrived." I get up and grab a McGriddle. This whole situation requires fat and protein and salt, and whatever other unknown substances lurk in McDonald's fast food.

"We tried to call. Your phone was off, Addle Brain," Vic says, through a mouthful of cinnamon roll.

"Point." I wash a bite of McGriddle down with sweet, icy coffee. "All right, listen. Here's where I think we're at. Dad, you take the lead on the media spin. I'll check in with the caterer, but the menu and staff are already set, and I don't expect any trouble. Britt, I've got an invite list I made with Spiro, and I'll get you Leno's list from Owen. You're responsible for the final guest list. Everything okay with drinks, Vic?"

His mouth is full and he's making appreciative noises of the type required when eating one of Carmen's cinnamon rolls, but he gives me a thumbs up.

"If you can get me logged into the Leno and the Lonely website, I can set up the T-shirt orders," Carmen offers.

"That would be amazing," I tell her. "I'd be so relieved. Jax and Sig should have the log in info."

"Consider it done," she says. "Also, I know a guy who can help with decorations if you want."

"You're an angel. We've got a budget, and we can pay him. And you."

"So, the last and biggest problem is the band," Vic says.

"Not a problem." Britt grins at us all. "The contract still stands, right? I mean, it's not canceled just because Spiro is out."

"But they were already missing Leno," Vic says. "I mean, Sig and Jax are awesome, but they can't possibly carry it alone. I'm afraid we're back to the DJ idea."

"What if I told you Gary was coming? Already got a flight.

The other guys know, and they're still game. I talked to Sig this morning—they are spitting nails that Spiro would have pulled any of this shit. Can you believe they didn't know those songs were Owen's? Only Spiro and Leno knew, apparently. So, they will do whatever it takes, they said, to help Leno set that right."

I drop my food to run across the floor and hug Britt. "You are absolutely the best. I would walk to the store and get yogurt for you."

"Not looking like that, for the love of God," Vic implores.

"I've got fruit and yogurt in my fridge," Carmen says. "I'll get you something to eat, Britt." But instead of getting up, she turns to look at me, her expression unusually dark. "Was it really fentanyl that killed him?"

"We know his tox screen was positive for fentanyl," Britt says. "How it was delivered, we don't know for sure. Autopsy hasn't been done, so we don't even know if that's for sure what killed him."

"That Roxy bitch deals fentanyl," Carmen says. "Stuff is lethal."

A glimmer of an idea drifts into my awakening brain. "Draco said that when he last saw Leno, he was lighting up a joint. Could weed get contaminated with fentanyl accidentally?" I ask.

"Not my weed," Carmen says darkly. "Can't speak for Roxy but wouldn't put it past her."

"What if it really was an accident? What if Spiro scored some pot from Roxy's network and it was contaminated? I read a news story about some girl who died that way. Spiro could have given the weed to Leno and—"

"She'd have smoked some herself, and she'd be dead too.

Can't imagine anybody going to so much trouble to cover up a murder they didn't commit," Vic says. "She's guilty. Stop fretting, Addy."

"But what if she's not?"

"Not your problem. Leave Alex and the legal system to take care of justice."

"Go have a shower. You'll feel better," Britt says.

"Fine. But there had better be a cinnamon roll left when I get back." I finish my McGriddle, stow what's left of my macchiato in the fridge, and head for the bathroom. I'm in the middle of a blissfully hot, steamy shower, lathering my hair with way too much shampoo, given that there is now so much less hair to lather, when Britt knocks on the bathroom door. "Somebody here to see you."

"They're going to have to wait." I close my eyes and lean my head back into the spray of hot water, feeling like it's washing away more than grime.

"It's a courier," Britt says. "With a package. You have to sign for it, apparently. I said I was you, but she asked for ID."

"I didn't even know there were couriers in Fox Valley."

"Life is full of surprises lately," Britt says, which is certainly true enough.

Five minutes later, clean and reasonably presentable, I step out in a cloud of steam to find the courier sitting at the table with a mug of something in front of her, eating the last cinnamon roll. Everybody turns to look at me, and the only one of them with the grace to look guilty is the courier.

Wiping her mouth and hands with a napkin, she shoves back her chair and turns to face me. She's young, maybe twenty or so, wearing a navy uniform jacket and khaki pants. A carrier pouch and a clipboard rest on the table beside what is left of her—make that *my*—cinnamon roll. She smooths a hand over her already perfectly smooth hair and asks, "Are you Addison Winters?"

"That depends? Am I about to be served with a lawsuit or something?" I glare at my supposed friends, and my twin and my father, who are not only fraternizing with the possible enemy but giving away a piece of delectable food I had already laid claim to.

The courier smiles, dark-brown eyes crinkling at the corners. "I'm not a process server, just a courier. My instructions are to deliver this document into the hands of Addison Winters on Wednesday, June 19th, as close to 9 am as possible. My apologies that it's late. There were two deliveries before yours, which is weird because this is like the first time ever we've even had one delivery out here in Fox Valley. And I had to hunt one of those customers down because they weren't at the address I was given."

"I'm Addison. Did you need to see ID?"

"Yes, thank you," she says.

I grab my bag and dig out my driver's license. She checks it over thoroughly and asks me to sign the form on her clipboard. Then, she unzips her messenger bag and extracts a large and official-looking white envelope.

"Have a good day," she says. "Thank you all so much for the tea and that cinnamon roll. You are all so nice! I should move here." She beams at all of us, and Vic ushers her out and closes the door behind her.

I stand there with the envelope in my hands, equal parts curious and terrified. "I've never been couriered anything before," I say.

"Well, I doubt it's a bomb or anthrax or anything," Carmen says impatiently. "Open it already. We've been waiting."

"I see how you've been waiting," I retort. I can almost taste cinnamon and butter and perfectly baked doughy goodness. With a sigh, I go to the fridge and retrieve my drink, then drop into a chair and use the paring knife Britt hands me to open the envelope.

Inside is a legal document. I catch the words Last Will and Testament of Leonard William Masterson, then read the hand-written note stuck to the page with a piece of tape.

Addy, on the chance that I wasn't able to get you on board with my plans before my date with death, forgive me for afflicting you with this extra responsibility. This is a new copy of my will, updated and signed on June 13th, which, yes, I had done before I ever talked to you. You're in it now, by the way. Draco was weird about it, and I'm not entirely sure I trust him to do the right thing. My brother, Owen, is my executor and should have also received a copy this morning, but would you check with him? Again, my apologies. I needed somebody from outside the family, and you're it. I'm so sorry for being such an asshole in high school. You were the best friend I ever had, and I totally screwed you over.

Sorry for this, too. Guess I'm still a manipulative asshole, even beyond the grave.

Leno

"Well?" Vic says. "What is it?"

"Leno's updated will," I say when my mouth catches up to my brain.

"And he sent it to you because?"

"Because he didn't trust his lawyer."

"You think Draco killed him after all?" Britt asks in a hushed tone. "Like, the Ice Queen lied for him?"

"I don't know what I think."

"Let me look." Vic sits down with Leno's Last Will and Testament and starts to read. I watch his eyes as he scans the first couple of pages. He stops in the middle of page three, goes back up to the top, and reads down again.

"Well, he left you the condo, for starters," he says, still reading.

"Why would he do that?"

Vic turns to the next page, and here he comes to a full stop. A low whistle escapes between his teeth. "That would do it," he says.

Right then, my phone rings.

"You got a copy, I presume?" Owen asks when I answer.

"I did. Listen, I didn't know about the condo."

"Come get me, would you?"

"Um, okay?"

"Sorry. Please? We need to talk to Draco."

"When were you—"

"As soon as you can get here." He hangs up.

I sit there, stupidly still holding the phone to my ear, as I ask Vic, "What exactly did Leno do now?"

CHAPTER 27

"WHAT WERE YOU THINKING?" Owen shouts.

Not at me, to be clear, but at Draco, who is slumped in the chair behind his desk, wearing the haunted expression of a man gazing into the abyss.

"I can't believe you were going to suppress this new will!"

"You don't know that," Draco says, trying to square his shoulders, but even I can tell he's lying.

"I *do* know that! You gave me what you said was the final copy of the will the day after Leno died. You gave an identical copy to Mother. It wasn't this one. What were you going to do, shred it? Pretend it didn't exist?"

"Sylvie needs that money!" Draco flashes back, his spine straightening. "The family business needs that money."

"Doesn't matter what you and Mother think, does it?" Owen challenges. "Only what Leno's last wishes were. This... thing...you're having with her has totally obscured your judgment. And corrupted your morals, apparently."

"Everything okay in here?" Vic sticks his head in through the open door, a reminder that he's out in the waiting room, just in case anybody in this office has murderous intent. He insisted on driving us in his own vehicle and then on hanging around in case things get violent.

"Everything is *not* okay," Owen snaps, "but nobody is waving guns around. Yet. You don't have a gun in your desk drawer, do you, Dawlish?"

Draco just glares at him.

Vic, having made his presence known, retreats back down the hallway and leaves us to it.

"Would somebody maybe tell me what he left to Lisa and Jackson in the original will?" I ask. "Just so I understand this all better."

Owen runs both hands through his hair, then lets them fall to his sides. "There was a provision for her to continue to receive what she's been getting all along. Three thousand a month, on auto deposit into her bank account. A college fund for Jackson. And then, when he turned twenty-one, the monthly payment switching over to him."

"And he changed it to a million-dollar trust for Jackson, with Owen and me as responsible parties, and absolutely nothing for Lisa? Did she know about this?" I ask.

"Leno said he'd told her what he was planning, and it didn't go well," Draco says. "She was getting married to that Brad guy, and Leno was worried the money would get siphoned off for his business and not go to the kid. She had apparently already been dumping a lot of the monthly payment into her own business-expansion plan. When Leno questioned her on that, she said the kid was fed, clothed, educated and had everything he needed, and his having a happy life would be a direct result of her having a happy life, so she should get the money to spend however she saw fit."

"Some truth to that, to be fair." I sink into a chair and turn to the page about the trust fund to read it for myself. It's hard work wading through the legalese while still paying attention to the conversation, and I'm grateful Vic explained it to me earlier.

Draco shrugs. "She should have left well enough alone, and he probably wouldn't have pushed the issue. But she came after him for more. She'd signed an NDA when Jackson was born, which meant she couldn't tell people who his father was. And then, after Leno got cancer, she came after him, asking for a hundred grand, or she couldn't guarantee that there wouldn't be a leak to the media about Jackson's parentage. To which, Leno told her he was dying anyway, and frankly, he was glad to know he had an heir and didn't care less if the whole world knew about it. They had a big row right here in the office a few days before he died."

"But he hadn't actually made the changes yet. He'd just told her he was going to?" Owen asks.

"He hadn't made the changes," Draco confirms. "He was informing her of his intentions. He wanted me as a witness."

"Some witness you are," Owen retorts. "You sure you didn't kill him yourself, Draco? A million bucks that was going to go into the family estate suddenly going elsewhere, that's a lot."

"There was no need to kill him," Draco says. "All I needed to do was what I was going to do anyway—quietly destroy this final will after he died. Nobody knew about it but me and my secretary, and she's easy enough to buy off. But I guess Leno saw that coming. I underestimated him."

"We all did," Owen says quietly.

I stop reading, mark the spot with my finger, and ask, "Is there any chance Leno drove Lisa home after that meeting?"

"He did, actually. He'd picked her up from work and took her back after. Surprised she didn't kill him then and there. She was furious."

"She was still in love with him," I murmur, rereading the line where my finger is marking the place.

"Why on earth would you say that?"

"It was her ring. The one we found in the car. AR. Annelise Rosen. Lisa is a nickname."

"Funny thing, that," Draco says. "Now that I think about it, he did always call her Annelise. But I can't imagine why you'd think she was still in love with him. Wasn't she engaged?"

"He must have bought her the ring, for starters, back in high school. Her family didn't have that kind of money. She still had the ring and apparently still wore it."

"Lots of people get stuck in high school," Owen argues. "I know guys who still wear their class rings."

"This one is real silver. A quality sapphire. Lisa was money-hungry, so something stronger than class spirit kept her from selling it for cash. And she'd have needed to be pretty seriously pissed off to throw it at him, which is really the only way it could have ended up where I found it. Money, love, and revenge make for a pretty potent motive."

"She wasn't at the condo that night, though," Owen objects.

"Besides, she got over it," Draco offers. "When I went over the night he died, he said she'd come by the day before. She was all apologetic and said she appreciated him looking out so brilliantly for Jackson and that, of course, their son was her first priority, too. Actually wanted to smoke a joint together and hang out. Only he said he declined because the morphine was making him fuzzy enough already and he had things to do."

Owen's eyes meet mine.

"Carmen says Roxy deals fentanyl, as well as pot," I say slowly. "Roxy was Lisa's client. She was actually at *Foxy Lady* when Lisa went ballistic on my hair. And I'm telling you, that was not the behavior of a woman who had made peace with Leno."

"So, you think Lisa brought him a joint that was laced with fentanyl? On *purpose*? And when he didn't smoke it, she just left it with him for later?"

"Can you imagine the waiting? Wondering every minute whether he's finally smoking the stuff, whether it worked."

"You could almost feel sorry for her," Owen says.

I think about my hair. About Leno dying before he was ready. And whatever I'm feeling as I dial Alex's cell, it is certainly not pity for Lisa. It's Jackson I feel a rush of compassion for. His father murdered, his mother going to prison. Poor kid.

"Why do I have a feeling I don't want to hear this?" Alex asks by way of greeting. "Are you going to unravel my nice, neat little case?"

"I'm going to make sure justice comes for the right person," I say, and then I tell him what I know.

☙

FlatzandSharpz Live

"Flatz and Sharpers, you are not going to believe the latest. Legendary, badass female drummer, Spiro, was released from jail today—apparently, the cops had things all wrong, and she did not kill Leno Masterson after all.

"'But Lindy,' I know you are all saying. 'Who did kill him? Or did he just kill himself?'

"Just wait, just wait, until I tell you this.

"The local detective—who is, as an aside, yummy, I do love a sexy man in a uniform—is keeping the details locked up tight. Tighter than he locked up Spiro anyway! But here's what we know. Lisa Rosen, owner of the one and only hair salon in Fox Valley—*Foxy Lady*, which you can see behind me here—has been arrested.

"Why would a hair stylist kill a rockstar? Rumor has it that her son is Leno's secret love child. That's all we know. How she did it, or even why, is still under wraps. But I'll find out, don't you fret for a minute...and you'll be the first to know when I do."

SUNDAY

CHAPTER 28

LENO'S PARTY is almost over—and I think I can safely call it a win.

I stand at the back of the banquet hall, watching all of the famous people swirl and eddy, doing their best to see and be seen while eating, drinking, and dancing. The doors out to the patio and the gardens are open, and more guests are drinking and dancing and chatting outside under the fairy lights strung through all the trees.

Leno's proposed guest list included contact numbers and emails, which greatly assisted in getting out the invites. The four of us—Owen, Britt, Vic, and I—vetted the influencers and reporters and invited a select few, keeping the total guest list to three hundred and fifty.

Dad is in his element, with microphones and cameras and interview requests coming at him from all directions. He is good at working a room, I have to admit. His bruises just make him look like a hero. I got Dad to read Leno's goodbye letter and his prepared statement about Owen and the copyright stuff, which let me stay in the background, yellow polka-dotted dress and all.

Unlike at Geneva's funeral, my dress is conservative—comparatively speaking. We included a note on the invitation that anybody in black would be turned away at the doors, so bright, jewel-toned colors are everywhere.

Speaking of turning people away at the doors, there's a lot of that going on. The company we hired for security has had their work cut out for them, what with fans, influencers, and reporters all trying to bribe, schmooze, or otherwise sneak into the party. I strongly suspect that despite the wrought-iron fence around the gardens, there are a few uninvited people outside, which is fine. I have respect for motivation and gumption. If they've managed to sneak in, more power to them.

Vic is glowing; the comments about Raven Brews have been overwhelmingly positive, and a couple of well-connected people have talked to him about contracts for regular supply shipments.

Britt, breathtaking in a red, curve-loving, sleeveless dress that manages to be casual and glamorous at once, has been helping him with everything but serving drinks.

The band, with Gary on drums, is a huge hit. All three of the guys have taken turns with the vocals, which makes it sound weirdly like they're a cover band, even though they're playing their own tunes. The music just can't be right without Leno, but since that is sort of the point, it's actually okay.

Spiro isn't here. She is out of jail but not out of the woods. Even though she didn't murder Leno, she interfered with an investigation, and there's an obstruction of justice charge against her. Draco says she'll likely get off with a fine, but it might be a bit before any band wants to be associated with her. Anyway, she's gone back to Seattle, and Sig and Jax have made it clear that they will have nothing more to do with her. They invited Owen to sing for the party, but he caught a flight back to Chicago last night.

First, though, he took me out for a proper dinner at Fox Valley's one real sit-down restaurant. "It's not that I'm against the party," he said when I tried to cajole him into sticking around. "I just can't handle all the hype right now. I don't know how I feel about anything. Even you."

He was holding my hand when he said that last thing, and later he kissed me in the car, so I'm putting a positive spin on the comment.

"Are you going to be okay?" I asked him. "With the business stuff, I mean. And the debts and whatever."

"Leno designated enough to pay the big debts," he said. "Plus, I'll be getting royalties on the music. There's compensation for being the executor, too. I'll be fine."

"And your mom?"

"She's talking about selling the house. Maybe she and Draco will move in together. Who knows?" He laughed a little bitterly. "Maybe I'll see you sometime," he said.

"Right, next time I'm in Chicago I'll look you up," I said.

He'd smiled, his fingers tightening around mine. "I'll be back. I've started proceedings to get legal guardianship of Jackson. His mother's going to prison, and I understand his grandparents aren't really capable. So, I'll be back in town off and on. Also, Chicago can always use a party planner. You've got creds and contacts after pulling this off."

"I haven't pulled it off yet," I'd told him.

He laughed. "You will. I haven't a doubt in the world."

That was when he kissed me. It was different than the goodnight or goodbye kiss, which had been tentative and brief. This was the sort of kiss that heated my body and curled my toes. When he pulled away, we sat there, breathing hard, gazing into each other's eyes. It was the sort of kiss that could have led to more. But he'd already told me he wasn't sure how he felt about me, and I wasn't entirely sure how I felt about him.

So, I let the moment pass, and now he's in Chicago, and I keep asking myself if I ought to have done something differently and answering myself that I'm still not sure.

He was right about me pulling off the party. It's almost over, and it's been a huge success. Not that I get to take the credit for that, not really. I used most of Leno's ideas, and I had a ton of help from my friends.

My phone buzzes with a text from Carmen, who has been sending regular updates about the T-shirt charity thing.

> Carmen: I'm closing down the store

> Addy: Why? The day's not over.

> Carmen: Out of inventory. Better to say the site crashed than not be able to fulfill orders.

> Addy: Wow! Amazing!

> Carmen: Right? Party still going well?

> Addy: Fantastic! Or at least it was. Alex just showed up.

> Carmen: OMG. If he tries to arrest you on obstruction, it's harassment. Update me!

I send a thumbs up and drop my phone into my bag. Alex

was definitely not invited. And he's in uniform, which means he's on official business.

He sees me, and I decide it's better to go to him than have him walk through a crowd of media people while he's in uniform, especially when they are all buzzing already about the murder.

"Looking for somebody?" I ask him.

"You. Can we go outside where it's quieter?"

He doesn't wait for my assent, and I follow him out into the front parking lot.

"What do you want, Alex?"

He shifts his weight uncomfortably, and his eyes slide sideways. "I needed to give you some information. We found the pickup truck that ran you and Owen off the road. It was abandoned up at the old quarry."

"But..."

He waits, letting me absorb the information.

"It's not Lisa's," I say.

"No. It was stolen from Spokane, actually."

"Are you sure it's the right truck?"

"Front end damage that correlates to the damage to the Maserati. Matching paint scrapings. I'm sure."

"So, who was it then?"

Again, that uneasy shifting of his weight. "We can't be sure, but I'd guess some of the people wanting to be paid by the Masterson business."

"My God." I shiver, blaming it on a spring breeze on my bare shoulders, but I know it's not the weather.

"I don't think you're in any danger," Alex says. "They all know by now that Leno is dead. Owen's in Chicago. Draco tells me arrangements are being made to get everybody paid."

"So, why are you telling me this?"

"Those are bad people, Addy. And now they know who you are. So don't be afraid, exactly just—let me know if anything happens that seems...off. Okay?"

"All right."

"All right. Well, that's all I guess." He lingers for a moment, then turns and starts to walk away.

"Alex!"

"Yeah?" He looks back over his shoulder.

"Thank you."

A smile touches his lips. Then he turns away and keeps walking.

I watch him go, feeling suddenly tired and maybe a little bit down. Leno's murder and his party have been my sole focus for days, and now that things are winding up, it's back to my ordinary life, which feels a little boring in comparison to solving a murder and planning a gala event. Although, maybe not quite ordinary, I remind myself. I'm still driving Hannibal. Leno's condo will be mine as soon as the will is probated.

Owen will be coming to visit.

I step back into the hall as the band transitions into "Light Me Home," the last number for the evening. It's a slow dance song, the sort of song that makes me feel lonely.

I see Vic hold out his hand to Britt, and the two of them swirl out onto the dance floor. Unexpected tears dim my eyes, and as I blink them back, I see a blur of color and movement on the stage, to the front of the band.

I blink again, and it coalesces into a familiar figure. Leno. Not the emaciated, skeletal, dying Leno, but the way I want to remember him. Young and vibrant and beautiful. He's looking right at me as if there's no crowd, no distance between us.

In the dark of night
When I'm all alone
Darling, light me home...

He smiles, brilliant and blinding. I blink against the light, and when I open my eyes again, he's gone. Just an illusion. My imagination. But the part of me that had felt so unsettled and unfinished is now resting easy, as I hope he is, too.

"Rest in peace, Leno," I whisper.

My job is done. The caterers will clean up the food. Vic will gather up bottles and empties. The decorators will retrieve their banners and balloons. So, I step back outside into the spring-scented dark of not-quite midnight and take out my phone to update Carmen.

A new text message catches my attention.

Unknown Number: Hi, my name is Kaleigh Wilson, and I'm dying. I'd like to hire you to throw me a big-ass party like you did for Leno Masterson. Can we talk?

The End

KEEP READING for an excerpt from *A Party to Die For...*

EXCERPT FROM A PARTY TO DIE FOR

Chapter One

"I'm dying. Please, can you help me?"

Obviously, this call should never have gone to voicemail. I blame Britt.

We're luxuriating in late morning coffee at *Grounded,* Fox Valley's one and only café, when it happens. Or at least, *I'm* luxuriating in coffee—my signature frozen caramel macchiato, never mind that it's twenty degrees outside and blowing snow. Britt, as usual, is drinking green tea, hot, no sugar. Not so much as a dollop of honey to add a little sweetness.

It's my belief that anything so overtly healthy can't really be good for you. It's Britt's belief that my icy confection will shave years off my life, whereas she's taking in antioxidants and magic tea juju that will make her live to be a hundred and ten.

"Besides all of that sugar forcing your poor little cells to exist in an acidic environment, and growing bacteria on your teeth, aren't you already freezing? We're in the middle of a blizzard." Britt shivers and snuggles deeper into her oversized sweater.

"Maybe if you added some sugar to your tea your poor little cells would grow some fat around themselves and not be shivering their way into hypothermia." I take a delectable lick of caramel and whipped cream before sucking up a supersized mouthful of icy goodness, waiting for the brain freeze to pass before I add, "Who wants to live to be old if you're forced to subsist on twigs and seeds and bitter green water anyway?"

And that's when the phone starts playing Toyah's *It's a Mystery*, in a key and tempo that clashes horribly with the rendition of Jingle Bells currently blasting out of the speakers.

"God, you do pick the most bizarre ringtones," Britt says. "Send it to voicemail. Rapido."

"That's my new client ringtone. I have to answer."

Britt grabs my phone and turns off the ringer. "Technically, it's not your new client ringtone, it's your unknown caller ringtone. They can leave a message. We're planning a party for ourselves for once."

She has a point. I'm moving into my new condo tomorrow, and three days after that it's Christmas, so we're planning a housewarming slash Christmas party to celebrate. This is pushing it, I know. It means I'll actually have to unpack right away and get the boxes out instead of dragging the process out over the course of a year like I did when I moved into my first (and last) apartment. I've taken the week off to move, get settled, and throw my own party. This, by the way, was Britt's idea and I'm having major second thoughts. I like planning parties for other people. For myself, not so much.

So I'm not working and it's probably a spam call and it makes sense to let voicemail handle it.

But.

I'm afflicted with the sort of curiosity that supposedly kills cats. I mean, what if this call is from a total dream client and they don't leave a message? What if I magically won a million dollars without playing the lottery, or a secret wealthy uncle died and left me his entire estate?

So when my phone vibrates to let me know that there is actually a message, obviously I have to check it out.

Britt sighs. "You won't be able to focus on anything until you listen. Put it on speaker, so I can hear too."

Grounded is full. There's a clamor of voices competing with the next tune on the play list, an absolutely awful cover of *Last Christmas*, this time performed by a pseudo rap group I've never heard of. It's my least favorite seasonal song to begin with, and this is the worst version of it ever. It's loud and annoying and when I press play, even with my phone on speaker and the volume amped all the way up, Britt and I are forced to lean down close to the phone to hear.

"I'm dying," a woman's voice says. "Please. Can you help me?" Ragged breathing, follows. A ragged sob. Then, "Oh God. I'm sorry. Voicemail – shouldn't have – too late..."

And then, nothing.

I glare at Britt, whose fault this is.

"Call her back," she says.

But I just sit there, feeling like one of those tiny little flies trapped in amber. All of my logic and motion circuits have gone offline. My heart is attempting a new world record for speed.

Britt, on the other hand, is a doctor's daughter and grew up in a house where her father was always being called out on emergencies. Maybe that's why she's always calm in a crisis, maybe it's just her more rational brain and all of the yoga and meditation. She grabs the phone and taps the call back option. The phone rings and rings and finally goes to voicemail.

"This is Johanna. I can't imagine how I missed your call, but you know I'll call you back." Same voice that left the message, minus the breathlessness and panic.

"That's not good," Britt says.

"You think?" My mouth has figured out how to work again, although my brain is still mostly offline. "Do you think she's dead already? Maybe a murderer was actually in her house and she just dialed a random number and then we didn't help her."

Britt taps at the screen. "If that were the case she would have called 911. I'll do that now."

One ring, then a professional voice says, "911, what's your emergency?"

"I got a voicemail from a woman who says she's dying and is asking for help. Can you send somebody to check on her?"

"This person's name and address please?"

"All I've got is a first name and a phone number."

The dispatcher takes the name and number, and then Britt supplies my name and cell number when asked.

She hangs up and looks at me blankly across the table. "How strange." She sips meditatively at her tea.

I suck up a freezing mouthful of macchiato and immediately feel better. A lick of whipped cream and a bite of my blueberry scone further aid my recovery. "I think what you mean is terrifying and unsettling. Strange is like—when the internet password stops working for no reason. Or Bruno steals the neighbor's Playboy tie."

"Why would this woman call you in the middle of some sort of crisis?"

I can practically see the question marks dancing above her head, all in sync with the ones in my own. "If I'd answered the call, maybe we'd know."

Yes, I'm snarky and this is blatant guilting. But my adrenaline rush has to go somewhere and Britt is the only person I can vent it on.

"Maybe we can find this Johanna person's address." Britt digs her laptop out of the backpack she always carries with her and starts tapping away at the keyboard. I shift my chair around to sit beside her where I can watch as she searches some obscure database for the phone number.

It only takes her a minute to locate our caller. I shouldn't be surprised.

Britt is all the things I am not. She's got a dancer's body, long and lean, wavy black hair cascading down to the middle of her back, big brown eyes, skin that looks sun-kissed winter and summer, and cheek bones to die for. Worse, this exterior, about as far as you can get from the stereotypical tech geek, houses a brain as sharp as her cheekbones.

She walked away from a high profile, six figure salary position in Silicon Valley to come home and be nearer her parents when her dad got diagnosed with leukemia. Now she has a remote parttime gig that allows her to help her mother with housework and meals and getting her dad to doctor's appointments and chemo. She's bored, although she'll never admit it, which is unfortunate for her but makes it easier for me to persuade her to set aside logic and caution and join me in my harebrained schemes.

"You're brilliant," I tell her now, reading the info on her screen.

She shrugs. "It's just reverse caller ID."

"Every time I try reverse caller ID I get asked for a credit card and it all looks super sketchy."

Her expression goes blank, which means she's trying to hide something. I store that away for later, since she's already calling 911 back.

"Just in case they didn't find the address yet," she says.

By the time she's done relaying information, I've packed up my own belongings, stacked our cups on a tray, and am on my feet.

"No, Addy." She reaches for her cup. I yank the tray out of her reach and carry it toward the designated "leave your shit here" zone.

"We are not going to that woman's house!" Britt calls after me.

I don't even bother turning around to look at her, and of course she's right behind me when I open the door and step out into the swirling snow. She shivers, pulling up the hood of her parka.

"I don't see why we couldn't just let the police and EMTs do their jobs while we stay cozy and warm," she complains, but she still helps brush the snow off of Jezebel, my battered old harridan of a Crown Vic. "I also don't understand why you persist in driving this old wreck when you could be driving the Maserati."

"Shh. She'll hear you. Plus, Hannibal isn't a snow car."

"Jezebel isn't a snow car. Or any season car. Also, she can't hear, doesn't have feelings, and won't be jealous if you drive the Maserati."

Which just proves that after years of explanations—and demonstrations—Britt still doesn't understand thing one about Jezebel. I pat the steering wheel to mollify her (the car, not Britt) before she (still Jezebel) decides to play dead.

"I love you and only you," I tell her, and when I turn the key I'm rewarded by a cough, a shudder, and then the asthmatic sound of a long-suffering engine that would like me to know she doesn't appreciate the cold.

"You didn't drive the Maserati in the summer, either," Britt says, struggling with a recalcitrant seatbelt, and shivering dramatically. "I bet that car has seat warmers." But she pulls up the address on her phone so she can give me directions while I focus on navigating snowy streets.

Once we turn onto Shady Grove Way, there's no need to pinpoint the address. A police car and an ambulance are already parked in the second driveway on the left. Despite the weather, neighbors in snow boots and jackets are clumped together on the sidewalk across the street, staring and chattering.

I pull up to the curb and park, then wrestle open the door and brace myself against the swirling snow. If there is anything to know, someone in the little cluster of bystanders will be sure to know it. By unspoken agreement, Britt and I walk over to join them.

"What's happening with Johanna?" I ask, as if I know the woman and have the right to an answer. "Is she all right?"

Animated faces instantly turn guarded. After a long, uncomfortable silence and a complicated series of exchanged glances, an elderly woman with close cropped gray hair and skin two shades darker than Britt's plants her hands on substantial hips and says, "I don't know whether you're reporters or some of those influencer people, but Johanna is none of your business."

Emboldened, a reedy, pale little man in a Santa hat steps forward to stand beside her. He's beardless, snaggle toothed, and there's not a pinch of fat anywhere on him. He takes a drag on a cigarette held between two nicotine stained fingers, blows the smoke in our faces, and says, "You've never been here before even the once. So if you heard about this from one of them police scanners and you're here to sniff out a story, you can just sniff some place else."

"She...called me and asked for help," I protest, finding myself at a highly unusual loss for words.

Britt shifts her position a little to get out of the direct path of the smoke. "We're the ones who called 911," she says. "We wanted to make sure Johanna was okay."

"What would she call you for?" the spokeswoman demands.

I judge this to be one of those occasions where it's best to go with the truth. I can't say I'm Johanna's niece from out of town, because surely they will have seen pictures of all of Johanna's relatives. Probably they know their names and where they live and what they do for a living.

"Honestly? I have no idea. Wrong number?"

"There, you see? You didn't even talk to her," the skinny mutant Santa says.

"She left me a voicemail that said she was dying and asked for help."

Again there's a complex exchange of coded glances. "We don't know anything," the spokeswoman concedes. "We were all going about our day when the ambulance and the cop showed up."

A young woman balancing a toddler on one hip adjusts a woolen hat down over the kid's forehead. "If Johanna is dead in there they'll have to knock down a wall to get her out."

"Reckon they'll bring her out through the door like anybody else," mutant Santa says.

The kid, now half blinded by the hat, squirms in her mother's arms and pulls it off, flinging it into the snow.

"Ashley, I swear to God." The young mother bends down to get the hat and shakes the snow out of it. "You ever seen Johanna come in or out of that house? Only reason for somebody never leaving the house is she's too big to walk through the door. Like that show *Supersized*. With the guy who weighed like a thousand pounds and couldn't get out of bed?"

She puts the still snowy hat on the kid's head, and the kid starts to howl.

"Johanna doesn't weigh a thousand pounds," the spokeswoman says.

"How do you know, Serena? You ever seen her? Has anybody here ever seen her?"

"If that woman wants to stay inside and keep to herself, that's her business," Serena says.

"Surely she must go out sometimes," I say, inspecting Johanna's house. Her sidewalks have been shoveled in the recent past. Christmas lights festoon the eaves and the neatly trimmed shrubs. A tall privacy fence conceals the back yard. There's a small gap between the curtains, where someone on the inside could peer out without being seen.

"How does she eat?" Britt asks. "Who shovels the snow and put up the lights?"

"Gets her groceries delivered," Serena says. "Once a week, on Mondays. She paid somebody to do the Christmas stuff. And she pays a kid to shovel snow. She gets Amazon deliveries on the regular."

"Bet she's one of those hoarder types." The speaker is a pale, middle-aged woman in a puffer jacket who has been quiet up until now. "I watched that Hoarders show – some of those people let their dogs shit in the house, did you know? Surprised the ambulance people aren't wearing gas masks."

"She hasn't got a dog," Serena says.

"How do you know that?"

"You ever heard a dog in there? It would bark."

"Maybe she keeps it muzzled. Or, I know, puts one of those bark shock collar things on it and zaps it whenever it tries to make noise."

"She has a cat," mutant Santa says. "We've all seen the cat."

The door to the house opens and I brace myself for the sight of a woman being wheeled out on a stretcher—maybe with an oxygen mask and an IV. Maybe dead, with her face covered by a sheet. But there's no stretcher, and the emergency response people come sauntering out like they're just returning from brunch.

First out the door is a compact Black woman in police uniform. I know who she is – Officer Michelle McCarty – but she's an import to Fox Valley, so she hasn't got a clue who I am and there's no point trying to get information from her. The EMT who emerges next is also a Fox Valley import. But the last one out is our old classmate, Perch. We're far from friends, but he's possibly approachable.

"Well, show's over I guess," Serena says. "Johanna's fine, or they'd have done something. You'll be leaving now."

"Maybe not just yet," I murmur, because as far as I'm concerned, this was just the opening act. I'm looking for my backstage pass, and I'm hoping Perch can give it to me.

"Perch, wait up!"

He turns, puts his hands up to ward me off, and takes a step backward as I slip and slide through the snow toward him. "Whoa, Addy. I swear I'm not the one who hit him."

I skid to a halt a couple of feet away from him, trying to process his reaction. Perch is a big guy – six-foot-three, build like a linebacker. He's got a shaved head and skull-and-cross-bones tattoos and I've always suspected there's a swastika etched into his skin somewhere. So Perch looking scared of little old me is every bit as unexpected as Johanna's voicemail.

"It's not about Dad," I say, because there's really only one thing he could be referencing. "He told me what happened."

"Wasn't sure he'd remember," Perch says. "Alvin clocked him pretty good and then someone threw a chair. I'd have given him a ride only the chair hit me. I was out cold."

Truth is, there have been plenty of times in my life I've contemplated violence toward my father, myself. I'd have totally understood if Perch had been the one to flatten him.

"Dad's fine. No hard feelings."

Perch still doesn't lower his hands. "What are you doing here, Addison?"

"Johanna Myers. She called me and said she was dying. We just want to know if she's okay."

His partner is brushing snow off the windshield. Perch glances at him, then back at me.

"So is she?" I ask. "Okay?" Surely they wouldn't just leave her there if she was dead. But what do I know about dead-on-arrival procedures? Maybe Johanna has advance arrangements with *Ever After*, Fox Valley's one and only funeral home, and they'll come and get her. But the panic in that message didn't sound like someone who has been making funeral arrangements. It sounded like somebody terrified of dying immediately.

"I can't tell you anything about her, Addy. You know that. Confidentiality and all." Perch edges toward the ambulance, gets a hand on the door, then stands there. I can pretty much hear the ponderous thought wheels turning.

"You gonna help clear the snow or what?" his partner asks.

Perch holds up a hand to indicate his forthcoming compliance. "Theoretically speaking," he says, "People are allowed to refuse treatment. But if someone was, say, unconscious, then we'd never leave them alone. Unless, of course, they had one of those death with dignity things like your boyfriend Leno had."

"He wasn't my boyfriend. And you've told me absolutely nothing I couldn't have figured out for myself. Either she's dead, or she's well enough to refuse treatment, or she's unconscious but the law says you can't interfere with her dying. Which is it?"

"I gotta go."

He turns around and starts brushing snow of his side of the ambulance windows and I trudge back to Britt. The bystanders have vanished, presumably all into their own houses, not one of them making a beeline to check on Johanna.

"That's weird."

"Which part?" Britt asks. "Some random lady calling you to say she's dying, or Perch being scared of you?"

"The neighbors. If the ambulance and the cops were at my

mother's house, everybody within a ten block radius would be knocking at the door with one pretext or another, trying to find out what happened."

Britt frowns, looking around at the now deserted street. "Point. Same at my house, really. An ambulance came for Dad that one time when he had a bleeding episode, and neighbors were in and out for the next three days trying to get the inside story."

"Exactly." Decision made, I head up the sidewalk toward Johanna's house.

"I'm sure she's fine," Britt calls after me. "They wouldn't have just left here there if she wasn't."

"Did she sound fine to you?"

"Well, no, but. Listen. Maybe she'd done this sort of thing before. Maybe she cries wolf all the time. Maybe she's a psychopath. Or a serial killer, even."

I see the drapes move, and I'm pretty sure Johanna is watching us.

"You can wait in the car if you'd rather." Holding onto the snowy railing, I carefully make my way up the slippery steps.

There's no knocker and no doorbell, so I use my knuckles, already stinging from the cold, and rap three times. There's no answer. But I know Johanna is in there and I'm pretty sure she's seen us.

I knock again. Still nothing.

"Come on, let's go," Britt says, joining me on the porch.

But then I hear the sound of approaching footsteps. They stop on the other side of the door, and again there is silence.

"Johanna, it's me. Addy Winters," I call out.

"Go away."

"I want to make sure you're okay."

"Fine as I'm going to be."

Britt tugs at my jacket sleeve. "Come on. Let's go."

I lean in closer to the door. "You left me a voicemail. You asked for my help."

There's the sound of a bolt sliding back. The door opens, only a crack, revealing a narrow strip of pale face and one hazel eye. "You," she says, accusingly. "You're the reason the ambulance came. And the cops."

"You said you were dying," I retort. "What did you expect me to do?"

"I hate voicemail," she says. "Never know what to say."

"I hate it too, but don't usually tell people I'm dying."

"But I am," she says. "Dying." She bites her lip, looks me over, adjusts the crack in the door so she can inspect Britt, too. "I called because I thought you might throw me one of those death parties. Like you did for that rockstar."

"Could we maybe come in and talk about it?" I ask.

Her eyes widen and the crack in the door narrows.

"Or you could come out? I usually meet my clients at *Grounded*."

She laughs, then, a rusty, awkward sound as if it's not something that happens often. "I don't come out," she says. "Surely they told you that, the neighbors? I haven't walked through this door in seventeen years."

💜

A *Party to Die For* is coming soon. Join our newsletter community at www.allthingskerry.com to make sure you don't miss it!

ACKNOWLEDGMENTS

I can't even remember how the idea of this book came to me... only that it showed up and wanted to be written. The fact that it actually progressed from that spark of an idea to a "real book" is a miracle of sorts, and so many people had a hand in that.

For my Viking—your ongoing faith in me, despite all of the obstacles and roadblocks along the way—means everything.

Sandi and Pam—your early reads and assurances that you loved this book—well. Let's just say that without your early support, the book might well have been consigned to the discard pile.

And again to Sandi (aka Maddie Dawson) and Jennifer Moorman, my friends and collaborators in the creation of everyday magic and the One Happy Thing podcast, thank you for helping me create a new publishing reality for this book.

Which brings me to everybody on The Dream Team!

Jodi Warshaw, you are the best developmental editor I could ever hope to meet and I loved having your invaluable insights on this book.

Denise Birt, cover designer extraordinaire — you literally deserve a medal for creating countless concepts and variations of concepts in the Dream Team quest for the perfect cover. I appreciate your patience and sense of humor more than you will ever know.

Stephanie Walls, copy editor—thank you for being the detail person who organized my usual chaos of erratic punctuation and style choices and helped make every word shine.

Theresa Baker, audio book narrator—you and your amazing voice are such an inspired addition to the Dream Team. Thank you for bringing Addy and the other characters to life.

Dream Team Avid Readers—you rock in so many ways! From helping in the choice of a cover, to catching pesky errors, to reviews and social posts and feeding my author ego with your positive comments—you've been a vital part of this adventure. This couldn't have happened without you.

And reader, I am above all things grateful to you for joining me in this little adventure.

Happy reading!

Love, Kerry & Kerry

ABOUT THE AUTHORS

Kerry Schafer (aka Kerry Anne King) is an Amazon Charts and Washington Post bestselling author. An incorrigible genre hopper, Kerry has written fantasy, paranormal mystery, and book club fiction. Known for her lyrical writing and memorable characters, Kerry weaves deep emotional insights, humor, and often a touch of magic into all of her tales. *Party Planning Can Be Murder* is her fourteenth novel.

In addition to writing, Kerry co-hosts the One Happy Thing podcast with bestselling authors Jennifer Moorman and Maddie Dawson and runs Author Genie, where she provides virtual assistant services to fellow authors.

Kerry lives in a small town in northeastern Washington with her real-life Viking and a crew of neurotic rescue animals —two dogs and four cats—whose favorite pastime is interrupting her writing.

Visit her at her website, www.allthingskerry.com.

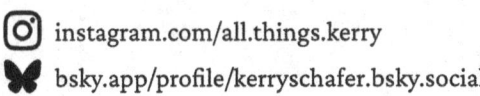

instagram.com/all.things.kerry

bsky.app/profile/kerryschafer.bsky.social